The Plus One

ALSO BY MAZEY EDDINGS

A Brush with Love
Lizzie Blake's Best Mistake

A NOVEL

MAZEY EDDINGS

ST. MARTIN'S GRIFFIN
NEW YORK

First published in the United States by St. Martin's Griffin, an imprint of St. Martin's Publishing Group

THE PLUS ONE. Copyright © 2023 by Madison Eddings. All rights reserved. Printed in the United States of America. For information, address St. Martin's Publishing Group, 120 Broadway, New York, NY 10271.

www.stmartins.com

Designed by Jen Edwards

Library of Congress Cataloging-in-Publication Data

Names: Eddings, Mazey, author.
Title: The plus one : a novel / Mazey Eddings.
Description: First edition. | New York : St. Martin's Griffin, 2023.
Identifiers: LCCN 2022048568 | ISBN 9781250847041
    (trade paperback) | ISBN 9781250847058 (ebook)
Classification: LCC PS3605.D35 P58 2023 | DDC 813/.6—dc23
LC record available at https://lccn.loc.gov/2022048568

Our books may be purchased in bulk for promotional, educational, or business use. Please contact your local bookseller or the Macmillan Corporate and Premium Sales Department at 1-800-221-7945, extension 5442, or by email at MacmillanSpecialMarkets@macmillan.com.

First Edition: 2023

10 9 8 7 6 5 4 3 2 1

For those who hurt, those who've healed, and those who are somewhere in-between. You are worthy of love even on your hardest days.

And for the younger me that still gets stuck in the bad place. You make it out.

CONTENT WARNINGS

Hello, my dearest reader!

While this book is a romance with a very happy ending and some laughs along the way, it also addresses heavier topics. Please be aware that the following are discussed throughout the novel:

- PTSD from losing patients as a medical provider in emergency situations
- Emotional repercussions of growing up with divorced parents
- Moving on after a past partner cheats

Also of note, the Global Health Care Organization mentioned throughout the book is fictional, created from various elements of existing systems and organizations, and is not representative of any singular group.

Please take care of yourselves as you read. I did my best to handle the above with nuance, respect, and compassion.

All my love,
Mazey

The
Plus
One

CHAPTER 1

Indira

T-MINUS FIVE WEEKS UNTIL THE WEDDING

Indira knew, rationally, it wasn't doing her much good to keep canceling her therapy appointments.

But, irrationally, it was a hell of a lot easier to ride the wave of a decent week than to sit down on Dr. Koh's beige couch and sift through her feelings until she realized she'd been deluding herself and her week was, in fact, total shit.

Indira also knew, as a psychiatrist herself, that this was called avoidance. And it was *bad*.

Fatal flaws, et cetera, et cetera.

Pushing away the tiny pang of guilt she felt for canceling, she stopped at the market a few blocks from the apartment she shared with her boyfriend, Chris, to buy ingredients for her mom's old chicken parm family recipe and a way-too-expensive bottle of wine, hoping to surprise him. While Chris worked from home, he wasn't much into cooking, and most nights Indira was too tired from her long shifts at the children's outpatient center to want to whip anything up. They were in a rut of delivered food eaten in silence as they scrolled through their phones, together in the most disconnected way possible.

They'd moved in after only five months of dating, riding a high of decent sex and early relationship happy hormones. But after almost a year of on-again, off-again whiplash, the relationship was starting to feel more like roommates than romance, and they both knew something had to change.

At least, she thought they both knew that. It wasn't like they talked about their relationship. They didn't talk about much, if she were being honest . . .

But it would all be okay. If the emotional roller coaster of Indira's childhood had taught her anything, it was that there wasn't a problem out there that couldn't be (at least temporarily) fixed by her mom's red sauce.

Indira checked out, even grabbing an impulse-buy of dessert to try and lift her glum mood.

Practicing her brightest—albeit forced—smile, she made her way through the cool October evening to their apartment, giving herself a pep talk. Chris was, at his core, a good guy. And Indira could get over her mental blockade of past relationship failures mixed with melodramatic ennui and get this one to work. Besides, she'd been down the whole single-and-searching-on-dating-apps road. The grass was definitely not fucking greener; relationships take hard work; insert platitude here; blah blah blah.

Indira hiked up the stairs of her building and let herself into the unit, sweeping into the kitchen with a flourish.

"Surpri—"

The unexpected sound of lusty moans killed the greeting in her throat.

For a moment, Indira wondered if she'd walked in on Chris watching a particularly vocal porno.

And then she saw.

Oh, the horror of the things she saw.

There was writhing.

And grinding.

And an . . . open jar of peanut butter? . . . (???)

Indira's jaw was on the ground as her fucking boyfriend groped—

with very little finesse, skill, or sensuality, thank you very much—a stranger on their fucking couch.

With peanut butter smeared on their faces.

(Seriously, what the hell?)

Her mind was slow and sluggish to process the tableau of betrayal she was witnessing in real time. The entangled couple finally registered her presence, separating their sticky faces long enough to stare back at her. The shocked silence held them all captive.

It was the soul-shattering howl of her cat, Grammy, that finally snapped Indira out of her daze.

Her head whipped around, looking frantically for Grammy, who had a propensity for inserting herself in the center of most human interactions. A little paw batted under the crack in the pantry door.

Indira saw red.

Oh no. There's no way this dickhead locked Indira's cat in a closet to pat down the titties of some rando without interruption.

"What the actual *fuck*," Indira shrieked, stomping to the door and ripping it open. Grammy darted out, back legs skidding across the tile as she booked it to the bedroom.

Besides Grammy's continuous wailing, a piercing silence fell between everyone as they continued to stare at each other.

Then Chris turned himself into the world's douchiest cliché. "Indira, it's not what it looks like."

That trite little phrase set off a trip wire of rage in Indira's chest.

"Really, Chris?" she yelled. "Because it looked like you were tongue-punching the tonsils of a stranger on the couch I paid for. But please, explain to me what I'm actually seeing."

Chris's face turned an alarming shade of mauve as he spluttered, and the woman's jaw dangled open.

"And why the fuck is there so much peanut butter?" she added, her hands turning into claws at her sides. "That shit is *organic*. And *expensive*." Indira stared expectantly at the duo.

"We . . ."

"I . . ."

Chris and the blond woman looked at each other with a combination of fear and longing that made Indira want to dry heave.

"We both really love peanut butter," Chris eventually whispered, saying it like he was delivering the world's most melodramatic line in a play.

Indira slow-blinked at him for a moment before throwing her head back and shrieking out a laugh. If she didn't laugh, she'd scream.

"Un-fucking-believable," she said. "I'm out of here, you piece of shit."

Indira darted to the bedroom, ripping through the closet and grabbing any bags she could find. She moved like an efficient tornado, shoving shoes and chargers and shirts into duffel bags as she went.

Grammy added to the drama with her ceaseless cries in the background. Indira didn't even know a cat could *make* noises like that. She made a quick mental note to ask Harper, one of her best friends, if earth-shaking screams were normal in felines or if Indira had unwittingly adopted a demon-possessed creature instead of an old, docile ball of fluff. But at the moment she had more important things to deal with.

"Indira, hold on," Chris said, standing in the doorway, hair mussed, pants unzipped, and shirt on backward, globs of peanut butter visible under the fabric. "Let's just calm down and talk about this like adults."

"That would require you to be one, Chris. And from where I'm standing, you're a cheating, cat-imprisoning man-child with the emotional intelligence of a rusty nail. So, no. I won't be calming down."

She marched to the bathroom, picking up what she could from the floor as she went, then used her entire arm to swipe her toiletries into a bag.

"You don't understand. This is different. You and I . . . we haven't been happy for months. I—"

Indira stopped in her tracks, eyes so cold and hard Chris slammed his mouth shut.

Months? In that moment, Indira didn't think she'd *ever* been happy with the asshole.

"Get out of my way," she said through clenched teeth. Chris at least had the decency to lower his head and slink back to the couch.

She stormed through the apartment, dropping bags on the kitchen counter as she gathered up odds and ends.

Moving back into the bedroom, Indira took a deep breath in preparation for her final mission: saving Grammy.

Grammy was no one's idea of cute. She perpetually looked like a bolt of lightning had just jolted her wiry frame, sooty hair standing on end at wild angles and back permanently hunched like a dramatized Halloween cartoon. To top off her loveliness, she had a half-missing ear, a curled lip that always displayed one stained fang, and the spectacular ability to infuse havoc into any situation.

This dazzling creature was currently hanging (sagging) from the bedroom curtains, her claws gouging through the fabric in long tears and head thrown back as she continued to howl as though she were being electrocuted.

"*Get a cat*, they said. *It'll be fun*, they said," Indira muttered to herself. *They* primarily being Harper, who had enabled Indira's impulse decision to adopt a furry companion to fill the dull and gnawing sense of loneliness that hit Indira regularly.

But, observing the unearthly noises and mentally preparing to lose at least a nipple, if not an entire boob, to Grammy's claws in what was about to go down, Indira wondered if she was making a fatal mistake.

With no other choice, she walked across her bedroom, unlatched Grammy from the curtain, and winced as the cat's claws slammed into her skin. The torture continued as she pried Grammy off herself—Indira's sweater gaining some lovely rips in the process—and squeezed the poor gremlin into a cat carrier before moving back to the kitchen.

With rage still pumping through her system, Indira found a surge of superhuman strength and, like a mother lifting a car off her child, hefted all of her earthly possessions onto her back and into her arms.

"Don't fucking call me," she said to Chris, who had the audacity to stare at her like a startled owl. His companion still had her mouth hanging open.

Indira had her hand on the doorknob when the other woman cried out, "Wait!"

Indira stopped. She wasn't sure if it was the weight of the items she carried or the hurt that was radiating out from the center of her chest, but she realized she was trembling. She turned to look over her shoulder at the stranger.

"It's . . . We're in love," the woman whispered. By the look on her face, Indira could almost believe it.

"What's your name?" Indira asked, swallowing past the knot of emotion in her throat.

"L-Lauren," she replied, her big blue eyes shimmering. She was blond. Freckled. Beautiful.

"Well, Lauren," Indira said with a pitying smile, "good fucking luck."

CHAPTER 2

Indira

Indira made sure to slam the door behind her as she went, then flew down the stairs and out to the street. It took her a few minutes of wandering to remember what random-ass side street she'd parked on, but she eventually found her car.

A hysterical giggle bubbled up from her throat as she stared at her SUV.

Her tires were slashed. All of them. Every single one deflated and floppy . . . kind of like her ego.

She started laughing even harder.

Her entire body shook with cackling laughter.

Then something in her chest cracked.

And she was bawling.

Indira collapsed against her useless car, tears streaming down her cheeks and a pained howl tearing from her throat Grammy decided to harmonize.

Indira couldn't pull herself together, so she leaned into the sadness, letting it pour out of her.

Eventually, with a final, rattling breath, she cried herself dry. Then considered her options. Lizzie, another of Indira's friends, lived in an apartment less than a mile away, but she also had a gorgeous partner and an eighteen-month-old tottering around and a total of zero doors in her studio apartment. Indira was a firsthand witness to the lack of self-control Lizzie and Rake had when it came to keeping their hands off each other in public; she couldn't imagine what occurred behind (not) closed doors.

Indira's other two closest friends, Harper and Thu, also lived reasonably close, having recently moved back to the area from New York and California, respectively. But they, too, lived with their significant others in one-bedroom apartments. While a night or two on their couches wouldn't be the worst thing in the world, Indira knew anything longer than that would leave her with a sore neck and back probably for, like, ever. Getting older sucked.

That left her older brother, Collin, and his fiancé, Jeremy.

The pair was intimidatingly put together, their cushy doctor salaries granting them a spacious three-bedroom home in Manayunk, one of Philadelphia's more residential neighborhoods a few miles northwest of Center City.

Indira and Collin were close, having leaned on each other since they were little ones trapped in the crosshairs of a messy divorce, and she knew he wouldn't mind her crashing at his place. In fact, despite the longer commute she'd have to endure for work, she felt a tiny bubble of excitement at the opportunity to spend time with her brother while she figured out what to do next.

Besides, Collin and Jeremy were getting married in a little over a month and had so many pre-wedding events planned—most of which seemed more like exploitation of the wedding party for free labor to make decorations and goody bags than actual celebrations—she was already planning on being there quite a bit.

Maybe watching horror movies and ordering pizza like she and Collin had when they were teenagers would help her through this outrageously awful situation. This wasn't likely, but if listening to Taylor Swift since she was a die-hard teenage superfan had taught her anything, it was that healing from a breakup was a slow, treacherous process and any attempt at feeling better was worth it.

Indira shot Collin and Jeremy a quick message in their group chat, telling them that something had happened with Chris and she'd be crashing at their place for a bit, knowing they were probably in surgery at the hospital and wouldn't see it for a few hours.

Straightening her spine (as much as she could under the tremendous weight of all her shit and pseudo-feral cat), Indira left her vandalized car to be dealt with on a day that sucked ass just a little less and walked to City Hall to catch a train out to Collin's.

Collin and Jeremy, like Indira, were doctors. Collin and Jeremy, unlike Indira, were anesthesiologists, earning them a level of respect in the medical community (and a giant salary) that Indira would never scratch as a psychiatrist.

Physicians and surgeons and psychiatrists alike all had the goal of healing, but because Indira wielded a complex system of therapies and medications instead of a scalpel, her work would never be as valued. Psychiatry lacked the instant gratification of surgery, and just as mental illnesses were ridiculously stigmatized in society, those who treated them were held in lesser regard.

Not that Indira gave a shit. To her, the brain was the most vital human component, and she was humbled to have the privilege of helping her patients cope and heal theirs . . . even if she struggled with her own sometimes.

Arriving at the station and swiping her pass, Indira draped a scarf over the outside of Grammy's carrier, hoping the general loudness of the city would divert notice of any bizarre screeches the creature decided to let out. She picked a window seat in a fairly empty train car, dropping her stuff around her in a mess.

The train pulled out a few minutes later, and Indira watched the city blur into streaks of gray and green. The steady vibrations of the ride relaxed her tense muscles, and the commotion of the past hour hit her unguarded heart.

How could Chris do that to her? How could he betray her like that?

Indira had twisted herself into knots to be a chill girlfriend. A fun girlfriend. To be exactly the type of person she thought Chris would like.

That had worked fucking well.

The train pulled to a stop at the next station, and Indira blinked away the tiny stars in her vision, focusing on the view outside her window and hoping the onboarding passengers wouldn't see her tear-stained cheeks. It was a useless effort, fat droplets squeaking out and plopping on to her lap.

Indira was so damn sick of being left by the men in her life—first her father, then every guy she'd offered her heart to after—and just once, she wanted to be someone worth staying for.

She tended to fall too fast. Too hard. Care way too much. It was why Chris had seemed so *safe*. The thought of him had never made her heart swoop or her head float. Liking him hadn't felt like anything more than . . . well, liking him, and she thought not feeling too much would be a safeguard from another emotional car crash.

So much for that plan, because now she was sitting here, bawling on the fucking train, and careening off a cliff to rock bottom.

She rubbed the heels of her hands into her eyes, willing herself not to cry (again). She was done crying over all these people who hurt her. She was done letting anyone hurt her, period.

She finally arrived at the Manayunk station, gathered her crap and cat, and trudged out of the platform and up the disgustingly steep hill to Collin's home.

Collin and Jeremy's cars were parked in front of their tall, brick row house, which meant they were likely sleeping, coming off a long shift.

Grammy was well on her way to scratching a hole through the cat carrier as Indira clutched it to her chest, balancing the rest of her stuff precariously as she moved up their stoop. She didn't *want* to wake Collin or Jeremy, but with her arms filled to the brim with baggage and mood darker than a storm cloud, Indira (oh so gently) pounded her foot as hard as she could against the base of the door so one of them would open it for her.

After a few moments of banging, Indira heard footsteps on the other side and stepped back, ready to put her shit down and collapse on Collin's expensive leather couch the second he let her in.

But, when the knob turned and the door swung open, Indira's battered heart somehow managed to sink even lower at who she saw.

The person she'd loathed since childhood.

Overlord of darkness and killer of fun.

Her older brother's best friend.

Jude.

"Oh great," she said, blowing a stray curl off her forehead as she glared at him. "It's you."

CHAPTER 3

Jude

∞

There were very few people Jude enjoyed spending time with.

Collin Papadakis, Jude's closest friend since they were kids, historically topped the list, despite his many extroverted tendencies and tediously charming personality that would annoy Jude in any other person. Collin's fiancé, Jeremy, was also fun to be around, primarily because he made his best friend happy.

But at the very bottom of said list where the most aggravating of people existed, written in red pen and underlined for good measure, was Indira fucking Papadakis. She was the counterpoint to every facet of his personality and she never failed to fracture his composure, the duo growing up bickering more than they ever actually talked.

"Great to see you too, Dira," Jude said, fixing her with a bland look, taking in her wild mane of hair and watery eyes as she stood on Collin's doorstep. "It's been awhile."

"Not long enough," she said, pushing past him and walking into the house. Jude sighed, then closed the door with a flick of his wrist.

This was not what he fucking needed.

Jude, to put it delicately, did not like Indira. Ever since they were children, she'd managed to rub him the wrong way. It would be easier to explain their mutual loathing if there were some grand event of childhood betrayal or a deep-rooted blood feud—something he could point to and say, *There. Right there. That's the reason we don't get along and never will.* But nothing could ever be easy when it came to Dira, and their animosity didn't have a source so much as it was a fact of nature. The sun rose in the east. Set in the west. Indira annoyed Jude. Jude annoyed her back.

She was intensely sensitive and had a way of . . . of *staring* at people with those big copper eyes like she could see beneath their skin. Read their thoughts. The overall effect was horribly unnerving.

Jude was barely holding it together as it was; he didn't need her . . . *seeing* him.

"Where's Collin?" Indira asked, depositing some of her bags on the floor but still clutching what looked like an animal carrier close to her chest. "Did the shock of your ascension from hell kill him?" she added, looking over her shoulder and arching an eyebrow.

Jude flinched like she'd slapped him, and the surprise on her face made embarrassment flood his veins. Indira didn't know how spot-on her little joke was.

He'd spent the past few years witnessing some of the worst atrocities that could be inflicted on a human body. Hell would be a welcome reprieve from his service with the Global Health Care Organization.

Jude was a doctor specializing in emergency medicine, and the rapid accumulation of student loans in med school had pushed him to sign on the dotted line for a scholarship with the GHCO. In exchange for free tuition that saved him close to half-a-million dollars in debt, Jude promised four years of his life, going wherever the GHCO sent him to perform emergency medicine in areas of conflict, natural disasters, and great need.

Sometimes, he wished he could say he'd joined the GHCO for something altruistic, some deep, insatiable desire to serve humankind. It made his shell of a body feel that much hollower to know that all he'd seen, all the times he'd failed, were all to avoid monthly loan payments.

Desperate times . . .

"What are you doing back?" Indira asked, her voice losing its usual combative edge in exchange for gentle curiosity. It made Jude's skin crawl.

"I couldn't miss Collin's wedding," Jude said, rubbing a hand across the back of his neck. "The agency gave me an extended break for my three years of uninterrupted service. My next assignment starts a couple weeks after the wedding." Jude's voice cracked as he spoke and a familiar type of panic slithered down his spine as he stood there.

He wasn't sure when talking got to be so hard, but every interaction since he'd touched down in America had sent his system into a tailspin—sudden and random emotions stampeding through his chest and roaring in his ears, disrupting the safe numbness he'd built. Jude needed that numbness. Survived only because of it.

"And you're . . . good?" Indira asked, tilting her head as she studied him far too closely.

Jude made a dismissive grunting noise, looking away.

"Dira?" a sleepy voice called over Jude's shoulder. Collin came into view as he walked down the steps, rumpled and pajama-clad. He stopped next to Jude, clapping him on the back with a grin, making Jude flinch again.

Collin and Jude had grown up as inseparable best friends, spending every day together and leaving the younger Indira behind. She'd always been a pestering plus one and they'd lacked the patience to include her in their adventures.

"What're you doing here?" Collin asked Indira, smiling through a yawn and dragging a hand through his golden hair. "Wait, is that Grammy?" he added, gesturing at the cat crate in her arms.

Indira looked down at herself, her hair falling over her hunched shoulders like a violent ink splat to match the mascara streaks down her cheeks. Her cat completed the horrifying look by punching a furry fist through her carrier and latching it onto Indira's sweater, punctuating it all with a howl.

For the first time in what felt like forever, something close to a laugh almost reached Jude's lips, but it died somewhere in his throat. He hadn't laughed in a long time. Sometimes he wondered if he'd ever laugh again.

Indira chewed her lip, shifting on her feet. "I . . . um. I-I sent you a text but I need . . . Well, I was going to ask to stay here, but I'll go. I didn't realize you have, uh, whatever." She made a flapping gesture toward Jude.

Lovely.

Collin let out a forlorn sigh, moving toward Indira and gingerly unhooking Grammy's paw.

"What did that piece of shit do this time?" he asked, taking the carrier from her arms and opening it. A mangy-looking animal tumbled to the floor and sprinted away like a bat out of hell. Jude stared after it.

"Nothing! Well, just—"

"Collin! Look at this massive fucker!" Jeremy yelled, bursting through the back door and making everyone jump. He brandished dirty gardening gloves in one hand and an alarmingly giant squash in the other. "Oh, hey, Dira. I didn't know you were coming over," Jeremy added, giving her a broad grin.

"Pretty sure your lovely cousin had something to do with the impromptu visit," Collin said quietly, shooting him a look.

"Collin, you ass, shut up," Indira snapped, hitting her brother on the shoulder. "There's nothing to talk about. Don't drag Jeremy into this."

It felt like Jude's muscles were ripping with the force it took for him to stop his body from jerking at the sudden noises, to keep his hands pinned at his sides instead of shooting to his ears or covering his head.

Instead, he stood there, wanting to seem normal. Wanting to *be* normal.

"What did that mouth-breather do now?" Jeremy said, voice rough as his gaze flicked between Indira and Collin.

"Indira brought all her stuff, so it must be bad," Collin said, fanning the flames. Jeremy's face twisted in outrage.

"Collin, hold my squash. I need to kick some ass." Jeremy thrust the vegetable into Collin's arms, then dove across the kitchen counter for his cell phone.

"I got your squash, baby. Tear him apart."

"Would you both stop it?" Indira said, snatching the phone out of Jeremy's hand. "You're making way too big a deal out of this."

And overwhelming the fuck out of Jude. He took a deep breath, closing his eyes and cracking his knuckles with his thumb as he tried to calm his painful pulse.

He'd promised himself he wouldn't do this. Wouldn't carry this dark cloud of awfulness that hovered around him like a second skin into Collin and Jeremy's special time. This was his best friend's wedding, and Collin had asked Jude to be there. Jude knew he was too broken to be fully anywhere, but he'd do his best to pretend.

Slowly, his senses dulled a bit, the adrenaline ebbing from his limbs like a retreating tide. The fog that cradled him was good, and he leaned into it as he opened his eyes and fixed them on the group, not really seeing anything at all.

"I have half a mind to kick him out of the wedding party," Jeremy said.

"Oh my God, please don't make this into a thing," Indira said, eyes wide as red splotches spread across her fair cheeks. "Everyone needs to calm down."

Yes, calm would be *excellent* right about now. Jude was about ten seconds away from getting on his knees and begging for it.

Jeremy grimaced, then said quietly, ". . . Kicking him out would mess with the symmetry of our altar moment."

"That's a really good point," Collin whispered back. The couple shared a meaningful stare.

"Okay," Jeremy said after a pause. "Chris isn't out of the wedding party. But he can't keep doing this on-again, off-again game." He turned to Indira. "You both aren't getting any younger. It's ridiculous at this point."

"It was *mutual*," Indira spat. "We both, like mature adults—

unlike some people I know"—Indira gave Collin and Jeremy a pointed look—"had a discussion and decided we . . . I don't know. Aren't well-suited. Again, a mutual decision."

"Which is why you look like you've been sobbing for hours?" Collin said quietly, arching an eyebrow at Indira.

She landed a punch on his shoulder. "Something can be mutual and still painful, jackass."

Collin's face softened. "I'm sorry, Dira. I don't mean to make a joke of it. Come here."

He stretched his hands out to her, but Indira wrapped her arms around herself instead, back hunching.

Jude understood that. He worried that if someone touched him, he'd crumble.

It was much safer to hold himself together.

"It goes without saying that you can stay here," Collin said, gesturing at the pile of her stuff she'd left in the living room.

"Are you sure?" Indira asked, shooting a glance at Jude. He blinked away. "I don't want to crowd you."

"Don't be ridiculous." Jeremy waved her words away. "We have plenty of room, and having two of our bridal party members here at the ready for emergency situations will end up being a blessing, I'm sure."

Indira shot her brother and Jeremy a skeptical look. "Oh, goody. Can't wait to be of service."

"I'm choosing to ignore that dripping sarcasm, sweets," Jeremy added, tapping Indira on the nose as he passed her.

Collin grabbed Indira's suitcases from the floor while Jeremy slid the duffel bag strap off her shoulder, the pair moving up the stairs before Jude could even blink, let alone wrap his head around the past fifteen minutes.

That'd been a problem for him lately, this inability of his brain to process the things happening around him, this constant disconnect from his body.

"This will be fun," Collin called down, "the three of us living together for a bit. Just like when we were kids!"

Jude and Indira were left in the foyer, the vibrant energy of Jeremy and Collin settling around them like dust in the long, silent moments.

Indira cleared her throat. "So . . . how long are you home for?" she asked, shifting from foot to foot.

"Seven weeks," Jude answered tersely.

Indira nodded, eyes bouncing around his face. "Where, uh, have you been stationed?" she asked.

Jude really wished she'd give up on the small talk.

"Finished a five-month assignment at a women's clinic in Sierra Leone," he said with detachment, even though pieces of his broken soul still lingered in the small graveyard attached to the clinic's adjacent church.

Indira opened and closed her mouth a few times, questions getting caught in her throat.

"You okay?" she finally managed, speaking softly, eyes full of curiosity.

Jude's head jerked back in surprise, the question sending his thoughts somersaulting in multiple directions.

Of course he was okay, he wanted to tell her. He was alive and in Collin's house and not staring down at a bloody operating table, and he was getting really good at not feeling anything most of the time.

Except for when he felt everything.

"Fine," he choked out, voice rising an octave. "Totally fine. Why?"

Indira shrugged, taking a step forward. "You seem, I don't know . . . different." She tilted her head, looking at him like she could read every awful secret written on his skin.

"I'm just, uh . . . tired." Jude pretended to yawn. Indira didn't look convinced.

Damn her.

"Are you *sure* you're okay?" she asked, taking another step toward him. She reached out, her fingers landing on his wrist in a friendly gesture.

The touch sent a jolt through his skin, straight to the marrow of his bones, zapping down his spine, while a matching heat spread through Jude's chest.

His head swam at the disorienting familiarity of the touch. The gentle comfort of it.

It felt . . . *good*.

He jerked his arm away, hands clenched into fists at his side as he sucked in a breath.

That wouldn't do.

Jude wasn't allowed to feel good when he was the reason some people couldn't feel anything ever again.

They stared at each other, Indira's lips parted as she blinked at him.

"Sorry," Jude said, clearing his throat. "That, uh, tickled."

Indira pursed her lips, not looking convinced, but she nodded. They continued standing there, Jude wishing desperately to escape but unable to break away.

"Do you want to get lunch with me? Or dinner?" Indira asked suddenly, tipping Jude's axis upside down.

"I don't eat," Jude blurted out, spouting off the first excuse he could think of. But he couldn't possibly do something as intimate as share a *meal* with *Indira* and expect to make it out alive. He couldn't sit across from her at a table when the weight of his memories was dragging him straight to hell.

Oh no. She'd ask one question, maybe two, and all the awfulness in Jude would come pouring out of him like an unstoppable tidal wave of truth and she'd have to live with knowing his sins too. Nope. Not happening. He didn't even like her; he wasn't about to pour his soul out to her.

"You don't eat," Indira repeated, the familiar cynicism she'd addressed him with since childhood returning to her voice.

"Kicked the habit," Jude said with a mild shrug, trying to save face by being sarcastic too.

Indira stared at him for another moment, her tender curiosity shifting to insulted disbelief before she huffed out a breath and looked around the entryway.

"Cool," she said at last, her olive branch withering between them. "Cool cool cool cool. Well, welcome home. Enjoy your malnourishment."

With a scowl, she brushed past him and hiked up the stairs.

Jude let out a pained breath, hitting the heels of his hands against his forehead before dragging them down his face.

Well, being back was going well.

Jude moved toward the steps, wanting to escape into the sanctuary of his room—Collin's guest room—the space quiet and safe and terrifyingly lonely. But the muffled voices of Indira and Collin above, cut short by the sound of a door slamming and Collin's heavy footsteps moving up the second set of stairs to the main bedroom on the third floor stopped him in his tracks. It was then that Jude realized the cherry on top of this fucked-up sundae.

Collin's other guest bedroom was directly next to Jude's.

Meaning approximately five inches of wall would be separating Indira and Jude for the foreseeable future.

Jude was, to put it lightly, so fucked.

CHAPTER 4

Indira

Indira decided that if there were ever an appropriate time to call an emergency session with her therapist, it would be right about now.

"I'm fucking sad. All the time," she said, voice cracking as she blinked away tears. She didn't want Dr. Koh to see any of them fall. "My gut is constantly twisted in knots and my heart feels like there's a fist squeezing it to a pulp. The sadness is so heavy it sometimes feels hard to breathe."

Dr. Koh nodded gently.

"And you know what I can't stop thinking about?" Indira said, face scrunching up in disgust. "Why peanut butter? *Why?* I'm not here to kink-shame or yuck anyone's yum, but I truly cannot think of a less sexy food than thick-ass peanut butter."

"Well," Dr. Koh said after Indira was silent for a minute. "That is quite a lot to think about."

Indira shot Dr. Koh a look at that massive understatement.

"What are these feelings surrounding the situation with Chris bringing up in you?" Dr. Koh asked gently.

"That I'm not sure I'll be able to enjoy PB and J sandwiches ever again."

"Fair. But what about on a more emotional level?"

Indira blew out a breath. Fuck if she knew.

"Fuck if I know," Indira answered honestly. "And I think that's part of why I feel so shitty."

Dr. Koh pursed her lips. "Tell me more. I'm not sure I follow."

"I feel . . ." Indira grappled with adjectives and emotions, none of them fitting right. "I don't know how I feel. And *that* makes me feel uncomfortable."

"How so?"

Indira's knee started bouncing. "I'm a psychiatrist. I'm supposed to have all this emotional intelligence and well-developed coping skills and I . . . I can't even figure out what I'm fucking feeling. How am I supposed to be of any use to my patients, or anyone for that matter, if I can't help myself?"

Dr. Koh sat back, brow furrowed. "Why do you think your personal, emotional experiences will prevent you from being there for your patients as they undergo treatment?"

"I . . . I don't know," Indira said, throwing her head back against the couch as she stared up at the ceiling. She wished she could shout the words. "I just feel useless. I feel like I'm this broken mess that will fail others because I can't even fix myself."

"Are you emotionally projecting your current struggles onto your patients?" Dr. Koh asked.

Indira's head jerked forward to look at Dr. Koh. "No. I . . . No."

"Are you interfering with their sessions by discussing your own feelings or personal difficulties?"

"Of course not."

"Are you abusing your patients? Are you manipulating them? Are you acting bored in your sessions and not engaging? Are you neglecting them?"

"No," Indira said, her voice rising. She cared about her patients—their well-being, their path to wellness—so deeply, it was offensive to even imagine doing those things.

"Then, Indira, I hope you can understand that you experiencing personal struggles—ones that you deal with in your *personal* therapy sessions on your own time—isn't preventing you from serving your patients. If anything, it's you putting in the work on yourself so you can be more present for them."

Indira chewed on her lip as she turned this over. She'd spent so much of her life feeling like she wasn't good enough for people—someone who always got left behind no matter how hard she tried—it was hard and obscenely uncomfortable to accept this line of thinking.

Dr. Koh cleared her throat. "Do you think that some of these feelings that are being churned up, making you question your adequacy, might come from your father's—"

"Nope," Indira said, popping the *p*. "That was a hiccup in my timeline. Not worth discussing."

Dr. Koh tilted her head, giving Indira a look that said it was very worth discussing, but Indira turned her focus to her phone.

"Oh gosh, that looks like time. I don't want to throw your schedule off," Indira said, brushing her hands over her cheeks to make sure no tears had escaped before standing.

"I appreciate your conscientiousness regarding my schedule," Dr. Koh said, glancing at her watch. "But I do assure you that our session running a bit overtime to have an honest discussion would not a disaster make."

Indira pressed her lips together, nodding. "Right. Right. I just don't want to be *that* patient, ya know?" She moved toward the door.

"Indira?" Dr. Koh said.

Indira stopped, eyes lowered as she glanced over her shoulder, hand poised on the knob.

"I have no doubt you are wonderful at what you do. Psychiatry takes a special understanding of where chemical imbalances and emotions meet. But when you come to these meetings, I hope you know it's okay to take off that hat."

"I . . . uh . . . I don't wear hats," Indira said, staring at the floor. "Rather prone to hat hair."

Dr. Koh indulged her with a chuckle. "Fair enough. But what I'm saying is, in our sessions, you don't have to be a put-together doctor. You don't have to be a source of wisdom or strength. You don't have to be anything but human. I'm here to listen to you. Be here for you. It's okay to lower those walls in this one hour you take for yourself each week."

Indira was silent, teeth clenched and jaw ticcing. Part of her wanted to shatter. To crumple on Dr. Koh's ugly carpeting and pour her soul into the room. She wanted to talk about the ache that never went away. The hole in her heart that no one seemed able to fill. She wanted to sob out every fear that tore at her seams.

How her deepest want was just to be loved, and how she wasn't sure anyone ever could.

But admitting that, shining a floodlight on those dark corners of her thoughts, would make all that hurt she kept bottled away more real. More painful.

Instead, she straightened her spine, swallowed past the lump in her throat, and looked up to smile at Dr. Koh.

"Thank you," she said. "I appreciate you saying that. I really do feel like I get a great deal out of our sessions."

After a nod from Dr. Koh, Indira scuttled out of the building and onto the street, deciding that was enough of sitting with her feelings for one day.

She worked hard to keep her messy bits hidden from others, and the raw honesty of being a patient in a therapy session always left her off-kilter. Shaking it off, she boarded a train and headed toward Collin's, holding herself together with the promise of a nice cry facedown on the bed as soon as she got home.

The one silver lining in this shit sandwich Indira was smooshed between was that she certainly didn't care about being a mess around her brother and, by extension, Jeremy. She and Collin had supported each other through so many messes growing up, she felt incredibly safe letting her guard down around him.

Even annoying ass Jude didn't elicit Indira's usual need to be the best version of herself. She'd known him far too long—and they'd both observed each other's worst awkward teenage years—to care what he thought of her. Some small comforts, even from the world's most annoying source, would never change.

CHAPTER 5

Jude

∞

Living with Indira, Collin, and Jeremy was, to put it plainly, a sensory assault. The siblings seemed to honor their Greek and Italian roots primarily by seeing who could talk louder, with Jeremy reveling in the noise. Jude wasn't sure three people ever laughed so fucking often and so fucking noisily. Except for when Lizzie Blake, one of Indira's best friends since high school, visited. That was a new level of sound.

Over the past few days, Jude had discovered one way to hang out with Collin without putting his eardrums at risk (for the most part): watching *Grey's Anatomy*.

"Pick me. Choose me. Love me," Collin whispered in time with Meredith Grey on the TV, pressing his head against the back of the couch as he blinked past his tears.

When the episode ended, Jude stood up, pacing a circle around the living room, hands planted on his hip as he fought off crying too.

"Told you it's a good show," Collin said, shooting Jude a shit-eating grin, his red-rimmed eyes crinkling at the corners.

"It has its moments," Jude conceded, finally getting his bearings and widening his eyes against the pressure building behind them. Jude *never* cried . . . What was *wrong* with him?

"If the actors knew how hard you are to please, they'd probably cherish that admission more than any of their Emmys."

Jude rolled his eyes as he walked to the fridge and grabbed a water.

"So, uh, next episode?" he said as casually as possible, stepping over Collin's long, outstretched legs to take his seat back on the couch.

"Thought you'd never ask, superfan," Collin said, cueing up the next episode. Jude grunted in response.

They got through the first few minutes before Collin paused the show, turning to Jude.

"I'm really glad you're here," Collin said, smile earnest. "I've missed you."

And dammit if Jude didn't almost break down into hysterical sobs right then and there. What was it about the simplest comments that had the power to break down every wall?

"Of course," he said, tongue thick and mouth numb as he tried to shrug past the tiny crack fissuring through his chest. "You know I wouldn't miss your wedding."

"I know. But it still makes me happy you're here."

Jude didn't know what to say without turning his heart inside out with all the feelings weighing it down, so he nodded and took a sip of his water.

"And . . . everything's good? With you?" Collin asked, his voice dripping with false casualness. "You're doing okay with the GHCO job and stuff?"

Dammit. Jude hated this question.

There weren't really words for just how not okay he was, but if he pretended hard enough to be, he wouldn't have to face that truth.

"I'm fine," Jude lied, pushing the words through his clenched teeth as he peeled at the label on his water bottle with his thumb. "The position has given me plenty of opportunities to put my specialty to use."

And plenty of opportunities to fail hundreds of people.

Jude used to love being a doctor. It'd been his dream since he'd found out it was a profession. Emergency surgery in particular held a spark, a high, almost spiritual in its intensity, and Jude had worked toward it with undeterred focus through med school and his first year of hospital-based residency.

There was no feeling more powerful than being the sole reason a life was saved, being witness to the hidden brokenness of a body and knowing how to fix it, and Jude had chased the rush of it.

But not anymore. He didn't lust after that power now, but ran from it, knowing it was the most terrifying thing a person could face.

"Okay," Collin said, dragging the word out, another question following close behind. "But if you want to talk—"

Luckily, Indira's voice cut through the precarious conversation, sharp and piercing.

"Collin!" she yelled, her feet slapping the steps as she ran down them.

Acting on impulse, Jude jumped up, moving to the foot of the stairs, a familiar surge of fear punching along his spine, part of him pulled toward the sound of someone needing help, the other part wanting to sprint away from the noise. Indira stopped two steps from the bottom, tears in her eyes and her mouth twisted as she gave him a confused but challenging look.

"Uh, move, please," she said, nose crinkling and eyebrows furrowing as she pushed past him into the living room.

His body was slow to catch up to the fact that he was standing in Collin's entryway—not under attack, not in danger—and he tried to shake off the fog.

"Glad to see you're making so much progress with your manners," Jude mumbled.

He was finding that annoyance was one of the easier emotions to lean into, especially with Indira. The sensation was so familiar around her, it bordered on comforting. Not nearly as terrifying as all the other feelings that were trying so desperately to kick down the doors in his mind.

Indira whipped her head around to look at him, profile limned in the soft light seeping through the windows. She licked her full lips, giving him a pretty smile that, for some bizarre reason, made his pulse punch against his skin.

"How clever, Satan," she said, the smile curling into something sinister. "But I don't have the energy to pretend to listen to you today."

She turned back around, stomping to the couch and plopping next to Collin, leaving Jude looking like a fool trying to come up with something to say.

Jude was discovering that one of his newest issues with Indira— on the very long list—was that she'd grown up to be terrifyingly beautiful, and it regularly caught him off guard. She was all long-limbs and graceful curves, her mass of hair framing her face like a flower in bloom.

And those damn whiskey-colored eyes. They'd only increased in their intensity as she aged.

She still had that unnerving energy about her, like she walked around perceiving the world with heightened senses. Seeing into the very core of everything and everyone, each movement she observed being translated into a detailed report in her head that she studied from all possible angles until you were left feeling like she knew things about you that you didn't even know about yourself.

And dammit if she hadn't figured out how to constantly poke Jude's buttons and disrupt every shred of calm fortitude he had. Or pretended to have, at the very least.

"What's wrong, Dira?" Collin asked, attention absorbed in playing with the settings on the TV.

Indira thrust her phone under his nose. "Did you know about this?" she asked, her voice quiet, fracturing on the words.

Collin blinked at the phone, his eyebrows furrowing deeply with his frown. "What . . . what is this?" His gaze bounced between Indira and Jude like Jude had any clue what they were talking about.

"He's having another kid," Indira said, jabbing her finger at the screen.

Jude's heart sank. He'd heard Indira say *he* in that way—dripping with disbelief and disdain—enough times to know she was talking about their father.

Mr. Papadakis was, to put it lightly, an asshole deadbeat. Collin didn't talk about his dad's leaving often, but when he did, it came out drunkenly and saturated in hurt; in questions of loss and confusion.

On a few even rarer occasions in college, Indira and Collin had talked about it together in front of Jude, crying as they dug their fingers into the unhealed wound of his empty promises that never stopped in their frequency.

"Did he call you?" Collin asked, the tiny touch of hope in his voice plummeting Jude's heart even lower. Collin was a naive optimist, and Jude hated seeing his friend hurt.

Indira scoffed. "Of course not. I found out on Facebook. Stepmommy dearest posted a fucking photo shoot of it this morning."

She scrolled down a bit, tilting the screen to Collin again. Jude glanced over their shoulders.

Mr. Papadakis was standing with his third wife, Brooke-Anne, their toddler twins clad in matching outfits and clinging to their parents' legs. The adults held up a sonogram in front of them as they kissed. The caption read, *Our perfect family is getting a little more perfect.*

Collin's mouth dangled open for a moment, and Jude could see him trying to spin the truth, find a way to make another excuse for the man who so regularly disappointed him. Indira, on the other hand, was nothing but steely anger, eyes sharp, jaw clenched tight as a muscle twitched.

"I'm sure he was waiting until the wedding to tell us," Collin said, meeting Indira's eyes. "I bet he wanted to surprise us with the news in person. You know how obsessed Brooke-Anne is with social media, though, so she probably didn't know the plan or think it through."

"You seriously can't be defending him right now," Indira said, mouth twisting. "He shouldn't even be invited."

"Indira, I'm not having this fight again," Collin said, pushing to stand up from the couch. Indira followed him, the pair tracking an angry path around the room.

Jude was rooted to the spot, the tension and emotions seeping into his skin, locking his muscles and tendons, as they made loops around him.

"It doesn't need to be a fight if you just think about it for even a minute. He's the worst, Collin. Why are you opening yourself up to more hurt?"

Jude's heart thrummed and his palms turned clammy at the increasing volume, the noise resting like a weight on his chest as he tried to breathe normally.

"Excuse me for wanting a relationship with the man," Collin said, throwing his arms out to the side, making Jude flinch at the sudden movement. "But you're right. Being pessimistic and jaded like you is definitely the healthier choice."

Indira's head shot back, and she opened her mouth to reply.

"Can I borrow your car?" Jude yelled, jolting a step away from them, clenching his shaking hands at his sides.

They blinked at him for a moment like they'd forgotten he was there.

"Sure," Collin said at last, giving his head a mild shake. "Keys are in the bowl in the hallway."

Jude nodded in thanks, then darted out the door, gulping down the cool October air through his closing throat.

He locked himself in the car, then started the engine and whipped out of the driveway without looking, trying to steady his shaking hands and roiling stomach, cold sweat breaking across his skin and making it prickle. No matter how many breaths he took, he couldn't slow his spinning brain.

It was all so much. Too much. The noise and the tension and all of it ripping down his spine, leaving him feeling like he'd be split in two.

After a few blocks, he pulled over and cut the engine, gripping the steering wheel for a moment before slamming his fists against it, yelling out all the hurt that was trying to crack him open.

What the fuck was wrong with him? Who had he become? He didn't know himself anymore, and it scared the fuck out of him.

Jude had heard Indira and Collin bicker before. Hell, growing up, neither of them had had a conversation without someone ending up raising their voice. But all of a sudden, he couldn't handle it.

He couldn't handle *anything* anymore. And Jude fucking hated himself for it.

He was supposed to be in control of himself, of his world. He'd always been a rational, even-keeled, *skilled* doctor. His entire life's purpose revolved around helping people. But here he was, a man in absolute shambles and no clue what to do to fix it. He was disgusted with himself.

Thoughts and emotions rushed across his brain in blinding flashes, none sticking around long enough for Jude to make any sense of them. It didn't matter. Nothing had made sense to him in a long time.

Eventually, Jude got his breathing under control, and his heart stopped threatening to punch out of his chest.

Body spent and tingling with a settling numbness, he restarted the car. Without much thought—he was too fucking tired of thinking, to be honest—he started driving, following a path he knew all too well.

He passed across highways and cityscapes and twists of green hills, driving to a place he'd been avoiding since he'd gotten back.

Home.

CHAPTER 6

Jude

∞

Without registering much of the drive, Jude eventually pulled up to his childhood home, the car idling as he stared at the squat house with white siding and a deep-green door.

Jude loved his parents. Admired them endlessly.

Which meant he was swamped with self-loathing at the resentment that darted through him every time he thought about seeing them.

Jude's parents had always just scraped by—his dad was a machinist for Philly Gas Works, and his mom a preschool teacher during the day and waitress at night.

They were one of those working-class couples cursed with frequent and near-devastating financial hits ranging from exploding carburetors to freak accidents and a fair amount of medical emergencies thrown in.

Get out of the car, Jude told himself, staying firmly seated as his heartbeat sawed against his sternum. *Go in and see your parents. Smile at them. You did this for them.*

Jude had watched debt eat away at his parents in this home, every paycheck stretched so thin that some months there was nothing left, placing brick after brick of stress on their backs as they tried to stay afloat.

Jude had vowed that would never be him. He wouldn't live this life where every action was dictated by the crushing weight of bills stacking up on the table and bank accounts being overdrawn.

He'd vowed to stop it from being their reality too.

Scrounging up any inner-strength and calmness he could muster, Jude got out of the car, walking along the perfectly kept yard and up the three stone steps to stand in front of the door. The door he'd always dreamed of buying for his parents.

Jude didn't earn as high a salary as his hospital-based colleagues, but GHCO did pay him well enough and his lack of general expenses meant he always had a surplus of money.

He'd directed most of it toward his folks.

He'd never felt prouder than the day he'd been able to write to them, explaining that he'd paid off their house, a financial burden that had been poised to force his parents to work until they keeled over on the job. Now, they even had retirement in sight because of Jude.

It made everything he'd seen worth it.

Almost.

With one last deep breath, Jude knocked on the door, taking a step back as he waited.

His mom's face appeared through the glass door, her plump and sweet features morphing from greeting to confusion then to pure, screaming joy.

"Oh my God," she cried, pushing the door open and throwing her arms around her son. Jude was much taller than her, but it didn't matter. Maria clung to him, pulling him down and holding him close.

"My sweetheart," she cried, pressing her nose into the crook of Jude's neck and shoulder, breathing him in. "You're here? What are you doing here?"

Before Jude could respond, Maria pulled away, calling for Jude's dad. "Don," she hollered, dragging Jude in the house behind her. "Don, get over here."

Don, an imposing but gentle man, quiet in nature, walked in, eyes going wide as he took in Jude. With a sharp inhale, Don moved forward, embracing his son.

"Hey, Dad," Jude whispered as he hugged him back.

"Don't hog him," his mom eventually said, wedging her way in and hugging Jude again.

The tiny woman oh-so-gently manhandled Jude into the sitting room, plunking him on the couch. Jude looked around the room, taking in the small trinkets over the mantel, Dad's chair in the corner, the old maroon carpeting marked with perfect lines from the vacuum cleaner. It wasn't much, but every fiber of this home was infused with pride.

"What are you doing home, sweetheart?" Maria asked, eyes wide with wonder and happiness.

Jude cleared his throat. "My GHCO director gave me an extended leave to attend Collin's wedding."

Maria clapped in excitement, shooting a smile to Don, who sat in his chair with a serene look on his face. "That's so wonderful. How long are you home for? When did you get in? Why didn't you tell us you were coming? Are you staying with Collin? Do you want to stay here?"

Her questions were delivered with such dizzying speed, Jude could only blink at her.

"You're so thin," she continued, clucking her tongue as she held his face between her palms. She rubbed her thumbs over the hollows below his cheeks. "And you look so tired, honey. Are you not sleeping well?"

Jude couldn't force any words out of his mouth, staring at his sweet mom and her round face and warm smile, comfort spreading like a ball of warmth through his chest.

But as the good feelings flooded in, fear came close on their heels, chasing away anything that made him feel safe.

He was once again frozen by the all-too-familiar weight of his disjointed mind, slow to process, distrusting of everything good.

"Don't worry," she said, patting his cheeks and grinning. "I'm making sauce. We'll fatten you right up."

Maria ushered him to the table, dragging her husband along with them. With both men seated, she whipped around the small kitchen, grabbing plates and plopping pasta on top.

"You have perfect timing, sweetheart," she said, sliding a large dish of linguini with red sauce in front of Jude, then spooning heaps of parmesan cheese on top. "But you always could smell my sauce from up the block, so I'm not surprised." She winked at him before scooping parmesan with gusto on to Don's plate too.

Jude managed to smile at this. Regardless of the stress his parents faced while Jude was growing up, they'd always made Sunday lunch—served precisely at three p.m.—a priority.

Don would spend his Sunday mornings making the noodles while Maria would get her sauce simmering before Jude even woke up, her hair frizzed from the humidity of the kitchen. Jude always had to be home at a quarter till, washed up and setting the table so they could enjoy together.

"I'm so glad nothing's changed," Maria added, scooting her chair close to Jude's and pressing her palm lovingly against his cheek again.

Jude's heart tipped out of his chest, shattering on the linoleum floor.

God, how he wished that were true. It felt like his gut was being squeezed through a metal tube, panic oozing out of his skin.

Somehow, Jude found that little trap door in his brain—the one that let him slip away from chaos, drift into numbness—and he disappeared through it. Numbness was easier than looking at his sweet parents and telling them just how much everything had changed.

Jude's leg started bouncing, and he picked up his fork with shaky fingers, pretending to dig in, trying to swallow past the closing of his throat as his parents continued to talk.

"Your best sauce to date," Don said through a mouthful, smiling at his wife.

"You say that every week," Maria responded, giving him a playful swat.

Jude let himself slip further away—dissolve into the gray space where things passed through him. He retreated so deeply into himself, he was shocked to realize that two hours had passed and the meal had been eaten, not remembering any of it outside of the basic mechanics. In some far-off, disconnected way, he knew they'd asked him questions. He'd answered. He'd asked his dad about work, his mom about her latest class of kids, letting them carry the conversation without being present for any of it.

"Are you okay, sweetheart?" his mom asked quietly, taking his hand in hers. Her eyes traced his face, and Jude blinked away.

Guilt eroded his insides like acid at the soft and subtle worry lining his mom's features, but he couldn't let himself go there. If he opened the door to anyone, even a crack, all the badness would flood out.

"Fine, Mom," Jude said, giving her hand a quick squeeze before pulling his own away. "Stuffed to the brim," he added, trying to put on a smile while he patted his stomach. Every inch of him felt hollow. "And it's getting late. I actually better start heading back."

Maria's look was skeptical. "Do you want to stay the night? We always keep your room made up."

"No," Jude answered. Too fast. Too harsh. But he also knew spending the night in this cozy house with his wonderful parents would hurt far too much.

"No thanks," he said, softer now. "I really just need to get back."

He stumbled through goodbyes, hugging both his parents and promising to come back soon.

The tension holding his body taut unwound a bit on the drive home, Jude losing himself in the glow of headlights. In these moments, when he hovered in his body, not deep enough to actually feel its hurt, he could almost convince himself he was okay. That his sharp and fluctuating reactions to things weren't out of the norm. That no one sensed a change. That being back, even for these short weeks, would be okay . . . wouldn't destroy him.

Part of him did like being home. He enjoyed being around Collin, watching his best friend happy and in love.

Jude even kind of . . . liked seeing Indira. Mainly because his annoyance by her was untouched after all these years. It was nice to know there was at least one thing in his life that was never at risk of changing.

When he finally pulled into Collin's driveway, he was exhausted, wanting nothing more than a hot shower and to collapse facedown on his bed. He quietly let himself in, leaving Collin's keys on the entryway table before dragging himself up the steep staircase.

He stopped at the bathroom, the first door on the left, to quickly rinse the day off and brush his teeth before calling it a night.

He pushed the door open, one hand on the hem of his shirt while the other reached behind him to shut the door.

And a sharp intake of breath set off a domino effect through his system, every sense being slapped awake.

First, was the feel—hot and humid air already pressing against his skin as he stood in the bathroom. Next, was the smell—something earthy and soft and undeniably sensual, mixing with the heat to envelop him like a hug. His eyes were delayed in processing, going in and out of focus as some of the steam lifted. But when his vision cleared, he saw everything—every single inch—in high definition.

Hot-pink toenails accenting a foot propped up on the toilet seat. Hands halted around the calf of a long, lotioned leg. Miles of olive skin. The curve of a hip. The dip of a waist. Sharp points of elbows. Soft ellipses of shoulders. Dark tangles of curls plastered against a slender neck and the angle of a jaw.

His gaze finally stopped traveling when he landed on wide brown eyes and a parted mouth, staring like a horrified owl at Jude.

Who stared, equally horrified, back.

The bloodcurdling scream came last.

"What the fuck are you doing?" Indira shrieked, jolting upright in a movement that dragged Jude's eyes down.

"No. No!" Jude bellowed back, slapping a hand over his face as he hurled his body against the closed door.

"Get out!" Indira yelled, the sound of her hitting the glass shower door emphasizing the point.

"Oh my God, no," Jude repeated, fumbling for the door handle, which seemed to have dissolved away in the seconds since he'd witnessed Indira Papadakis. Naked.

He'd seen Indira naked.

He'd seen her naked and she was undeniably hot as fuck and Jude absolutely did not know what to do with any of this information because his brain was short-circuiting and his heart was slamming against his chest and his brain kept looping the different parts of naked fucking Indira and her sleek, gorgeous skin through his head.

The notch of her ankle. The curves of her collarbones. The slopes of her . . .

"I'm going to kill you, Jude Bailey!" Indira said, chucking something that felt like a wet loofah at Jude's head. It landed on the tile with a squelching noise.

"Get me out of here!" Jude howled, turning fully to the door as he continued to search for the handle.

"Open the door, you loser!"

Jude finally wrenched it open, tumbling out into the hall and scrambling down the stairs, scaring Indira's lurking cat in the process. Grammy let out a disturbing growl as she jumped, then latched onto his pant leg, sinking her claws in.

"Jesus Christ," Jude said, tripping and landing with a loud smack on the hardwood floor.

Freeing himself from Grammy's clutches, he jumped up and started pacing the living room, panic and horror and something that felt way too close to lust pumping through his veins. He needed to get as far away from that bathroom as possible, but he couldn't actually get his brain to work long enough to have him *go* somewhere.

Pounding footsteps overhead and doors slamming made his pulse double, and he tried to cram all mental images of a wet and thoroughly moisturized Indira into a box in his brain that he could then set on fire and never think of again.

There was one peaceful, blessed moment of silence that lasted long enough for Jude to delude himself into thinking the chaos was over.

Then the stairs started creaking and groaning with Indira's descent.

Jude launched himself onto the couch, scrambling to situate his limbs into what he hoped was a casual position that also hid his aggravating (and confusing) half-hard cock . . . Jesus, what was happening? He wasn't supposed to get an . . . an *erection* from Indira. This was madness.

Jude grabbed the remote and hit about forty buttons to get something—anything, dammit—to play on the TV, hoping the noise would somehow drown out the thoughts Jude should definitely not be having about Indira fucking Papadakis.

Indira finally entered the room. From the corner of his eye, he could make out that she was fully clothed, in a dark and bulky mass of a sweatshirt and pajama bottoms. Which was good. Great.

But they didn't do much to replace the images Jude was still working to throw out of his clogged brain.

"Seems like pretty advanced stuff for you," Indira said coolly, nodding at the TV that was playing a children's show at full volume. A cartoon pig sprouted wings and started to fly while counting stars.

"I like to push myself," Jude responded, eyes glued to the screen and palms sweaty as he grabbed the remote and clicked to Netflix's homepage.

Indira moved to stand in front of the TV, crossing her arms over her chest—which Jude had *totally* forgotten the naked image of—and looked at him expectantly.

Jude swallowed once.

Twice.

Cleared his throat.

Coughed for good measure.

"Good weather today, huh?" he mumbled, eyes looking somewhere in the vicinity of her shoulder.

"Excuse me?" Indira spat out, moving her hands to her hips. Also areas Jude no longer had naked images of.

"Think it might rain on Tuesday," he said, cracking his knuckles and switching his gaze to her other shoulder.

"Don't you dare attempt small-talk after walking in on me naked," Indira said, pointing at him. "What the fuck was that?"

"It was an accident," Jude said, dropping his head to the back of the couch.

"An *accident*," Indira repeated, disbelief dripping off every word. "You *accidentally* opened a closed door with a light on inside and *accidentally* shut it behind you while someone else was in there?"

"You didn't have the door locked!" Jude pointed out, then cowered at the fury on her face.

"The lock is broken," she hissed. "So try another excuse, creep."

Jude's gaze snapped to hers, his own frustration rising in his chest. "You act like I *wanted* to see you naked!" Jude said, pushing to stand. "Trust me, Dira, you are the last person on this planet I would want to see naked."

Indira's mouth dropped open, a deep red spreading across her cheeks like ink on paper as silence filled the room.

"Choke on your toenails," she said at last, whipping around and heading to the kitchen. "*Accidentally* walk in on me again, and I'll castrate you," she added from the other room, the sound of the fridge opening and closing echoing after her words.

The house fell into an agitated hush, and Jude collapsed back down on the couch, reeling. The soft hum of running water and dishes being put away traveled from the other room, and Jude's heart seemed dead set on slamming itself out of his chest, a fresh spark of memory lighting across his mind with every beat.

Out of nowhere the sound of shattering glass erupted from the kitchen, followed by a sharp "Ow. *Fuck!*" from Indira and the scrape of Grammy's claws on the floors as she sprinted from the room.

Jude jumped up and stalked to the kitchen, where he found Indira crouched on the floor, clutching her hand as rivulets of blood dripped to the tiles.

"Are you okay?" Jude asked, darting to her side.

"Fine," she said, squeezing her eyes shut and digging her teeth into her lip.

"Let me see," Jude murmured, reaching for her hand.

"Think you've seen enough of me tonight, thanks," Indira mumbled, little beads of sweat popping up on her forehead.

"Indira." Jude said it more firmly, taking her hand and curling back her fingers to analyze the cut. It was about three inches long in the fleshy part at the base of her thumb, the depth of it worrying Jude.

"Come here," he said gruffly, gripping beneath her elbows and lifting her to sit on a chair at the kitchen table. He moved quickly, grabbing paper towels for her to press against the wound before digging under the kitchen sink and in the pantry to find a broom and a dustpan and sweeping up the shards of glass.

"I can do that," Indira protested, still clutching her hand.

"Stay here. I'll be right back," he said, putting away the broom and moving out of the kitchen.

"Jude, I'm fine. Don't worry about—"

Jude ignored her objections, taking the steps two at a time as he ran to his room. Rifling through his duffel bag for a moment, he finally found his suture kit and hurried back to the kitchen.

"Are you allergic to iodine or anesthetics?" Jude asked in his detached, clinical voice as he unzipped the nylon case.

"No," she said softly. "But Jude, it's fine. I can suture it. I'm left-handed anyway."

Jude focused on pulling out what he needed, pulse pounding sharply in his temples and tongue curling behind his teeth, a small tremble traveling down his spine.

He tried not to think of the last time he'd stitched someone up, just days before he'd left his post to come home. He'd been treating a minor laceration on a woman's calf when his brain glitched, and he teetered between that present moment and a haunting memory. His nimble fingers had turned stiff and clumsy while his vision tunneled. He'd stepped away from the patient, gruffly telling a nurse to finish up while he did everything in his power to walk slowly out of the room instead of leaving in a dead sprint. He'd crammed himself into a supply closet, trying to catch his breath and instead hyperventilating until he nearly fainted.

But Jude wouldn't let that happen again. Not now. Not when Indira needed him.

After snapping on a pair of gloves, he grabbed an iodine swab and some topical anesthetic, then turned back to her, kneeling at her feet.

He reached again for her hand, but she pulled it back. "Seriously. You don't have to."

Jude swallowed, then licked his lips, looking up at her.

"Let me do this for you, Dira," he uttered, holding her gaze for the first time since he'd been back.

Indira blinked, then slowly held out her hand for him.

"Okay."

He rested it against his palm, the heat of her skin seeping in through the gloves and making Jude's breath tangle in his throat.

Gingerly, he dabbed at the wound, cleaning the area. It felt like something sharp hooked into his chest at her intake of breath from the sting. He placed the topical anesthetic over it to make her more comfortable. When she was numb, he checked more closely for any lingering shards of glass, holding the palm of her hand close to his face and tilting it in the light.

When he was satisfied that the area was clear and sterile, he got to work. He picked up the needle, hand trembling slightly. Holding surgical tools had once made Jude feel powerful. Infallible. Now it just felt damning.

With a deep breath, he steadied himself, carefully stitching her up, the only sounds in the room their off-rhythm inhales.

"There," he said after a few minutes, smoothing a bandage over the area. He dragged the pad of his thumb against the rough material. "All done."

Indira's fingers closed around his hand for a moment, and he couldn't look away from the spot where she touched him. He had the bizarre feeling that he'd fall backward the second she let go.

"Thank you," she whispered.

Jude managed to drag his eyes away from their hands and up to her face. "Of course," he said through a dry throat, blinking rapidly.

They stared at each other for a moment, an odd cord of electricity tethering them together, pulling them just the tiniest bit closer.

Suddenly, a crash from upstairs, followed by Grammy's howl and the sound of her running, jolted them both out of the trance.

Indira shook her head, letting out a huff of a laugh before pulling her hand away.

"And while I'm still not happy with you and the . . . uh . . . events that transpired earlier—"

A vibrant heat filled his cheeks at the roaring images that stampeded through his mind.

"—I don't actually want you to choke on your toenails."

Jude's lips quirked, the closest he could get to a smile. "I'll give it my best effort not to."

"Better go check on the monster," Indira said, eyes rolling toward the ceiling.

Jude nodded, gaze tracing down the long line of her neck before falling to the floor. He pushed to stand, then turned away from her and roughly dragged his thumb across his forehead.

He heard her chair scraping against the tile and then the pad of her steps, but he couldn't watch her leave.

"Jude?" she said, voice soft.

He risked a glance to where she stood in the doorway, an odd surge of feelings he couldn't name rising in his chest.

Indira licked her lips. "Seriously, thank you. I really appreciate it."

Jude nodded, then looked back to the ground. "Of course."

After standing there for a few minutes, waiting for the noises above to stop until he was confident she was settled down, Jude collected his things and headed up the stairs.

Making a beeline straight for his room, he collapsed facedown on the bed, feeling like he'd sink into it, completely spent and exhausted from the coiled tension of his muscles, chest aching and breathing short like he'd run a marathon. He hated how much work it took for his body to do the things that should come naturally.

But, even in the heavy weight of all the aches, a foreign warmth glowed in his chest.

And Jude couldn't shake the feeling that the warmth had originated at the touch of Indira's fingers against his skin.

CHAPTER 7

Jude

∽

Jude had picked up running during the summer GHCO assigned him to various areas around Indonesia after a series of devastating earthquakes. It started as an escape, a way to lull his screaming thoughts. He was about eighteen months into his GHCO service and was desperate for a distraction.

The punishing heat on his shoulders, the muscle-twisting hills, all of it turned his attention away from the memories that haunted him.

Running was the one constant Jude had from place to place, giving him some momentary peace as he pushed his body.

Jude was searching for a similar escape when he'd laced up his sneakers that morning—hoping to outpace the constant stream of Indira that had looped through his dreams all night.

Instead, he got an extremely chatty companion.

"I really don't think there could be a worse time to plan a wedding," Collin said as they turned a corner. "Everything is so expensive and there's supply-chain issues . . . Like, we had to go through five different invitation designs before we got one that could reliably be sent out on time."

"That's rough," Jude said, concentrating on the burn in his legs.

"But that was nothing compared to agreeing to tuxes. We went back and forth for probably six weeks over that. Jeremy was trying to convince me we should wear these hideous burnt-orange plaid suits," Collin said, voice straining as they ran up a hill. "I mean, Beetlejuice's wedding ensemble would have been a better option than *that* ugly thing."

"That's wild," Jude said, sucking in lungfuls of cool air as he picked up the pace. He wanted to put miles between himself and the flooding memories of Indira's naked skin, the way her hands dragged over it.

"And he tried to argue that we're having a November wedding and the color palette would match the autumn vibe," Collin said, pushing his hand through his wavy golden hair as he kept up. "But I didn't want to be walking down the aisle in something that's more of a Halloween costume than anything else."

"Oh wow." Jude pushed his legs even harder.

"And then pigs flew and I vomited up a kitten after binge-drinking with Bruce Springsteen."

"That's—" Jude did a double-take. "Wait, what?"

Collin laughed, then stopped running, putting his hands on his knees. Jude reluctantly slowed down, circling back to his friend.

"I know you've always skewed toward the moody and aloof," Collin said, fixing Jude with a good-natured smile as he squinted up at him. "But you could at least pretend to have some interest in what I'm saying." He straightened, hands fixed on his hips. "I plan on only getting married this one time so I'm allowed to obnoxiously indulge in all the mundane wedding details."

"I-I . . . I was listening . . . I mean, I heard . . . I . . ." Jude hung his head. "I'm sorry," he said at last. He was an asshole. He'd come back to celebrate Collin and Jeremy, but his brain was always a million miles away.

"Jude, come on, I'm just kidding," Collin said, patting Jude on the shoulder. "I'm getting to the point where I'm annoying myself with wedding talk. If you'd asked me two years ago if I'd have an opinion on napkin rings and bow ties, I would have laughed in your face. Now I have multiple Pinterest boards, for fuck's sake."

Jude let a huff of a laugh through his nose. "Why are you being so, uh . . . detail oriented?"

Collin laughed again, dragging a hand through his sweaty hair. The slow smile that curved his lips was infectious. "Because it's kind of . . . fun?" he said. "Jeremy's been dreaming up wedding plans since he was a kid, and he loves this stuff. And I love getting swept up in things with him, I guess."

Jude nodded, a weird achy weight settling on his shoulders as he tried to relate to the feeling. He couldn't.

"It's no different than our lawn and garden," Collin said, green eyes crinkling at the corners with his soft smile. "I never thought I'd give a shit about grass length or hedge trimming or sun exposure on a patch of dirt, but now we're both obsessed with it all. We'll spend hours working on the garden and even more hours talking about it. It's surprisingly fun to indulge in the details or something. Get lost in the complex simplicity of it all. It can be . . . I don't know, really nice getting caught up in the small things with someone you love."

Jude nodded again, knowing he'd never have that type of closeness with someone. Knowing he'd always exist as this empty shell, none of life's small details affecting him because all the big ones had chewed him up.

"I'm glad you have that," Jude said.

Collin smiled again "But, erm, I did want to talk to you."

Jude's stomach sank. He hated talking.

The pair started walking down the block, Collin chewing on his bottom lip as he searched for words.

"I can't help but get the feeling you're . . . I mean, it's not even a feeling. It's a fact. You aren't yourself." Collin glanced at Jude, worried lines creasing his forehead. "It's like you're somewhere else. Or thinking about something that's . . . I don't know, bothering you. You've always been quiet, but this seems different."

Jude didn't know what to say to that. He wasn't himself. He'd probably never be that person again. He felt uncomfortable in his body, like he didn't deserve the space it took up. Like it didn't fully belong to him. He tried so hard to be normal, to avoid burdening anyone with the guilty weight cinched around his neck, but apparently Collin had noticed.

"And I guess, uh—" Collin cleared his throat, dragging a hand down his mouth and chin. "I guess I want you to know that if you need to talk about anything, we can. Like I said, I know I'm ridiculously focused on the wedding and stuff, but that doesn't mean we can't . . . you know . . . talk. And shit. Or whatever."

"Wow," Jude said, shooting Collin an impressed look. "That was really beautiful. And here I thought Indira was the psychiatrist."

Collin laughed as he punched Jude's shoulder. "Okay, asshole. Bury those feelings all you want. But just know the offer doesn't expire."

Jude stopped, cracking his knuckles as emotions clogged up his throat. Collin stopped too, looking at Jude, carefully studying him.

Jude jerked forward a bit, almost reaching out and wrapping Collin in a hug. He knew Collin would hug him back, let Jude collapse against him if he needed.

But Jude feared if he gave an inch of himself to someone, he'd crumble completely. And he couldn't handle breaking more than he already was.

So, instead, he clapped a hand on Collin's shoulder and attempted a smile.

Collin smiled back, genuine and warm. "Love ya, man."

Jude's friendship with Collin was the most effortless relationship in Jude's life. They'd been best friends since kindergarten, close as brothers through high school. Roommates in college and med school. Jude had even been there the night Collin and Jeremy met.

Something about his bond with Collin always made him feel safe.

Which made guilt churn in Jude's stomach and flood down to his toes as he thought about how many minutes of the past day he'd spent picturing Collin's little sister naked.

Which was so ridiculous. Obscene, really. Jude didn't even *like* Indira . . . not that much anyway. Being around her was never easy. She was obstinate and annoying and seemed to find perverse joy in being a pain in the ass. A constant challenge. Collin was safe, but Indira was terrifying, and being back with both of them was twisting him into knots.

"Tell me more about the wedding," Jude said through a tight throat, walking down the street again.

Collin didn't need to be asked twice.

He talked about flowers. The mountain venue. Cake tastings. Listed at least three variations of an engagement party, one of which was happening *after* the wedding. Jude decided not to ask too many questions on that one.

"And, in a mildly shocking turn of events, my dad is going to give me away."

"Not your mom?" Jude asked, thoroughly shocked. Angela had raised Collin and Indira—and Jude, considering how often he had stayed over at their place—alone after their father, Greg, had left.

Even when they were younger, Collin didn't talk about it much, but from what Jude had picked up over the years, Greg had abandoned his family to start a new one with his mistress in Florida, accumulating a few additional wives since. There had been many broken promises over the years, but Collin seemed incapable of not falling into the traps.

"They'll both walk me," Collin said with a shrug and a smile.

"And your mom is going to be okay with that?" Angela made no secret of her hate for her ex-husband.

Collin waved away the question. "I talked to her about it and she's fine. They're both adults. They can deal."

"I certainly wouldn't want to be the one trying to defy your wedding orders," Jude said dryly, trying to tease Collin like he used to. Collin laughed, and Jude felt a tiny ping of happiness.

"Glad to hear it," Collin said as they turned the corner to his house. "Because there's been a small logistical change. Indira and

Chris were supposed to walk down the aisle together, but now that they've broken up—"

"Yeah, what happened with that?" The words poured out of Jude before he found any self-control to suppress the question he had no right asking. Jesus Christ, when did he lose the ability to think before he spoke? And why was he suddenly so curious about Indira?

Collin shrugged. "They've been on and off for the last year or so. I've never really understood the pairing. I mean, between you and me, I think Chris is a bit of a dickhead. But he and Jeremy have always been close, I guess, I don't know. From an outsider's perspective, Chris is that relative you know is a bit of a shit but you end up being reluctantly bonded to."

Jude came from a very tiny family, both of his parents only children and Jude without siblings, so he didn't fully get this, but he had also learned long ago not to question Collin when he gripped at an assumption with both hands and refused to let go.

"But what I was getting at is we obviously can't have Chris and Indira walk down the aisle together—I doubt Chris would make it to the altar in one piece," Collin said casually. "So, we're going to have you and Indira paired up for the ceremony."

Jude tripped over his feet, nearly belly-slapping the pavement. Collin caught him by the elbow.

"Oh my God, there's no need to be so dramatic," Collin said with a chuckle. "I know there's always been some animosity between you two, but you'll be able to deal . . . Right?"

More of that guilt pumped through Jude's veins.

"I . . . uh . . . does Indira know about this?"

There was no way she'd be okay with it if she did. They'd be more likely to kill each other than actually make it through the ceremony.

Collin sighed. "You don't have to look so afraid; she's outgrown her biting habit."

Jude's entire body flushed with a very lewd image that he absolutely should not be having.

"Regardless," Collin said, hopping up his front steps and unlocking the door. "I have faith you two can dig deep, deep down and behave yourselves."

Jude shot up a silent prayer to whatever deity was listening to prove Collin right.

CHAPTER 8

Indira

T-MINUS FOUR WEEKS UNTIL THE WEDDING

Indira was wrong before: rock bottom wasn't bawling hysterically on a train. Rock bottom was, in fact, getting wasted at a Cheesecake Factory on thick and creamy cocktails while sitting across from your shithead ex, the latest love of his life, *and* the guy you'd known since childhood who recently walked in on you naked. And screamed in horror.

Being an adult was fun.

Indira chugged down the last of her cranberry cheesecake martini, signaling the circling waiter for another one, as she tried to listen to Collin and Jeremy's highly specific instructions for putting together wedding favors.

"So each of you has multiple mini easels and canvases," Jeremy said from the head of the table, gesturing at the supplies in front of himself. "And we want you to use them to express yourselves. Specifically, express what love represents to you. Each tiny painting will be a priceless keepsake for our wedding guests. And we request you make about thirty each."

Indira stared darkly at the three-by-four-inch canvas in front of her, wishing her eyes alone could light it on fire and char it to ash. She raised her hand like a kid in class.

"Yes, Indira," Collin said, falling easily into a teacher-on-a-power-trip role.

She cleared her throat. "Seeing as you two pull in a combined salary of seven figures, and were able to rent out this entire party room, wouldn't it be better for you to just buy wedding favors instead of forcing us to arts-and-crafts our way through them? In a Cheesecake Factory, no less?"

"Don't you dare disrespect the Cheesecake Factory," Lizzie cut in with an unnecessary amount of passion.

Indira shot her a dirty look, but it was quickly replaced by a melting smile when Evie, Lizzie's toddler, popped between them and gave Indira a sloppy kiss.

"Cheesecake!" Evie shrieked, before crawling onto Indira's lap. Indira, a hopelessly adoring aunt, was wrapped around Evie's pudgy little finger. Lizzie and Rake beamed at their daughter.

Rake and Collin had become close over the years with how much time Lizzie and Indira spent together, earning him a groomsman spot. Jeremy and Lizzie had also formed a special bond, particularly after Jeremy discovered Lizzie's immense talent for erotic baked goods. Not only was she his groomsmaid, but she was also making the wedding cake. There was no chance it wouldn't be perverse.

"I know this can't be fun for you," Lizzie whispered, tracing her knuckle across Evie's soft cheek, "but that's no reason to blaspheme the Cheesecake Factory."

Indira shot Lizzie a bland look. *Fun* wasn't even in the top one-thousand words she would use to describe this night.

"Don't hog the sweet angel," Thu said, leaning toward Indira and blowing raspberries into Evie's neck. She let out a squeal and squirmed on Indira's lap.

Thu wasn't technically part of the wedding party, but she was close to Jeremy and Collin, and also known to bully her way into any event that provided free food.

"I'm absolutely not sharing," Indira said, hugging Evie closer. "I need all the cuddles right now."

"Feel free to keep her for a day or year," Rake said from Lizzie's other side. "She's become quite the cot escape artist. I haven't slept through the night in nearly two years."

"Don't be modest, dear," Lizzie said, patting him on the cheek. "They know the real reason you're up all night . . . As insatiable as ever," Lizzie said, shooting Thu and Indira a lascivious wink. Rake blushed crimson.

"Say the word and I'll verbally annihilate him," Thu said, taking a prim sip of her drink and shooting a dark look across the table. Chris and Lauren rubbed their noses together while Jude silently studied his piece of bread.

"Don't tempt me with a good time," Indira said out of the corner of her mouth, sharp prickles radiating across her skin. She was surprised, albeit relieved, at how little she missed Chris, but seeing him flaunt his new infatuation was a particularly bitter pill to swallow.

"I've been storing up insults for that man for as long as I've known him," Thu whispered, an evil smile ticking up the corner of her mouth.

"Go on," Indira encouraged, taking a big gulp of her drink.

"I'd start with how Chris is the most embarrassingly stereotypical example of the frosted-tip frat-boy-to-cryptocurrency-bro pipeline. I'm even considering making a PowerPoint that showcases every time he unironically used the terms 'on that grind' and 'the city is my playground' in a conversation, and how I believe I'm entitled to compensation for emotional and intellectual damages as a result. But if I need to go off the cuff at some point tonight, I'll go for a quick but deeply personal attack on how unsettling his Vineyard Vines polo collection is, and end with an empirical review of how his favorite IPAs reflect all of his worst, and only, personality traits."

Lizzie nodded in agreement.

Indira stifled a laugh as she took another sip of her drink, a buzzy type of warmth filling her. "I can't let you destroy him without Harper around to witness. She's quietly hated him more than you this past year, I think."

"Her on-call schedule is really interfering with my hobbies," Thu said, pouting. "She needs to reassess her priorities." The three women giggled.

"I don't mean to interrupt," Collin said from the head of the table next to Jeremy with a voice that very much conveyed the opposite. "But it seems like you haven't started any of your paintings. I just want to make sure you're taking this seriously. Look at Rake—he's already completed two."

Rake blushed and bowed his head with a smile like a teacher's pet.

"Oh, I'm taking this *soooo* seriously," Indira drawled, jamming her brush in black ink and dragging it over the canvas. "Don't you like it?" She turned around the tiny canvas to show Collin a rough outline of a hand giving the middle finger. "Inspired by how much I love you."

Collin's handsome face fell into a scathing frown, causing wondrous satisfaction to flood through Indira. "You're so immature," Collin snapped.

"Maturity is a social construct upheld by the patriarchy with an incredibly narrow, white, cis, neurotypical scope to enforce conformity and then implemented as an othering and shaming tactic for anyone that steps outside of that paradigm."

Collin blinked at Indira, a notch deepening between his eyebrows as he processed that.

A rough sound from across the table grabbed Indira's attention. It was the echo of a memory, rusty and worn, but still recognizable.

Jude had laughed.

Indira stared at him, and Jude looked back, eyes wide like the sound had surprised him too.

Jude was quiet by nature, but his silence since he'd been back was different, tinged with an undercurrent of hurt that Indira didn't fully understand.

Their gazes held, and Jude's face lost a bit of its tension, a bit of its strain, something close to warmth and maybe even happiness peeking out of those coffee-black eyes.

Indira's throat constricted painfully, a little voice in her head saying, *Ah, there you are.*

Evie suddenly decided she wanted in on the painting, lunging forward in Indira's lap to grab a brush. In the process her chubby fist tipped an empty water glass onto a plate, creating a sharp and loud clatter that made everyone jump.

"Oopsie!" Evie yelled, pulling a booming laugh from her mom. Lizzie righted the glass, accidentally banging it against the plate a few more times and creating more noise, before grabbing Evie and cuddling her on her lap.

"Let's get you painting over here, missy," Lizzie said, pressing her nose to Evie's orange hair. Evie shook her fists in excitement.

With the sudden commotion settled, Indira looked back across the table, desperate to soak up more of the Jude she recognized.

But any openness on his face was now sharp lines and a pained expression, his entire body tense like the sound had been a physical blow.

His eyes darted back and forth across the room before he pushed back from the table and hurried away.

Indira shouldn't follow him. If he was upset, it wasn't her business. He'd made it very clear he didn't want her involved in his life. But Indira was Indira, and she had a rather unfortunate and incurable need to help people.

Taking the final sip of her drink, she excused herself from the table and walked out of the party room, scanning the restaurant before making a beeline for the bathrooms down a dark hallway.

Jude was leaning against the wall in the shape of half a heart, head bowed, back curved, and legs stretched in front of him. She cleared her throat gently, drawing his attention so she wouldn't startle him.

Indira's eyes traced his profile, his expression one of weary surrender, before walking to him, stopping about a foot away.

"Mmm. Explosive diarrhea." Indira nodded sagely, looking between Jude and the bathroom door. She couldn't help herself. Being around Jude turned her into a snarky teenager ready to battle, and after that taste of his laugh, she wanted to pull him back out. Just like old times.

Jude closed his eyes and huffed out an amused breath. "I'm not sure if you meant that as a question, but it certainly sounded like a declarative statement, so don't let me stop you." He waved toward the door.

Indira spluttered, unable to think of anything to save face. She stood there, looking at Jude looking at the ground. Her chest ached as she felt the hurt radiating out of him. An odd urge to reach out to him, hug his wiry frame, swamped her, and she had to work to keep her arms pinned to her sides.

She should pull herself away, march into that bathroom, and splash icy water on her face to jolt her out of these bizarre feelings she was probably projecting onto him.

But she'd had one gross cocktail too many, and common sense failed her, so she stepped closer to Jude instead, leaning her back against the wall next to him.

"You know, you don't have to lurk in the shadows like some creature of the night. Everyone's been warned you'd be here, and they were given instructions on how to prepare accordingly."

Jude rolled his neck to look at her. Indira stared straight ahead, pressing her lips together.

"I'm assuming you want me to ask you what those preparations were?" Jude asked dryly, but Indira knew his voice well enough to catch the tiniest hint of amusement in its lilt.

Indira nodded. "I told them you'd likely materialize in a cloud of toxic gas, and they should try to ignore the smell as best as possible. I also explained that one of your coolly appraising glances is liable to make both babies and puppies cry, and that you are deathly allergic to joy and laughter, either of which will make you break out into festering boils."

"So clever," Jude deadpanned. "How long did it take you to think of those zingers?"

"Only like, twelve hours," Indira said, turning to face him. "I couldn't decide between the cloud-of-toxic-gas bit or a staircase for your ascension from hellfire," she added in a self-deprecating tone before crossing one eye to look at her nose, the other fixed straight ahead, then reversing the whole bizarre thing on the other side.

Jude stared at her for a moment, an almost-smile tugging at the corner of his tense mouth. He shook his head, letting out another small laugh.

Silence fell heavily between them again.

"You okay?" Indira asked. God, why did she care so much? She was annoying herself with how much she was asking.

"Fine," Jude said, voice cracking on the word. "Just, uh, weird. Being back. Being around so many people again after being gone for so long."

"Has it been hard?" Indira asked.

Jude looked at her questioningly.

"Your work with the GHCO, I mean. I can't imagine how jarring it must be to ship off to a totally new country every few months. And in areas of disaster or conflict, no less . . ."

Jude's body jerked, his jaw tensing and a muscle ticking like he just remembered he was supposed to keep it shut around her. The air turned chilly, more distance growing between them as they stood there until the chasm felt so much greater than when they'd *actually* been apart.

Without thinking, Indira reached out for him, wanting to touch him, wanting to take away some of that pain.

Jude flinched again and Indira caught herself before she made contact. Something about the curve of his shoulders and lines of his face told her that touching him would only make the pain worse.

"Jude," Indira whispered, balling her hands into fists and pressing them against her sternum. "You can talk to me. You know that, right?"

Jude looked up at the ceiling, and Indira watched his Adam's apple bob as he swallowed.

"Trust me," he said at last. "It's for the best if I don't." Then he turned and walked away.

CHAPTER 9

Indira

"I'm just gonna say it." Indira sucked down a rattling breath as she held back tears on Dr. Koh's couch. "There are few places more pathetic to get drunk and have an internal emotional crisis than a Cheesecake Factory."

Dr. Koh nodded sagely. "That does sound rather challenging."

Indira gave her therapist a pointed look. "The whole night felt like a massive disaster. And I can't stop thinking about it. I don't know what's wrong with me."

"What parts of the night does your mind keep returning to?"

A flash of the dark hallway. Jude's crestfallen face. The sound of his rough laugh and how she wanted more of it.

"I don't know," Indira said with a shrug. "Just . . . all of it."

"How was it seeing Chris with Lauren so soon after your breakup?"

Indira rolled her eyes and shook her head. "It wasn't fucking great, Dr. Koh."

Dr. Koh gave her a placating smile. "Let's dig a little deeper with the emotions at play here. What did it bring up in you?"

"Umm, I guess the overwhelming sense of abandonment?" A strangled laugh fell from her throat.

"From Chris's betrayal and new relationship?"

Indira chewed on her lip as she considered the question but shook her head. She hadn't been sleeping well lately, and plenty of hours staring up at her ceiling allowed her to untangle that the crashing and burning with Chris didn't upset her because she really loved him but because it meant he didn't really love her. They'd been a mess of make-believe, both letting the distance grow between them for months. It never would have lasted, but it certainly sucked how it ended.

And it was mortifying as hell to watch your ex and his girlfriend rub their noses together in a disgustingly overt display of affection.

"In all honesty, it kind of hurt more to watch Jude walk away from me than it was to process the end of the relationship with Chris."

"Why do you think that is?" Dr. Koh asked, tilting her head.

Indira shrugged. "You advised me to take my psychiatrist hat off during our sessions, so I'll defer to your interpretation."

That won her a genuine laugh from Dr. Koh, but that was all.

Indira leaned her head against the couch, staring out the window over Dr. Koh's shoulder. It was fairly annoying how much therapy made you actually think about things.

"I really don't know," Indira said, her knee starting to bounce. "Maybe because I've known Jude for so long and he's so . . . different? It worries me. Bothers me. Which is weird because we've never been, like, best friends or whatever. We've always fought more than anything."

"And this change in Jude is holding your attention and emotional energy more than Chris's infidelity?"

Indira nodded, digging her teeth harder into her bottom lip and swallowing down a sudden swell of feelings that threatened to overflow from her chest.

"It's weird, right? That Jude is what I'm more focused on?"

More of that therapeutic silence.

"I feel like maybe I kind of . . . expected this with Chris?" Indira admitted softly. "Or at least knew it was possible? Not the weird peanut-butter-cheating thing, but it ending. Or maybe it was that things never felt . . . *right* with him?"

"Does your relationship with Jude have a more correct feeling?"

Indira snorted at that.

"Why's that funny?" Dr. Koh asked.

Indira blew out a deep breath. "I've known Jude my entire life. He lived on the same block as us growing up, and he and Collin were best friends from the jump. But he and I have always been, like, these fundamental opposites. Even as a kid he was serious; had a certain sharpness about him. And I was nothing but soft spots."

Dr. Koh gave her a gentle smile.

"But despite that, I was always chasing after them, always forcing my way into their world. I wanted so badly to be their best friend too. Jude spent so much time at our house, always eating dinner with us or sleeping over. During the summer it was like he lived with us. And he and I fought *all the time*. And it was always about the silliest stuff. A snarky comment, a mean look, breathing too loud . . . I could always get under his skin, and I kind of loved it. It meant he saw me."

Indira rubbed her hand over her chest, a soft ache growing as she sifted through the memories.

"After my dad left," Indira continued, swallowing past the bubble of rage that burned her throat, "my mom wasn't able to hang on to the house, so we moved into this cramped two-bedroom apartment—don't even get me started on the turmoil of being a teenager and sharing a room with your older brother. It forced closeness on us."

The fondness in Indira's voice earned her another soft chuckle from Dr. Koh.

"But even then, Jude was still *always* around."

He and Collin playing video games. All of them eating pizza around the small table her mom insisted they have nightly dinner at. Jude was a constant in the shifting mosaic of her childhood.

"We didn't have much contact during college, but I had a year of overlap in med school with Jude and Collin, and we still battled each other like when we were little. Old habits and all that . . ."

Indira missed their constant teasing. Their bickering. It used to be . . . fun. She wasn't really sure what she wanted from him now, but she was filled with this overwhelming urge to *find* him under that cold and distant mask, pull the Jude she used to know up to the surface.

"His scholarship required him to go to areas of need or disaster or conflict zones to perform emergency medicine. At his going-away party, I kind of . . . panicked a bit."

"How so?" Dr. Koh asked.

"It wasn't any big scene or anything, but I remember spending the night with this knot of anxiety in my chest. This overwhelming dread that Jude would be . . . gone." She blinked past the sharp pinpricks of tears in her eyes. "Having him be this steady presence in my life for so long, it felt terrifying for him to leave, no matter how annoying he was. Is."

Dr. Koh let the silence linger for a minute before asking, "Have you talked to Jude about this?"

"Oh, fuck no," Indira said, eyes shooting wide in horror. "That would be, uh, rather mortifying."

"How so?"

"Because . . . I don't know. It would be weird. We're not . . . *feely* with each other. It's all surface level with us. It would be so random."

Indira was getting a bit sick of these extended silences of Dr. Koh's, hot damn.

"What would I even say?" Indira asked, throwing her hands up. "'Hey, you going off and doing that whole living-your-life thing like an autonomous adult is supposed to stir up complicated feelings of abandonment in me and now I can't stop worrying about you?'"

"Perhaps somewhat less sarcastic, but yes, something along those lines."

"Absolutely not," Indira said, shaking her head.

"Why?"

"Because I . . . It's fucked up."

"What's fucked up?"

Indira wasn't sure why, but she was crying. Tiny, hot tears burning her cheeks, her shoulders shaking with the force.

"I'm fucked up," she said at last, shrugging. "I panic when people leave. It feels as permanent as death and I react like that's what happened. Every boyfriend in high school. And college. And med school . . . I've had so many people walk out of my life after I cling to them too hard and it's embarrassing. I'm not about to put that on Jude, especially when any connection we have isn't one of emotional intimacy."

She took a shuddering breath, trying to calm the sharp jabs of her heartbeat. "I'm not looking to have a conversation with Jude that shows him how fucked up I am. I'm just not."

Indira fiddled with the hem of her shirt, the silence in the room crushing her as doubts circled around her shoulders.

"I sometimes wonder how I'm allowed to be a psychiatrist when I still carry all of these issues," she whispered, giving words to the fear that kept her up at night. The same one she'd tiptoed around at her last session. It pissed her off that she wasn't magically over this fear. "How can I be this damaged and still help people?"

The silence stretched until Indira thought she would snap from it. Finally, Dr. Koh cleared her throat. "Indira, you're self-aware, and that alone is half the battle."

Indira made a dismissive noise.

Dr. Koh leaned forward, resting her forearms on her knees. "If you're open to it, would you hear me out on something?"

Indira opened her mouth, but that question seemed a bit like a therapeutic trap. She opted for a shrug.

"You are incredibly early in your career, and doubt is a near-universal feeling, especially in those first few years. Offer yourself some grace as you navigate this new role."

Indira stared down at her lap.

"There's also this huge misconception," Dr. Koh continued, "that psychiatrists and any other mental health professionals are ideally self-aware and have perfect coping strategies and practices for every situation and have overcome all of their trauma and never crumble. That's a ridiculous standard to be placed on anyone, regardless of profession.

"We struggle too. We hurt. We handle situations badly or get depressed or anxious or anything else. We're all flawed. Your emotional struggles as a human are not a moral judgment of your worth, and they're not a reflection on your ability to help others."

Indira stared at Dr. Koh.

"Sitting with these feelings is a great place to start with healing from them."

"I hate sitting with my feelings," Indira mumbled. She thought back to all the times she'd told her patients the same exact phrase and wondered how much they had despised her and her advice in those moments.

"If sitting with them were comfortable, we wouldn't let them fester until they infected our hearts and our heads. But we avoid. We throw ourselves into work or vices or others because it's easier to focus on those things than our own hurt."

"That, unfortunately, makes too much sense for me to argue."

"I think that's what they refer to as a breakthrough," Dr. Koh said, her lips tipping up.

Indira blinked at her, then busted out laughing. "Dr. Koh, was that a joke?"

Dr. Koh was fully grinning now. "I've been known to make them from time to time."

Indira continued to giggle. Humor might be one of the most healing aspects of therapy.

"Do you think it's possible for you to view Jude as an acquaintance or even a friend?" Dr. Koh asked, redirecting. "Instead of as some sort of childhood adversary?"

"Do I have to?" Indira asked impertinently.

Another laugh. Indira was on a roll today.

"You don't have to do anything," Dr. Koh said. "But if you're going to be forced to see him until the end of this wedding, living in the same house as him even, perhaps it might be easier to sit with your emotions if you two can find level ground. Maybe even open up a dialogue to some of the emotions and worry you're experiencing."

Indira shrugged. That also, unfortunately, made sense.

"This week," Dr. Koh continued, "if I can encourage you to do anything, it's to sit with whatever emotions come up. Trace their source like a map in your body. Let them burn until they snuff out, if you're able."

Well, that sounded awful. But Indira nodded, blowing her nose one last time before gathering herself and leaving the office.

Out on the street, she caught herself trying to shake off all the feelings, all the pain that hovered on her shoulders like she always did after sessions. And she stopped. She felt the hurt, the heavy weight in her chest.

And, for once, she let it be.

CHAPTER 10

Jude

∞

Help. Please. Help. Please.

The desperate chant was a whisper but it released an avalanche of fear in Jude's chest. He needed to move. Do something. Anything.

But he couldn't.

It was like cement solidified through his veins, rooting him to the spot, unable to do anything but stare in horror, knowing how this ended. Knowing it was his fault.

No. No. No. I can't see this again. I can't. I can't. I ca—

Jude woke up in a cold sweat, heart slamming against his breastbone in a jagged pattern as he jolted up to sitting. He couldn't catch his breath, couldn't wash the phantom blood from his hands.

Slowly, reality settled around him, but not fully. Two fuzzy worlds were superimposed, the dark bedroom and the piercing light of the operating room. House and desert. Midnight silence and war-zone chaos.

He tore out of bed, needing to escape before he got stuck in the in-between permanently.

Jude wrestled his long limbs into running clothes. Running would save him. If he ran hard enough, long enough, fast enough, far enough, he could outpace the chaos in his brain. He picked up his sneakers, waiting to put them on until he got outside of the house so his steps wouldn't wake anyone up.

But as he tiptoed down the stairs, front door in sight, the soft glow and muffled hum of the TV caught his attention.

Indira was on the couch, wrapped in a tight ball with a blanket draped over her. When she noticed Jude, she jumped a bit then sat up, the blanket falling to her waist, her wild mane of inky curls surrounding her face like a dark cloud.

"Hey," she said softly, tilting her head as she looked at him. The TV offered just enough light for him to see the curiosity in her tired features.

"What are you doing?" Jude said with his characteristic roughness. He didn't mean to be so abrasive, but his throat always felt rusty and raw, especially when trying to form words for Indira.

Her face hardened at his tone. "What are *you* doing?" she shot back. "It's close to three a.m. and you're dressed like a highlighter," she added, nodding at his neon-yellow shirt and the stripes on his sneakers.

"I—" He gestured helplessly at the door before dropping his hand to his side. "I can't sleep," he admitted. He wasn't sure why he told her the truth.

Maybe it was because he was exhausted and disjointed and felt a fog of derealization sinking into his bones. Or maybe it was because of the way Indira's eyes pierced through him, even in the dark. Maybe it was the way energy softly radiated off her, a confusing mix of gentleness and hardness, that created the odd sense in his chest that she understood him.

But it was probably just the exhaustion.

"I can't sleep either," Indira said. There was a beat of silence. "Do you, uh . . . wanna watch TV with me?"

Jude's brain generated the word *no*, but his tongue wouldn't form it, wouldn't push the syllable out. He knew he shouldn't burden her with the subtle sickness that leaked out of him like a toxic cloud. He should leave her be and walk out that door, run his muscles into painful oblivion and spare Indira the trouble.

But something about her drew him in, like she had a rope looped around his chest that she gently and steadily pulled on.

His legs started moving, dragging his shattered self to the soft-looking couch with the sweetly sleepy-looking Indira as if any of it mattered. As if he could find comfort in any of it. He knew he couldn't.

"What are you watching?" he asked, sitting stiffly on the sofa with as much space between them as possible.

"*Bob's Burgers*," she said, hitting play on the paused cartoon. "But only the Thanksgiving specials."

Jude's mouth quirked. "Why just the Thanksgiving specials?"

Indira smiled, her eyes still fixed on the TV as a cartoon woman in a teal dress started singing about cranberry sauce. "I'm not sure. They make me happy, I guess. Slows my brain down and usually lets me fall asleep."

"Why can't you sleep?"

She shrugged, readjusting the blanket and draping part of it over Jude's lap. His thigh muscles jerked as if she'd dragged her hand over them.

"It's not always a problem, but sometimes work keeps me up. Or wakes me up, more accurately."

"Are you having trouble with work?" Jude kind of hated himself for the tiny blip of hope that maybe she was having a hard time with her career too. That maybe he wasn't completely alone.

But Indira shook her head. "No, not particularly. Today was actually a really good day. I've been working with this little boy for a few months now, but he wouldn't speak—and after what he's been through in such a short life, I can't blame him." Indira paused, chewing on her lower lip. "But I decided to try something new today and I took him outside to sit in the sunshine. He was hesitant at first, but slowly, he relaxed. He rubbed his sweet little hands over the grass, dug his fingers into the dirt. Raised his face to the sun and actually smiled. And then he talked—just a few sentences—but I almost cried I was so happy to hear his voice."

The noise of the TV was the only sound in the room for a few moments.

"I'm so hopeful for him," she whispered. "I love that I get to watch people learn to heal themselves. It's magic."

Jude couldn't look away from her mouth, the cadence of her words like a lullaby.

"Then why can't you sleep?" he heard himself asking.

Indira smiled—a small smile with the tiniest hint of hurt.

"I don't know; I worry about my patients, I guess. Even when things are going well. It sometimes feels like I'm missing a crucial piece to their puzzle and it makes me restless."

"You shouldn't let your work affect you like that," Jude said, sounding like a smart-ass even to his own ears.

Indira turned fully toward him, her face expressionless except for her eyes, which were endless pools of irony.

She looked at him like she *knew*. Like she'd seen every haunting dream, witnessed every one of his choked awakenings. She stared at him like she'd paced his room with him for hours until the sun rose, desperately wishing for sleep but dreading the idea of attempting such torture.

That stare caused his skin to prickle and his muscles to tense. He felt exposed under her consideration, and his heart stuttered in his chest.

"Want some chips?" she asked, keeping her voice level and her gaze locked on his as she reached down, then handed him a bag of Doritos.

"Okay," he said, swallowing on a dry throat as he accepted the bag, getting lost in the liquid copper of her irises. After what felt like an eternity, she finally blinked away and turned back to the TV.

Instead of feeling relieved and freed from the intensity of her stare, Jude had the distinct sense of falling backward, like she'd just cut the rope while he dangled over the edge of a cliff. What the hell was wrong with him?

And then she laughed. The sound was deep and goofy. A true, genuine laugh that seemed to set some of his discombobulated pieces back into order. At least for a moment. He sucked in a deep breath, grounding himself on the couch, absorbing the noises of the TV and Indira's breathing and the crinkle of the chip bag as she reached over and fished some out.

"This part's really funny," she said with a full mouth, nodding her chin toward the screen.

Jude fixed his eyes on the TV, but his body still felt on high alert. Tense and taut like dreams or danger would blow down the door.

He felt Indira's gaze on him, assessing him, in that careful, sensual way she had about her. Her looks usually annoyed him. Provoked him. But, for some reason, in the haziness of early morning hours and bad sleep, that look felt like a comfortable weight on his skin.

He glanced at her, and gave his most genuine attempt at a smile. It was slow and hesitant and probably looked more terrifying than anything, but he had to try.

Indira's eyes trailed to his mouth, tracing his lips.

Then she smiled back, and it, ever so slightly, tipped Jude's world upside down. His breath caught at the top of his throat, heart dipping then doing a wild circuit around his torso while a steady shimmer of warmth shot down to his toes.

Slowly, so slowly Jude could tell Indira did it for his benefit, she reached out her hand across the inches that separated them, and picked up his. She scooted her body a little closer, still leaving plenty of couch between them, and rested his hand on her lap.

Jude wondered if she had any idea of the bolt of sensation she'd just sent through his whole body. It was like every nerve ending had fired and flooded him with good hormones when she'd broached the distance, touched him.

Both of their eyes back on the show, Indira lazily started massaging his hand, working her thumbs into his palm, pulling gently at each joint.

A foreign sense of calm trickled from the back of his neck down his spine, slowly spreading across his chest. Into his arms. Down his legs.

And it was good.

For the first time in months, he was feeling something that wasn't numbness or shame or fear. He was feeling . . . contentment. It was delicious and warm and disorienting.

Part of Jude feared it. If he indulged in the good feelings, it would hurt all the more when they inevitably left him. But, with the glow of the TV, the softness of the blanket, and the gentleness of Indira's fingers, it was impossible to resist. So, he didn't.

And, for the first time in so long, he felt almost normal. He felt like a real life human being, sitting on a couch, watching TV and eating junk food. He could almost laugh at how such small things brought him overwhelming relief. But in the same instant, his throat felt choked and clogged, like he was a moment away from weeping, like all the pain he kept closely in check would burst out of him.

He had to get a grip. He had to find control. He crammed all these conflicting, confusing emotions into tiny separate boxes, dragging them to the furthest corners of his mind, hoping they'd stay locked and collect dust. Jude wouldn't waste this brief reprise on analyzing his response. He'd sit on the couch and listen to Indira laugh.

It happened so gradually, Jude didn't notice at first, but as they made it through season after season of Thanksgiving-themed episodes, Indira moved closer to him on the couch until she was pressed lightly against his side, his hand still cradled in hers, her body melting around him in comfortable warmth. He felt the rise and fall of her chest against his biceps, the vibrations of her laugh against his shoulder and neck. Even her bizarre, mangy cat joined in, perching on the arm of the couch and staring at him with intermittent slow blinks.

It was the first time he'd been touched like this in . . . forever. He couldn't conjure a single memory of someone touching him for such an extended period of time so comfortably. It should have disconcerted him. He'd been deprived of substantial touch for years now; the only contact he made with another was when their body was broken on his table and his hands were the only things that could put it back together again. He'd started avoiding touch as much as possible—like it would singe his skin if he allowed anyone too close. But Indira's warmth and comfort lulled him to an almost-drugged state of euphoric calmness. And, without thinking, without stopping himself, Jude leaned back.

Then he fell into the deepest sleep of his life.

CHAPTER 11

Jude

∽

"Oh my God, Jude! How *are* you?"

It was about the fifteenth iteration of the same greeting Jude had heard in as many minutes as he hovered on the outskirts of Collin and Jeremy's latest engagement/pre-wedding party.

His body tensed as he was pulled into another crushing hug by someone he only vaguely recognized from med school.

Collin and Jeremy, damn extroverts that they were, had invited all their friends from medical school to come out to Dusty Luke's, a dive bar most Callowhill students had drowned their sorrows in at least once or twice. Which basically meant their entire graduating class was packed into the tiny West Philly pub.

And every single one of them seemed dead set on randomly touching Jude and speaking loudly in his face over pumping music and colliding voices.

"You were stationed overseas, right?" Brad, someone Jude distantly remembered from cadaver lab, asked, leaning far too close into Jude's already invaded personal space. This was the first time he'd been out in a crowd this large since coming home, and he was thoroughly wishing for the lonely safety of his room. He'd thought the Cheesecake Factory had been overwhelming, but this was next level.

"Were you in the military?" Brad's wife, Marta, asked, also getting close.

"Not exactly," Jude mumbled, gulping down his water, hoping it would cool the burning feeling in his gut and limbs. Jude had seen the consequences of war, though, the horrific injuries people inflicted upon each other. The reminder of it regularly punched him in the throat.

Brad opened his mouth to ask another question, but a loud tapping on the microphone at the front of the bar commanded everyone's attention.

Jeremy and Collin stood on the small stage in the corner, cheeks rosy as they smiled at their friends.

"Hello, everyone!" Jeremy said, gripping the mic. "We have a few things we'd like to say. First, thank you all for coming to our little pre-wedding bash." The pair beamed at the scattered applause. "Everyone says it's so easy to be caught up in the day that you miss your own wedding, so we decided to celebrate it as many times as possible!"

"And tonight," Collin said, taking the microphone from Jeremy, "we thought it would be fun to throw back some beers, eat cheesesteaks, and host a little bit of trivia! It'll be a mix of general knowledge and facts about us as a couple, and the winning team will get a prize."

"What's the prize?" a voice near Jude called out. He could recognize that voice anywhere. He scanned the area around him until he saw Indira standing at a nearby high top, elbows propped on the table as she slid her glass between her hands.

Jeremy took the mic again. "Glad you asked! It's a super-cool, custom-made, limited-edition, extremely fashionable and not at all tacky . . ." Jeremy and Collin looked at each other with matching grins, then created a mock drum-roll by slapping their thighs. ". . . *Jellin* shirt!"

Jeremy grabbed something from the table behind him, then held it up to the crowd with a flourish, a T-shirt unfurling from his grip.

It was . . . something. That's for sure.

Large caricatures of Collin and Jeremy hugging each other were airbrushed in the center with *Jellin* (which apparently was their couple name and wedding hashtag) written in large cursive at the top.

"Amazing, right?" Collin said, voice cracking on a chuckle as he looked adoringly at Jeremy. He pulled the mic away from his mouth as another laugh shook him, closing his eyes for a moment to collect himself. "Get ready, because we'll get started soon."

The crowd cheered and whooped, but Jude didn't miss Indira's rather vocal heckling. She was such a little shit. Jude smiled as he moved closer to her.

Everything about her drew him in, and Jude made a conscious effort to stop his feet from moving.

The past few days had been a rather shocking exercise in restraint. Jude was trying, somewhat desperately in his mind, to sever any growing threads between the two of them since their bizarre couch . . . cuddle . . . thing.

He didn't want Indira seeing him too closely, noticing the damage in him. But living under such tight quarters with her was a surprisingly visceral type of torture—her laugh traveling through the wall they shared as she talked on the phone, the sound of her rough and lovely voice as she sang in the shower, her soft and earthy scent embedding itself into everything Jude owned—all little tugs at a spot below his ribs, tempting him to . . . to . . .

To just exist around her.

So, naturally, he'd been trying to avoid her as much as possible.

He stepped back, tucking himself into the corner, hoping to disappear into the bar's dark and chipped paint while the hum of the space threatened to cut him open. He hated that subtle noise. It set his teeth on edge and made his heart pound against his chest.

He tried to focus on the faces of people—study their features until everything else blurred at the edges—instead of absorbing the overwhelming amount of bodies around him.

That was when he spotted Chris at the high top next to Indira, talking to his (very) new girlfriend, Lauren, as they swayed in a rhythmless dance. It didn't take a rocket scientist to put two and two together with that one.

Jude risked another glance at Indira, who was staring with a bland look at her ex. When Chris placed a particularly sloppy kiss on Lauren's cheek, Indira grimaced, then shifted so her back was to them, a disgusted look lingering on her pretty features.

Indira must have felt the weight of Jude's stare, because her gaze flicked to him, their eyes locking. Jude couldn't pull away. Her lips parted slightly, a tiny pucker forming between her eyebrows.

After what felt like an eternity, she lifted her hand in a tiny wave, one side of her mouth kicking up.

Jude didn't know what to do. He felt so disconnected from his limbs and body, it was hard to know what a normal response would be. But he felt himself mimic the gesture, and Indira's small smile grew a bit.

Suddenly, Chris swayed backward, throwing his head back as he laughed at something Lauren said. He bumped into Indira, pitching her forward and causing half her drink to slosh over the rim of the glass. She whipped around, a snarl on her lips.

Chris turned, his jolly smile morphing into a look of surprise, then horror. Then pity.

Jude couldn't fathom a universe where Indira would take that reaction well.

Sure enough, the tone of her voice carried to where Jude stood. He couldn't make out exactly what she said, but he could tell she wasn't happy. He didn't blame her. Jude knew things were really heating up when she started pointing her finger at Chris's chest.

Without fully processing that his legs were in motion, Jude strode over to Indira.

"Hey," he said, standing a bit too close to her for it to be natural. Indira blinked at him.

"Hey," she managed, tilting her head back to look at him.

Jude wasn't sure what to do next, why he was even standing there. For some bizarre fucking reason, he made a sort of jerky and indecisive movement toward her, Indira's eyes widening in alarm and horror.

Ah, fuck it.

Jude leaned in and gave Indira an awkward, one-armed hug. Indira was stiff at first, then her body softened, feeling oddly familiar pressed against his side. He dropped his arm, taking a small step back.

Jude glanced at Chris, who was staring at him with a confused look on his face, like he couldn't quite place Jude despite having met him several times at all the countless pre-wedding events.

Jude turned his attention back to Indira.

"Wanna, uh, stand in the corner with me?" he asked, nodding to his hideout.

Indira was silent for a beat, then flashed him a sardonic look. "I'm sure you use that line on all the girls," she said dryly.

"With excellent success," Jude shot back with a small huff of laughter.

Indira smiled at him, then mouthed the words *Thank you* before shifting toward the spot, Jude following close behind.

Before they made it, Collin picked up the mic again, sharp and painful feedback piercing through the room. Jude stopped in his tracks, his neck stiffening painfully and hands shooting up to cover his ears, his entire body pivoting to red alert.

"All right," Collin said through the noise, adding a layer of static to the auditory chaos. "It's time! Please divide up into teams of five or six."

The bar erupted in movement and sound—the scrape of chairs on the sticky floor and the bang of tables as they were pushed against the wall, Collin holding his phone up to the microphone as he played the *Jeopardy!* theme song—all of it wedging apart Jude's nerves.

Something in Jude's brain glitched, his world tipping. It was the deep bass of the people in the bar laughing and yelling and the screeching feedback of the microphone and the thuds of barstools that sounded like gunshots . . . and . . . and *everything*.

"Jude." Indira's soft voice cut through the disarray of his senses, and she bobbed into focus in front of him.

She looked calm. Soft. Steady.

She looked like everything.

His head swam. He wanted to ask her for help, but he didn't know how. He wanted . . . wanted . . .

"I'm going to touch you," she whispered, holding up her palms. "Is that okay?"

Somehow, he managed to nod, and she reached out, fingertips stroking Jude's fisted knuckles. He forced his muscles to relax, letting Indira coax his fingers apart and slide her palm into his.

"We're going to get out of here," she said, keeping those big brown eyes locked on Jude. Anchoring him.

She started walking, tugging gently at Jude's arm.

And he followed.

There was nothing more he was capable of doing at that moment than following Indira out of the chaos of that bar into the cool night air.

CHAPTER 12

Jude

The world was still spinning as Jude let go of Indira's hand. He slouched against the brick wall of the adjacent alley, shoving his fingers through his hair and tugging at it as he dropped his head.

Indira's shoes entered his line of sight as he stared down at the concrete.

He couldn't bring himself to look at her. His breaths were coming short and tasted bitter, his stomach swooping. Was this his life now? Either feeling absolutely nothing or feeling everything all at once? What a miserable fucking existence. Such a lonely one.

"In this moment, you are safe," Indira said softly.

The words caught Jude so off-guard, his head jerked up and he met her eyes.

Her face was serene, gently observing Jude. He wanted to drown in her calmness.

"You are here in this alley," she continued. "And I'm here with you. The October night is cold and the air a little smelly. But we're both safe. We're both here."

The lovely rasp of her voice lulled Jude's somersaulting thoughts.

But the comfort was as scary as chaos. Jude felt both sharply. Painfully. Both existed outside of the safety of numbness. The softness of Indira's voice, the closeness of her body, cracked him open, busted down the doors to the pain he kept tightly shut. It made him desperate to escape those feelings.

"H-hold me," Jude choked out. "Please. Please hold me."

Indira moved immediately, wrapping her arms around his waist, squeezing him, hugging him tightly to her. He clutched her back like he could melt into her skin.

And then he was crying. His chest heaved, lungs threatening to burst as he choked down air and emotion flooded him.

Jude couldn't think of the last time he'd cried. Not from broken bones as a kid, or grandparents' funerals. Not from anger or stress or frustration. Not even as he witnessed all the death and pain and hurt wrapped around the globe.

It hurt, this crying. It grated against his throat and stripped his skin. He couldn't stop.

Indira held him through it all. She pressed onto her tiptoes, plastering herself against him. Anchoring him. One hand rubbed circles across his back, imprinting care along his spine, while the other rested on the nape of his neck as he rested his head on her shoulder.

He eventually cried himself dry, and Indira held him in the after, stroking the hairs at the back of his neck and making a gentle humming sound as he caught his breath.

A bizarre mix of relief and shame pushed through him, but all he could really focus on was how glad he was to feel a little less of the hurt, like he'd stripped off a weight strapped to his neck. It was a bit terrifying to realize how much he felt he needed Indira in that moment. He wanted to stay in her arms forever.

"Do you want to talk about it?" Indira asked softly against his shoulder.

Jude shook his head first, then nodded, then shrugged.

"Not really," he said, the words muffled by Indira's thick curls.

"Do you *need* to talk about it?"

With a sigh he pulled away, stiffly untangling himself from her warmth. "I . . . I don't know. I want to tell you I'm fine, but I also know how contrary you are, so it seems a bit pointless."

He scrubbed his hands over his face, then attempted a weak smile. She stared at him with those endless eyes. Waiting.

With a rattling breath, he started talking.

"The GHCO has sent me to a lot of places. Beautiful places. But places with . . . I don't even know how to describe it. Just tremendous need." Jude stared at the brick wall opposite them.

"And I was so arrogant going into it. I thought my one year of residency in a Philly hospital would teach me everything I needed to know . . . I thought it would be . . . I don't know, simple. I'd go where they sent me, set a broken bone here, deliver babies there, stitch up wounds . . . I'd do whatever was needed without a hitch. All with this unwavering motivation to do it to save myself from student loans."

He paused, eyes flicking to Indira.

"Isn't that disgusting? I was so selfish in wanting to save a fucking buck that I really thought I'd go around the world playing God here and there. I hate myself for it."

"Don't say that," Indira whispered. "The burden of what we face with those loans and interest can be absolutely debilitating. You aren't a bad person for dedicating years of your life to serve in areas of need to reduce that burden."

"I'm a bad person because my interest wasn't in being some global humanitarian, it was purely selfish." Jude arched his head back, looking up at the sky.

He blinked a few times, trying to unscramble the confusing strings of emotions and put them into words. Explain them to Indira.

This happened to him a lot lately. Trying to think would wrap his brain into knots, impossible to unravel. His mind used to be so agile, seeing steps ahead in conversations or action. Now, it seemed incapable of even completing the simplest of processes.

"Everywhere I went, I was losing someone. I wasn't quick enough to cauterize a wound or smart enough to recognize the underlying ailment. I saw people lose their eyes. Their legs. I saw civilians bombed in the middle of a normal day or villages laid flat from a hurricane. Entire families snuffed out of existence in their homes . . . I saw people in the most primal states of pain, and more often than not, I seemed to leave them with just as much of it. It started to feel like I was the one that brought it to all those people."

Jude was haunted by those bodies on his table, their pleading, pained eyes looking at him for salvation when he couldn't deliver it.

"Jude," Indira whispered, reaching her hand toward him. He didn't take it. She left it hovering. "Doctors aren't infallible healers. You're put into impossible situations and all you can do is your best."

"My 'best' resulted in people dying, Indira. How can I ever forgive myself for that? How can I ever erase the idea that I inserted myself into situations I wasn't ready for, when someone else, someone more capable, could have been doing the job?"

Indira's eyes flicked across his face. "I don't understand what that means," she said, a certain helplessness to her voice.

Jude fisted his hands in his hair. Fuck. Why was talking so hard?

"It's like, I applied for this program, right? I submitted an application for the spot; I went through interviews. I painted the best version of myself to review boards for the sole purpose of getting money for school. Not for helping. Not for saving people. But to avoid all this debt. To unburden myself from a loan payment every month. But who's to say I didn't steal the spot from someone more capable? Someone who could have actually saved all these people? How am I supposed to live with myself when my shortcomings could be the reason people no longer exist?"

Great, Jude was crying again.

Indira chewed on her lip. "Jude, have you ever talked to a therapist about all of this?"

He let out a hard, bitter laugh. "Believe it or not, therapy isn't often readily available in the places I'm stationed."

"But have you approached anyone at the GHCO? Maybe a supervisor about protecting your mental health? Or maybe—"

"Indira, stop," Jude said through clenched teeth, his head swimming.

He felt so much shame. So much embarrassment. So much plain fear at how unhinged he was. He didn't have the tiniest clue who he was supposed to talk to about any of it when he was in the middle of areas of civil unrest or war. His inability to cope was so insignificant compared to the trauma civilians were facing every day just to survive. It would be another selfish act.

Indira pressed her lips together, but her eyes told Jude how much she wanted to push the issue. He'd caused those worried lines across her forehead, the tension in her mouth.

One more thing to hate himself for.

He wanted to reach out to her, hug her again, bask in her lightness—her goodness—until he could convince himself he was good too. But he couldn't do that to her. He was feeling far too much around Indira for that to be safe. He'd only hurt her.

Jude ducked his head again, dragging the toe of his shoe into the cracks of the concrete.

"What about the moment in the bar triggered your reaction?" she eventually asked, moving to stand next to him against the wall.

"The noise, I think," Jude said, pressing his hands into the rough brick behind him. "And the amount of people. A lot of the places I was stationed experienced frequent bombings or attacks. It . . . Sometimes I have trouble remembering that I'm not there when a noise surprises me."

Jude saw Indira nod out of the corner of his eye.

"Thank goodness Collin and Jeremy are so low-key with their wedding events. Would hate for you to experience weeks of extremely loud and dramatic gatherings."

A startled laugh bubbled from Jude's throat. Indira's head whipped to him, her eyes on his mouth. He watched her smile bloom.

"I feel like a dick," Jude admitted, gesturing toward the bar. "I want to support them. I came back to support them. Collin's my best friend, and he's always been there for me, you know? I don't want to miss all these important moments because I'm so fucked up."

Indira looked away, something flashing in her eyes.

She cleared her throat. "Is there anything I—we—can do to make it easier? I can talk to them. See if they can cancel one of the forty additional parties they have planned or something. Or tone them down."

"Don't," Jude said, voice far too loud. Way too rough. Indira jumped.

"Sorry," he said, softer this time. "But don't tell them. I don't . . . I don't want to distract from their wedding. I don't . . . I guess I don't want them to know."

"They wouldn't want you hurting like this," Indira said, eyebrows furrowing.

"I . . ." Jude didn't know what to say. He knew his friends wouldn't want him feeling this way, falling to pieces at moments that were supposed to be joyous. But there wasn't any fixing it, so why include them in the consuming guilt?

"This helped," Jude said, gesturing around the alley. "Being around you has helped."

Indira went silent, and Jude cleared his throat, awkwardness wedging them apart.

"Speaking of hurting," Jude said, oh-so-casually delivering that drastic change in subject. It was uncomfortable to admit how lost he was, that he'd never find his way back. He needed a break from talking about it. "I can't believe you haven't lost your shit on your ex with all the groping he's been doing. That level of maturity isn't like you."

Indira let out an indignant gasp, jaw falling open as her gaze whipped toward him. Jude tried to hide his smile, but it was impossible. She narrowed her eyes at him in a withering glare, but her own smile won out, and she let the subject switch.

"I mean, in all honesty," she said, "it's taking what very limited self-control I have to not go into a complete meltdown every time I see them. And there's still so many more things Jeremy and Collin have planned for the wedding party."

"I'm, uh, sorry things didn't work out," Jude said, staring down at his shoes. He was surprised to discover it was a bold-faced lie. But some weird, selfish, foreign part of him was kind of . . . *glad* that she wasn't pining after Chris. He wasn't sure what that meant. Probably just a protective thing from having known her for so long.

"Don't be," Indira said with a flick of her wrist, the smallest hint of sadness in her voice. "The only thing that hurts is my pride at this point. It's rather mortifying to walk in on your boyfriend hooking up with someone else. But it's probably for the best."

"You don't hope to reconcile things?" Jude asked, his heart hammering like a hummingbird's wings in his chest.

"Hell no," Indira said, tugging at one of her curls. "I'm done with relationships for the time being. It's the last thing I want."

Oh.

That was . . . a statement. A pretty innocuous one. So why did Jude's rusted-shut heart simultaneously jump and sink at it?

"I wish I didn't have to see them parading around while I'm standing like a loner in the corner, though," Indira continued. "It doesn't help to be the only one of my friends single too. Would be nice to have a date just to distract from all the disgusting displays of affection happening around me."

A small, dangerous idea blinked into existence in Jude's brain, then ping-ponged around his skull. It was a bad idea.

So. Bad.

Knowing this didn't stop his damn mouth from opening, though.

"I could . . . I don't know, pretend to be your boyfriend when Chris is around, or something?" Jude blurted out. He pressed his shaky palms hard into the brick wall behind him.

Indira looked at him, her face twisted into something between confusion and disgust.

Well . . . ouch.

"To like, keep you distracted, or whatever. Give you an excuse to get away from all the adoring couples or . . . I don't know. Someone to dance with at the wedding . . ."

"I've seen your dancing, Jude, so I'm not sure why you're framing that as an incentive."

Jude rolled his eyes, then bumped his shoulder against hers.

"Fine. No dancing. You'd probably crush my toes with your giant feet anyway."

"I've grown into my feet!" Indira said with outrage, kicking up a foot. It wasn't like she had clown feet, but they'd always been a bit big for her body. Especially as a kid, she'd looked like a Great Dane puppy, this small, wiry body, with giant paws slapping around.

It was kind of . . . cute.

"Sure you have," Jude said dryly. Indira huffed.

Silence lingered between them, and Jude resisted the urge to push the matter. It was a ridiculous idea. He shouldn't be inserting himself into Indira's life.

"Why would you do that?" Indira asked, staring straight ahead. "Be my fake date, or whatever. What's in it for you?"

Jude shrugged. "I don't know. Like I said, this is all overwhelming, but being around you, it seems to help."

Indira shot him a look.

"Believe me," Jude said, cheeks heating. "It's the last thing I expected either."

With a growl, she elbowed his side.

"It would . . . I guess it would give me reasons to escape some of the social situations without causing a big scene. Act as a buffer from all of the . . ." Jude gestured vaguely in front of them.

Indira was quiet again, and Jude risked a glance at her. She looked wounded.

"I would hope you know me better than to think I need some sort of bargain to help or support you," she finally said, her voice even and flat.

Jude's heart tripped over itself as he fumbled his words. "Shit. No. I'm sorry, I didn't mean it like that, I just . . ."

"Just what?"

"I feel really useless," Jude admitted, his voice sounding far away. "Like, all the time. I feel like I don't have anything good to give to anyone and I . . . I guess I saw it as maybe something I could offer you for once. I didn't mean to offend you."

Jude felt Indira's eyes on him, but he couldn't meet her gaze, a weird thump of embarrassment surging through him.

"I know we haven't always gotten along . . ." Indira said, stating the obvious. "Part of me does want to . . . I don't know. Be friends? With you? Or at least frenemies?"

"Friends?" Jude echoed, the word tasting odd in his mouth.

"I'm leaning more toward the frenemies bit, gotta keep that spark about us," Indira said, bumping her shoulder against his.

"You want to be my friend?" Jude repeated, a bit too earnestly.

Indira chewed on her bottom lip, staring straight ahead. "Yeah, I'd like to be your friend."

A small, golden surge of warmth spread out from his chest.

"And your fake date since you're throwing yourself at me," Indira said with her usual level of sarcasm as she pushed away from the wall.

"Yeah?" Jude asked, the warmth slipping down his limbs to the tips of his fingers and toes.

"As long as you buy me fake flowers and fake diamonds and very real meals from DoorDash. Fake-girlfriend tax and all that." She fixed him with a teasing smile.

Jude smiled back.

"All right, frenemy," he said, pushing away from the wall too. "You've got yourself a deal."

CHAPTER 13

Indira

Their first task in their giant lie was to tell Jeremy and Collin the truth.

Delivered with as much shock value as Indira could muster because she refused to miss an opportunity to mess with her brother.

"Jude and I are madly in love," she announced, waltzing into the kitchen as Collin, Jeremy, and Jude sat around the table, eating their breakfast in peaceful silence. All three men broke out into choking sounds.

"As such," she continued, perching dramatically on the arm of Jude's chair, her hip leaning against his biceps, "we're each other's dates to the wedding."

She was caught off-guard by the sudden swoop of her stomach. The ache in her chest that didn't make sense.

"Excuse me?" Collin said between hacking coughs.

With an inflated smile, she (awkwardly) rested her hand on the top of Jude's head. He swiveled to look up at her with confusion and horror. Collin's eyes bulged as they bounced between Indira and Jude.

"Isn't that right, *darling?*" Indira purred, punctuating the ruse with a lascivious wink. She placed two fingers under his chin, closing his gaping mouth.

"What is happening?" Jeremy whispered.

Jude made an odd gargling noise.

"But you're . . . He's . . . This literally would never happen. You two? No. I—" Collin started choking again on air or spit or confusion, and Jeremy thumped him on the back.

Indira laughed, hoping if she did it loudly enough, the soft pokes of misplaced sadness wouldn't flood her.

"Calm down. I'm kidding," she said, sliding away from Jude to take her own seat while they blinked at her. "It's fake," she explained, flourishing her hand like that should be obvious. "He's my fake date for the wedding. And the lead-up to it, I guess."

"I'm sorry, *what*?" Jeremy asked, now rubbing circles on Collin's back, who was turning an alarming shade of red. "Are you telling me you're cosplaying some sort of direct-to-Netflix rom-com?"

Indira rolled her eyes. "Not that it's any of your business, but I'd like to attend your wedding with a shred of dignity while Chris eye-fucks his new girlfriend the entire night. Jude's gonna help me do that. By being my *fake* boyfriend."

She poured herself a steaming cup of coffee from the carafe in the center of the table, taking a sip then smiling serenely at everyone.

"This is weird," Collin finally said.

"I'm not going to put much stock in the opinion of a man who still wears *Grey's Anatomy* merch from 2008." Indira nodded at the old and stained T-shirt Collin was wearing, the picture of the show's cast members worn and crumbly.

"This is a rare, vintage item," Collin said, gripping the fabric. "Guarantee you it will be worth a small fortune someday."

"It has holes in the armpits."

Jude let out a noise that Indira could have sworn was a laugh, but he disguised it as a cough. Collin shot a look at Jeremy for backup, but he just stared up at the ceiling, lips tucked into his mouth while the corners kicked up at the side.

"Let's refocus," Jeremy eventually said, massaging Collin's curled shoulders. "What exactly does this little stunt entail?"

Indira shrugged. "It's really not a big deal. We pretend to be a couple so I have a good excuse to stand with Jude in corners while we trash-talk everyone around us or disappear for a bit. And it'll make me feel like less of a loser with Chris parading Lauren around."

"I'm sorry about that," Jeremy said gently. "We don't have to talk about it, but I get the feeling Lauren might have played a role in your 'mutual' breakup?"

"I mean, I'm definitely not about to start a Lauren fan club, and it's objectively shitty to sleep with someone's partner, but Chris was the one in the relationship. I prefer to focus my anger on that flesh-bag of disappointment."

"Do you want me to talk to Chris?" Jeremy asked. "Seriously. If this is too much, or you need me to ask him to sit out of the wedding—"

"No," Indira said quickly. She wasn't going to let her failed relationship force Collin and Jeremy to warp their special day to fit her. "I shall survive. Even if it means saddling myself to this one for the next few weeks." She jerked her thumb toward Jude.

He gave her a bland look. "Yes, please continue your relentless roasting. Makes me so thrilled to help you."

Indira giggled.

"And what's in this for you? Why would you agree to it?" Collin asked Jude, looking at his friend as though he'd admitted to voluntarily French-kissing a possum.

Jude swallowed thickly. "You know me, always looking to serve those in need."

Indira poked her fingers into a spot at Jude's side that she knew was particularly ticklish—she'd exploited it constantly when they were kids—and was happy with the tiny squeal he let out.

Collin pushed away from the table and took his bowl to the sink. "I for one can't wait to watch this awkward shit show unfold. Thank you for the early wedding present."

"Does this mean I don't have to get you something from your registry?" Jude asked.

"Absolutely not."

"Don't worry, sugarplum," Indira said, scrunching her nose up as she smiled at Jude. "Since we're a hopelessly devoted couple, we can get them a joint gift."

Jude and Collin both grimaced.

"Wow, it only took five minutes for this to be unbearable," Jeremy said with a smile, following Collin's lead and cleaning up his plate.

"Aww, don't be jealous, Jeremy. I can give you sweet nicknames too! How's pooky sound?"

"I've never been more excited for work," Jeremy said, Collin nodding in agreement. They both had elected to take extra-long Saturday shifts at the hospital in preparation for their honeymoon. The pair left the kitchen with equally disgusted looks.

Indira and Jude smiled at each other, their gazes locking for a beat too long. Too intimately. Jude cleared his throat, looking away, and Indira's heart sank down to the floorboards. They sat in silence for a few minutes, Indira alternately sneaking shy glances at him and sipping her coffee.

"What do we do now?" Jude asked, squinting up at the ceiling.

Indira blew out a raspberry. "Well, my sweet blossom, we probably need to figure out a way to be less fucking awkward around each other."

"I imagine ending this little nickname thing here and now would help with that."

"Not on your life, booger."

That won her a quick glance and a reluctant smile, soft and sweet.

"I actually should do a little work today," Indira said. "Review some case files for the week." As a psychiatrist, Indira did her best to be holistic for the kids she treated, engaging in psychotherapy but also incorporating pharmaceutical interventions and monitoring their effectiveness.

"How's work going?" Jude asked.

An unstoppable smile broke across her lips. "Amazing," she said, reverence in her voice. "It's challenging sometimes. And emotional. I don't ever think I'll get that tough doctor skin of clinical detachment, but I can't think of a job more fulfilling."

The outpatient center she worked at partnered with the hospital's inpatient unit so children could continue receiving intensive care once released. She often saw kids in some of the worst mental places of their lives, and she had the humbling privilege of treating them.

"Isn't it . . ." Jude swallowed, playing with the tines of his fork.

"Isn't it what?" Indira tapped him on the shin with her toes.

"I, uh . . ." Jude cleared his throat, tugging at his collar. "I don't know why the whole concept of it makes me nervous," he said at last. "Therapy, I mean. It seems so weird. I don't know how you do it."

Indira let out a small laugh. "I mean, therapy *is* weird."

Jude looked at her like she'd just divulged definitive proof that aliens existed.

"Think about it," she continued, shrugging. "You sit down and unpack all of your deepest feelings. You share the rawest truths of who you are to another person. One you don't even know. Of course that makes you nervous. I think it makes lots of people nervous. It's a nerve-racking thing."

"Oh, do go on," Jude said, waving his hand. "You're really selling it. They should have you do infomercials."

Indira laughed again. "But that's also what makes it *amazing*. You show up for an hour, maybe two, and you have no other responsibility in the world than to focus on yourself. Your feelings. Your thoughts. It's dedicated time to find yourself fully and deeply, with another person there to help when needed. Therapy is scary because it requires you to be brave. It's one of the most radical forms of self-love."

Jude stared down at the table, his jaw tense as he pressed the pad of his thumb against the fork's points.

"Are you . . . considering therapy?" Indira whispered, leaning toward him. "Because, if so, I have tons of recommendations for incredible psychiatrists and psychologists. I could reach out, see if they're—"

"Indira, stop."

Jude's tone wasn't exactly mean, but it was spoken with such stony finality, it made her flinch.

"Sorry," she said, voice small.

Jude glanced at her, his tense features drooping into a defeated look. "I didn't mean to be a dick. I . . . I'm sorry. I was just making conversation. I mean, my next assignment starts in six weeks. I couldn't start therapy even if I wanted to."

Indira opened her mouth, ready to argue. Ready to problem-solve every issue he could come up with. But the look he gave her, raw and weary and pained, had her shutting her mouth.

"Work's good," she finally said, voice quiet, as she retreated to the mundane parts of the conversation, trying to keep it safe. "I better get to it," she added, standing from the table and gesturing toward the stairs.

Jude nodded, trying for a smile. It didn't reach his eyes, didn't create happy brackets around his mouth.

Indira hovered, wanting to say more; so many words were crowding her throat it was a miracle she held any back. But this wasn't the moment to push. She wasn't sure if she'd ever get the privilege of that moment. If he'd ever trust her enough to let her in, no matter how much she wanted to help him.

His words from last night whispered across her mind. *I feel really useless.*

Well, maybe that was something she could fix.

"Hey, Jude?" Indira said, picking at her nails as she stood in the doorway.

He looked up at her, gaze wary. She gave him a smile, and her heart glowed when the tension around his eyes eased a bit.

"Wanna go on a fake date?"

CHAPTER 14

Indira

∞

"I don't mean to be rude—"

"Anyone who starts a sentence like that automatically knows they're about to be rude as fuck," Indira cut in.

Jude sighed. "Okay. With full intended rudeness, if this is your idea of a first date, I can understand why you don't have a particularly satisfactory romantic history."

Indira took one hand off the steering wheel, trying to land a punch on Jude's thigh. He dodged it easily.

"I don't know why you're complaining so much," she said, glancing out the rearview mirror as she changed lanes. "I told you I'd buy you a special treat for helping."

They were headed toward Chris's apartment to get her stuff. Her tires had finally been replaced and the car returned to her, and there seemed no better time than the present to get the rest of her things from that cesspool. Apartment hunting was going terribly—she couldn't find anything halfway decent that wasn't at least fifteen-hundred dollars over her monthly rent budget—and it looked like she'd be bumming off Collin and Jeremy for at least a few more weeks.

"Okay, first of all," Jude said, ticking up his index finger, "I'm not a toddler. Bribing me with toys and Happy Meals isn't a decent incentive anymore."

Indira shot Jude a skeptical look.

"Second, you told me this would be trial-by-fire fake dating practice in front of Chris, and now you're telling me he won't even be there, so explain to me what purpose I serve besides a mover."

Indira huffed. "Okay, Nancy Drew, you caught me. I told Chris not to be there and I don't want to move all my shit by myself so I'm using you for labor. You have the truth. Are you happy now?"

She'd originally pitched the idea by telling Jude it was crucial groundwork in their fake dating scheme as the wedding loomed closer. This was all a concocted crock of shit, of course, but if she and Jude were going to try this whole friendship thing, she might as well exploit him as such.

Jude mumbled something along the lines of *No, I'm not happy at all* as he crossed his arms over his chest.

"Do you want the cheesesteak after or not?" Indira asked, eyes wide as she shot Jude a menacing look. "Because I'll turn this car right around if you're going to keep up the attitude."

Jude's lip curled a bit and he turned to gaze out the window, so sullen Indira had to bite back a chuckle.

"I want the cheesesteak," he grumbled a moment later. Indira fully laughed at that.

She took the exit for the city, steering through the narrow streets and going over the endless potholes that made up Philly's infrastructure. Getting near the apartment, she braced herself for chaos as she looked for a place to park.

After about four (failed) attempts at various parallel-parking spots, two extremely minor curb jumps, a gentle bottoming out over a road plate, and the tiniest bumper bump on a lamppost, Indira paid thirty bucks for a spot at a nearby parking lot and cut the engine.

They sat silently for a moment, Indira trying to get her jack-hammering heart to calm down after the stress. Having a car in a big city was a lot like owning cast-iron cookware—it seemed almost like a luxury at first, but ended up being a way bigger hassle than it was worth.

Out of nowhere, Jude erupted into laughter, making Indira jump. She stared at him in horror as the rusty noise echoed through the car, his shoulders shaking and throat working as he leaned over, resting a large palm on the dashboard.

"What's so funny?" Indira hissed, her lips kicking up at the sides as his giggles turned into a wheezing noise.

"You might be the worst driver I've ever seen!" Jude choked out, his face red and eyes watering.

"I am not! I'm a great driver!"

"By whose standards?" Jude asked, trying and failing to pull himself together.

"You and Collin are the ones that taught me, smart ass. That's a reflection on you." She had a few too many points on her license to continue defending herself.

Jude snorted. "Oh yeah . . . we were. I guess I must have blocked out the trauma."

"Lucky you. Collin's screaming still haunts my dreams sometimes."

"I seem to remember you threatening to drive us the wrong way onto the highway if I made one more snarky comment."

"A vow that does not expire," Indira said, trying to look serious but her face crumpling with giggles at the memory of their teenage dramatics.

"I believe it," Jude said, reaching over and tugging at one of Indira's wild curls and watching it spring back up.

Indira sucked in a breath, the gesture sobering her up. It felt as intimate as a lover's caress, and her heart twisted in her chest as echoes of past touches played across her mind. Small ones. Innocuous.

She remembered the rough shoves as little kids. The awkward and stiff hugs as teenagers. The more affectionate one she'd given him at his going-away party—the way his thumb had gently stroked twice between her shoulder blades when he'd hugged her back.

Jude blinked rapidly, looking at her like he remembered too.

Which was ludicrous.

So, *so* silly.

The ridiculousness of it was confirmed when he shifted away, getting his body as far from hers as possible.

He cleared his throat. "Ready to go in?"

She stared out the window. Mmm, not really. It didn't feel good to go back to the place she'd tried so hard to squeeze herself into. The space where she'd labored to pretend everything was good.

But instead of admitting any of that, she said, "Yep," and got out of the car.

CHAPTER 15

Jude

Something was seriously wrong with Jude (besides the whole emotional trauma thing).

He couldn't, for the life of him, get Indira out of his head.

Her ridiculous jokes and raspy voice and all that softness just beneath her prickly exterior looped around in his mind, shooting odd jolts of feelings through him at random moments.

Which was all so weird. He needed to get a grip. Needed to stop getting tangled in daydreams of her curly hair. Needed to stop wanting to touch her skin that looked so soft and warm. He needed to knock it all off because any feelings this intensely persistent couldn't be good.

Indira flipped through her keys, then jammed a gold one in the lock, turning the knob and stepping into the apartment, Jude close behind her.

And then she jerked back so hard her hair whacked Jude in the face, a few rogue strands poking him in the eye.

"Oh, what the *fuck*," Indira said, voice loud as she stepped to the side, revealing Chris standing just a foot inside the entryway, wringing his hands as he gave her a puppy-dog expression. Chris's face morphed into confusion when he saw Jude.

"What are you doing here?" Chris asked, locking eyes with him.

"What are *you* doing here?" Indira said, taking a step forward and inserting herself firmly between the men. "I texted you and told you not to be here." She shook her phone at him.

"I know," Chris said, giving her a pleading look. "But I've been trying to talk to you. I've been calling."

"And I've been ignoring them," Indira said, lifting her hands in an exasperated gesture.

"I just . . . I really want to talk about . . . everything." Chris's eyes flicked to Jude again. "Alone."

Jude's jaw twitched in annoyance, his hands curling and uncurling at his sides.

"No," Indira said, crossing her arms. "I'm not interested in talking. Please give me some privacy while I collect my things."

"Dira, come on." Chris took a step toward her, hand outstretched.

Without thought, Jude reached out, wrapping his arm around Indira's waist and pulling her close to his side, her hip pressing against his. Her head swiveled and he could feel her eyes on him, but he kept his gaze steady on Chris.

"She asked you not to be here," Jude said, voice low. "The least you can do is respect her request. She shouldn't have to keep asking."

"I need her to hear me out," Chris said, brow furrowing as his eyes bounced between their faces and the spot where Jude's hand rested on Indira's hip.

"I think you've lost the right to be heard," Jude said. "Do you want to hear him out?" he asked, turning his attention to Indira.

Her face transformed from wide-eyed confusion to a vindictive smile. "No, I do not."

"There you have it," Jude said, pulling Indira even closer as he looked back at Chris.

Chris's lips parted. "What's going on here?"

"We're dating," Jude and Indira said in unison. He squeezed her hip lightly, electricity dancing up his arm.

"That . . . that was fast," Chris said, voice cracking.

Indira's jaw hit the floor, then she snapped it shut, grinding her teeth together.

"Your audacity truly knows no bounds," Indira said, pulling away from Jude and moving around her ex to get to the kitchen. "I'll text you when we're done."

Chris stood there for a second longer, hurt and confusion on his face as he watched Indira open various cupboards and place items on the counter. Eventually, he straightened his shoulders and moved to the door.

Jude placed a hand on Chris's shoulder as he walked out, stopping him before he made it down the hallway.

"Someone else shouldn't have to step in for you to listen to her, or anyone else, for that matter," Jude said, voice hushed but sharp as a knife's edge. "Don't let that happen again."

Chris swallowed audibly, the noise wet. He nodded and Jude released his grip.

Then shut the door in Chris's face.

CHAPTER 16

Indira

⤜∞⤛

Indira made quick work of packing up her stuff, getting a spiteful thrill as she shoved everything into the last of Chris's garbage bags.

As Jude packed up her car—complaining the entire time about the outrageous number of shoes she had—Indira ran to the Bed Bath & Beyond two blocks away to buy some storage bins to transfer everything into when she got back to Collin's. She had a thick stack of sweet, sweet 20-percent-off coupons that catapulted her into a near-euphoric state when she used them.

Back in the car, she maneuvered them out of the city with only three close calls and level-ten dramatics from Jude.

"Want to do Dalessandro's?" Indira asked as she merged onto the highway. She and Jude hadn't agreed on much growing up, but Dalessandro's cheesesteak supremacy was an undisputed fact between them.

"Oh my God, yes," Jude said, punctuating it with a groan that he probably meant to be funny, but made Indira's belly swoop and cheeks heat instead.

She accidentally jerked the steering wheel a teeny-tiny bit, the entire vehicle swerving into the right lane and eliciting a few honks from other cars. Jude lurched with the sudden movement, one hand slapping the dash, the other large palm landing directly on Indira's leg, fingers sliding over her leggings and grazing her inner thigh.

Indira absolutely, 100 percent *did not* automatically squeeze her thighs tight together at the contact. And she also didn't choke back a gasp at the bolt of sensation it sent through her. Or didn't send through her . . . whatever double or quadruple negative of denial she was working in at that point.

Jude, for his super-chill part, flung himself to the opposite side of the car with as much gusto as a wallflower protecting their virtue in a historical romance novel.

The rest of the drive was nothing but awkward silence.

"Do you want to call ahead and put in our order?" Indira eventually asked. "We're less than ten minutes out."

"On it," Jude said, lifting his hips to pull his phone from his back pocket, then searching for the number.

Indira cleared her throat. "I'll have—"

"Whiz-wit, mushrooms, tomatoes, mayo, ketchup?" Jude finished for her.

Indira blinked at him in surprise. "You remember my order?"

A touch of pink kissed Jude's cheeks. "Well, you made me get them for you often enough in high school and college." There was an awkward pause. "And Collin too, obviously. I know his order."

Indira continued to stare at him until Jude shot a nervous glance at the road. Indira refocused her eyes on her driving.

"Right. Of course," she said, swirling the past minute around in her head as Jude called and placed the order.

Either her standards were exceptionally low, or Jude retaining her cheesesteak order for the better part of a decade was the most romantic thing to ever happen to her . . .

Both things could be true.

She parked next to Dalessandro's and reached for her purse, but Jude hopped out of the car before her fingers touched her wallet.

"I've got it. I'll be right out," he said, shutting the door and jogging up the ramp to the entrance.

Indira sat in a shocked silence.

Paying too? Was he trying to kill her and her silly, aching heart? This needed to be taken to the group chat.

> **Indira:** Jude remembered my cheesesteak order
> **Indira:** and paid
> **Indira:** do you think this means anything?

Texts back from her friends were almost immediate.

> **Thu:** oh *WOW*! Another man doing the bare minimum of decency! How shall we celebrate?
> **Lizzie:** where's the cheesesteak from?
> **Harper:** is this a fake dating outing or . . . are you two hanging out just to hang out?
> **Indira:** . . . I guess both?

Indira had filled her friends in on the fake dating thing because . . . well, because those three could sniff out a secret from miles away and weren't against public humiliation and coordinating massive, dramatic scenes to get answers. It was just easier to tell them the truth.

> **Thu:** call me jaded, but it's just a cheesesteak.
> **Lizzie:** once again requesting further details on where the cheesesteak is from
> **Lizzie:** and what toppings were procured?
> **Harper:** Thu when did you become such a cynic?
> **Thu:** Harpy . . . have you met me?
> **Indira:** he's walking back to the car this was useless bye

Indira shoved her phone back in her purse as Jude opened the door and then sat down, the heavenly scent of sandwiches and French fries filling the car.

"You didn't have to pay," Indira said, backing up the car and making her way to the house.

"Not a big deal," Jude said, tapping his fingers against his thighs.

"Seriously. I can Venmo you. Or I might even have cash back at Collin's. I—"

"Dira," Jude said, softly. "I wanted to, okay? Let me do this one thing."

Indira tried to swallow past the lump in her throat, but she didn't trust her voice, so she nodded instead.

Collin didn't live far from Dalessandro's, and Indira pulled into the driveway a few minutes later. Jude left the plastic bag of food on the dash, hopping out of the car and immediately starting to unload bags from the trunk. He'd managed to lug six of them up the front steps and into the house before Indira even got out of the car.

She fisted the last two bags in one hand and grabbed the food with the other, waddling into the house and up to her room.

Jude hovered outside her door, half the bags resting on the ground, as he looked nervously around.

"You can open it," Indira said, nodding at the handle, a bit winded after dragging her shit up the stairs.

Jude nodded, biting the inside of his cheek as he did what she asked. Indira gestured him in, then followed. He stopped after a few steps, blinking around the space like he was scared to let his gaze linger.

"You okay?" Indira asked, maneuvering around him.

Jude shook his head. "Yeah. Sorry. It was almost like I was expecting to see your old room when I walked in here."

"Sadly, I can't convince Collin to share a bunk bed with me anymore no matter how much I beg." Indira and Collin regularly lamented about the horrors of sharing a room for the entirety of their teen years. "I am making headway with him agreeing to some *Doctor Who* posters, though," she added.

"You always had an eye for design," Jude said.

Indira beamed at him with a smile too big. Too vulnerable.

But it felt like the old Jude was peeking back out again.

With Indira's next step, a hanger poking through one trash bag sliced the other open, and an avalanche of books and notebooks skittered across her floor.

Indira swore as the corner of a particularly thick hardcover landed on her foot, and she plopped onto the ground, dropping the bag of food next to her.

"You okay?" Jude asked, making a move toward her. He stopped, hand hovering between them, a look of uncertainty on his features.

"Fine," Indira said, sliding off her shoe and rubbing at the tender spot.

"Wait." Jude's head swiveled back and forth a few times before he committed to a full turn. Something in his eyes sparked when they landed back on Indira. "Are these your diaries?"

"No!" Indira lied. "Go away." She scrambled onto her hands and knees, sweeping the journals to her chest.

"They so are!" Jude said, childish joy in his voice. "I would know with how often Collin and I stole them."

"Monsters, the both of you," Indira growled, aiming a feeble kick at him. Jude laughed.

"I love that you kept these," he said, his voice quieter as he sat down cross-legged on the ground, reaching toward a pale green notebook with a shiny cover. He took it in his hands, dragging his fingers along the edges, and Indira's heart thumped painfully in her chest like he was doing the same to her cheek.

"You were *always* writing in them. I feel like I rarely saw you without a pen and diary in your hand when we were kids."

He wasn't exaggerating. Indira loved journaling when she was growing up. Even before she knew how to write, she was filling pretty notebooks with swoopy scribbles. As an adult, she still had a dangerous notebook-buying habit, but rarely took the time to fill them.

Indira picked up one of the books and flipped to a random page, cackling as she read the first line.

"Oh my God, if this isn't perfectly on brand," she said, angling the notebook so Jude could read too. He scooted closer to her, and Indira could feel the warmth of his body. He tilted his head and they both read.

> Jude is a bad boy but mama told me I need to be nice. Mama also taut me a new word called compeshin and said it would be nice if i had it for Jude like i have it for baby birds i find in the woods because his parents work a lot so he is with us a lot. I'm going to write Jude a letter so we become friends.

"That's so fucking cute," Jude whispered, tracing his finger over the indents in the paper.

Indira flipped to the next page. Sure enough, there was a letter to Jude, but it was sporting a giant X through the center of it.

> Dear Jude.
> Hi how are you I am good. Do you know what the word compashen means? Mama taught me today it pretty much means being nice to people. I think that I will show you compashin and you can show me compashon and we can be best friends.
>
> Thank you.
> Dira

The diary entry on the adjacent page read:

> Jude is still bad and he dunked me in the pond today. Got water up my nose. I'm done giving him campashin.

"Oh my God, I remember this day," Indira said, jabbing her finger at the last entry and gazing up at him.

"You do not," Jude said, giving her a skeptical look. "We were so young."

"I think I was like six or seven, but I seriously do remember it. Collin was being all sweet and gentle helping me get into the pond in the woods by our house, and you came up and pushed us both under."

Jude started laughing. "That doesn't sound like something I would do *at all*."

Indira rolled her eyes. "And that got Collin all riled up so then he started dunking you and then next thing I know I'm being splashed from every direction by you two ding-dongs."

"Okay, actually, I do kind of remember that," Jude said, his eyes lighting up. "You were *screaming*. But your hair looked like a deflated poodle draped across your head and Collin and I couldn't stop laughing. You whined about that for hours."

"Yes!" Indira said, jabbing a finger in his chest. "No lies were reported in my journal! You *were* bad."

"The *worst*," Jude deadpanned.

Indira scrunched her nose up at him. "A menace to society. And our parents wondered why we never got along."

Indira had overheard countless conversations between her mom and Jude's parents, the three of them shaking their heads in defeat as they tried to understand their kids' heated dislike.

"You just had it out for me," Jude said, all puppy-dog eyes and innocent lilt to his voice. "Never gave me a chance."

"Not to be a know-it-all—"

"It seems like you're going to go for it anyway . . ."

Indira reached over and smacked Jude's arm. "I was always the one following you and Collin around, begging to play with you. If anyone's to blame for our reasonless feud . . ."

"It'd be me," Jude said, all humor faded from his voice. He paused for a moment, looking down at the diary. "I truly am sorry for always excluding you and teasing you."

The tinge of remorse in his voice had Indira's heart stretching till it ached. Acting on instinct, she reached for Jude's hand, giving it a gentle squeeze that sent ripples of golden warmth up her arm. "Stop. You don't have to apologize. We were both little shitheads. I think it's what made us . . . us. I like our past."

Jude's smile was hesitant but earnest. "You like that I've never been a particularly nice person?"

Indira snorted, chewing on her lip as she looked at him. "You might not necessarily be nice, but I've always known you were kind."

Jude's eyes were dark. Intense. Tracing across her face with a vibrant type of openness that made her pulse double.

Indira felt too much all at once, and she pulled her hand back, pretending to flip through more pages of her notebooks as she tried to cool the hot flush of her cheeks.

"God, those summers were always so fun," Jude said after a few moments of heavy silence. "Exploring the woods. Our little 'hikes.' Climbing that big oak. Every summer we got a little higher."

"You and Collin got higher," Indira said, jumping at the safer conversation topic. "I stayed firmly on the ground. Humans weren't meant to climb trees. It's none of our business what's going on up there and, quite frankly, it's rude to the birds making their nests and trying to raise a family. You two were basically home invaders."

"That's a lot of words to say you were, and apparently still are, afraid of heights."

Indira rolled her eyes. "Yeah, how weird that I don't want to fall from high places and break every bone in my body."

"I miss those summers." His voice was soft from equal parts nostalgia and wonder as he looked back down at the notebook.

"I miss that house," Indira said, trying to ignore the sudden and sharp prickling along her nose and eyes. While her dad had been decent enough to let her mom keep the house when he abandoned the family, Angela hadn't been able to hold on to it, despite working two jobs to make ends meet.

"So many memories there."

Indira remembered her bedroom, with its pink comforter and

shaggy purple rug. She remembered running down the wooden steps to the kitchen every morning, the third from the bottom always squeaking in greeting. She remembered the small rectangle of stained glass above the front door, the afternoon sun casting a rainbow into their entryway, turning the dust motes into fairy sparkles Indira would conjure stories from.

"What other gems are you hiding in these?" Jude asked, gingerly picking a different journal.

"The inner workings of a highly profound and complicated teenage girl, I'm sure," Indira said with a haughty sniff. She grabbed a black velvet notebook, one she recognized from her moody high school years, and flipped to a random page and began reading out loud. "*Math isn't real and its textbooks are consumerist propaganda. Nobody needs sixty-two watermelons . . .* see, told you these books were full of genius."

Jude chuckled.

She flipped to another page. This one had a green sticky note taped to the inside. Indira was surprised to see Jude's messy handwriting scribbled across it.

> Movie wasn't half bad. Might let you pick more
> often. Your singing is the worst though.
> P.s. I thought you looked nice in your dress.

Now there was a memory that transported her right back to the moment.

Indira had been a gangly teen with a mouth full of braces going to homecoming for the first time. She'd gone with a group of somewhat popular girls after Tamar, the queen bee of the group, had recently acknowledged Indira's existence.

Tamar had been so nice to Indira the few weeks leading up to homecoming, even advising her on how to text Matt, the boy Indira would have put money on that she would fall in love with and marry and have lots of kids with and never get divorced and live happily ever after. In retrospect, the texting "advice" was more like Tamar instructing Indira to bombard disinterested Matt with endless questions.

At the dance, instead of Tamar setting Indira up with Matt like she'd promised, she'd told Indira that her dress was pretty but would be more flattering if she actually had boobs to fill it out, then proceeded to dry hump Matt on the dance floor, making out with him while Indira watched in horror. She remembered how that night was the first time she and Lizzie ever talked, Lizzie calling Tamar an asshole and solidifying what was to become their decades-long friendship.

"I had to *beg* you to drive me home," Indira said, remembering the instant onslaught of tears as she ran around the gym looking for Collin and Jude, her legs wobbly and unstable like a baby giraffe's as she navigated emotions and high heels.

Jude's mouth was tense again. "We were kind of assholes about it."

Indira waved him off. "You were horny teenage boys with dates and plans . . . You two were *not* subtle about your intentions for how the night would end."

Jude let out a surprised bark of a laugh.

"I can't say your reluctance to drive me home was misplaced."

Jude glanced at Indira, his look hesitant. Gentle. Indira smiled, and his muscles relaxed a fraction.

Collin had begged and bribed until Jude finally agreed to drive Indira back to the Papadakises' apartment. The car ride had been tense, Indira quietly crying, Jude giving her the courtesy of pretending not to hear, waves of annoyance radiating off his shoulders.

But when they'd pulled into the complex, he'd surprised her, asking if she wanted to watch a movie to take her mind off things. He had even let her pick and Indira had made a few jabs about how chivalry wasn't dead after all.

That was the first time they'd ever spent time together just the two of them, and Indira had assumed it would end quickly with their usual arguing.

But that night had been . . . fun.

Indira remembered how she'd felt something close to . . . *liking* Jude. She'd picked *Across the Universe*, and it hadn't taken long for them both to be absorbed by the moody sixties aesthetic and soundtrack composed entirely of hits by the Beatles.

Jude had even laughed till his cheeks and nose turned pink as Indira stood on the coffee table scream-singing along to the rendition of "Hey Jude" toward the end.

"I feel like that night was the first time I made you laugh," Indira said, tracing her finger over the edges of the Post-it.

She'd woken up on the couch, a blanket draped over her and the Post-it stuck to her forehead, Jude's shoes gone from their spot near the front door. She'd felt a weird pang at his absence, like by missing his departure, she'd missed some key opportunity to solidify that comfortable closeness as their new normal.

Maybe she'd been right.

Indira handed the journal to Jude and grabbed a different one, flicking through its pages.

"Oh shit, I totally forgot about the food," Indira said, shutting the book and looking over at the bag. "It's probably cold."

"I certainly don't care," Jude said, reaching across her to grab one of the plastic handles, his arm brushing her shoulder. Something warm and bright danced across Indira's skin and melted into her bones at the contact. She wanted more of it.

Jude pulled out the sandwiches, handing Dira hers. "Good meal, even better entertainment," he said, waving one of the notebooks. "You tricking me into free labor has its perks, it turns out."

Indira snorted so loudly that Jude jumped at the noise, making her laugh even harder.

They sat on the floor for hours, eating and reading and remembering.

CHAPTER 17

Indira

"But think about it," Indira whispered to Lizzie, Thu, and Harper as they stood in Collin's dining room about a week later. The four friends hadn't been able to coordinate a hang-out in far too long, so Indira had invited them to Collin's latest wedding-prep party, her brother glee-ridden to have more helping hands.

"*Peanut butter*. Like, have you seen a dog get peanut butter stuck on the roof of their mouth? It's chaotic!"

"Willingly incorporating it into foreplay is a bold choice," Harper whispered.

"It's the work of the devil," Thu said out of the corner of her mouth before sipping her wine and risking a glance across the room at Chris.

"It completely lacks an ideal viscosity for food play," Lizzie added. "Trust me, I would know."

"Thank you all for coming," Collin said, cutting off their conversation by clapping his hands and moving to the head of the table.

"Like we had a choice," Indira whispered to Jude, who was hovering at her shoulder. He bit back a giggle.

"We've been having such a blast bonding with you all during wedding preparations," Collin continued, flashing a handsome smile at everyone. "And I think this one will be extra fun. Today is all about the art of the flower—"

"Is that a euphemism?" Indira asked.

Collin shot her a dirty look across the filled table. Bushels of flowers ranging from a soft pink to a brilliant crimson were stacked high in the center, while each seat had a plastic container of an ominous-looking yellow goo.

"As I was saying," Collin continued, turning back to the group. "The wedding symbolizes a new beginning, the blooming of the next chapter of love."

Indira shot Jude a sidelong glance that had him twisting his lips together to prevent a smile.

"And as such," Jeremy picked up, wrapping an arm around Collin's waist, "we will not tolerate a single wilted flower at our wedding. So today, we're waxing."

"You know quite a bit about waxing, don't you, Harper?" Thu said innocently, nudging her friend.

"That was *one time*," Harper said, blushing as brightly as she did the day she'd suffered through a traumatic bikini-waxing incident four years prior. Lizzie laughed so hard she almost snorted up the petals from the rose she was sniffing, causing her to choke. Thu thumped her on the back.

"If you four can't behave yourselves, I'm going to have you escorted from the room," Jeremy said, brandishing a dahlia at them like a weapon.

"I didn't do anything!" Harper whined.

"Teacher's pet," Thu said through a fake cough.

"Guilt by association, darling." Jeremy offered her a sad but knowing smile.

"Can we focus, please?" Collin continued, raising his hands in exasperation. Everyone quieted down, and Indira pretended to scratch her nose while flipping Collin off. He pretended not to notice.

"We're going for a whimsical, rustic, cottagecore vibe, but with an overture of luxury and refinement. Follow?" Collin said. "Tonight we want to get the pieces for the end of each row of seats done. We're envisioning a sort of random, wildflower, natural-esque look. To pull that off we've come up with a precise formula for composition."

Jeremy went on to explain the value of having a three-to-two ratio of anemones with snowberry sprigs, and to never mix dahlias with the scabiosas. Indira peeked around the room, and was glad to see that everyone from Chris to Rake looked dazed and confused at the words being thrown at them.

"And once you've put together your bouquet, it's time to wax!" Jeremy said, like he'd just explained something as simple as hopscotch.

Collin cleared his throat as he prepped for his part in this odd demonstration.

"So, we've heated the soy wax." Collin gestured at the tubs of yellowish goo on the table. "And you simply dip the head of the flower in—not too long, don't want it to be weighted down—and then you let the excess drip off over the edge before setting it to the side."

"Sorry, I'm confused," Indira said, raising her hand. "Can you show me again?"

"Of course. You take the flower." Collin held up a deep-red rose. "Dip the head into the wax. Then let any extra drip off."

"Hmmm." Indira tapped her cheek as she tilted her head to the side, eyebrows deeply furrowed. She shot Jude a look and he nodded in confused solidarity.

"Sorry, Collin. Are you saying to let it drip first? Or dip first?" Jude asked, cradling his chin in his hand.

"Dip," Collin said earnestly.

"Gosh," Jude said, rubbing his temples. "I'm still getting all confused." Indira snorted but disguised it as a cough. "Can you show us one more time?"

Collin let out a sigh but nodded. "Of course. You take the flower—"

At this point, both Indira and Jude erupted into giggles, shaking and spluttering, and thoroughly enjoying being little shitheads. Indira rested her forehead on Jude's arm as they continued to laugh, and he placed his large hand on the small of her back.

The heat of his palm on her body stole all humor from Indira, every nerve ending rerouting itself to the spot where he touched her. It felt too good for it to be safe. She pulled back, trying to create space from the intimacy of it.

Then she remembered they were fake dating and, technically speaking, touches like that were *supposed* to happen, and she kind of . . . jerked forward a bit, accidentally knocking her forehead against the point of Jude's shoulder, then stumbled back. Jude reached out, stopping her from tripping into the wall by cradling the back of her head, his fingers tangling in her curls and tugging gently, sparking a sensation that traveled down her spine.

If that first touch felt intimate . . .

"You both are annoying little prigs," Collin said, frowning at them.

Jude dropped his hand from Indira as Jeremy reached across the table, smacking them each on the head with a stem of leaves to defend his fiancé's honor.

"I liked you two much better when you bickered," Collin continued. "At least then you subjected each other to your evil and left me alone."

"Quite the endearingly obnoxious couple, aren't you?" Thu said in a sweet voice, scrunching up her nose with a cutesy smile.

Indira's face heated to the point of discomfort, and she lifted her heavy curls off her neck.

"You know all about obnoxious, don't you, Thu-Thu?" Indira shot back in a wobblier mimic of Thu's tone.

"How long have you two been dating?" Lauren asked, all earnest eyes and friendly smile.

Indira and Jude shot each other horrified looks, all sense of time darting out of their heads. How long had it been since they started this? Two days? Six months? Who was to know, being put on the spot like this? *Dammit, Lauren.*

Jude opened and closed his mouth a few times while Indira blinked.

"Great question," Indira said, at last, turning to Lauren. "Remind me, how long have you and Chris been together? That helps me keep track. Minus a few weeks, I'm assuming."

Lauren and Chris both had the decency to pale at that. Lizzie, gotta love her, gasped like she was watching a soap opera, smacking one hand to her mouth and using the other to dramatically grip Rake's shoulder.

"Well, if things weren't awkward before . . ." Thu said, shooting Indira a look.

"Sorry," Indira said to the room at large, skin prickling and hot. "Excuse me."

Indira made a beeline for the bathroom, locking the door behind her and propping her hands on the sink, staring at her flushed cheeks and wild hair.

What the hell was going on?

One touch should not undo her like this.

It was fake. All of it was fake.

So. Fake.

And getting very real . . . flutters . . . of the . . . pelvic region . . . was *not* something she should be experiencing from her older brother's best friend. Satan himself. Indira needed to get her shit together.

She clapped her hands against her cheeks a few times before squeezing them together, making her lips pucker like a fish.

Shockingly, that didn't do anything.

What's wrong with you? she asked herself as she stared at her reflection. Like a bolt of lightning flashing across her brain, the thought *I wish it weren't fake* jolted through her.

Indira slammed her eyes shut and shook her head like she was dislodging water. No. No, no, nope. That didn't happen. No.

With a sigh, she washed her hands and left the bathroom.

Chatter punctuated with loud laughs filled the dining room as she returned. Everyone was seated around the table, cautiously dipping flower heads into the wax, no open seat in sight.

Lauren and Chris were seated at the nearest end of the table, holding flowers to each other's noses as they gazed longingly at one another.

Gag.

Harper and Thu were near them, chatting away, while Lizzie kept reaching over and messing up Rake's perfect arrangements, causing him to huff out defeated sighs mixed with indulgent smiles while she giggled and kissed his cheek.

Collin and Jeremy paced around the room, overseeing the progress with way too much intensity. Indira was tempted to trip Collin on his next pass.

Jude sat across from Chris, his spine curved and eyes darting around as different sudden noises battled for his attention. She took a moment to look at him, really look. Body like a rubber band. Dark hair. Long nose. Ears that stuck out and limbs that were endearingly gawky.

Her brain slowed down long enough to relearn his details—the freckle by his right temple. The subtle notch between his brows, marking his frequent frowns. The curl of his hair at the nape of his neck and the way his throat worked when he swallowed.

She'd known him her entire life, but this felt like the first time she was ever really seeing him.

He glanced at her, eyes shifting away then shooting back like he'd finally found a safe spot to dock. Indira walked to him.

"Okay?" she whispered into his ear, leaning down and pretending to inspect a maroon dahlia.

"Yeah. A bit, um . . ." Jude swallowed, then sucked in a deep breath.

Indira nodded. "I'll bring over a chair. Sit tight, peanut."

"Really don't think the pet names are necessary."

"Does 'my delicate pony' work better?"

Jude closed his eyes and sighed. "You're insufferable."

"Back atcha, boo," she said with a wink, straightening. Indira glanced around the room like a seat might magically appear for her to squeeze in next to Jude.

"Problem?" Collin asked.

"I need somewhere to sit."

"Uh . . ." Collin looked around. "Can I offer you some floor space?" he asked, gesturing at the corner.

"Can I offer you a kick to the shin?"

"There's no need to be so combative," Collin said, trying to keep his angry tone quieter than the general chatter. "Just get over it and—"

Suddenly, Jude grabbed Indira's elbow, giving it a gentle tug. His touch sent a bolt of electricity through her arm and down to her knees, making them wobble. She collapsed like a house of cards.

Directly onto Jude's lap.

Indira blinked rapidly, accidently whipping Jude with her hair as she swiveled her head to look at him.

"We'll share," he said gruffly.

Indira was pressed so close she felt the words vibrating in his chest.

"Right," Indira said, meeting his eyes, her voice breathy and soft.

Her heart hammered and head swam as sensations flooded her. The scent of flowers and Jude and his coffee-black eyes and the press of his thighs under hers and how she felt every twitch of his muscles echoed in her own. She couldn't resist leaning into him a bit more.

Jude cleared his throat, and Indira, once again, tried to pull herself together. Which was a relatively impossible endeavor seeing as a sweet ache was gathering between her thighs, every movement making it more intense as a growing heat surged through her.

Indira felt Chris's eyes on her, and she managed to tear her gaze away from Jude's profile to look at him. Chris was staring, lips parted and brow furrowed.

"Need something, Chris?" Indira asked innocently, picking up a flower and spinning it between her fingers.

He shook his head and blinked away. Jude gave Indira's arm a quick and friendly squeeze, and they smiled conspiratorially at each other.

Collin inserted himself in her line of sight, giving her a borderline angry look, one brow raised and lips pressed into a firm line as his eyes scanned his little sister perched on the lap of his best friend.

Fake, Indira mouthed to him, then she flicked her eyes in the direction of Chris, whose focus was bouncing between Indira and Lauren. Collin's jaw relaxed a touch and he gave an almost-imperceptible nod.

"Doing okay, my . . . gorgeous goblin?" Indira whispered to Jude, getting to work on her flower waxing. She felt his nod against her shoulder.

"Yeah. Better," he whispered back as he leaned forward to use the wax. His words tickled across her neck, creating goose bumps. "You're like a human shield from sensory overload."

"I'll make sure to add that to my résumé."

Jude chuckled softly, and they fell into a quiet flow, focusing on their pile of flowers while the other noises in the room faded to the background.

Good. This was all good. Their little ruse was working. Jude was feeling at least a bit more comfortable. Chris was getting a taste of his bitter medicine.

And Indira . . .

Well, Indira was once again trying to remind herself how very fake all of this was.

But Jude's warmth was real and his touch was there and his heartbeat was a steady thump against her back.

Indira's own heart was swelling with all the very real things she felt in this very fake moment.

The group continued their dipping and chatting, Jeremy making sure no one's wineglass got too low on rosé. For the sake of catalyzing creativity, of course.

"It's keeping me up at night," Indira heard Collin saying to Lizzie and Rake. "But we can't decide."

"Decide what?" Indira asked, shifting a bit on Jude's lap to face her brother.

"What color to make Dad's boutonnière," Collin said, holding up a richly purple flower in one hand and a burnt-orange bud in the other. "I was originally going to give him the same as the wedding party, but I'm wondering if it would be cute to have him and Mom stand out with a pop of different color. I think it would look nice in wedding photos to have variety."

Indira's heart plummeted down to her gut, sharp pangs dancing across the chambers.

"You know what would make the photos look really good?" Indira said, focusing on dipping a flower into the wax while the sound of her boiling blood rushed through her ears.

"What?" Collin asked.

"Not having that deadbeat in them at all," she said, giving him a fake smile, her lips curling.

Collin set down his flowers, the room hushing to an awkward quiet. "Wow," Collin said, shaking his head at her. "Real nice, Dira. That's our dad you're being so rude about."

"*Sperm donor* is a more apt title than *dad* for how involved he's been over the past few years, don't you think?"

"Dira," Harper whispered softly, reaching out a hand when Indira's voice rose.

"Why are you being like this?" Collin said, mouth twisting.

"I just don't understand why you even invited him."

"Because it's my wedding and I want him there," Collin shot back.

"But *why* would you want him there?" Indira said, disentangling herself from Jude as she stood, getting eye-level with her brother. "He left us, Collin. You saw how Mom struggled. It's such a slap in the face to then be like, *Oh, here, Father that abandoned us, have this starring role in my big day and stand next to the person that actually raised us.*"

"Believe it or not, Dira, I don't have to justify my choices to you."

Indira opened her mouth to say something, but Collin cut her off.

"And you're the only one who hasn't grown up enough to get over it. Mom and I talked about it, and agreed it's fine. Everyone's moved on except for you."

The silence in the room was sharp. Startling. And it pricked at Indira's skin, opening her to a rush of embarrassment as she felt so many eyes on her.

"I think we've done enough for tonight," Jeremy said gently, placing his hands on Collin's shoulders and giving Indira a soft look. "All this pollen has gone to our heads. Why don't we call it quits and walk to the brewery down the hill? First round on me."

Collin's mask of anger slowly fell away, but his eyes remained cold as he looked at Indira. "That's a good idea."

"We're down," Chris said after a beat, clearing his throat and holding up his clasped hand with Lauren. Jeremy smiled.

"And you all?" Jeremy asked, looking at the remaining people circled around the table.

Thu, Harper, and Lizzie shot Indira questioning glances. She gave them a tense smile and an encouraging nod. "You should go," she said softly.

They stared at her for a moment longer, but she nodded more encouragingly this time, and they agreed.

"I'm gonna stay back," Indira said. "I have an awful headache and probably should head to bed."

Collin opened his mouth, his eyes no longer cold, but Indira held up her hand.

"Seriously," she said. "Go have fun. I need to pop some ibuprofen and crash." They looked at each other, a silent understanding that the argument would be let go and the harsh words left behind passing between them.

Collin nodded. "All right," he said, glancing around. "Let's get our coats and head out?"

Everyone moved to get organized.

"Dira, we can stay," Harper whispered, moving to Indira's side.

"Yeah, we don't have to go. Do you want us to stay here?" Lizzie asked, big golden eyes warm and comforting.

"I swear, I'm good," Indira said, rubbing her neck. "I just need some alone time."

"Jude, you coming?" Collin asked, looping his scarf around his neck.

"Think I'm gonna stay back," Jude said. "Someone needs to clean this up," he added, gesturing at the table. "Shouldn't be the grooms, though, right?"

"You're too good to us," Jeremy said, giving Jude's shoulder a squeeze as he passed by. "But don't kill yourself over it. I'll get it organized when we get back."

Indira glanced at Jude and found him staring right at her, intensity in his dark eyes as he studied her face. That look made her feel far too seen. Far too exposed. She blinked away.

"See you later," Collin called over his shoulder as he led the group out the front door.

The resulting silence did something to the minimal composure Indira had mustered, and she deflated as the door clicked shut. She stumbled to the couch, plopping down on it and cradling her head in her hands, stinging pain building in her throat and behind her eyes. A few rogue tears slipped out, and, like a dam cracking, she started quietly crying.

Collin was right—she couldn't get over it. No matter how hard she tried, how much work she put into letting those feelings go, that anger, that hurt, always welled up in her, endlessly deep and shockingly toxic.

Indira was so alone in her misery, she jumped when Jude cleared his throat. She looked up at him, his sharp features in half shadows as he leaned against the wall. He took a step toward her. Then another.

"How . . ." He cleared his throat again, a touch of color gathering at his cheeks. "I want to help you," he whispered. "Can you tell me how?"

CHAPTER 18

Jude

Jude wasn't exactly sure why Indira laughed when he asked how to help her, but at least it stopped her crying. He hated when she cried.

"While I appreciate you being such a diligent fake boyfriend, I'm fine," she said, voice wobbly.

"You definitely look it," Jude deadpanned, taking another step toward her as he tried to shake off the prickle of annoyance at the term "fake boyfriend." That's what he was to her. It shouldn't bother him.

Indira snorted, then scrubbed at her tear-stained cheeks.

Her eyes roamed over him. His feet. His nose. His forearms. His eyes. Jude felt her gaze on every corner of his body and it made his skin prickle with awareness.

She patted the cushion next to her, and Jude had to hold his body back from sprinting to the spot. He settled himself with plenty of inches between them, letting the silence linger.

"It pisses me off," she said at last, waving vaguely toward the table. "Everything about my dad pisses me off. I hate that man so much. And I want Collin to hate him too." Indira tugged at her fingers, cracking them one at a time.

"I don't want to see him at my brother's wedding. I don't want to hear about his perfect third wife and his new set of perfect twins. I don't want to see pictures of their perfect house and its perfect lawn and the perfect boat tied to the dock out back. I don't want to be reminded how, to get all of that, he left us behind."

Jude had witnessed the eye of the storm when Greg left. The subtle changes in Collin. His paper-thin patience for his sister, the weight of taking care of his mom that he saddled to his shoulders.

He also saw how Indira became so quick to cry in those early days. How she always clung to Jude and Collin with an almost terrified ferocity. Jude hadn't fully understood their hurt, but respected it, nonetheless.

Indira was silent for another moment, a fresh, fat teardrop slipping out, her long lashes spiky as they rested heavily on the tops of her cheeks.

Jude wasn't sure what came over him, but he scooched closer, wrapping an arm around Indira's hunched shoulders.

She trembled slightly, but, after a moment, leaned into him—only the tiniest bit—her warmth spreading across his chest.

"No matter how many years pass, it still feels as fresh as the day he walked out," Indira whispered against his chest. "And Collin's right, I'm not over it. And I don't know why I can't find that closure. But having him at the wedding, being charismatic and charming and stepping right in to this shiny role of supportive dad makes me furious. We weren't enough for him as kids, but suddenly him gracing us with his presence at their special day will make up for the constant messes he left behind?"

"You two were—are—more than enough," Jude said, his voice a rough growl. "He's the one that didn't come up to scratch."

"Clearly not," Indira said with a bitter laugh, brushing the tears off her cheeks. "Because he's happy and thriving and living this lovely cookie-cutter life and I resent him so fucking much for it. I wish I didn't care. Why can't I stop caring?"

Indira looked at Jude like she actually expected him to have an answer. His heart stuttered for a beat, then pounded in double-time.

He was suddenly desperate to give her an answer that would soothe the ache etched across her features.

But he had nothing.

Indira blinked away, and Jude hated that he was one more disappointment causing that weariness in her eyes.

"Caring is kind of your thing," Jude said at last. "I've known you since you were what, five? Six? Even when you were little, you cared about everyone. Everything. I imagine it's hard to stop something that's your nature."

Indira stared at him in that way of hers, like she was reading a secret inscription at the very core of him, seeing him in a way that left him far too vulnerable. The effect was always unnerving. . .

At least, it used to be. Now, Jude found a sort of odd . . . *comfort* in it—that look shocking his system, but leaving a pleasant buzz in his veins.

Indira was silent for a moment, staring straight ahead at the carpeting as she bit the inside of her cheek.

Then her face crumpled. All of her crumpled, honestly. Her head fell heavily forward, her spine bending into a defeated curve as she sobbed into her knees.

And Jude . . .

He panicked a bit.

He didn't know what to do with this outpouring of emotions and feelings, and he acted on instinct, sort of . . . awkwardly draping himself over her back. Holding her tightly, one hand rubbing (in what he hoped was a soothing manner) up and down her arm. It was weird and the angle caused a twinge in his neck, but Indira seemed to soften at the touch. At the pressure. So he stayed still. Very still. And held her as she cried.

Eventually, Indira's tears stopped and she let out a deep breath. Jude disentangled himself from her, his cheeks hot and stomach rolling as she sat up, her shoulders maintaining a protective hunch.

"I'm sorry," she said at last, still not looking at him. "I'm a weepy mess tonight and I'm sure it's annoying to deal with. There's just been so much that's happened the past few weeks and I'm feeling a bit overwhelmed by it all and . . . yeah. It's a lot. I don't mean to emotionally dump on you like this."

Without thinking, Jude reached for her, resting his hand on the back of her neck. She turned, looking at him with wide, vulnerable eyes.

"Don't," he said, his other hand cupping her cheek, guiding her to fully face him, little bolts of electricity ricocheting up and down his spine at the heat of her skin. "Don't apologize. You're allowed to tell me—anyone—when you're upset. You don't have to pretend to be okay."

Indira's eyes traced across his face, then she let out a tiny hiccup of a laugh.

"When did . . . this . . . *compassion* happen?" she asked, scrunching up her nose as she waved her hand at him. "Talking to you used to feel like the verbal equivalent of a boiling enema."

It was Jude's turn to laugh, but it came out breathy, doing little to untangle the knot of tension in his stomach. "Trust me, I'm as horrified at this expression of feelings as you are. You bring out the worst in me."

Indira rolled her eyes but smiled. And Jude felt that smile. He felt the way her cheek stretched and moved under his palm that still cupped her face. He felt it in the warmth that shot through his fingers straight to his chest.

Their gazes clashed, and, in the same moment, they both became aware of how intimately Jude was touching her. How they'd drifted nearer, their mouths only centimeters apart. The soft puffs of hot air on skin as they breathed so closely. Jude continued to search her face—for what, he wasn't sure—but the moment clicked into place like the turn of a lock, and Indira's body swayed, almost imperceptibly, toward him, creating an echoing tug in the center of Jude's stomach.

Jude was frozen by a flood of sensations—terrifying and unsettling and achingly sweet. Like he couldn't breathe but at the same time his lungs were flooded with air.

She arched an eyebrow and sucked in a breath, parting her lips like she was going to ask a question. No words came out.

Jude was simultaneously relieved and terrified at her silence. A question would break him out of this bizarre trance. It would wake him up and jolt him far away from Indira and her warm skin and dangerously close mouth. But that would also mean he'd stop touching her. And, for some maddening reason, he didn't want to stop touching her.

In the space between a breath and a heartbeat, Indira's face morphed from a question to something different. Something soft and open and the tiniest bit hungry.

And before Jude knew what was happening, she pushed forward.

And kissed him.

Her lips were hot and searching, and she threw her arms around his neck, pulling him closer.

Jude went without a fight.

He kissed her back, his brain unable to keep up with all the sensations pummeling him at once. The slide of her tongue against his. The brush of her hair against his cheeks. The taste of her lips as he took them like a starving man.

A tiny whimper escaped from Indira, the vibrations rattling straight into his chest.

That noise, quite simply, turned Jude inside out.

He growled in response, pushing her against the couch cushions. Getting closer to Indira.

Indira.

Oh God, this was *Indira*.

He absolutely should not be kissing Indira. Shouldn't be gripping her hips, pulling them snugly against him. Shouldn't be angling her hot and hungry mouth to seal perfectly against his.

Indira, his best friend's little sister, shouldn't be dragging her hands through his hair, pulling at it until he grunted in pleasure at the sensation.

Her name repeated on a loop in his mind—*Indira. Indira. Indira.* He couldn't hold back the groan of it against her mouth as he took the kiss deeper. Harder. As she arched against him. As she tilted her head for even more.

Jude thought he knew the human body. He knew muscles and blood vessels and bones and organs and how they all worked in miraculous harmony. But this kiss, apparently, had the power to reroute nerve endings. Turn blood into smoke. Set fire to every cell. Indira was a fever, one that had been biding its time, waiting to compromise his system.

Her hands clawed down his chest, landing at the button of his jeans. He kissed her more, tasting the dangerous sweetness of her silky mouth. Biting those lips that always had a ready retort.

"Holy shit," Indira whispered, dragging her teeth down the column of his neck. "What's happening?"

Jude didn't know how to answer. He had no words for whatever alternate universe they'd tumbled into. All he knew was that it shouldn't be happening.

It had to happen.

He didn't want it to end.

Through their panting breaths, a new sound emerged. It was far away. A tinkling. A nearly imperceptible warning they both wanted to ignore. And then the unmistakable sound of a key entering a lock, the turning of a bolt, jolted them both back to reality.

Their heads whipped to the side, Indira's hair getting caught in Jude's gaping mouth, his body heavy as he pressed her against the couch. They watched in fear as the doorknob turned.

Indira finally got some sense between the two of them. With a tiny squeal, she slid out from under him, Jude pitching forward and banging his face on the arm of the couch. She scrambled to standing, then sprinted to the bathroom.

Jude rolled off the couch at the last second, bouncing to his feet and fixing his pants and hiding his throbbing erection just as Collin walked in through the door.

"Why are you home!" Jude yelled. Then cringed as Collin's head jerked back. So chill.

But, truly, what was the proper reaction for his best friend almost walking in on him feeling up his sister?

"I live here!" Collin yelled back in a mocking tone. "Did you forget?"

"I mean . . . why are you back so soon?"

"I left my wallet. Didn't realize till we sat down, so I ran back home." Collin grabbed his wallet from the ceramic dish on the entryway table, slapping it against his palm as he looked around. "And, uh, I wanted to check on Dira. Talk to her. Where is she?"

Jude's mind went completely blank. "Outer space!" he shouted.

Collin blinked. "What?"

"I . . . She . . ."

A flush and the sound of water running interrupted Jude's fumbling, and Indira walked out, looking perfectly put together, except for deep red splotches that stained her cheeks.

"Hey," she said, giving Collin a limp wave.

"Hey. Can we talk for a minute?"

Indira nodded, then led them to the dining room table. Jude stayed put, pressing his back against the hallway wall and trying to calm his swimming head. A few words drifted in on the soft murmur of their voices—*sorry* and *I love you* and *everything's fine*—but Jude couldn't process them with the memories of Indira's moan flooding his brain.

After a few minutes, Collin reappeared by the front door. "Sure you don't want to come grab a beer with us?" he called over his shoulder.

"I'm good," Indira called back from the other room.

Collin shot Jude a questioning look, but Jude shook his head and gave him what he hoped was a casual smile.

"I'm good too," Jude said, guilt sinking his stomach. There was no way he could sit across from Collin, bullshitting over beers, with Indira's lips still imprinted against his skin.

"Okay," Collin said. "See you later."

As soon as the door clicked shut, Jude darted to the dining room to find Indira.

"We can never mention what happened," Jude said, planting his hands on the table across from her, forcing his eyes not to land on the fullness of her mouth.

"Don't even know what you're talking about," Indira muttered, taking a sip of water as she tucked a lock of hair behind her ear.

"Good. Because that"—Jude gestured wildly in the direction of the couch—"should never have happened."

His friendship with Collin was one of the only good things Jude had left in his sad little life. He couldn't convince himself he was doing anything to honor that relationship by feeling up Collin's little sister.

"Again, can't say I know what you're talking about," Indira said, but her lips were pursed, an undercurrent of anger causing her eyes to narrow.

"And that won't *ever* happen again," Jude said, apparently unable to help himself. "This thing between us is fake. Purely fake. You get that? All clear?"

Maybe the more times he said they couldn't touch each other again, the easier it would be for his protesting brain to accept it.

At that point, Indira stood up, mirroring him by also planting her hands on the table and leaning forward. The movement was immediately predatory and a quick jolt of fear shot down Jude's spine.

"Not sure why you're choosing to be as dense as possible right now, but you repeating over and over that we can't talk about it is, in fact, you talking about it. So, allow *me* to make it clear. You seem to be the only one that needs confirmation that something like that"—she mimicked his earlier gesture toward the couch—"will never, ever happen again. You can fixate on how good it felt to stick your tongue down my throat all you want, but you'll keep all further comments locked in that big head of yours. Like you said, this is fake. That's all it will ever be."

Jude's jaw dangled open. Indira patted him on the cheek, then moved around him.

"Glad we had this talk," she whispered, then left the room.

CHAPTER 19

Indira

∞

"So you and Jude are . . . lying? Am I understanding this correctly?" Dr. Koh asked, pressing her hands together as she looked at Indira with an arched brow.

Indira squirmed from her spot on the couch. "I mean . . . I guess in the most stripped-down sense, yes. But Collin and Jeremy know. And my friends know. So, really, it's more like just lying to Chris."

And to yourself, you heartsick dummy.

"And . . . you think this is a wise idea?"

"Well, when you use that tone, I don't," Indira said, staring up at the ceiling. "But Jude said it will make the sensory overload of it all easier to deal with. Gives him an excuse for us to make an escape without eliciting a ton of questions. They'll think we're off doing . . . coupley stuff in dark corners or whatever."

"Have you talked to Jude about why he's struggling? Where this is coming from?"

"I've tried," Indira said with a defeated shrug. "He's told me a bit. About how much blame he's internalized for patients that didn't survive or had less-than-ideal outcomes. And I think he's seen a lot of violence in the areas he's been stationed."

Dr. Koh nodded. "Is he talking to anyone about that?"

"No. And I wish he were. I'm just . . . I'm scared to push him. I'm scared to ask him too much, suggest too much. He's only recently started confiding in me, and I don't want to then kick open the door and bust down the walls. And—" Indira swallowed, then looked to the side.

"And what?" Dr. Koh prodded.

"I don't want him to see me as his psychiatrist. Or for him to think that I'm trying to analyze him like some case study. I don't know."

"Why does that idea bother you?" Dr. Koh asked quietly.

Tears pricked at Indira's eyes, then spilled over, hot as they rolled down her cheeks. "Because . . . fuck, I don't know? I want him to see me as me? Not as a psychiatrist and not as Collin's little sister . . . I want being me to be enough."

Dr. Koh leaned forward, resting her elbows on her thighs. The silence was thick, and Indira could almost hear Dr. Koh thinking as she studied her.

"Indira," she said, tilting her head. "There's something I want you to understand. Something crucial. Regardless of how Jude sees you, regardless of if he gets help or lets you in or any other path his journey may take him on, you are perfectly enough, exactly as you are."

Indira blinked rapidly, unable to meet her therapist's eyes.

"Where do you think this fear of not being enough comes from?" Dr. Koh whispered.

"Are you going to make me say it?"

Dr. Koh shook her head. "You don't have to say anything you don't want to in here."

Tears still rolling down her cheeks, Indira sighed, looking away while her leg bounced so hard the entire couch vibrated.

"I was young when my dad left. And little kids . . . they digest the actions of adults and those around them differently—this isn't a secret." Indira's voice was detached, looking back on her childhood self like she would a patient. "And when your mom's a mess and your brother won't talk to you and your world feels like it's crashing down, it's hard not to find something easy to place blame on. And, like, obviously, I developed these thoughts that maybe if I had been a better daughter or done something different or . . . been enough, none of this would have happened."

Indira looked at Dr. Koh, soul weary.

"And I . . . I don't know. I guess I started seeking that approval wherever I could get it. However I could, because maybe then it would prove that I am enough and I'm worth sticking around for."

The silence ticked through the room, and Indira let out a defeated sigh. "I know it's not a rational thought. Like, I one hundred percent recognize that these fears and this need for extrinsic validation doesn't determine my worth. But it doesn't stop me from *feeling* it."

The problem with being self-aware and introspective while also being, admittedly, emotionally damaged was that Indira could reason through her feelings and their source and how they didn't serve her, but she also couldn't stop the ruminating circles of feeling them.

"We place these expectations that being aware of our brain or emotions lying to us means that we should automatically be able to get over it," Dr. Koh said, eyes locked on Indira. "That's simply not how it works. We wouldn't expect someone with asthma to recognize they have asthma and then be able to go and sprint a mile without needing an inhaler. Healing from those internal wounds takes time. Sometimes a lifetime. But it's the willingness to work on it that matters."

"I'm tired," Indira admitted on a small, choked-back sob.

"I know, dear," Dr. Koh said, eyes filled with understanding.

"What do I do?"

"You rest up. And then, when you're ready, you keep working."

CHAPTER 20

Jude

"Are you excited for Saturday?" Collin asked, twisting Jude's tie into an elaborate knot as he tried on his groomsman suit at the tailor's.

"I actually really am," Jude said, tugging at the sleeves of his jacket.

Collin shot him a look. "I'm going to pretend to not pick up a double meaning in there that you haven't been equally excited for all the other wedding-adjacent events."

Jude gave his best attempt at looking sheepish.

He had found an open date in Collin's packed schedule and asked him to go camping, like when they were kids, pitching the idea as pre-wedding rest and relaxation.

Jude loved the outdoors. He and Collin had spent most of their adolescence roaming in the woods that bordered the back of Collin's house, camping out in the backyard through the summer and as much of the fall as their parents would allow. The idea of hanging out with his best friend in the peacefulness of nature was like a soothing hand rubbing over his sternum.

"I think we'll have good weather too," Collin added, frowning at the tie and then undoing it, fingers moving quickly as he gave it a second attempt. "Maybe we could even try to do some fishing Sunday morning."

Jude could practically hear the babbling brook, and he was giddy with anticipation. But there was a tiny, nagging void in all their weekend plans.

"So," Jude said casually, pushing Collin's fiddling fingers away from his tie. "Should we invite Indira?"

"Dira? *Camping*?" Collin snorted. "No. Never. I don't think I've ever met someone so outdoors adverse."

"Oh?" Jude's heart dipped. When had that happened? As kids, Indira always loved being outside. And why did it bother him so much that he didn't know how she'd changed?

"She literally once told me she thought the ocean sounds from a white-noise machine were more beautiful than the actual ocean. So, no, I don't think she'd be that interested."

Jude nodded, trying to swallow past the sudden lump in his throat, and ignore the odd aching in his chest, that little voice whispering that he'd missed so many important things right in front his eyes.

It was for the best Indira wouldn't go. They could probably use some space from each other. Like, miles of space. And protective barriers from touching. Or looks. Or any of the countless tempting aspects of her. They'd been awkwardly scuttling around each other the past few days, little hermit crabs retracting into their shells.

Plus, Jude didn't like how much he'd started to enjoy being around her even pre-make-out-that-shall-never-be-consciously-thought-about-again-(dreams-don't-count-because-he-has-no-say-in-those).

He had another GHCO assignment looming in a few weeks, and being thrust back into that terrifying world where people relied on him to live or die—where every moment felt like water slipping through the cracks of his fingers—wouldn't be made any easier by missing Indira's presence.

Space was good. Necessary. Protective.

The best thing for them both.

"This looks great on you, by the way," Collin said, brushing his hands over Jude's shoulders.

Jude snorted, glancing in the mirror. The suit did look nice. Crisp lines and a striking hunter green.

He wondered what Indira would be wearing as they walked down the aisle. How peeks of skin would glow against a similar green or how the skirt might hug her curves and frame the sway of her hips, his hands itching to trace down the path of her spine to rest on the small of her back. Jude's heartbeat echoed in his ears as he imagined gauzy fabric draping along her collarbones, accentuating her long neck. Falling to highlight the swells of her—

"You good?"

Collin's voice cut through Jude's haze, and he blinked rapidly out of his daydream, smacking his overeager imagination on the nose.

"Yeah, sorry. Zoned out for a sec."

Collin shot him a look of *Yeah, I'll say.*

"Are we done with the try-on?" Jude asked, not waiting for an answer as he darted for the fitting room, almost plowing over a short old man organizing ties on the display table.

"Uh. Seems like it," Collin called from the other side of the curtain. "You sure you're okay?"

"Fine," Jude wheezed out, collapsing onto the bench, biting his knuckle then burrowing his head in his hands, willing his inconvenient boner to fuck off.

He wasn't supposed to be fantasizing about Indira or her . . . neck . . . among other areas . . . all of which Jude was officially banishing from his brain because holy shit he needed to stop getting a half chub from his best friend's little sister. Especially when said best friend was standing *right there.*

What was wrong with him? What was this bizarre obsession with Indira?

She's safe.

The thought rocketed through Jude, zipping away before he could even find its source. But it was kind of . . . true?

Indira was familiar. And funny. And regularly annoying as hell. But there was something undeniably safe about being around her.

Which all makes sense, Jude reasoned, clawing for his rational brain to take over. That was the crux of the reason they'd started this arrangement. He'd known her for so long, she was a natural anchor for him when the world started tipping.

That was all.

And that's all she would continue to be.

Jude arranged himself as he got changed and then met Collin at the front of the store.

"I was able to find my second tent in the basement for you to use this weekend," Collin said, picking up the thread of conversation Jude had long ago lost. "It's old, but should do the trick."

"Thanks. I really am so excited."

Collin clapped Jude on the back. "Glad to hear that. It'll be great. Super low-key and chill."

Jude nodded then smiled, following Collin to the car.

Low-key and chill. Exactly what he needed.

* * *

Saturday, shockingly, was neither low-key nor chill.

Jude stared in silent horror at the unadulterated chaos filling the foyer as Collin and Rake wrestled with camping equipment while Lizzie and Jeremy laughed like banshees every few minutes. It didn't take long for Jude to realize his fatal mistake: Collin, demonic extrovert that he was, had applied his signature "the more, the merrier" mentality to Jude's desperate attempt at a peaceful weekend in nature. He'd done similar things in college and med school, handing out camping invites like candy on Halloween. It hadn't bothered Jude much back then.

He hated himself for how much it bothered him now.

"Oh my God, what is happening?" Indira asked, appearing at the open front door, earbuds hanging around her neck and face flushed from her run.

Lizzie hurdled over a tent and a cooler like an Olympic track star to smack into Indira with what Jude assumed was a hug. It resembled more of a meteor crashing onto earth with its force.

"Howdy, camper!" Lizzie said, wrapping her arm around Indira's shoulders and ushering her into the house, shutting the door with her foot. "There's still time for you to join us on our outdoor adventure." Lizzie offered a sweeping gesture at the shit storm in the hallway.

"I'm sorry, what?" Indira asked again, face scrunched up as she looked at Lizzie.

"We're going camping," Rake explained, examining a dented cooler.

"You should come!" Lizzie said, bouncing on her toes.

"It'll be fun," Collin added with a smile, zipping up a backpack.

"Absolutely not." Indira's eyes danced around the mess, landing on Jude for a beat longer than anything else. Then she turned to her friend. "Lizzie, I didn't even know *you* liked camping." Indira's eyebrows were furrowed so deeply it made Jude want to laugh . . . if he wasn't absolutely freaking out at his crumbling plans for peace.

"Well," Lizzie said, "this will actually be my first time. But I'll try anything once. And I'm also fairly desperate to get a little time away from Rake's screaming spawn."

"Yes, because Evie obviously gets her volume from me, love," Rake deadpanned, making Lizzie cackle.

Unfortunately, Indira caught the way the sudden noise made Jude flinch. She studied him for a moment, and Jude's pulse punched at his chest as he wondered if she could read his panic. He didn't want her to see how chaotic every emotion was. How damaged he was.

"I . . . I thought it was just Jude and Collin going?" Indira asked, her expression mirroring Jude's own internal confusion at how things had spiraled into such a massive event.

Lizzie shrugged. "From what I understand, Jude invited Collin. Collin obviously invited Jeremy. He also invited Rake. And I invited myself with the full intention of turning this into a homemade *Naked and Afraid* moment." She shot Rake an overt wink.

"Did you even ask Jude if this was okay?" Indira asked, rounding on Collin. "Or did you just steamroll through his plans?"

Collin shot Indira a confused look. "Why are you being so combative right now? Jude was the one who suggested inviting you in the first place. Why would he care if our other friends came along?"

Indira's eyes shot to Jude, and he looked to the floor, pangs of embarrassment slicing through his haze of sensory overload.

"That's . . . that's not the point," Indira spluttered out.

Collin let out a sigh. "Do you want to go camping or not?"

"No, I don't want to go camping!" Indira flung up her hands. "I also don't want to intrude on or alter Jude's intentions for the trip."

"Oh my God. Not everything has to be made into some big deal," Collin said, rolling his eyes.

"You didn't even think about his feelings!"

"Would you just chill? It's camping, not some soap opera. It's going to be a fun weekend away, but if you're going to be like this you don't have to go."

"I don't *want* to go!" Indira screeched. She opened her mouth to say something else, but Jude cut her off.

"Indira, stop."

His voice cracked like a whip across the room.

And he hated himself for it. For the harsh way his words slammed her jaws shut. The way her lips twitched and face fell.

But he couldn't help it; their rising voices felt like needle points injected directly into the nerve endings along his spine. He was sweaty and dizzy and trying to figure out what to do about the spiraling chaos unfolding before him.

Indira's big copper eyes flashed to Jude. The anger on her face shifted, the obstinate clench of her jaw and the firm lines between her eyebrows morphing into soft hurt as she studied his face.

"You're right, Collin," Indira said, her eyes sticking on Jude's for a second longer before she dragged them away to look at her brother.

"I'm clearly the asshole here. So, yeah, I'm going to politely decline the invitation to sleep on the ground in the freezing cold. I have a bunch of work I need to get caught up on anyway."

Collin frowned, shaking his head as he continued gathering supplies. Indira wrapped her arms around herself, plastered on a fake smile, and took a step back from the group.

After a moment, Rake followed Collin's lead, and Lizzie moved to Indira's side, giving her hand a subtle squeeze as she whispered something to Indira that Jude couldn't hear.

Jude had hurt her feelings. She was trying to protect him and he'd snapped at her. And he wanted to punch himself in the face for the subtle sadness in her features.

But he didn't want it to be a *thing*. He wanted to be fucking *normal*. He didn't want the unruliness of his brain to be obvious to anyone.

He wished so desperately he could be the guy who wouldn't have a problem with last-minute invites. Someone who didn't feel this desperate, almost primal need to escape the structure of the city.

And he thought maybe he was doing an okay job pretending to still be that guy.

But Indira, with her goddamn perceptive eyes that could read his thoughts like they were written on his skin, wouldn't let him pretend.

Things were spinning out of control. Jude couldn't process the number of people. The noise. The spontaneity of it all. A pressure built in his skull, dull and dangerous and ready to lay him on the floor.

"Please come," he said suddenly, seeing only Indira. He needed her. He couldn't do it without her.

Indira looked at him, eyes wide and cautious, shoulders curved in defense.

"Please," Jude repeated, keeping his eyes locked with her. Looking at her for longer than he'd allowed himself in days. "I—" Jude swallowed.

I want you.

I need you.

I already miss you.

"It wouldn't be the same without you."

When she continued to stare at him in silence, Jude attempted a smile. It felt stiff and foreign and probably looked absolutely horrifying based on the way Lizzie did a double-take before turning away, following Rake and Collin out the door with a handful of supplies.

Please. This time Jude mouthed the word, only for Indira. She watched his lips, licking her own before meeting his eyes, nodding, and giving him a tentative smile that pulverized his heart to dust.

"Okay," she said with a resigned sigh. "I'm ready to suffer in the great outdoors."

CHAPTER 21

Indira

As Indira drove her SUV full of people toward the mountains—how did she get suckered into using her car for this damn thing?—she thought of all the things she'd rather do than go camping:

1) Lick the needles off a cactus.
2) Cut her own bangs knowing full well the emotional turmoil that would haunt her for the next year.
3) Listen to a boomer talk about student loans.
4) Eat cigarette butts off the filthy Philadelphia sidewalks.
5) Sit through a man playing devil's advocate on literally any topic.

Indira tried to find the bright side to her predicament. But, between being annoyed at her brother and worried about Jude, the situation was, to say the least, not fucking ideal.

"Turn here," Collin said, leaning up from his spot in the back to point at a gravel path to the left.

Indira held back a gasp. "If my car suffers a single ding from this ridiculous, off-roading nightmare of a weekend, I will skin you alive, Collin."

"It's a gravel road on flat land—I'm not having you traverse the Grand Canyon here."

"Feels like it," Indira mumbled as the car jostled over a dip.

Collin scoffed and sat back in his seat.

"Just imagine the larger bumps are you running over his big head," Jude whispered to her as he leaned forward to turn down the radio's volume.

And Indira nearly crashed the car with how fast she jerked her entire body to face Jude. He'd been so closed off with her the past few days, retreating in on himself after their . . . after that moment they would never speak about. Was this real? Did Jude just peek a millimeter out of his shell to roast Collin on her behalf?

Jude looked at her with wide, cautious eyes for a moment before offering her a hint of a smile.

It was crooked and kind of awkward and the most endearing thing Indira had ever seen. She couldn't tell if the earth was shaking from the power of that devastating little smile or just another pothole.

She found some inner strength to pull her gaze away from that growing grin and safely navigated through the winding road. When the trees were thick and the gravel turned to dirt, Collin had Indira pull over at a patch of browning grass that he referred to as a campsite.

Indira felt it would more accurately be described as a dump, but then again, her primary hobbies included eating soft pretzels in bed and online shopping, so she might not have been the best judge of the spot's character.

"Oi, this is great," Rake said, hopping out of the car, Collin close behind. Lizzie and Indira shared a skeptical look in the rearview mirror, but Lizzie shrugged, then grinned, following the others.

Indira sighed, scrunching up her nose as she continued to take in her bleak accommodations.

"What happened to Dira, nature girl extraordinaire, that I grew up with?" Jude asked quietly, casually, still sitting in the car with her as the others opened the trunk and started to unpack.

Indira's heart thrummed against her breastbone at the sound of his voice, low and edged with roughness.

"She was introduced to the finer things in life like mattresses and running water and bathing regularly," Indira said, turning her head slowly to look at him. She let her eyes flick up and down his body. "Shame that last one never took with you."

It was delayed, Jude seeming to process in slow motion, but—ah—there it was. That whisper of a smile back again, slow like honey and just as sweet. Then he laughed, rusty and hoarse, but genuine.

And Indira's heart, quite simply, expanded to twice its size at the combination of the two.

"Personal hygiene habits aside," Jude said, leaning in almost imperceptibly, "between the two of us, I think you're the one more likely to have something nest in that hair of yours while on this trip. I'd be careful."

Indira, creature of indoor pleasures and fearer of nature that she was, did not have the wherewithal to come up with something witty, her hands plunging into her curls and eyes going wide.

"I will—and I cannot emphasize this enough—lose my ever-fucking shit if *anything* tries to make a home out of my hair."

Jude chuckled again, then shook his head, the smile slowly fading and his features taking on that serious look that shielded him.

Indira wanted to grab his face. Make him look at her. Demand that smile to come back. But she couldn't do that. The past few moments felt crucial. Monumental. And she'd cherish them for exactly how long they'd lasted. She had no reason to be greedy for anything more.

"We should probably help set up," Jude said, his eyes sliding to Indira's mouth, then quickly flicking to look out the windshield.

"Yeah, you probably should," Indira responded, hoping her voice sounded lighter than her sinking heart. "I'll stay in here and . . . not do any work."

Jude laughed at that, opening his door and then sliding out. Indira pressed her head against the seat, trying to pull herself together.

"Dira?" Jude whispered, leaning down to peer into the car.

She arched an eyebrow.

"Thank you for coming. Thank you for . . . for being willing to help me."

Indira's throat constricted, heart squeezing.

"Don't mention it," she said with a smile. Jude smiled back.

A single, small tear rolled down her cheek when Jude shut the door.

* * *

"This is ass," Indira said under her breath a few hours later, burrowing deeper into her coat as the wind picked up. "Camping is just life but harder."

Collin, Rake, and Jude had already spent an annoyingly long time trying to start a fire the "good old-fashioned way," by smacking sticks together. And, as each minute of failure ticked on, warmth seemed more like an elusive fantasy than a basic tool for survival. Lizzie, Jeremy, and Indira were huddled together, stuffing marshmallows in their mouths and quietly narrating their Neanderthals' dismal survival skills like sportscasters covering a game.

"Collin's recent tantrum before the commercial break certainly lacked a level of sportsmanship," Jeremy said quietly. "But he's regained his composure as we kick off the next quarter."

"It seems as though Rake is going for the thick stick again after recently benching it for injury recovery. Could this be a reflection on his own phallus and using it as a guiding force? Our player expert, Lizzie Blake, is here with the details," Indira said, handing an invisible microphone to Lizzie.

"Thanks for the introduction, Dira. While yes, Rake does have a confirmed hammer dick packed into those tight pants, said penis has more of a leftward curve than the thick stick he is aggressively rubbing against yet another stick. Insider knowledge leads us to believe that, more than anything else, our resident himbo's choice of fire-making tools is directly correlated to having absolutely no clue what he's doing. Back to you."

They all cackled until they were crying, provoking dirty looks from the other three who were sweaty and irritated by this point.

"Why must I do everything?" Indira sighed, standing and brushing off the back of her jeans.

She walked to the pile of gear by her car, rummaged for a second, then found what she was looking for. Per Collin's instructions—who'd binge-watched one Saturday's worth of *Man vs. Wild* and suddenly considered himself a survivalist—the guys were crouched near the side of the firepit, trying to light the small bundle of tinder that they'd then move to the logs if they ever got it going.

Indira used her hip to bump Collin out of the way, the others tumbling like dominos after him. She then popped the lid off the lighter fluid, giving it a good squeeze over the wood before tossing it to the side. With sharp movements, she grabbed a match, struck it, and tossed the tiny flame into the firepit, grinning in delight when large flames burst up with a quiet but powerful *poof*.

Dusting her hands off, she turned to the group. "S'mores, anyone?"

Lizzie started slow-clapping.

After mild grumbling that was soon replaced with full mouths and fuller bellies, the group thawed by the fire. Lizzie and Jeremy kept everyone entertained for hours, the vivacious storytellers feeding off each other until Indira was close to tears with laughter and Rake was doubled-over, holding his sides as he wheezed. Even Jude looked more relaxed. He didn't smile, exactly, but it was like, for the first time in weeks, some of the tension in his body was finally releasing.

Indira kept catching him looking at her across the circle, his eyes shooting to his feet the second their gazes met. The dancing flames cast shadows on the hard lines of his face—amplifying the sharpness of his nose, the angle of his jaw—but the amber glow warmed him, making him look fierce but beautiful in the darkness that settled around them like a blanket.

When the fire was burned down to weak embers, everyone made the silent decision that it was time for bed.

It wasn't until Indira was gathering up the bundle of quilts and pillows she was using in lieu of a sleeping bag that she realized her sleeping situation was about to get extremely awkward.

Rake had brought a sturdy, reliable, two-person tent for the trip, which Lizzie had managed to mangle into a knot for an hour while the two bickered and giggled as they put it together. Collin and Jeremy had their own sleeper that barely seemed to fit the pair as they wrestled their limbs into it.

Which meant, nightmare of all nightmares, Indira's only option for sleeping was to curl up on the dirt and hope she didn't roll into the firepit while she slept.

Or . . . share with Jude.

Her stomach swooped up while her heart bottomed out of her chest.

"'Night," Collin mumbled before closing himself and Jeremy in, the scratch of the zipper's teeth amplified in the quiet of nature.

Indira and Jude stared at each other in mutual horror, scrambling for a solution that wouldn't have them pressed against each other in a three-by-five space for the next eight hours.

"I can sleep out here," Jude said, jamming his hands in his pockets and looking down at the ground.

"No. Don't be ridiculous," Indira said, tugging at her curls. "It's your tent. I can . . . I'll sleep in the car. Blast the heat too instead of dying of hypothermia tonight." Her words were punctuated by a nervous cackle of laughter that made them both flinch.

"And drain your car battery? Genius."

Indira was caught off guard. Not because Jude was being a snarky twat—she knew that was fundamental to his being—but because he said it with something almost like . . . playfulness. A teasing that reminded her of when they were young, but with a subtle undercurrent of something different. And dammit if her soft and traitorous little heart didn't melt a bit at that.

Was being roasted her love language? What the hell *was* this?

"Listen," Jude said, dragging a hand across the back of his neck, then dropping it heavily at his side. "There's only one tent. We'll just . . . I don't know, squeeze some blankets in between us. Problem solved."

Indira opened her mouth to argue—mainly because arguing with Jude felt as natural as breathing—but a loud groan from the vicinity of Collin's tent cut her off.

"Would you two mind, oh, I don't know, shutting the hell up and going to bed? Thanks."

With that oh-so-subtle scolding, Jude pushed Indira into the tent, following close behind.

Indira was eternally thankful for the pitch blackness of the space. She didn't want Jude to see her hands trembling, the swirling thoughts written on her face, the unbelievably awkward and graceless way she shoved herself under her heap of blankets.

She made the impulsive, self-protective decision to sleep opposite Jude, her head lined up with his legs, so she wouldn't do something mortifying like reach out her arm and snake it around his chest or lean her head on his shoulder and whisper every real feeling she was having about their fake dating into his ear.

After a few seconds of frantic shuffling and thrashing on both their parts, they fell as silent as the dead, laying just as stiff.

Indira wondered if Jude could hear the *thump thump thump* of her hammering heart. Every breath was shallow, as though breathing too deeply would jolt the earth off its axis or do something worse like make her accidentally touch Jude. Every cell in her body prickled with awareness of him, how only a few layers of fabric separated their skin.

Torture wasn't a strong enough word.

"This might be the most uncomfortable night of my life," Indira said into the darkness after what felt like hours. It was likely only seven minutes. She heard Jude's head turn in her direction.

"Really? Because I absolutely *love* sleeping with your stinky feet in my face," he said dryly.

Indira's mouth dropped open. Without thinking, she used their positioning to dig her sock-clad foot into Jude's cheek and ear, satisfaction ballooning in her chest at the *Aarghhhhhhh* Jude choked out before grabbing her ankle.

He paused for just a beat, like he was checking an impulse, but something shifted in the way he touched her—firmer, surer—and he used his other hand to rip off her sock and start tickling her foot mercilessly.

Indira swallowed a shriek, writhing like a fish on land to get out of his grip. But part of her—a detrimental part—couldn't ignore the sharp jolt of joy that speared through her chest at his touch. At his teasing.

She turned her head, sinking her teeth into Jude somewhere in the vicinity of his thigh through his sleeping bag and pajamas.

"Oh my God, no biting! You know that's against the rules," Jude hissed, trying to keep his volume to a whisper. He dropped her foot, trying to disengage her bite.

"The rules," Indira mocked, matching his hushed tone. She took advantage of his releasing her, squirming upward until she could roll her deadweight on top of him, pinning his hands in the process. "The rules were for when we were kids. We're adults now and this is a *WWE SmackDown.* All bets are off."

Jude and Collin had gotten really into wrestling one summer, coaxing Indira into joining their tournament-style matches, which basically equated to them tossing her around like a ragdoll until she'd go feral and sink a good bite into them or "accidentally" knee them in the groin.

Jude tried to roll out from under her, but his sleeping bag restricted his movements. All his thrashing pushed Indira further up his body.

She was shaking with silent giggles as he continuously cursed under his breath.

"You're"—*grunt*—"so"—*thrash*—"annoying."

Indira laughed harder.

Jude managed to free his hands, shooting both out to Indira's sides and digging in. She made a mortifying sound like a screeching pig, and Jude became the one laughing.

"It's not so funny now, is it?" he said, voice dripping with smugness, an arrogant grin on his mouth that shone even in the darkness.

She found a reserve of superhuman strength and ripped his hands off her body, slamming his wrists to the ground.

"I'm not letting you win this, kitten—" Indira whispered sweetly into his ear. "Surrender."

Jude bucked under her one more time, and she reinforced her hold, knowing she had him pinned.

But victory was short-lived, instantly replaced by a hyperawareness of her body and his.

Their suppressed giggles died in their throats as the intimacy of the position crashed around them. Indira suddenly felt like the one held captive. A bolt of sensation rocketed through her as they both sucked in a breath at the same time, their stomachs meeting, neither willing to break the contact to exhale.

Jude's arms were pinned over his head, Indira's chest pressed against him, her thighs straddling his groin, and her lips just centimeters from his.

And Jude stirred with the proximity, his sudden erection prominent between her thighs.

An involuntary whimper of desire clawed out of Indira's throat.

Well . . . fuck.

Even in the dark, Indira could see Jude's eyes go wide with horror, and she scrambled off him as he squirmed uncomfortably, sitting up and shifting to the farthest corner of the tent he could.

They stared at each other, their shallow breaths mixing with the wind and rustling leaves outside their tent.

"I . . . uh . . . Sorry . . . um," Jude spluttered out. "That didn't . . . That wasn't . . ."

Somehow, all those disjointed words made the situation ten times worse.

"Goodbye," Indira said quickly, moving in a flash to unzip the tent and bear-crawling out of it. She grabbed her shoes, rolling onto her back in the damp grass to jam them on her feet.

"Where are you going?" Jude hissed, popping his head out of the opening.

"Air," was all Indira managed to choke out, scrambling to her feet and doing an awkward walk-run away. She needed space. She needed to not let the traitorous memory of the feel of his body buzz around her brain like a horny little fly.

"You can't take off into the woods in the middle of the night alone," Jude said, crawling out of the tent and jogging to catch up.

"I am a fiercely independent woman with immense survival skills and perfect night vision," Indira lied.

Jude scoffed in response.

After a few minutes of stumbling in the woods, she begrudgingly pulled out her phone, using the flashlight to follow a short trail that led to a small creek.

Indira stopped at the water's edge, out of options.

"What's wrong? Not gonna plow through the stream?" Jude asked, shooting a look at Indira's exceptionally flimsy, but extremely chic, tennis shoes.

She sighed, turning to face him. "Should we just . . . get this conversation out of the way?"

Jude nodded, eyes dropping to the ground. "I'm sorry I . . ." Jude cleared his throat, gesturing at his body.

"Pitched your own tent?" Indira supplied.

Jude shot her a look of horror, their gazes locking for a solid thirty seconds.

And then they both dissolved into nervous giggles.

"It's . . . uh . . . been awhile," he said quietly, rubbing a hand across the back of his neck and looking off toward the river. "It didn't mean anything. I promise."

Okay, ouch. Perhaps the only thing more awkward than feeling an inconvenient—and rather forbidden—boner between your legs was said boner-owner then telling you that it didn't mean anything.

"I, um, yeah. I figured." Indira wanted to crumple her silly heart into a ball and chuck it into the garbage for making her wish it meant something. "If it's any consolation, it's, er, been awhile for me too."

Jude's eyes snapped to her incredulously, and Indira, quite simply, wanted to die.

Holy fuck.

Why did she say that? *Why?*

She'd blurted out the words before she could process them, and now she wanted to choke on her own damn tongue.

"It's only been a few weeks since you and Chris broke up," he said carefully, tiptoeing on the edge of this conversation that shouldn't be happening between them.

She let out a self-conscious laugh, tucking her hair behind her ear. "Dry spells exist in relationships too."

There was a long pause, and Indira felt forced to fill it, more far-too-honest truths pouring out of her. "I think Chris and I lost any connection we originally had a long time ago. It was almost like we stopped actually seeing each other. Like going through the motions of being together was easier than the work being single would take."

Indira wasn't sure they ever did feel *right* together, but having someone around with the potential to love her had felt better than being alone. Being lonely.

Indira wanted so badly to be loved.

Still more silence from Jude. More babbling from Indira. "And while the circumstances around it were shitty beyond belief, the actual ending of the relationship didn't feel like that much of a surprise. So, all this to say, uh, physical intimacy wasn't a huge thing for us."

They were quiet again, Indira locking her jaws shut for good measure. She heard Jude swallow, noticed the way his gaze kept landing on different places of her body and then darted away, everything in her heating with a mixture of mortification and desire.

"Should we . . ." Indira waved a hand at the grass before plopping down. Jude looked at her for a moment before following her lead.

They let the night sing its quiet tune around them, its rhythm washing away their embarrassment, the sharp bite of the wind attempting to lift the heated tension between them. Indira didn't think Mother Nature was particularly successful on that front.

"I do feel better out here," Jude said after awhile, plucking at the grass. His hands paused, like he'd just accidentally said something way too honest and raw.

Indira could let it go. She could pretend he hadn't said anything indicating he'd been feeling less than fine, despite the obvious. Or she could reach out, one more time. She could softly, gently, ask him to trust her, if he wanted to.

"What do you mean?" she murmured, saying it low enough that he could act like he didn't hear if he wanted. But he glanced at her instead, and Indira felt his look like a caress against her cheek.

"I guess . . . I don't know. Something about the fresh air makes me feel . . . lighter. Like all the oxygen is cleaning out my head." He tilted his neck, staring up at the stars. "That probably sounds silly."

"It doesn't."

Jude was silent, and Indira let it linger. She knew that all the greatest conversations happened in silence. Discoveries, breakthroughs, puzzle pieces snapping into place, all occurred when two people let themselves think in comfortable quietness. It seemed like Jude needed all the silence he could get, and Indira wasn't going to take that from him.

Indira lay down on her back, looking up at the stars dotting the inky-black night. For a second, it felt like she was floating, leaving gravity behind and sinking into the lovely sky. Then she thudded back onto earth at the shocking feel of Jude lying down beside her. It wasn't long before their breathing was in sync, matching the gentle flow of the creek and the crickets singing around them.

"The trip up was kind of nice too," Jude said after a few minutes. "Despite your awful driving."

Indira let out an indignant noise. "Wow. *Wow.* Don't be surprised if I abandon you here. Have fun living off dirt and marshmallows."

Jude started laughing. "Oh my God, I just thought of something—"

"Don't strain yourself."

Jude bumped Indira's shoulder, laughing harder. "Do you remember that summer when we were teenagers and you tried to take up cooking and your mom would make us all sit there and eat every bite of those disgusting meals?"

"Disgusting?" Indira screeched, propping up on her elbows to look down on him in shock. "I was basically a culinary prodigy!"

"Indira, you made us ramen with peanut butter, hot dogs, and American cheese. Please acknowledge how objectively gross that is."

"It was a bold and brave take on a classic."

"It tasted like dog shit."

"Something I know for a fact you're quite the expert on," Indira said primly.

"Okay, that was *one time* when I was nine and only because Collin bet me twenty dollars. *One time.*"

"You know how many times I've had dog poop in my mouth, Jude? Zero. I can go to my grave knowing that truth."

"Oh, come on, twenty dollars feels like a million when you're that age."

"All I know is you are, quite literally, full of shit."

Jude let out something like a growl and Indira threw her head back, cackling.

Memories continued to flow from them like water in the brook, gentle but determined. The once-irreparable annoyances and transgressions of their childhood turned into glowing, perfect memories that threaded them together.

"What made you choose psychiatry?" Jude asked suddenly. Quietly. Like her answer scared him a bit.

Indira chewed on her lip as she considered the question. "I guess, in a lot of ways, I have my parents' divorce to thank for setting me on the path."

The grass rustled as Jude turned his head to look at her. Indira kept her eyes trained on the sky.

"It probably sounds dramatic, but it really fucked me up," she admitted to the stars, licking her lips. "I woke up one day and my dad was packing up all his shit while my mom cried and yelled. I knew they fought a lot, but I guess I never understood that people can just . . . leave." She swallowed past the lump in her throat. "And then I watched my mom lose herself in the wreckage."

Indira's mom, Angela, had spiraled after he left, to the point Indira didn't recognize her for awhile. She hid herself in a fragile shell that eventually turned into endless broken pieces. Tear-smudged pillows. Lipstick-stained wineglasses. Angry sobs when she thought no one was home.

"Missing is such a painful emotion," Indira said, digging her fingers into the dirt. "So painful. And I missed my dad so much after he left. But while missing him, I also missed my mom. The carefree woman she once was, replaced by this hurt and wounded person." Indira sucked in a shuddering breath.

Indira had felt so clueless and useless as a little kid witnessing complex adult emotions while feeling so many of her own. And, as she grew up, it was a new type of pain to see her mom as human, lovely and wonderful, but flawed and messy all the same.

"And Collin wasn't much better. On the outside he handled it well." She felt Jude nod beside her. "He kind of shut down for a bit, walking around with these walls up, all feelings pinging off. He told himself he was the man of the house and nothing could convince him otherwise. He channeled all of it into school. I know he loves what he does, but I can't help but think he found medicine because he was searching for stability. A career that was safe. Employable. Would make him enough money so our mom would no longer have to struggle.

"And they both continued on their trajectories, my mom collapsing in on herself, Collin building up shell after shell. And I was caught in between. I always felt like this raw nerve. Everything touched me. Every feeling hit me with an overwhelming force. I'm sure you remember how sensitive I was as a kid and teenager."

She turned her head to look at Jude, and he was staring at her like she was the center of the world.

"It was . . . a lot," she said at last, thinking of the swells of emotions that had swamped her when she was young. The bellyaches and head throbs when things felt like too much for her. "And while my mom hadn't handled the divorce perfectly, she realized the toll it took on both of us, and she was quick to get us to counselors."

It had been transformational for Indira. A weekly space to pour her heart out. To fall apart. To have someone listen. During college, she'd gotten out of the habit of going, convincing herself she'd healed enough. But her med school program had required her to participate in counseling as a patient on a rotation, and it had inspired her to keep going to Dr. Koh.

Indira was surprised by how difficult it was to open up in the sessions as an adult. How hard she pretended to be okay. She was sick of pretending.

"And . . . yeah. That's how I discovered I wanted to do something in the mental health field. When I realized how much I liked chemistry and pharmacology, psychiatry ended up being the perfect fit," she said. "I wanted to help people—especially kids—who felt everything too. Or nothing at all. Or some mixture of both. Because feelings matter. They're chemicals mixing with experiences and some deep, unknown part of a human soul. They make us who we are and I always wanted to help people find a way to steer their ship when those feelings had them lost at sea."

They fell into silence again, the cold night biting at Indira's cheeks and the tip of her nose. Maybe it was Jude lying beside her, but she felt exquisitely, comfortably warm.

"Thank you for telling me that," Jude said. "I . . . It means a lot."

"Of course," she said casually, waving her hand. She bit back the words that she had a terrible desire of wanting to tell Jude everything.

Indira cleared her throat. "You can talk to me too, you know. If it would help."

Jude was quiet for a minute. "I don't want you to be my psychiatrist, Dira." The words were spoken on a fractured sigh.

"I don't mean it like that. I mean . . . I don't know. Talk to me as a friend. Or as just a person."

"You aren't *just* anything."

Neither said anything after that.

Eventually, cold and sleepiness forced them from their sacred little spot back to the tent. Without thinking, Indira laid her head next to Jude's with an ease of intimacy that was startling and inevitable.

After a moment of awkward silence, they crafted a small barricade of bedding between their bodies, much of their newfound closeness left down at the river's bank.

But Indira couldn't suppress the happiness that lit up like sparklers in her heart at the tiny steps they'd taken back toward each other. She fell asleep with a smile on her face.

When she woke up to the early chill of the October morning, she found the barrier of blankets and pillows down the center of the tent still intact.

But, sometime in the night, they'd both reached across it to hold hands as they slept.

CHAPTER 22

Jude

∽

T-MINUS TWO WEEKS UNTIL THE WEDDING

"What are you *wearing*?" Jude choked out, his eyes nearly popping from their sockets.

"Like it?" Indira asked, giving a quick twirl. She was dressed for Halloween in what appeared to be a . . . bee suit? The potato-shaped sack had a zip up the front with alternating shiny black pleather and fuzzy yellow panels, the whole thing filled with stuffing to create a giant bumble butt, all of which was cinched right above her knees.

The stuffing continued its trajectory after she'd stopped turning, the bottom of the suit whipping around her and making her laugh.

"I'm a bumblebee," Indira clarified, as Jude continued to stare at her in wide-eyed horror. "It's cute," she added, crossing her arms over her chest and frowning at him.

Jude's eyes flicked to her face. He was certainly losing his mind. That was the only reasonable explanation for the fact that Indira's ridiculous, shapeless mass of a "costume" was close to giving him a heart attack.

But it was so fucking *adorable*. And *cute*. And the silliness of it mixed dangerously with Indira's potent sensuality, the sex appeal she radiated in waves that seemed designed purely to draw Jude in. Tempt him endlessly.

Things had changed dramatically for Jude after camping—like the entire trip had shifted the tectonic plates of his heart, creating a devastating earthquake that made constant thoughts of Indira rattle through his mind. Not that he hadn't been thinking about her before. But now . . . well, now, the knowledge of her touch, the snug and perfect way her palm fit against his, what it was like to have her looking down on him, her legs straddling his body, were all imprinted on his skin.

Not things he seemed capable of forgetting. Even for a second.

Which was bad. Very, *very* bad. But he had trouble reminding his cock of that fact.

"I'm not exaggerating when I say I'll kill you both if you let anything happen to my home tonight," Collin said, his voice (thankfully) derailing the horny trajectory of Jude's thoughts as Collin walked into the room and pulled on his jacket. "It will be a slow death. Merciless. One that involves hours-long PowerPoint presentations about my lawn-maintenance procedures."

Indira rolled her eyes. "Collin, when you say stuff like that, it makes me want to vandalize your yard myself."

"I mean it," Collin said, pocketing his keys and fixing Indira and Jude with stern stares. "Jeremy and I have had to work every Halloween since we moved in here, and the house *always* gets egged or TP-ed since we can't pass out candy. But you two are now officially on trick-or-treater management, which means the destruction of my property won't happen again. Right?"

Jeremy had already left for a scheduled surgery in the late afternoon, and neither would be home until tomorrow.

"That whole thing sounds like a you problem, not an us problem," Indira said, waving a hand between herself and Jude. Something about that *us* made Jude's heart flip in his chest.

"It will most certainly be a *you* problem when you're the ones cleaning it up. You have one job: feed these rabid animals masquerading as youths enough candy so they don't attack my home."

"Did you ever think that maybe the reason you're a target isn't because you don't pass out candy, but more because you're a crotchety old man stuck in a thirtysomething's body?" Jude said, feeling a light and bubbly sensation through his torso and arms when Indira grinned at him, a golden thread connecting their chests as they joined forces in teasing the hell out of Collin.

Collin's eyes flicked back and forth between Indira and Jude. He pursed his lips. "I liked it better when you two hated each other. At least then I knew peace."

"We—No—"

"There's not . . . No way . . . Fake . . ."

Indira and Jude spluttered over each other, making Collin's rather innocuous joke one hundred times worse and painfully awkward.

"Oooookay," Collin said, narrowing his eyes.

Jude and Indira made the mistake of guiltily glancing at each other at the same moment.

Which was so silly! The whole thing was ridiculous! They weren't a thing! They were nothing! Maybe they were . . . kind of friends? Jude seemed to be doing an okay job managing that without hurting her. But then again, the past few years had shown him just how capable he was of inflicting lasting damage.

"You two are so weird," Collin said at last, looping his scarf around his neck and heading toward the door. "Protect this house by whatever means necessary. I don't care if you have to stand out there and pour sugar straight into their mouths, just guard my lawn like you would your own child."

"I bet dentists love you," Indira yelled right before he shut the door.

Jude let out a small laugh before a piercing silence cinched around them.

Indira and Jude looked at each other for a beat before shooting their gazes in opposite directions, Jude squinting up at the corner of the ceiling where a miniscule crack was forming, Indira scuffing her toe over the floorboards, bee costume swaying gently.

After the camping trip, they'd slowly—cautiously—tiptoed into more familiar territory. A few quiet minutes sipping coffee together in the morning before she left for work. A movie watched by all four of them on nights when Collin and Jeremy weren't on-call. Some über-polite texts asking if the other needed anything from the store.

It was all dismally controlled and restrained, and while Jude knew the friendly distance was necessary—ideal, even—each sterile inter-action chipped even further at the painful fissure in his chest. Ever since their kiss there was always a buzzing sensation right below his skin. A cord of tension—a twisted rope wrapped around both their waists, tugging them closer no matter how far away they walked from each other—that had the memory of her feel just within reach. It had taken all his self-control not to kiss her again that night under the stars.

This was the first time since then that they were by themselves in the house and actively choosing to be in the same room as each other. Jude felt like a teenager being left alone with a girl for the first time: clueless and awkward as fuck. Also, desperate to get closer to her.

Which was BAD. And he needed to STOP IT.

Grammy, food-motivated tension breaker that she was, let out a howl from the kitchen and pulled Indira's attention from her feet.

"Better go feed the monster," Indira said, giving Jude a tense smile before waddling off.

Jude blew out a raspberry, trying to pull himself together.

After a minute or two, Indira emerged from the kitchen, a wiry Grammy trotting behind her and licking her chops.

"I don't think she even chews," Indira said, looking down at Grammy with a concerned frown. "It's like she unhinges her jaw and swallows the food whole. Hoover would have been a better name for her."

"What made you get a cat?" Jude asked, mimicking the forced breeziness Indira was using for their small talk.

She shrugged. "I looked at my life one day and realized I wasn't devoting enough of my time to being at the beck and call of an arro-gant fluffball that thinks she's God and licks her own asshole."

"Ah. A very common milestone. I think I'm at a similar stage myself."

"Lick your own asshole a lot, huh?"

Jude's head jerked back and, for the life of him, he couldn't think of a single witty thing to say. His face must have shown his surprise, because Indira's own was filled with pure glee.

"Did I win that one?" she crooned.

Jude nodded appreciatively, giving her an exaggerated frown. "Expect a witty comeback text in seven to ten business days."

She laughed so hard she started to wheeze. Jude would be damned if it wasn't the most beautiful sound he'd ever heard.

He absolutely loved making her laugh.

After a few more moments of obnoxious giggles, she collapsed onto the couch—her costume swallowing her whole—then grinned up at Jude. Her smile melted into his skin and through his blood, flooding him like a fever. Some primitive part of him wanted the exclusive right of making her smile.

Quietness fell between them again, but this time it was more . . . comfortable. Soft. Like they were still communicating through the quiet.

And Jude had the overwhelming and disastrous urge to broach the distance between them and kiss Indira until she couldn't maintain silence for a moment longer. An urge that had tugged at his self-control for weeks and was becoming harder and harder to resist.

But, before any further dangerous thoughts overtook his brain, the doorbell rang, the ding sharp and unexpected, making him jump up. Indira glanced at him, her eyes lingering for a beat before she hefted herself up and trotted to the door, candy in hand and giant bee suit quivering around her.

Jude could hear her cooing and complimenting the children's costumes; he even saw her swoop into a small bow and address one of the children as "your royal highness." But Jude couldn't move. His muscles were tense and his heart beating too fast, too violently, for him to ignore.

Not now, not now, not now, he silently begged his hyperactive nervous system. This night was supposed to feel normal. A nonissue. But the familiar muffling of his senses descended upon him, making him simultaneously feel less than alive but also sharply aware of his fear response. He didn't want that. He was scared of the pain but he was similarly starting to fear the numbness. Especially when he felt it around Indira.

The noises of a few more groups of trick-or-treaters stopping by filtered through the door, but Jude stayed rooted in place, trying to collect himself. To focus on breathing.

After a few minutes, Indira walked back into the living room, eyes locking onto Jude. She smiled at him, lips full and looking dangerously soft.

She set the bowl down, walked toward him, grabbed one of his stiff hands, and marched them toward the couch. With a flourish, she dropped onto the cushion and grabbed the remote, flicking through streaming services.

After a moment of Jude continuing to stand near her—staring at her and her curly hair and soft skin and eyes so kind they had the power to destroy him—she tugged on his arm and he rigidly sat down next to her.

"Do you still like *Scooby-Doo*?" Indira asked, gaze fixed on the TV.

Jude swallowed and shook his head, trying to clear out the thick fog up there. "Shocking as it may be, I graduated to watching big-boy shows about ten years ago."

Indira scoffed. "Wow, Jude, so cerebral of you. Color me impressed."

A smile twitched at the corner of his lips, and Indira caught it, her own grin melting his insides.

"I had a thought," she said, turning back to the TV.

"Your first?"

She landed a punch to his shoulder that, for some reason, felt as wonderful and delicious as a hug.

"I was thinking it'd be fun to watch *Scooby-Doo*. None of the shitty new animation, obviously, but the classic old-school ones from when we were little."

The suggestion sparked countless happy memories, sleepovers at the Papadakises', late nights giggling with Collin, early mornings of cartoons and pancakes with both siblings.

"I like that idea," Jude said softly. Indira smiled like a kitten in cream.

She clicked over to the show and scrolled through the options, mouth pursed as she read through descriptions. Jude stared at the little divots it created in her plush lips, the way time had kissed her features, still vibrant and fresh, but with subtle lines of vulnerability that she wore proudly around her eyes and mouth.

"Didn't this one used to be your favorite?" Indira asked, bringing up a thumbnail with a character in an eerie submarine costume.

"Wow. Yeah, it was. I can't believe you remember that."

Indira opened her mouth like she was going to say something smart and biting, but nothing came out as she looked at him. Something about the way she studied him, saw him, made warmth spread from the center of his chest like sunshine appearing from behind a cloud.

"Memories of you are inevitable," she said at last.

She returned her attention back on the TV, goofy cartoon voices filling the room.

Jude, despite taking himself incredibly seriously as an adult, quickly lost himself in the nostalgia and fun of the show. He was mortifyingly riveted by an animated crew of mystery solvers.

So, when the doorbell rang again about fifteen minutes later, it caught Jude off-guard. His spine went taut and his heart rebounded off his breastbone. Indira must have felt the reverberation of his shock, her head snapping up to look at him. Their gazes held and Jude swallowed.

The trick-or-treater hit the doorbell again in rapid-fire mode, ding after ding clashing over each other, propelling Indira to move. She grabbed the bowl of candy, enthusiastically greeting the next group of kids at the door and leaving Jude stuck in his spot, a hot and sticky pulse of fear slow to ebb out of his system.

After a moment, she came back into view, chewing on her lip as she thought, eyes fixed on the candy in her hands. She smiled slightly, then bolted up the stairs. Jude could hear her muffled footsteps as she zipped around the upper level. She came charging back down the stairs, then turned into the kitchen, rogue bite-sized sweets trailing after her.

When she reappeared a few minutes later, she clutched all the (highly excessive) bags of candy Collin had bought for Operation Please Don't Destroy My House and a piece of paper.

She held the sheet in view for Jude to read as she moved toward the door.

Happy Halloween, Ghouls and Goblins! Doorbell broken. Help yourself, the words written in green and made to look like slime. Indira deposited her armloads of candy on the porch, ripped off a piece of duct tape that was looped around her wrist, and stuck the sign over the doorbell.

She walked back into the house and shut the door with a proud thud, dusting off her hands as she made her way back to the couch and plopped down next to Jude, restarting the show.

Every muscle in Jude's body felt locked in place, a prickle of sweat irritating his skin as he tried to breathe. He couldn't get himself to relax, couldn't snap out of whatever brutal impulse propelled his body headlong into this state.

"Can I hold your hand?" Indira asked, eyes still trained on the TV. Jude looked at her.

"My hand?" he echoed, slow to process what she meant.

"Yes. This episode is scarier than I remember and I could use some comfort." She scooched toward him a bit.

Jude cleared his throat, the corners of his mouth ticking up. "If you must," he said with as much melodrama he could muster. His heart started to thud with something like triumph instead of fear when he saw Indira smile.

She reached out, more direct and self-assured than she'd ever touched him, and picked up his hand resting on his thigh, twined their fingers together, then leaned slightly against him.

And the feeling of being touched in such a soft and deliberately comforting way seemed to let every muscle sigh with relief.

Her touch made him feel . . . safe. Grounded. Gave him the physical anchor that allowed him to push his way through his jumbled-up thoughts and resurface as himself.

Without even realizing it, he felt himself leaning back, letting go, just a bit, and allowing Indira to support some of his weight.

It felt delicious and indulgent and like coming home.

Jude felt drugged by the happiness flooding his brain, the familiarity of childhood comforts, the lovely trill of Indira's laugh, the way she gently scoured her nails up and down his arm, making every hair on his body stand tall in pleasure.

As minutes ticked on and they watched episode after episode, they kept drifting closer.

Somehow, Jude's arm moved around her shoulders, her head tucking into the crook where his neck met his shoulder. At one point, her giant bee costume bunched itself further up toward her hips, the warmth of her thighs pressing against Jude through her leggings.

And, eventually, the show stopped playing, Netflix asking if they were still watching.

They weren't.

They were looking at each other, gazes locked, bodies close.

But they needed closer.

They needed more touch and skin and warmth.

They needed each other.

Indira shifted slightly on the leather couch to fully face him.

And an extremely loud farting noise reverberated around the sensual silence they'd been basking in.

Indira's jaw dropped, her eyes going ridiculously wide and cheeks burning a luminescent red as the noise echoed around them. She blinked a few times, her mouth opening and closing like a dying fish.

Her mortification was palpable, and Jude pressed his lips together in a failed attempt to hide his smile.

After a moment, Indira cleared her throat. "Needless to say, that was my costume against the couch."

"Yeah?" Jude said, unable to hide a choking laugh. "Make it again."

"What are you, twelve?" Indira shrieked, pressing up so she hovered slightly over him in what he could tell was an attempt at intimidation.

"I'm not the one who just farted after watching a scary *Scooby-Doo* episode," Jude said with obvious glee.

Indira's face scrunched up in mock fury. With a haughty sniff and as much dignity as she could muster, she aggressively rubbed her ass over the couch.

Silence.

She rubbed again.

More silence.

"You're an asshole," she said at last, throwing her arms up.

"I just like making you squirm," Jude said, his gaze hot as he watched Indira's thighs move and press against the couch.

She caught his stare.

And their eyes held—locked and heavy and dangerously close.

Jude became hyperaware of every subtle movement Indira made. Her widening pupils. The rise and fall of her chest. The way the corner of her eyebrow quirked and her gaze dropped to his lips as he licked them. Jude pressed his knuckles to his mouth, dragging them across his lips in a vain attempt to hold back every raw and honest word that wanted to rush out of him. But it was useless.

One thousand things were said in between the seconds of that look.

And, in that final moment before he threw himself off the edge of the cliff and dived headfirst into the feelings that threatened to drown him, Jude knew he was both lost and found in the loveliness that was Indira Papadakis.

With the inevitability of magnets colliding, Indira's hot, soft lips clashed against Jude's, urging him—begging him—to join her in the frenzy.

And he did.

Nothing else mattered but where their bodies touched, where the heat of her gasps and the scorch of her kiss branded his skin. Jude's mind quieted, and he lost himself in the pleasure swamping his senses. The fractured cadence of her breathing. His own pulse pounding everywhere she touched him. The trace of his tongue across her lip when he pulled back just a bit, savoring her taste. The simple, exquisite comfort of knowing Indira.

A deep moan rumbled through his chest, and Indira seemed inspired by the sound, pushing him further against the couch, then straddling his lap, never breaking the kiss.

Jude gripped her hips like gravity had ceased to exist and she was the only way he'd stay grounded on earth. His fingers pressed into her thighs, her ass, any part he could press his palm against. He caressed and squeezed and touched her like he'd die if he stopped.

Except her giant fucking bee costume was presenting many, *many* roadblocks.

"Take this off," Jude growled, fumbling with the zipper.

Indira laughed, deep and husky, rewiring circuits of Jude's brain to erupt in pleasure at the sound. She found the zipper and ripped it down, squirming out of the enormous thing with record speed.

She was down to just a bra and her leggings, and Jude, who was already aching, went painfully hard at the sight.

His hands and eyes scoured over every inch of her as she reached behind her back and unclasped her bra, tearing it off her arms and flinging it to a far corner of the room. Jude felt primitively satisfied at how her desperation seemed to match his.

His fingertips grazed over her breasts, learning the shape, the softness, the decadence of her hard nipples under the pad of his thumb.

Indira tilted her head back and moaned as his touch skated over her, pebbling her skin. Making her press closer.

"I need more," she said roughly, threading her hands in his hair and pressing hard kisses against his mouth. Jude kissed back, giving her everything. His fingertips trailed down her ribs, the muscles of her back, the divot of her spine, to rest at her waistband.

"Is this okay?" he asked, tugging lightly at the elastic.

"Fuck. Yes," Indira said against his lips, her hips grinding mindlessly against his lap.

He pulled the fabric down around her thighs, revealing her sweet, wet cunt.

"Show me," he said, gripping her wrist and leading her hand to her clit. "Show me what you like."

Indira glanced at him, eyelids heavy with desire, smile dripping with satisfaction. And she did as he asked, showing him the rhythm and speed that brought her pleasure, the broad circles punctuated by quick flicks. The way she dipped her fingers into her wetness and dragged it along her slit. And Jude, God bless him, was a quick learner.

He removed her hand, bringing her wet fingers to his mouth and sucking deeply, lapping her taste off them, while his other hand repeated her instructions.

Indira pulled her fingers from his mouth, scraping her nails against his scalp as she ground against him.

"Inside me," she panted. "Please."

Jude obliged. Who was he to ignore such excellent manners?

He slipped two fingers inside her, moving and pressing until he found a spot that made her groan and her hips buck.

"Yeah?" Jude grunted out, continuing the movement.

"Yes. Yes. God, yes," Indira babbled, hips pumping to match his fingers and brush her clit against the heel of his hand.

Indira became almost frantic in her noises and movements, and Jude was lost in the sounds of her pleasure. He couldn't take his eyes off her, unable to decide where to look. Every millimeter of her was the most beautiful fucking thing he'd ever seen. Indira tugged on his hair again, bringing his head closer to her chest, and Jude gleefully took the hint. He pulled one of her nipples in his mouth, rolling his tongue around it before sucking deep, biting gently.

Indira gasped—the noise sharp and clear and the most erotic thing Jude had ever heard—before her body went stiff, then shook with the force of her climax. Jude continued what he was doing, giving her everything he could until she finally slumped against him in a boneless heap.

Jude withdrew his fingers, reveling in the feel of her hot and labored breaths against his neck. He readjusted her leggings, then smoothed a hand over her curly hair, tucking her head securely under his chin, arms wrapping around her.

There weren't really words to describe what it felt like to hold Indira Papadakis.

Over the past month, Jude had spent more hours than he cared to admit picturing Indira's body, imagining its feel, its textures. He was a fool for thinking he could ever imagine anything close to this.

He now knew what her heartbeat felt like against his own chest, the luxurious feel of her hair sliding between his fingers, the decadent bite of her nails into his skin. He'd learned what she tasted like and he wanted to repeat the lesson over and over again.

Indira stirred, pulling her head back to give him a smile that felt like sunshine being injected directly into his veins. She leaned in and kissed him, achingly tender and soft. Jude kissed back, lacking technique or finesse, and making her smile again against his lips all the same.

Indira's hands started roaming, caressing down his neck, his chest. He was still hard between her thighs, and it didn't take long for her wandering fingers to start stroking him through his jeans.

"It feels like I've been wanting this forever," she whispered into his ear before giving the lobe a soft bite. She returned to kissing and rubbing him, filling Jude with endless sensations of want and desire.

But he was simultaneously flooded with something tinged in bitterness. Anger at all the time that had been stolen from him. That he hadn't seen what was right in front of him when he'd still been whole. He was drowning in loss for the memories they could never make.

All things good were fleeting, and he already missed her, knowing this would be a happy blip in his endless path of numbness. He missed her with a bright and sharp type of pain, one that had teeth and gnashed its jaws in his chest even though she was right there with him.

Because Jude knew.

He knew his finicky brain and his stained past would always keep him painfully separated from her. He'd been witness to too many awful things to ever be with her the way she deserved.

And Jude, who'd been damming up countless emotions for so long, felt them all at once.

He tore his mouth from hers, locking her curious and tempting hands in his grip. "I can't," he gasped out.

"What?" Indira asked, shooting him a confused smile that turned into something deliciously wicked as she rubbed her pelvis against his erection.

"I can't," he repeated, finding his last fragment of self-restraint and lifting her off him. "We can't do this."

Indira blinked rapidly, eyes still glazed but smile falling.

"But we—You—I—" she stuttered out, her cheeks turning a dusky red. "What did I do wrong?" she finally managed, unable to meet his gaze.

Jude raked his hands through his hair. "It's not you," he said, his breaths still coming in near-painful pants.

Indira made a small noise somewhere between disbelief and embarrassment.

"It's *not*," Jude said, reaching over and holding her chin between his thumb and forefinger, tilting her head to meet his gaze. "I promise."

"Then what is it?" she asked, her eyes glistening.

She looked so vulnerable like that, with her shirt off and cheeks flushed, her face destroying him with its open vulnerability. And he wished he had words. He wished he could get his brain to work so he could articulate everything he felt. That she was the most tempting thing he'd ever seen. That her moans made him weak. The heat of her body drove him out of his mind with wanting.

But he also wanted to tell her how little he trusted himself. That he didn't know if the smallest thing would set him off, take him out of a moment and back to that place where the past and the present merged into a waking nightmare. He wanted to explain that he didn't deserve sex and he was too broken for intimacy.

"It's . . ." He swallowed once. Twice. The words almost there. "It's not you," he repeated weakly, moving away from her.

"Wait. No no no no no," Indira said, scrambling onto her knees. "Don't."

"Don't what?" Jude asked, absolutely frozen by her wide, copper eyes.

"Don't crawl back into that brain," she said, reaching up and gently placing her hands on his cheeks. "Don't retreat. You've already come so far. Stay with me. Please. We don't have to do anything, but don't leave me." She placed a kiss to the center of his forehead.

"I'm not . . . I don't . . ."

"Jude," she said softly, moving her arms to wrap him in a hug. "Talk to me. Say anything. I promise no matter what you tell me, you can't screw this up."

A cold, bitter laugh escaped from his throat. "*This*," he spat out, putting his hands on her hips and moving her off him again, then pushing to stand, "doesn't exist. It can't."

"I refuse to accept that," Indira said, standing too. She seemed to register that she was topless, and crossed her arms over her chest, looking around. Her bee costume was the only option, and she bundled it up in her arms, a gigantic fluffy shield. The absurdity of it all made Jude almost laugh, but the pain etched around her eyes cut him straight to the core.

"This is real," Indira said, her voice level and powerful. "Whatever this is between us is real and it hurts and it's beautiful and it matters. And I won't let you deny that. You deserve happiness, Jude. *I* deserve happiness. And I think we can have that. Together."

Happiness? Indira thought he deserved *happiness*? Jude could say, unequivocally, he did not deserve anything close to happiness.

"Don't you get it?" he shouted, turning on her. "I *can't* do that. I can't do *anything* anymore. I can't think. I can't sleep. I don't feel anything but numbness or anger or fear. I can't trust myself to have sex with you because I'm scared I'll hurt you. Because that's what I do. I hurt people and break things and taint every single thing I touch. And I can't do that to you, Dira. I can't risk anything happening to you because you matter too much. You're too important to me."

His chest was heaving, his eyes wild as he stared at her. Indira was still. Incredibly still. But Jude didn't sense her fear like he should. Instead, he could almost hear her thinking.

"For fuck's sake," he said. "Do us both a favor and leave me alone."

That was when he meant to leave. When he fully intended to turn on his heel and walk up the stairs to his room.

But he didn't.

Couldn't.

Because Indira, with those goddamn eyes that saw straight through every wall he tried to build, kept him rooted to the spot.

"Is that what you actually want?" she said, voice even. "You want me to leave you alone?"

Jude swallowed. He tried to say yes—was desperate to force out the syllable. But his mouth refused to let him lie to her.

"Because I think, what you actually want, is to grab this moment with both hands, and never let it go. I think your brain has convinced you that you don't deserve to be cared for. Well, I'm calling bullshit. Because I care. And I'll keep caring. I care now. I cared yesterday. I'll care tomorrow. Every single day, I will sit outside your doorstep. And I'll wait. I'll wait until you need me, and I'll be ready. Nothing you can say will change that."

Jude's pulse pounded so hard, he felt it in his palms, every joint of his fingers. His entire body ached from the building pressure.

"People get so few moments," Indira said, her voice cracking as she stepped toward him. "And you've had so many robbed from you. I'll never, ever be able to fully understand what you've been through but I'm not going to let you walk out of here and pretend that neither of us care."

She took one more step toward him. Within reaching distance. He could do it. Do what she said. Reach out with both hands and hold on to the thing he really wanted.

"So let me in, Jude," she whispered, two teardrops racing down her cheeks. "Even if it's just tonight. Please. Let me in."

Jude had no fight, no restraint, left in him. He wanted her too badly. He wanted her smile and her laugh and her biting sarcasm. He wanted the warmth of her skin and the way she made him feel alive. He wanted her comfort. He wanted Indira.

Jude closed the remaining space between them, one hand plunging into her hair, the other gripping her hip. He kissed her, pouring every overwhelming emotion into the touch. If it was just tonight, he was going to give her all that was left of him.

CHAPTER 23

Jude

Indira's giant bee costume was dropped and forgotten as Jude picked her up, one hand cradling her ass, the other braced against the wall as he turned, pressing her into it. Indira's legs cinched around his waist, holding him snugly against her as their teeth clashed and tongues dragged over each other.

"Upstairs," Indira groaned before kissing and biting his neck. Jude happily obliged.

Or tried to, at least. He tripped after the second step, and they plopped apart, both breathless and giggling in a heap on the steps.

"So smooth," Indira said, wasting no time and crawling on all fours up the stairs. Jude's cheeks heated, and he smacked her on the butt as he frantically followed, eliciting a shriek and more giggles from Indira.

They kissed down the hallway, bouncing off the walls as they consumed each other, unable to ever get close enough. Crashing through the door, Jude shut it behind him with his foot, then walked Indira to his bed, watching her fall against the white comforter.

Jude paused, forcing himself to savor this moment. Savor Indira. He didn't want to miss a second. Her hair spread out like ink in water across the sheets, pupils blown out and breaths coming short as she looked up at him.

After a moment, Indira sat up, reaching out her hand, eyes locking with Jude's. He took it, braiding their fingers together, and meeting her on the bed.

They touched each other slowly, the intimacy of every caress intentional as they removed each other's remaining clothing with reverence, peeling away all the layers between them. They lay down, kisses deep and tender and tinged with desperation, lips molding together in delicious torment. Jude wanted to devour her.

Indira climbed over him, straddling his lap, pressing her chest against his. It felt like his entire body, every nerve, every muscle, every cell, sighed in sweet relief at the feeling of skin against skin. Indira's softness and warmth and the delicate scent of her scrambled his brain.

She rested her cheek right over his pounding heart, taking a deep inhale, then letting the breath out with a sigh of happiness, the warmth of it traveling through his skin to swirl around his chest.

Jude felt her heart knocking against his, and he wondered if the rhythm of their heartbeats matched.

"Should we get a condom?" he asked, fingers tracing up her thighs, memorizing their curves.

Indira looked at him, her tongue making a slow glide across her bottom lip. "I'm on birth control and got tested after everything with Chris. If you're in a similar spot . . ." Indira's cheeks flushed a decadent pink. "I think I'd like to feel only you."

"I'm negative too," Jude said, fire licking through his body.

He didn't miss her wicked smile before she started kissing him again. Indira dragged her lips and teeth down his neck and chest, hands working between them. She stroked his length softly at first, like she wanted to commit every inch to memory.

"I want you to feel good," she said, the words sinking through his skin and lodging firmly in his heart. "Does this feel good?" she asked, and Jude groaned his assent, her touch firm and electric.

"Tell me what you like," she whispered, the words hot and hoarse and safe. Jude's hands trembled as they roughly traced along her body, gripping her hips and pulling her closer, Indira's moan punctuating the moment.

He felt clumsy. Disoriented. It'd been so long since he'd been this close to someone else, let them in. He felt his body tense as he scrambled between mindless pleasure and overthinking every moment.

Indira must have noticed the shift, and she pulled back slightly. She continued to touch him—fingers greedy up his thighs, the vault of his ribs, the nape of his neck—as she looked at his face, her big, whiskey eyes making him drunk with want.

"Do you want to take control?" she said, her voice filled with husky promise.

And Jude realized that's exactly what he wanted. He wanted to direct this overwhelming pleasure building inside him. He wanted Indira to drown in it too. He wanted to feel it all without fear he would disappear in it. Indira—gorgeous, intuitive, wonderful Indira—knew that offering to let him lead was exactly what he needed.

Jude nodded, and Indira's smile was sinfully satisfied as he flipped their position, laying her beneath him.

While every pulse point in his body thrummed with *want want want*, urging him to move faster, he paused, staring at her in awe.

Jude had thought he'd lost his faith watching the horrors humans could inflict upon each other. But, hovering over Indira's long, naked body, he felt something almost spiritual in its intensity. He needed her. It was a desperate and basic type of need to be close to her. His Indira. His touchstone. His person.

Indira stayed still on her back, her tangle of curls like a violent, beautiful ocean around her head, her sharp inhales the only movement as she watched him. Waited for him.

He reached out, slowly dragging his fingers across her mouth in a featherlight touch that moved to her jaw, then down her throat as she swallowed. He felt her pulse beneath his fingers and, this time, he was certain its jagged rhythm matched his own.

Jude's hand moved along her body, rougher now as his palm

grazed her nipple and she arched in response. He lingered there, toying with the hardened points, testing the sensitivity of the luscious skin on the underside of her breasts.

His fingers continued down, brushing over the soft triangle of hair before feeling the slickness between her thighs. A groan tore from his throat.

"Let me kiss you here?" he said between clenched teeth, gently pushing her knees further apart, looking at the glistening wetness between her legs. He licked his lips.

"Yes," she said, without hesitation, placing her hand over his where he gripped her thigh. "God yes."

An unmatched type of joy swirled in his chest at the want in her voice.

Jude whispered her name like a benediction as he bent his head to worship between her thighs.

He started slowly, reverently licking her plump pink lips, blowing lightly on her wet flesh, and he memorized every moan Indira made, every press of her hips closer to his mouth, the way her fingers threaded through his hair and pulled him closer still.

"I want to taste you forever," he growled against the softness of her inner thigh before softly biting the spot. Indira's entire body bucked beneath him as she let out a cry.

When her legs were trembling and her breaths were sharp pants, Jude focused in on her clit, licking in a tight circle, then sucking until her back bowed off the bed and she fisted the sheets in one hand, pulling on his hair with the other.

He looked up at her over the planes of her body, and nothing, *nothing* in the world, was more earth-shattering than seeing Indira Papadakis fall apart on the tip of his tongue.

He extended the pleasure as long as he could, reading her body, doing what she needed, wanting her jolts and tremors to never end.

Eventually, when she unfisted his hair and collapsed into a boneless heap on the pillows, he removed his mouth from her, kissing lightly along her hips, dragging his mouth up her belly, grabbing that hand that fisted his hair so fucking good and licking and sucking on her fingers, thanking her for letting him touch her.

"I want more," Indira whispered, softly scratching her nails on his scalp, dragging her palms to cup his face. "Can we do more?"

"Holy fuck yes please," Jude rushed out, a beat of silence following his less-than-smooth words. And then they both started to giggle, silently at first, until they were gasping with it, pressing their sweaty foreheads together as they laughed.

Indira snaked her hands down his body, ending the laughter with kisses. She wrapped her fingers around his length, and he was heavy and hot in her palm. It wasn't long before he was rocking into her grip, threads of pleasure weaving through his body.

"Now, Jude," she said, the neediness in her voice almost making him spill then and there as she lined him up with her opening. He grabbed her wrist, pulling it up and pressing it against the mattress before twining his fingers through hers, holding her hand.

He hovered over her, feeling vulnerable. Exposed. Excited.

But the way Indira looked at him—her heart in her eyes and trust on her lips—he couldn't wait a second longer. He bent his head and kissed her.

Jude pushed into her, his panting breaths mingling with Indira's raspy groans, sliding forward, chest rubbing against hers, their temples pressing together as he seated himself fully in her. They both took a moment to feel their bodies together.

It was raw and real and the most alive he'd felt in a long time. Like her body was made to hold him.

"You feel," he grunted out, heart threatening to punch through his chest, "so fucking perfect."

Indira's responding whimper spurred him to move, hips thrusting in a rhythm that totally lacked finesse. But the way Indira started moaning his name, gripping his ass and clawing down his back, led him to believe she didn't mind his technique.

Jude cupped her breast, leaning down to suck her sweet nipple between his teeth, loving the way she arched into him. He reared up on one hand, licking the pad of his thumb on the other and pressing it in tight circles right above where their bodies met.

"Okay?" Jude grunted out at the hiss of breath Indira released, clenching around him.

Indira managed something between a choked sob and a groan in confirmation, nodding her head for emphasis, and Jude smiled, a wolfish, delicious smile of satisfaction.

He flipped them, fingers digging into her hips as she moved over him, urging her into an almost frantic pace that matched the fire surging through his blood.

"Fuck," Indira ground out, arching back, pinching her nipples between her fingers, her brow furrowed and sweat on her temples.

"That's it," he said, moving his fingers to rub against her clit, his whole body bucking beneath her at the way she squeezed his cock. He kept up the tempo, loving how she moved faster and faster over him, the way her voice grew hoarse and needy and raw.

But he was greedy and lost and wanted more, more, *more*.

He wanted to press every inch of his body to hers until there was no space, nothing separating them.

"Hold on," Jude said, and Indira slowed, too far gone to fully stop the drag of her hips. Jude sat up, cinching one hand around her waist and using the other to scoot back against the pillows.

"I feel like I can't get close enough to you," he said, nuzzling his face against her chest, whispering the words into her breasts.

Indira hummed, taking on a lazy rhythm as she slid and circled over him. "I know, baby. I feel it too," she said, knotting her hands in his hair and tilting his head, bending down to kiss him, deep and messy, and beautiful.

And something about hearing those words—knowing she was right there with him—while being held by her body, ripped away any remaining walls Jude had. He sank his teeth into her shoulder, letting go completely, kissing and sucking and thrusting until she came again, and he followed her over the edge, a molten and sinuous pleasure lighting every nerve in his body on fire as he lost himself in her.

They continued holding each other, sliding down to lay tangled on their sides as Jude started to soften, but stayed inside her. Their hands moved in soft and comforting circuits up backs and down legs, through hair and along jaws. It wasn't long before they were rocking their hips gently against each other again. Never enough.

"Indira," he said, pushing her hair from her face, wrapping the curls around his fingers. She looked at him with those achingly familiar eyes. "I think I want more than just tonight."

Indira smiled, lips swollen from his kisses. "I think I do too."

CHAPTER 24

Jude

∞

The next morning, Jude lay on his stomach, his face buried in a pillow as tentative rays of sunlight cut through the blinds and curled across the bed. Indira's fingers trailed lightly across his back, tracing the planes of muscle and sinew, and he smiled at the soft, electric current her touch sent through him.

"Someone once told me that birthmarks and moles are markings of where lovers of your past lives kissed you the most," Indira said in her husky voice, propping up on an elbow to look down on him as she continued touching. "Seems like past-life you was *very* busy."

"Mmm, is that right?" Jude said, turning his head to face her. He was rewarded by the crisp white sheet slowly falling away from her chest. Indira's exposed skin, her collarbones, her breasts, all touched by the gentle morning light. She was the most beautiful thing he'd ever seen.

"Yes, and I've decided I'm jealous of every single one of them," she said primly, spreading out her fingers so each pad touched a different mark along his arm. "Isn't that ridiculous?"

"How do you know it wasn't you that caused them?"

"You think we knew each other in a past life?" Indira said, looking at him with a hint of seriousness, like the question shouldn't matter but it did.

"You're terrifyingly persistent. I'd bet that every alternate universe Indira has tracked me down."

Indira rolled her eyes, pulling her hand away.

But Jude stopped her, gripping her wrist, kissing the inside of it lightly.

"But I'd hope alternate versions of me would be smart enough to find you first," Jude said, taking a terrifying leap of vulnerability. All of this was uncharted territory, and he knew—absolutely *knew*—he'd fuck it up. But he'd be damned if he didn't at least try.

"I like that idea," Indira said after a long moment, her eyes matching his in naked truth. Jude could sense the fear in both of them, and all he could do was hope they'd make it through.

"Past-life me was clearly enamored with your back," she said, breaking the tension and sweeping her gaze over the smattering of marks there. She bent over him, planting soft kisses along his spine, in the center of his right shoulder blade, a ticklish spot right below his left rib, all the places where small birthmarks dotted his skin.

"My back and my ass," Jude said with a smile in his voice.

Indira tilted her head to meet his eyes, arching a skeptical brow.

"Look for yourself if you don't believe me," he said, his grin unrestrained.

Indira lifted the sheet that covered his bare butt.

"Are you going to kiss those too?" Jude asked, propping himself on his forearms to glance at her over his shoulder with a look of pure innocence as he wiggled his hips.

"You're the worst," Indira said, smacking him on the ass, then dissolving into a giggling heap on top of him.

Jude laughed too. It was a raspy, raw sound from lack of use. But it was genuine. And it was good.

The feel of Indira was unreal. The weight of her body, the warmth of her skin, the pure ecstasy of her breasts pressed against his back, all of it was nothing short of decadent.

"Come here," Jude said, shifting beneath her to lay on his back, pulling her up his body.

She came willingly, those gorgeous eyes like smoke and honey. Jude kissed her forehead, savoring the tickle of her curly hair against his face, trailing his mouth to her temple and cheeks until he finally made it to her mouth.

Their kisses were languid. Hot. Every moment stretching out into a tiny infinity before them like nothing else mattered besides their lips meeting and their tongues tangling. Indira wrapped her arms around Jude's neck, twisting her fingers into his hair while his hands mapped her body, exploring every inch that had so long been forbidden.

"Are you cold?" he whispered against her mouth, feeling the goose bumps along her arms.

"A little," she said back, smiling into another kiss. "Why do you sleep with the windows open in October? Don't you freeze at night?"

"I like the fresh air," Jude said, tucking her against his chest and pulling the blankets further over them. "And I've always liked the crispness of fall. Autumn just smells . . . good," he said.

"Wow, you're quite the word wizard," Indira said with mock awe.

Jude gently dug his fingers into her side, making her squeal and writhe.

"Stop it!" Indira said, biting his shoulder.

He stopped immediately and Indira nuzzled closer like she could burrow into his skin.

Who was Jude kidding? She was under his skin and in his bones and she'd been there for a long time.

After a few moments of squirming, she stilled, her long body pressed against his, their legs tangled together. "I have an idea," she said, then yawned.

"What's that, morning breath?" Jude waved away the air in front of his nose.

"Har, har," Indira deadpanned, plucking at his chest hairs. "What if you go be a chivalrous, sweet hero, and make us some tea, then come back in bed and we stay here for the rest of forever?"

"Tea?" Jude said, his nose crinkling. "You mean dirty plant water? No thanks. But *you* can go make us some *coffee*."

"Coffee is beans, dumbass. Hot bean water. Might as well boil some pinto beans."

"Indira, I've regularly seen you drink an entire carafe of coffee yourself, so don't pretend to be a pretentious tea drinker."

Indira huffed. "While you may be rigid and stuffy, I am a woman of multitudes and have the capacity to like many things at the same time. Shocking, I'm sure . . . Plus, I'll never miss a chance to be contrary toward you. It's my love language."

"So, your years of being annoying and combative have just been some sort of extended foreplay?"

Indira turned her head to glare up at him, but her eyes turned hot and sensual. She snaked her hand down Jude's torso, letting her fingertips gently graze the sensitive skin beneath his happy trail, making his stomach clench and dick harden.

"Perhaps," she said, her voice a husky whisper. "But something tells me you like it."

She cupped him below the sheets, then wrapped her fingers around him, eliciting an immediate and near-desperate groan from Jude that made her smile turn smug. Jude shifted, pressing into her fist and gripping her hair in his hands, ready to claim her mouth.

But the sound of the front door crashing open, a booming voice, and footsteps in the hall ripped through their haze like a needle scratching over a record.

"Collin is going to kill you two!" Jeremy yelled, voice growing louder each second. Jude could hear a muffled knock on Indira's door next to his room, followed by a banging on his own.

Jude and Indira froze in place, their faces only centimeters apart, causing them to stare in cross-eyed horror at each other.

"Wake up!" Jeremy's footsteps paced between the two rooms as he continued to bang on the doors.

Jude somehow managed to give his head a frantic shake, untangling his hand from Indira's hair to hold a finger to his lips in a sign of silence. Indira stayed frozen, her features almost like a cartoon character in their uncompromised fear. And the ridiculousness of that look, combined with the giddiness of waking up next to her and the absolute absurdity of it all, made a rough laugh bubble out of Jude's throat and roll off his lips.

"I can hear you, Jude," Jeremy said. "Our yard is fucking trashed!"

The unmistakable sound of a hand grabbing a doorknob echoed in the room.

Indira's face morphed into even greater horror, her mouth gaping open like the painting of *The Scream*. She started moving then, shaking her head and waving her arms at Jude like he wasn't also in sheer panic that her older brother's fiancé was about to walk in and catch them naked together.

"Don't!" Jude yelled. "I—It's—Wait!"

Indira clamped a hand over Jude's mouth but it was too late. As if in slow-motion, the doorknob turned, and they both stared at it.

The door started to glide open, Jeremy's angry voice trailing behind it. "You had one job! Protect our property from the youths!"

With stunning acrobatics, Indira log-rolled across the bed, projecting herself off the side of it with a not-so-subtle thud.

And taking all the covers with her.

Jude was fairly certain his brain would explode from being pulled in two opposite directions, one half scrambling to listen to Jeremy and formulate words that would get him to shut the damn door, and the other screaming at him that he was lying on his bed completely naked with a rather obvious boner and needed to get the sheets back from Indira. *Now*.

"There's a thousand forks in the lawn! Someone put pads all over the windows!" Jeremy continued to say.

As the door creaked the final inches open, Jude flipped over onto his stomach, a nice cool breeze caressing his bare ass that was now on full display to Jeremy.

"Oh shit," Jeremy groaned, catching sight of Jude. "God, didn't want to see that." Jeremy's gaze snapped from the mattress to the floor near the foot of the bed, one hand shielding his eyes.

There was an awkward beat of silence before Jeremy recovered his outrage.

"How did you two let this happen? Indira, wake-up!" Jeremy added, glancing at the wall she and Jude shared.

Jude wanted to tell Jeremy that he would pick up every fork with his teeth, buy Jeremy a new house, literally *anything* if he would get the ever-loving fuck out of the room.

But Jude couldn't do much besides make choked gurgling noises as he stared at Jeremy.

And that was when he saw Jeremy's face change from embarrassed sweeps of the floor to locking on to something at the foot of the bed.

"What . . . what the fuck?" Jeremy said, eyes going wide.

Dread curdling in his stomach, Jude slowly pushed up onto his elbows, following Jeremy's gaze.

And, sure enough, two big, adorable feet with pink-painted toenails poked out on the floor at the end of the bed.

". . . Indira?" Jeremy said, face going white, then a violent shade of pink.

In a flash that startled both men in the room, Indira jolted to standing, covers clutched around her body.

"What are you doing in here?" she screeched, pointing at Jeremy. "Get out!"

Jeremy, caught off guard, stumbled back a step, raising his hands in defense. "Sorry. Sorry. I . . . wait. No. What are *you* doing in here?" he asked, regaining some of his composure.

Jude—ass still fully on display—was helpless to do anything but stare at the soap opera unfolding in his bedroom.

"Out, man! Out!" Indira yelled, pointing her finger at the door in a menacing way reminiscent of her mother.

Jeremy tripped backward a few more steps, grabbing onto the

door handle. "We—I . . . What the fuck *is* this?" he said, eyes ricocheting between Jude and Indira like bouncy balls. "You're cracked if you think we aren't talking about this," he yelled back, moving out of the room and slamming the door behind him. "Get some clothes on and meet me downstairs."

"Don't think I will, thanks," Indira said, nibbling on her bottom lip and hopping from foot to foot.

"Jude, Collin is going to fucking kill you. Get some pants on." Jeremy stomped down the hall, a piercing silence filling the room.

Jude slowly rolled over and sat up, and Indira tossed him a blanket. They stared at each other in wide-eyed shock from across the room for a solid minute.

And then, without warning, Jude dissolved into laughter, a grin cracking across his face as he looked at Indira and her wild hair and barely covered body. She was a dream and a nightmare and Jude couldn't believe he was lucky enough to have her in his room. And the more the overwhelming joy filled him—the impossibility of it all pumping his blood through his body—the harder he laughed.

After a moment, Indira started giggling too, the noise like soft music.

When Indira laughed, she did so with her whole body—shoulders shaking, throat working, toes curling on the hardwood floor—and it was like watching a dancer move across a stage.

Jude reached out to her, and she went to him, the pair collapsing into a giggling knot on the mattress. Jude pressed his nose into her hair and breathed her in, the sound of their joy harmonizing and filling the room around them in an alchemy all their own.

Eventually, they both got a grip, trying to steady their breathing.

"So," Jude said, absentmindedly winding a strand of her hair around his finger, "that went well."

Indira smacked him on the ribs. "That was the single most embarrassing moment of my life."

"I'm sure everyone has an awful story of a family member walking in on them naked," Jude countered, tugging at her curl.

"That's a distant second to being caught in bed with *you* of all people," she said with another throaty laugh, pressing a soft love bite into his pec.

"Oh please. I'm not sure I'll ever recover my dignity after being caught canoodling with the enemy."

"Canoodling? Is that what you call it?"

"I'm a doctor. I like to use technical terms for bodily mechanics."

"Ha. Well, however you want to put it, your dignity and your body can rest in pieces based on Jeremy's threat," Indira said, untangling from him and standing, grabbing her leggings and stealing Jude's T-shirt so she could dash to her own room. "Let's get this over with. I have a feeling Jeremy might have a few questions about the, uh, 'mechanics' of our fake dating."

CHAPTER 25

Indira

∞

"Deplorable, inconsiderate, disrespectful, irresponsible . . . I could go on forever. How could you let this happen?"

Indira let out an indignant huff, crossing her arms over her chest as she stood next to Jude in the living room. "Who I fu—have relations with—is absolutely none of your business, Jeremy."

Jeremy turned on her. "You think that's what this is about? I could give a flying fuck about whose . . . uh, appendages . . . you're, erm . . . accepting—"

"Gross."

"I'm talking about my house! My beautiful yard! The eggs dried on my windows!"

"Yikes," Jude said, pulling aside a curtain to reveal endless sheets of toilet paper swaying gently in the breeze.

Indira pressed her face against the pane, taking in the massacre.

"They got you good," she said, unable to tamp down the laugh in her voice. She loved Jeremy like a brother, and, as all good siblings do, she took a certain type of joy in seeing him tortured. In a very healthy, mature, familial way, obviously.

"It's not funny, Dira!"

"It's a little funny," Jude said, pressing his mouth into a firm line. Indira didn't miss the tiny quirk at its corners.

Jeremy's face was a mask of horror as he looked between Indira and Jude. Then he threw his head back and groaned. "Is this how it's going to be now? You two living in my home, *rent free*, and tormenting me?"

"You are so dramatic," Indira said, stepping away from the window.

"Can you blame me? After coming home from a sixteen-hour shift to discover my vandalized home and my fiancé's best friend and little sister . . ."

"Went mattress spelunking."

"Stop it."

Jude buried his face in his hands while Indira laughed and laughed. Jeremy rubbed at his temples.

"So is this"—Jeremy brought his fist up to his mouth and cleared his throat—"like, legit? Are you two . . . Or is this some sort of fake dating method acting?"

Indira started fidgeting, hating that Jeremy had to ask the most annoying (albeit reasonable) question possible.

She didn't know what they were, but she knew her feelings for Jude were anything but fake. It all felt . . . private, almost sacred, to form that bond with Jude. Something that was just theirs. She was a greedy creature and wanted to keep it all for herself.

"I . . ."

"We . . ."

Indira and Jude both choked on words, looking at each other, then away.

"Please don't tell Collin," Indira finally managed. "Let us . . . figure things out first."

Jeremy pressed his lips together in a stern line. "Don't ask that of me, Dira. I can't lie to him. And it will be so much worse if he walks in on something like I did."

"I know," Indira said, waving her hands. "And he won't. But Jude and I . . ." She glanced at him, his eyes wide and vulnerable and a little bit scared.

But his mouth lifted at the corner, the tiniest hint of a smile. Indira smiled back.

"Please, give us some time to figure things out," she repeated.

Jeremy sighed. "Well, you can start figuring things out while you clean up the yard, but I'm not comfortable keeping a secret from Collin."

Indira's head jerked back. "Excuse me, but why wouldn't you also be helping to clean?" Indira said, trailing after him as he moved to the kitchen.

"Because you literally had one job while your brother and I pulled overnights at the hospital, and you failed spectacularly last night."

"I think I did pretty well for myself last night, actually," Jude mumbled quietly.

Jeremy stopped dead in his tracks and they both plowed into his back.

He did a full-body shudder. "I'm living in purgatory."

Indira started to laugh, but the giggle died in her throat as the sound of an engine cutting off in the driveway echoed around the room.

Jude and Indira's eyes whipped to each other, both full of panic.

A silent dialogue of *Oh fuck oh fuck oh fuck oh fuck* bounced between them as they stared at each other, then they turned to Jeremy.

Jeremy gaped like a fish for a moment, then gave a helpless shrug, shaking his head. "I can't keep a secret from him," he whispered.

Oh. Fuck.

Indira started bolting around the room like a frantic pigeon, trying to figure out what to do, Jude rooted to the spot, following her path with his eyes.

The front door opened, and Collin stepped in, groaning and rubbing his eyes as he dropped his keys on the entryway table.

"What the fuck happened?" he said, waving his hand toward the front yard.

All was silent, and he eventually looked around, his face morphing into confusion and worry. "What's wrong?" he asked. "Who died?"

Indira panicked a teeny-tiny bit.

"Jeremy walked in on us naked!" she yelled.

Each word dropped like a metric ton of concrete into the room before everything went silent.

Like . . . disturbingly silent.

Indira had watched a few documentaries about black holes, and her statement seemed to have a similar effect. All the air was sucked out of the room, sound and energy collapsing in on itself, Collin's gaping mouth the center of the pull.

Eventually, Collin blinked, closing his mouth and swallowing. "Excuse me?" he whispered.

"Naked," Indira repeated, as if it made anything even remotely better.

"But you . . . you two hate each other," he said, eyes bouncing between Jude and Indira. Jude took a step forward, arm outstretched like he was approaching a dangerous predator.

"Turns out we rather like each other," Indira said. "Believe me, I was stunned too."

Jude shot her a glare over his shoulder, and Indira tried her best to look placating.

"I . . . I'm having trouble thinking?" Collin said, looking around desperately until his eyes landed on Jeremy. "What the fuck is happening?"

Jeremy zipped to his side. "The apocalypse is upon us, it seems," Jeremy said, giving Collin a kiss on the cheek, and resting a hand on his back.

"This isn't just a random, one-off hookup."

It took Indira a moment to process that Jude was the one who spoke, and her eyes bulged at his admission. He glanced at her and blushed, then moved to hold her hand.

Collin looked like he was about to have a conniption. "But you . . . you're leaving after the wedding."

Jude nodded slowly.

"And you . . . you just got out of a relationship," he said, pointing at Indira. She shrugged. "And you're my *little sister*."

"Okay, turned a bit patriarchal there at the end, but keep going," Indira said, waving her hand encouragingly. "This verbal processing is good."

"I . . . How in the hell is this supposed to work? What even *is* this?" Collin rubbed his hand across his chest.

"We . . ." Indira fumbled for words because, truly, what were they? Fake dating was pretty damn far from what she actually wanted with Jude, but they also had so much to figure out.

"We're together." Although his face was tight with tension, Jude's words were calm. Steady. Sure.

Together.

She liked that.

They weren't perfect or fully figured out, but they were in it together. And that was all that really mattered.

Jeremy beamed, but Collin's expression was still a mess, his eyes wide and forehead lined with deep grooves as his gaze shifted between them.

"I . . . Don't hurt each other!" Collin blurted out, clutching Jeremy's hand.

Indira blinked in surprise. "What?"

"Don't hurt each other," Collin repeated, taking a step toward them, Jeremy in tow. "You two . . . you are my two favorite people. And I, uh, I don't want to see either of you hurt. And I can't lose one of you either."

"I'm not your favorite person?" Jeremy whispered.

Collin's head whipped to look at his fiancé. "I—We—Y-you—"

There was a beat of silence, then everyone erupted into giggles.

"This is so fucking weird," Collin eventually said, rubbing his eyes. "But I'm also too tired to do any more processing, so . . ."

"All's good?" Indira asked, squeezing Jude's hand.

Jeremy and Collin scoffed in unison.

"Hell no. You both still owe us extensive cleanup," Collin said, moving toward the stairs. "But I'm going to bed. My yard better be pristine when I wake up."

Collin and Jeremy retreated up to their room, leaving Indira and Jude alone.

They turned to each other, gazes tentative and shy. But, after a moment, Indira watched the strain on Jude's face melt into a smile that made her breath catch in her throat. It was open and vulnerable with deep brackets of hesitant excitement lining his mouth. Indira's heart barreled full speed off the side of a cliff.

She threw her arms around his neck, knocking him back a step with the force of her hug. Jude hugged her right back, pulling her flush against him and pressing his nose into the crook of her neck, breathing her in. A star glowed in her chest, heat and electricity radiating through her limbs at just how good it felt to be held so close.

"I'm a little bit terrified," Indira whispered into his chest.

He laughed at that. "You and me both."

"I think we have a lot to figure out," she said, pulling back to meet those deep, dark eyes.

Jude grunted in response.

They both knew it was an understatement, but it all felt so fresh, so deliciously theirs, she didn't want to ask the pressing questions. Solve the heavy problems that hovered in the space between them. She wanted to be naive and infatuated and enjoy just being with Jude.

She leaned in, pressing her mouth to his in a deep, decadent kiss.

"Oh *God*," Collin's voice cut through their bubblegum-pink haze. "I'm, like, mostly okay with this, but I don't need to see it."

Indira and Jude tore apart, giggling like two teenagers caught in a forbidden embrace.

"Sorry, Collin," Jude said, his cheeks burning red.

Collin mumbled something grumpy and disparaging as he stumbled to the kitchen for water, then back up the steps to his room.

"Yard! Now!" he called down, before slamming his door.

"Better get to it," Jude said after a moment, pressing his forehead against Indira's and smiling.

"Probably," she said, patting his cheek. "Good luck out there. Go as fast as you can, I'll miss you." She pulled away, then draped herself across the couch, scooping up the remote.

Jude stood there for a moment, mouth ajar, and Indira did her best to hide her smile as she pretended to focus on the TV.

"Fat chance," Jude said, snatching the remote from her hands and standing in front of her, hands on his hips. "I'm absolutely not cleaning it up on my own."

Indira pouted, looking up at him with puppy-dog eyes. "You can't possibly expect me to do manual labor after what you did to me last night. I'm simply *exhausted*."

"What I did—" Jude sucked in a breath, narrowing his eyes. "It doesn't have to happen again if it leaves you so feeble."

Indira's eyes widened and she perked up in her seat. "Let's not get hasty here—"

"No, no. If my sexual prowess is so potent, I'll refrain from sapping you of your energy. It's for your own good. Besides—"

"Joke's dead, Jude. You killed it," Indira said, clapping her hand across his mouth. "And if you ever use the term *sexual prowess* again, you'll never get another chance to demonstrate."

She felt his smile stretch under her hand, the heat of his lips warming her palm, filling her with an effervescent fizz of joy.

"Let's go," she said at last, releasing his mouth and grabbing his hand, dragging him out to the fresh air and sunshine. "The sooner we get this done, the sooner we can, uh . . ."

"Go mattress spelunking?"

Indira punched him on the shoulder.

The afternoon was spent with the two collecting reams of toilet paper from trees and bushes, finding countless reasons to laugh until they wheezed as they picked up forks from the lawn and did a half-assed job scraping egg bits off the bricks.

And kisses. They found every possible reason to kiss. Behind bushes. Pressed against the side of the house. In the garage, against her car.

And that night, they followed each other up the stairs, Jude only risking a tender squeeze to Indira's hand before leaving her outside her door. She went into her room, resting her back against the wall they shared, biting her lip to hold back a squeal and smiling up at the ceiling until her cheeks ached.

The softest tap at her door pulled her away.

She tiptoed across the room, then opened it slowly.

And Jude was there, eyes hungry, lips parted. He slipped inside, and Indira closed the door as quietly as possible, preserving the silence that let this moment be just theirs. Then Jude pushed her against it, claiming her as his regardless of any noise.

They were a blur of stripped clothes and whispered promises of leaving before the morning. Cries and groans held back with bitten tongues.

They held each other after. In those moments, it wasn't hard to be quiet.

They seemed to agree that some conversations could be left for another day.

CHAPTER 26

Indira

∞

T-MINUS TEN DAYS UNTIL THE WEDDING

Finally—*finally*—Indira found a decent apartment with rent that still made her sick to her stomach but at least wouldn't require her to sell a kidney, and she spent her birthday moving in.

Well, Jude was moving her in. Indira was spending most of her time facedown on the ground, trying to cajole a disgruntled Grammy out from her hiding spot under the bed. But what was the point of having a boyfriend if not for manual labor?

"I love it," Indira said, spreading her arms wide and spinning in her living room as the last box was brought up. "Happy birthday to me," she crooned, crossing the room and grabbing the front of Jude's T-shirt, giving him a deep kiss.

"Happy birthday," Jude said, rubbing the tip of his nose against hers. "I'm so glad you found a place you love."

"Only took me a lifetime," Indira said, plopping down on some plump cushions that were serving as a makeshift couch until she could buy a new one. Indira had sold most of her stuff when she'd moved in with Chris, so she had a lot of rebuilding to do, but it felt so unbelievably fucking delicious to have a place all her own once again, she couldn't be bothered to worry.

"You're lucky that mattress fit through the door," Jude said, glancing toward the long, narrow hallway that led to her bedroom, where a giant king-sized bed lay on the floor, her most recent, and rather extravagant, splurge item.

"I can always make things fit," Indira said with a dirty wink.

Jude cringed. "Nice one," he deadpanned, making her giggle.

She was about to ask him to grab her some water, when her intercom buzzed. Jude walked over and pressed the button.

"Grubhub," a voice crackled through.

"Be right down," Jude said back.

Indira raised her eyebrows in question.

"It's not a birthday without a delicious dinner, is it?" He shot her a wink, then slipped out the door.

Indira, mature, calm woman that she was, threw her head back and started squealing at the top of her lungs as she kicked her hands and feet. Holy *fuck* was she gone for this guy.

He was back in a blink, arms overflowing with various takeout bags. He set them gently at his feet.

"Oh shit." Indira scrambled across the floor to meet him. "Did you buy out an entire restaurant?"

"Try five," Jude said with a laugh, sitting cross-legged with her.

Indira stopped, hand on a bag, looking at him. "What?"

Dragging a hand across the back of his neck, he let out a nervous cough. "Well, uh, it's probably a poor reflection on my gift-giving abilities but I couldn't decide what you'd like best. So I got a little bit of everything." He waved over the bags.

Indira blinked for a moment, then squealed again, turning into a rabid raccoon as she tore through the bags.

"Nachos?" she cried, opening one Styrofoam container filled to the brim with chips and hot cheese. With a gasp, she opened a few more bags. "Cheesesteak? Pad see ew?"

She inhaled, eyes rolling back in her head. "Wait, is that Halal Guys?" she asked, hand darting for another container. "Oh my God, mac 'n' cheese." Holy shit, was she going to cry?

Jude cleared his throat. Indira turned to him, jaw dangling open.

"Happy birthday, Dira. I'm so lucky to spend today with you," he said, holding out a tray and looking at her with those coffee-black eyes brimming with emotion.

Indira's breath caught in her throat and her belly swooped as she blinked between his earnest face and the giant platter of parmesan, bacon, and truffle waffle fries with a single lit candle wedged in the center of it.

She scooched closer, watching the little flame dance. "This might be the most romantic fucking thing to ever happen to me," she whispered.

"That's extremely alarming."

Indira threw her head back and laughed.

"You have to make a wish," Jude encouraged.

Indira chewed on her lip, trying to think as happiness bloomed in her chest, roses and sunflowers sprouting in the spots between each rib.

She hated the pressure of wishes. She was always scared she'd make the wrong one, send a hope into the universe that would throw her entire life in the wrong direction.

Glancing at Jude, at the soft way he stared at her, like she was the most important person in the world, inspired an idea.

I wish to always remember the feeling of this moment.

She blew out the candle and smiled at him, leaning in to give him a kiss.

"Let's eat," she said against his mouth.

Jude laughed, sending an electric hum through her blood. They picked at the variety of food, Indira groaning every few seconds at how delicious it was.

She had the tray of fries cradled on her lap when Jude nodded his chin toward it.

"Give me a bite?" he asked, voice low. Perfect.

She picked up a fry, holding it out for him. Jude leaned forward, but at the last second, she popped it in her mouth.

"Oops," she said, pressing her lips into a remorseful frown as she chewed.

Jude narrowed his eyes.

"Here," she said, holding out another bite for him. Jude stared at her expectantly, eyes glinting and sharp.

Finally, he leaned in again, his mouth a millimeter from the food, before Indira snatched it up, eliciting a growl from Jude.

"Oh gosh, so sorry!" she said through her full mouth.

Jude gave up on her feeding him, reaching for his own bite. He opened his mouth, loaded fry dangling close, but Indira jolted forward, wrapping her lips around his fingers, tongue curling to take the fries into her mouth. She nipped at his fingers for good measure before pulling away with a loud *pop*.

Jude stared at her for a moment, then brushed his knuckles across his mouth trying to hide his smile and the touch of pink high on his cheeks.

"I'd be careful if I were you," he said, voice rough and hot. "Just because it's your birthday doesn't mean I won't bite back."

Indira stuck out her tongue, waves of heat rolling low in her belly at the very idea of his bite.

Jude caught her chin between his thumb and forefinger, brushing his nose against hers before kissing her with barely controlled passion. Indira pressed back, a soft groan vibrating in her throat as he threaded his fingers in her hair, tugging lightly and shooting sensation through her. Indira moved, crawling like a feral little animal across the space between them, legs kicking the food trays as she situated herself firmly on Jude's lap.

He grinned up at her. "Wow, should I threaten to punish you more often?"

Indira laughed against his mouth, dizzy with how much she felt for him. They continued making out like infatuated teenagers for a few more minutes.

"Bed," Jude grunted, pressing his hips up against her as she ground down on him.

Indira shot him a wolfish smile at the sharp edge of desperation in his voice.

"I've always said mac 'n' cheese is the world's most potent aphrodisiac," she said, nipping at his jaw before scrambling to standing.

They were a tangle of limbs and kisses, giggling as they tripped down the hall toward her bedroom.

Jude pressed Indira against the wall outside her door, dragging his teeth down her neck, hands snaking under her skirt and up her thighs to squeeze her ass. She threw her arms around his neck, knotting her fingers in his hair and tugging till his mouth met hers. They kissed until she was panting, a decadent type of pleasure coiling tight between her hip bones.

"Wait," he whispered against her throat, hands stilling. "Go get comfortable, I have one more gift for you."

"Give it to me later," she whined. "I have a few more important things on my mind." She felt his smile against her throat at her protest.

"I don't plan on letting you leave that bed once I get you on it," he said against her skin before nipping gently.

Indira melted. "Fine," she said with an exasperated sigh. "Do what you must."

He laughed as he pulled away, and Indira slapped his butt as he walked back down the hall, giggling and punch-drunk at the prissy look he shot her over his shoulder.

She went into her room, flinging herself on the bed as she waited for him. Her heart felt like it'd strapped on roller skates and was zipping a blurred, happy loop around her chest.

Indira considered getting undressed, but she loved watching Jude do that for her, the careful, adoring way he unwrapped her, like he could never get over the shock of seeing more of her skin as he stripped away layer after layer.

When he returned, he had a nervous look on his face, a wrapped rectangle partially hidden behind his back. But as he walked closer, he gave her a boyish grin that made her heart stutter.

She scooted to the edge of the mattress, and Jude sat down next to her.

"So, it's kind of silly," Jude said, pink touching his cheeks as he bounced his leg. "But, uh, here you go." He cleared his throat, handed her the carefully wrapped rectangle, then stared down at his lap.

Indira punched him on the shoulder. "You already got me literally all of my favorite food and moved me into my new apartment. Give a girl's heart a moment to recover."

Jude caught her hand, pressing a kiss to her knuckles before letting it go. "I think you should start having higher expectations from me," he said with a rough laugh. "Because you deserve the world."

Indira sucked in a breath, something sweet and intoxicating swelling in her chest, pressing against her ribs.

"It's seriously nothing big," he said, the pink turning deep and rosy, spreading across the bridge of his nose.

Indira tore into the paper, revealing the back of a frame. She turned it over, excited to see what picture Jude put in it, but instead of their smiling faces, a crumpled, old piece of paper sat front and center.

Indira brought it closer to her face, tracing her fingers over the cool glass. She recognized her own adolescent handwriting, big soft letters written in red crayon at the top of the page:

I ♥ Indira soooooooooo much
~Jude

Preteen Jude clearly hadn't been thrilled with her forgery, because he'd taken a black crayon and turned the big heart into a skull-and-crossbones, then circled her whole note and scribbled LIES!! in his own signature spiky scrawl.

It looked like they'd gone back and forth on the sheet for hours, Indira covering one corner with hearts and stars, Jude drawing a weird bird-man-monster punching said hearts and stars. They'd chased each other around the page until every inch was covered.

Indira stared at every letter, every line, until her vision blurred and the memories of them as children were projected onto her soul.

Jude cleared his throat again. "Sorry. I feel like it's kind of silly," he said. "I know the page is in bad shape and it's ugly. I'm not really sure what I was thinking."

He reached out like he was going to take the frame from her, and Indira clutched it to her chest and looked at him, eyes wide and brimming with tears.

"How old is this?" she asked in a whisper.

Jude shrugged, dragging a hand across the back of his neck. "I'm not sure. Probably close to twenty years old? It's the back of a menu from that pizza place your mom used to take us to when you moved to the apartment."

"You kept it for that long?" Indira's heart was in her throat.

Jude blushed harder, reaching for it again. "Yeah. I don't know why. I, um, well, it's super weird, but for some reason I took it with me when I left on that first assignment. I found it a few days before I was set to leave and something about it felt . . . I don't know. It felt like a small reminder of home."

Jude swallowed, eyes boring into the frame.

"I . . . I used to keep it in my pocket. The doodles were really indented in the paper and, um . . . running my fingers over the draw-ings when I'd get really stressed in the field kind of calmed me."

Could bones break from tenderness? Indira was worried hers might.

"Sorry. I should have known it was ridiculous to frame something so ratty. I, uh, clearly worked to cover up your cute doodles."

Indira shifted, placing the frame gingerly on the floor near the mattress. She then turned and launched herself like a torpedo on Jude. He let out an *oof* as he collapsed back on the pillows.

"This is the best gift I've ever gotten," she said, placing happy, sloppy kisses anywhere and everywhere her lips could reach. "Dam-mit, it's so us. It's so perfect."

"You like it?" Jude said, words muffled in the mass of her hair.

"I love it, you wonderfully clueless man," she said, pulling back just enough to look at him. Incandescent happiness radiated out of her, warming everything. He'd been writing love on every inch of her heart since they were kids, and he'd found the most beautiful, messy, ridiculous reminder of that and put it in a frame.

She started kissing him again in earnest, nibbling at his lips, pressing herself against his body until she pulled a soft groan from him.

"I feel like I should give *you* a present now," she said, giggling at the bubbly type of pleasure filling her chest. Jude shook his head.

"The best present you could give me would be lying on your back and showing me your pretty pussy," he said gruffly.

The sudden, dirty words shocked Indira, sending flames lapping through her veins like a struck match. She loved it.

She quickly and gracelessly rolled off him and lay on her back, ripping her skirt and tights off with record speed. She generally preferred to be as contrary as humanly possible toward Jude, but she was suddenly very keen to do whatever he asked of her.

Fancy that.

Jude hovered over her, his smile wolfish as he took her in. He stared at her for so long, her skin started to buzz, and she squirmed on the bed.

"I need you," she whispered, reaching for him.

Jude caught her hands, pressing them back to the mattress with a soft force that sent a thrill shooting though her body.

His smile grew.

"Too many clothes," he said, more to himself than to her, as he got to work on the buttons of her top, popping them free with self-assured flicks.

Jude pulled the edges of her shirt open, licking his lips as he stared at her body. Carefully, he moved her, tugging the blouse off and unhooking her bra. Indira watched him swallow, his pupils blown wide, before he bent his head and started kissing up and down her body.

Desire dragged down her spine, pooling low in her belly as his lips skimmed each inch of revealed skin, his clever hands caressing her curves, cupping her breasts. He spent his time there, alternating between thick drags of his tongue over her nipples with deep sucks on the hard peaks, placing light bites into her.

When Indira was shaking and panting, he continued his downward trajectory, her entire body buzzing with need.

"God, you're so fucking wet for me," he said, the words raw and full of want as he settled between her thighs, dragging one finger down her slit before bringing it to his mouth, tasting her.

A fractured whimper tore from her throat, and Jude smiled at the noise, looking at her like he could see the circuits going off in her body, every nerve aching for more.

He spread her, blowing a cool stream of air over her heated flesh. It was sweet and dark and wonderful, his mouth soft but demanding as he pressed against her. And Indira melted.

She groaned as he licked her, throwing her head back into the pillows as decadent pleasure ricocheted through her body.

"You taste so good," he grunted, emphasizing the point with a long swipe of his tongue over her cunt. "So perfect."

He continued to suck, dragging his face side to side, pulling cry after cry from Indira as delicious tension built and pressed through her body. She loved his touch and his praise and his mouth, and . . .

Her sudden, rough cry seemed to spur him on, his mouth turning determined. Focused. Licking and sucking and wrecking her in the ways he knew she liked best. Indira propped herself on her elbows, watching him destroy her. His dark hair falling across his forehead. The sweep of his lashes against his cheeks as he closed his eyes and savored her. His hips fucking against the mattress in mindless need.

Indira came, the force sharp and beautiful, body bucking as Jude dragged out the pleasure, making her tremble until she thought she'd die from the sensations zipping through her muscles, rewiring her system.

Only when she collapsed back, tugging on his hair to drag him up to her, did Jude relent, kissing a scorching path up her body.

"I need you," Indira said in a breathy whisper. She was a greedy creature who didn't want to waste a second.

"Hmm. Need me how?" Jude asked, fingers trailing over her thighs, her breasts, leaning down he kissed her, wet and dirty and delicious.

"Inside me. Now," Indira panted out, lifting her hips, grinding against him. Jude maneuvered away, eliciting a frustrated groan from her.

Jude clucked his tongue. "So demanding. Where are your manners?" Jude pushed two fingers into her, and her body clenched in response, a hot and aching need slicing through her. He pulled out far too soon.

"Jude," Indira whined. Wanting him. Needing him. Loving every minute of the drawn-out anticipation.

"Yes, Indira?" Jude said, the pad of his thumb whispering over her clit.

"Fuck me, Jude. Please. Please," she begged, wild fingers tugging at his clothes. "I need you so much."

"That's my good girl," Jude said, pressing his thumb against her in reward for a moment before undoing his pants and pushing them down.

She reached for him, gripping his shaft and dragging the head through her wetness and angling her hips to take him. Indira would never get over the luxury of touching Jude, the heat of his skin and the feel of his heartbeat.

Jude hissed out a breath as he seated himself fully in her, the sound cracking like lightning between their bodies. He paused for a moment, pressing his face into her neck, teeth bared against her throat.

"I could stay like this forever," he said, voice so low it was all vibrations from his chest to hers.

Indira held him tighter. She could never get close enough to Jude, never hold him in her body long enough. Nothing would ever compare to the way he adored her, cherished her, in these moments.

"I wish you would," she whispered back, dragging her nails down his back. The movement inspired Jude, and his hips started pumping, slow at first, then picking up an almost frantic rhythm.

Indira moved with him, clumsy and desperate and needing deeper and closer and more.

More.

More teeth biting into flesh. More hands fisted in hair. More raw moans and grunts and cries.

Until they were mindless with it.

"Come with me," Indira begged.

Jude's pace doubled, and he pressed his temple against hers, groaning as he did what she asked. Indira felt her pulse in every joint of her body as she threw herself over the edge of desire, each heartbeat saying:

He's mine.

   He's mine.

      He's mine.

         I'm his.

CHAPTER 27

Jude

T-MINUS TWO DAYS UNTIL THE WEDDING

"Why am I so nervous?" Indira whispered as she smoothed her hands over her hair in the car visor mirror. It sprang back up with a beautiful vengeance.

"I mean, it's pretty understandable," Jude said, reaching over and grabbing her hand, kissing her knuckles lightly. "I know how hard it is for you to make a good impression."

Indira's jaw dropped and nose crinkled as she landed a punch to his thigh. He grabbed that hand and kissed those knuckles too.

"One day that tongue of yours will go too far, and I'll have to cut it off."

Jude chuckled. "Well, based on the events of last night and twice this morning, I have a feeling you'd be the real loser in that situation."

Indira spluttered for a moment.

Jude threw his head back and laughed.

Indira freed one of her hands, using it to squeeze his chin in revenge. "You're the absolute worst."

"I know," Jude said, pressing his smile into the back of her hand before releasing it and opening his door. "Now let's go. They'll be so excited to see you."

With a sigh, Indira followed him out of the car, and they both grabbed their things out of the trunk and headed up the walkway to his parents' house.

The wedding was in two days, and Jude and Indira would drive the rest of the way to the mountain chateau tomorrow for the rehearsal, but they'd decided to spend the night at the Baileys' home on their way.

Jude let himself in. "Mom? Dad?"

Mrs. Bailey yipped in excitement from somewhere in the house, and the excited patter of feet echoed around them as she rounded the corner.

"Oh, my sweetheart. I'm so happy you're here." She crushed Jude into a hug, forcing him to stoop to hug her back. "Don!" she yelled, pulling her head away for a moment. "Don, get in here!"

Jude's dad padded into the hallway, smile serene as he took in his wife hugging their son.

"You've gained weight," Maria said, pulling back to look at him. "Thank God. You looked like a ghost last time I saw you."

"Indira keeps me well fed," Jude said, glancing at Dira and giving her a quick wink. "You remember Indira, right, Mom?"

"Indira Papadakis," Maria cried, turning to her. "My God, there's no way that's you. When did you grow up so fast?"

"I can't say for sure, Mrs. Bailey, but I promise all of it was against my will."

Maria laughed, pulling Indira into a warm hug. Jude's heart swelled as he watched them.

"We're gonna take our things upstairs," Jude said, giving his dad's shoulder a squeeze.

"Right, right," Mrs. Bailey said, fluttering around like an excited butterfly. "Dinner won't be ready for another thirty minutes or so. You two go rest up. Indira, dear, we'll have you sleep in Jude's old room," she said. "Jude, you'll have to make do with the pull-out sofa in the den."

Jude glanced at Indira. "This is where you insist on taking the shitty couch so I can sleep comfortably in my own bed."

Indira arched an eyebrow, then turned a beaming smile on his mom. "That sounds perfect, Mrs. Bailey. Thank you so much."

He followed her up the stairs, glancing over his shoulder to make sure his parents were out of sight before slapping her ass. Indira clapped a hand over her mouth to stifle a giggle, then sprinted up the remaining steps and into Jude's old room.

Jude pulled the door to his childhood bedroom shut behind them as quietly as possible before pressing Indira against it, gripping her hips and giving her a deep, playful kiss. She hummed in pleasure against his lips before opening for him, tongue sliding over his as she threaded her fingers through his hair.

"I'm going to miss you tonight," she whispered into the shell of his ear before biting the lobe. Jude groaned against her neck. "We could rip the Band-Aid off and tell them we're together so we can stay in the same room."

Jude shook his head, his stubble rubbing against a sensitive spot above her collarbone, making her suck in a breath. "It wouldn't matter. My parents are super-old-fashioned Italian Catholics. We'd have to be married for that to fly. And even then, there would be some raised eyebrows."

Indira giggled, moving her hands to wrap them around his waist.

"I, uh . . . I do want to tell them, though. If that's okay with you," Jude whispered against her skin, feeling a bit too vulnerable. A bit too exposed. They still hadn't had a conversation about what they were.

But Jude knew he was Indira's.

And that was all that really mattered.

She pulled back, looking at him with wide, eager eyes. "You do?" she asked, biting down on her lip.

Jude laughed, the sound rough. "Dira, I want to tell the world I'm with you. It's the way I want to introduce myself to everyone I meet."

Her lips parted, a smile lifting the corners. "I'm not going to stop you," she said, cheeks pink as she pressed a kiss to the edge of his jaw.

Jude hugged her to him then, pulling her tight and nuzzling his face into her hair. Breathing her in. She held him right back.

"Wait, I do want to see your room, though," Indira said, pulling away and looking around. "I never got to see it when we were growing up."

"I was terrified of catching your cooties," Jude said with a shrug. "Always been a consummate doctor."

Indira rolled her eyes, but turned a slow circle in the middle of the room, taking in the small space.

A narrow bed sat in the corner, bookshelves stacked with CDs and Marvel comics overhead, a small desk with an ancient desktop computer on the opposite side, some old textbooks still sitting next to it.

"Boring. Just as I anticipated," Indira said, turning to him with a smile. "Suits you."

Jude narrowed his eyes, and Indira giggled. She sat down on the edge of his bed, bouncing up and down slightly.

"What did teenage Jude fantasize about?" she asked, glancing at the sparsely decorated walls—all three *Lord of the Rings* movie posters were hanging near his desk, a few random indie bands from his teenage years littered in between.

He shrugged, shoving his hands in his pockets. Holy shit, why was he blushing?

"Natalie Portman, mainly," he said, a nervous giggle bubbling out of his throat.

"*Star Wars*?" Indira asked.

Jude shrugged again. "I mean, yeah. But, uh, *Black Swan* was a bit of a personal fav when I was sixteen."

Indira's jaw dropped, then her mouth morphed into a shit-eating grin. "Big fan of ballet, are you?"

Jude blushed even harder, a smile that made his cheeks ache winning out. "Huge supporter of the arts," he said with another giggle.

Indira arched an eyebrow as she continued to smile at him, a goofy type of happiness radiating through his limbs.

"Fine," he said, throwing up his hands and sitting next to her. "That movie was my first exposure to, uh, going down . . ."

Indira's eyes bulged. "Really? I'm kind of shocked it wasn't some porno or something."

"I mean, my mom checked my internet history so frequently, I was terrified to even try."

Indira cackled. "What a beautiful sexual awakening," she said, resting her head on his shoulder.

"What about teenage Indira?" Jude said, rubbing his cheek against her curls and nudging her thigh with his.

She snorted. "My sexual awakening? Probably *Moulin Rouge!*," she said, biting on her tongue as she smiled. "Seeing Ewan McGregor singing in suspenders changes a person."

"Wanna know a secret?" Jude asked quietly.

"Always."

"I'm wearing suspenders with my groomsman suit."

Indira nodded calmly. "Do *you* wanna know a secret?"

"Of course."

"I will definitely be jumping your bones at the wedding."

They both started laughing, a giddy joy buzzing around them. Jude was overwhelmed with the feelings that flooded him, soft and sharp and so decadent, he wasn't sure what to do with them, if he even deserved them. But God, did they feel good.

Indira was his softest spot, and he never wanted to let go of the happiness in this moment.

"What's in there?" Indira asked, nodding her chin at a stack of old shoeboxes by Jude's nightstand.

He frowned as he thought. "I don't actually know," he said, sliding off the bed to grab the boxes. He flicked open the lid.

It was filled with a hodgepodge of crap—movie tickets, plastic dinosaurs, a sample of Usher cologne, and some passed notes between him and Collin.

As he rifled through, he noticed more and more items with Indira's rounded, bubbly scribble. Notes she'd shoved under Collin's bedroom when they were very young, telling them to be quiet. Others from when the Papadakis siblings shared a room, telling them to enter at their own risk, specific memos to Jude to go home or lick lead paint. Always the charmer.

He'd never realized just how many mementos he'd kept of this woman. Granted, quite a few were thinly veiled death threats from a disgruntled tween, but they'd moved him enough to keep them some twenty-odd years nonetheless.

"Isn't this lovely," Jude said, handing her a torn piece of notebook paper. "Who knew you were such a poet?"

> A Haiku about Jude Bailey
> By: Indira Papadakis
> Jude. Rude. Fucking screwed
> Socially. he sucks asshole
> Personally. gross

Indira's eyes glided over the lines.

"I can't believe I didn't major in literature," she said, fixing him with a forlorn frown. "So much talent, wasted."

"Oh yes, you've really deprived the world," Jude said, nodding. Indira dug her toes into his thigh, pulling a laugh from the center of his chest.

"We better get downstairs," he said, as he flicked through more random mementos. "My mom doesn't tolerate dinner delays. Or my dad," Jude said, laughing lightly.

Indira stood up. "Say no more. I'm still in 'impress the parents' mode."

He shook his head, smiling up at her. "You'll have to be on your best behavior. Even that might not be enough for their precious son."

"You're annoyingly adorable and simultaneously intolerable," she said, tugging his hair lightly before walking to the door. "But fingers crossed, all the same."

CHAPTER 28

Jude

"I don't mean to be blunt," Maria said, all inflection begging to differ as they ate dinner. "But what is going on between you two?"

Jude and Indira both choked on their food, spluttering and coughing. Maria reached over and patted Jude firmly on the back.

"What do you mean?" Jude said, hacking into a napkin.

"Well . . . didn't you two always—hmm, how should I phrase this?"

"Despise each other?" Indira offered, taking a sip of water.

"Find the other the human embodiment of annoyance?" Jude supplied.

"Wish the other a slow and painful demise?"

Maria and Don blinked at each other across the table. "Well, er, yes. I suppose so."

Jude and Indira giggled.

"I convinced Indira to be my date to the wedding," Jude said, taking a bite of his gnocchi.

"Took so much begging," Indira whispered to Jude's dad. "Poor boy was desperate."

Don pressed his lips together in a silent laugh, and Jude gave her foot a playful kick under the table.

"Well, joke's on her," Jude said, nodding toward Indira while he looked at his dad. "Because now that I have her in my clutches, I don't plan on letting go."

Indira glanced at Jude through her lashes, reaching for his hand under the table.

"What does that mean?" his mom asked, eyebrows furrowed. "And why are you talking like a villain?"

Jude glanced at Indira. Color was high on her cheeks, a deep and dusky rose spreading across her skin. Her lips spread in a smile.

"Indira and I are, um, together," Jude said, clearing his throat. "She's . . . she's my girlfriend."

A beat of silence danced across the table before Mrs. Bailey erupted in excitement, clapping her hands. "Oh, how lovely," she said, beaming. "Don, you owe me ten dollars."

Jude's head whipped between his parents. "What?"

Don looked up at the ceiling, a defeated sigh leaving his lips before he reached for his wallet in his back pocket and pulled out a bill, passing it across the table to his wife.

"She bet me, probably fifteen years ago, that you two would end up together," Don said, his face a pitiful combination of happiness and disgruntlement. "The woman knows everything, I swear."

"I do," Maria said, winking at Don. "But this is wonderful," she cheered, turning to Jude and Indira. "You always seemed to have a knack for keeping him grounded."

Indira let out a loud laugh. "That's a very forgiving way of phrasing it, Mrs. Bailey."

Jude rolled his eyes. "I'll say."

Maria gave him a good-natured smile, passing him another roll.

"What's new in your life, Mrs. Bailey? Are you still at Better Beginnings?"

Maria let out a forlorn sigh. "That place would crumble to the ground without me, I'm just going to say it."

Jude nodded, trying to hide his growing smile. "So true, Mom."

She launched into a whirlwind story about cut funding and staff shortages at the preschool she worked at, the never-ending administrative issues she had to deal with. Even in the long list of problems, she still managed to tell story after story about a toddler doing something adorable. Maria loved to talk, and she didn't take a breath before segueing into some piping-hot drama with her neighborhood book club that was spilling over into the planning of the block's annual holiday party.

"All I'll say on the matter is you better be prepared to dust off all the skeletons in your closet if you start spreading a rumor like *that*."

"Those Andersons are nothing but trash," Indira agreed, keeping up with the neighborhood scandals far better than Jude.

Maria beamed at her before waving her hand to change the subject.

"Jude, sweetheart, when do you have to go to your next assignment?" his mom asked, taking another bite of food. "You have thirteen months left, right?"

Jude had forgotten how sudden it could be, that flip of a switch where one tiny, almost innocuous thing could release a sharp and wild type of anxiety snapping its jaws in Jude's gut.

The reality of his future trickled through him, a sticky type of dread that pooled in his chest, a reminder of all that pain and suffering that existed outside of the infatuated bubble he shared with Indira. He simultaneously felt everything and nothing, each nerve and muscle in his body short-circuiting as his brain disconnected with his body.

"Jude?" his mom asked softly, setting down her fork. "Are you okay?"

Jude blinked a few times, finally forcing himself to nod. Indira reached for his hand under the table, trying to hold it, but he pulled away.

He couldn't bear the comfort of her touch without crumbling. His heart was a shattered mess in his chest, the jagged pieces of his past ripping open all the scars.

It was hard to get his mouth to work, his jaw locking up, but he was finally able to force out the words, "Yeah. Fine, sorry." He cleared his throat a few times. "I'm set to go back in a little over two weeks. But they're hosting a few simulated emergency calibration sessions before I'm shipped out."

"Where are you headed?" Don asked, looking at his son closely. Jude couldn't meet his eyes.

"Don't know," he said with a shrug. "Usually find out last minute. Needs and coordination can shift so quickly."

Jude could feel Indira's eyes on him, begging him to look at her. He couldn't. Wouldn't.

All of this was such a mistake. A huge mistake. What was Jude thinking, letting his foolish fucking heart get him into this mess? Set him up to hurt Indira so thoroughly?

"We're so proud of the work you do, sweetie," Maria said, reaching out to pat his cheek. "You're a hero. It's amazing."

Jude had to choke back the sharp and acidic bile that rose in his throat.

His parents continued to ask questions and make small talk. Jude did his best to answer as normally as possible while the walls of his chest caved in on him, but he knew from the weight of the gazes around him that he wasn't particularly convincing.

Indira carried a lot of the conversation, her laugh like a knife twisting in Jude's side as he realized how much he would miss it. How much he already missed it. She was right there next to him but Jude could feel their time being stolen, a wall being laid brick by brick between them. With so much badness embedded in his DNA, where did his heart get off, longing for more?

Eventually, they started to clean up, Maria carefully placing leftovers in Tupperware containers while Don and Indira loaded the dishwasher. Jude made slow work of clearing the table, focusing on the feel of a plate gripped between his fingers, the press of a fork's handle against his palm.

Finally, a well-timed yawn from his mom inspired Jude's escape.

"I better head to bed," he said, glancing at his watch. It was barely past seven, but he didn't care.

"Oh," Maria said, her smile turning into a small pout. "So early?"

"We'll have to hit the road first thing tomorrow morning and . . . yeah. Super tired." Jude pretended to yawn.

His mom padded over, giving Jude's stiff frame a hug. He counted to three before pulling away, saying a few disjointed good nights before escaping out of the kitchen and heading to the den.

Indira wasted no time in following him.

"Jude." His name was barely a whisper. She might as well have screamed it at him the way it created an avalanche in his chest. He stopped just inside the doorway, head bowed.

"Talk to me," Indira said, extending her hands toward him. Jude didn't take them.

"I'm sorry," Jude said, voice cracking on the words as a sharp tear slashed down his cheek. "But I can't. I think it's best if you leave me alone."

And he shut the door.

CHAPTER 29

Jude

Indira abided Jude's request to be left alone, which, knowing her hard-headedness, was rather fucking disorienting for him. And it left him with way too much time to think.

Ghosts crept in, memories of injuries and agony and voices and cries all compounded with Jude's guilt until his brain was a swampy, clouded mess he couldn't wade through.

He sat on the edge of the pull-out bed, head in hands and heart thrumming painfully against his chest. Jude used to think he deserved all this pain—some sort of atonement for all the blood on his hands—but now that he remembered how happiness felt, he wanted nothing more than to be free of it. Unshackle himself from the weight of it hanging around his neck.

And the truth was, he didn't want to be left alone. Not by Indira. Because, around her, he felt better. Could breathe a little easier. And he was selfish and wanted more of that.

He felt like his time with Indira was being stolen, but here he was, wasting it. He got up, striding to the door and wrenching it open, desperate to be closer to her.

He jumped when he saw her standing in the hall, hand poised like she was about to knock.

Indira looked at him, wide eyes hesitant but determined. She swallowed, squared her shoulders, and stepped inside. She had on flannel pajama pants and a T-shirt decorated with Baby Yodas. She looked so adorable he thought his knees might give out.

"I think we need to talk," he said, turning to face her as he shut the door.

"Is that so?" Indira said, flashing him a soft but sad smile.

Jude's breath caught in his throat at a surge of overwhelming tenderness for this woman. For her steady perseverance. It seemed impossible to feel as much as he did for Indira—just breathing around her made his chest ache and his throat burn. And it scared the shit out of him. With so much pain already drowning him, he didn't want to ruin whatever it was that existed between them.

Indira stepped toward him, picking up his hand and holding it in both of hers, cradling it to her chest.

"Jude, I love you."

She said it simply, as though hearing those words didn't completely rearrange every molecule in Jude's body.

"I've always loved you. Even when I didn't like you, I loved you. You've been a permanent fixture in my life, someone steady to rely on, even when that reliance came with annoying each other or teasing. Because you let me tease you back. You've always been my person, Jude. My annoying, wonderful person. And I think I'm your person too."

Jude started shaking his head, tears pricking at his eyes as he stared at her. He pulled his hand from her, stepping back and scrubbing his palms down his face. He couldn't hear this. He couldn't possibly listen to something so kind and pure and sweet and survive it.

But Indira kept going.

"I know something happened to you," she said, holding his gaze. His skin prickled like a fever breaking. "I know you're hurting. You're in pain. I want to help you. I want to be here for you."

Jude's throat started working, opening and closing on words and feelings he couldn't get out.

"I'm scared," he finally managed, tears rolling down his cheeks. How could he love her wholly, the way she deserved, if he was nothing but a jagged fragment of who he used to be? "I'm really fucking broken," he admitted, the words ripped from his chest.

"I'm not looking to fix you," she said, staring straight into his eyes. "I'm here to love you."

Jude's head swam, bolts of feelings shocking his system as he tried to process any of this.

"Why?" he eventually asked.

Indira's eyes scoured over his face, and he could feel the heat of them on his skin. His fingers twitched with the need to reach for her, but he was too overwhelmed to move.

After a long moment, she spoke. "I'm going to speak in similes and metaphors for a moment, and you aren't allowed to roll your eyes." Her lips quirked at the corners as she said it, and the ghost of her smile nearly broke Jude in two.

She chewed on her lip, her eyes flicking to the bed. "Can I hold you while we talk?" she asked.

"Yes, please," Jude said, the words tumbling out of him rapid fire and a bit too loud.

"Okay." She smiled again, this one rich and glowing. "Lay down," she said, reaching out and tugging his hand.

He nodded, unable to say anything with that pressure still building in his throat, threatening to rip him in half. He let Indira guide him to the bed, and she gently pushed him to sit at the edge. He scooched back to lean against the pillows, legs stretched out in front of him. It felt like he couldn't get air past the base of his throat as she looked at him.

"Would you be willing to take this off?" Indira asked, tugging at the sleeve of his shirt.

Without a second thought, Jude nodded and pulled it over his head.

Indira's eyes traced over him, lingering on his exposed chest, the spot where it felt like his heart would punch out of his body. With a swift nod, she stripped off her own shirt, a delicate bralette of lace covering her breasts.

Jude's eyes traced over her skin.

Indira got in on the other side of the bed and, without hesitation, draped her torso over his.

"Everyone always talks about skin-to-skin contact in the context of babies and parents, but adults need it too," Indira said against his chest, trailing her fingers across his collarbone. "Probably just as much. Or maybe it's just me being touch hungry." She breathed out a soft laugh against his sternum.

Jude shook his head, his chin dragging through her curls. "This makes me feel so . . . calm. Safe."

They dissolved into silence for a few more minutes, their chests moving together as they breathed. Jude was probably just imagining things, but it felt like the rhythm of their heartbeats matched.

"Are you ready for the similes?" she said, and Jude could feel her smile press into his skin.

It took him a moment to remember what she was talking about, but when his brain could finally function, he nodded, then said yes.

Jude ran his hands over her warm skin, and she hummed at his caress, his fingers trailing down her shoulder and across her forearm, one hand settling in the dip of her waist, the other lacing his fingers through hers.

"Okay. Imagine your mind is a house," Indira said. "A good house. It has some wear and tear from years of use, but it's yours."

Jude nodded.

"Now, imagine, you have this house and one day, without your permission, a bunch of people show up and start having this massive party. They're throwing things and breaking things and moving shit around, but there's too many people for you to stop them all at once. You try to go and fix one mess, and ten more happen in another room. Are you following me?"

"Yes," he said in a hoarse whisper.

"Then, after what feels like endless days of partying, all those people finally leave. But they don't clean up any of the destruction. And you're sitting there, looking at this house you loved, and seeing pure chaos. Things are broken, piles of trash are everywhere, people even wrote on the walls. Your space was invaded, it doesn't feel like yours anymore. And you have no idea where to start with cleanup. Does that sound like something you could imagine?" Indira asked, the question soft.

He felt the gentlest press of her lips against his skin. "Yes. I can imagine it."

"And each day, the need to clean grows and grows, but you can't do anything about it. The tools are hidden or missing or destroyed. And it all adds to the mess. You feel paralyzed, because you had to watch your space get destroyed and it hurts and it's overwhelming and you start to shut down."

Jude held on to Indira, his fingers pressing into her, gripping with gentle pressure at her hip and side. She nuzzled closer.

"But then I show up. And I take in some of the destruction—not all of it, there are some rooms that are yours and will always be just yours. You might not even let me in the front door until you can decide if I'm safe and you trust me. That's fine, I'll wait outside as long as you need. But I decide I want to help you get it cleaned up. I want to help haul out broken furniture and scrub the walls and glue together broken plates. Because I know your house and I like your house. So, I ask you to let me help. I ask you to hand me some of the pieces so you can work on repairing the really big stuff."

"You—" Jude's throat locked around itself, but he tried to swallow past it, forcing the question out. "You like my . . . house?" His hand threaded up into the mass of her hair, tangling around the curls.

He felt Indira smile. Part of him wished he could see it, but the other part knew the force of it would obliterate him.

"Yes, I like your house, Jude. I've always liked your house. Even years ago when your house was more like a tiny apartment that was sometimes super stubborn and kind of douchey and—"

Jude slid his hand to cradle her jaw and tilted her face up, pressing his lips to hers.

Indira kissed him back, wrapping her arms around his neck and holding him close. Jude's stomach swooped at the sensation of her mouth against his. Her taste. Her everything.

After a few minutes, she pulled back slightly, resting her forehead against his.

"You don't have to talk about the things you've experienced on your assignments, Jude. You'll never have to tell me if you don't want to. But you also don't have to keep it inside either. Let it eat away at you for fear that I'll judge you. I could never do that."

After a moment, Jude nodded, deciding to trust that. To trust *her*.

So much of the past three years had been out of his control. But here and now, he had a choice. And he was choosing to give Indira whatever he could.

"I want to let you in," Jude said, pressing another kiss to her lips. "I'll probably be really shitty at it for awhile, but . . ."

"Take as much time as you need," Indira said. "I'm not going anywhere."

"Promise?"

"Promise."

"I'm . . . I'm scared," he whispered against her shoulder.

"Of course you are, Jude," she said, dragging her fingers through his hair. "You've been through hell. I think your brain may have convinced you that everything you've seen and experienced destroys your ability to be happy. That's not true. You can hurt and also be loved. You can feel sadness and also laugh and feel joy. Good emotions can coexist with hard ones. You can struggle and suffer and learn to heal while you also love. The best place to start is by giving yourself permission to feel with abandon. Feel everything."

Tears pricked at Jude's eyes as he held her as close as he could.

And, with a soft, sweet hum of satisfaction that reverberated through his bones, Indira held Jude back.

He pressed his nose into her hair, breathing her in, letting her feel his shuddering breath.

Then he started talking.

He told Indira about people he lost. About all the times he failed. He remembered the faces of every person who died on his table. Women who died from preventable diseases. Children caught in the middle of war and conflict, their futures ripped from them. People dying from random embolisms and plotted acts of violence.

His conscience was heavy, so fucking heavy, but speaking about it slowly unraveled the knot. It felt like for the first time in a long time, he could start to breathe again.

"It's hard to forgive myself," he eventually said, staring up at the ceiling.

"Forgive yourself for what, love?"

"For all the people I've lost."

Indira moved to sit cross-legged next to him. "But what about all those you've saved?"

Jude followed her lead, sitting up with his back pressed against the scratchy couch cushion.

"Indira," he said, feeling wrung out, but lighter. "I've lost more people than I've saved. That is, objectively, a terrible statistic for a doctor."

Indira opened her mouth to say something, then closed it, her face pinching into a look that could only be described as *yikes*. Jude saw the gears of her brain whirling around to spin that fact into something positive.

Something came over Jude as he watched his lovely girlfriend think about his awful truth, and he started to . . .

Well, Jude started to laugh.

It was rough and loud and totally, indescribably inappropriate. Indira's eyes went so wide, she looked like a horrified emoji.

And Jude laughed even harder.

"I'm so sorry, it's not funny," he wheezed, clutching one hand to his chest and shaking the other in front of Indira.

"Not even a little bit funny," Indira said, giggles of her own tumbling out, nervous but inescapable. She made a hiccupping noise that increased their laughter. "It's, like, genuinely awful."

Jude laughed harder still, slipping back down until he was flat on the bed. It just felt so *good*, like his whole body was humming on a new frequency.

"Why are we laughing?" Jude asked, snorting.

Indira reached for Jude, holding him close, both shaking as they laughed.

"Because sometimes," she whispered against the crown of his head, giving him a soft kiss, "the body needs to laugh instead of cry."

"Does this make me a bad person?" Jude said, eventually catching his breath.

"Laughing in this moment? No," Indira said with firm finality. "Your general priggish attitude? Jury's still out."

Jude laughed one last time. Then, quietly, he started to cry.

And that felt good too.

Indira slid down the bed until they were nose to nose, watching over him, dragging her nails through his hair. Small tears rolling down her own cheeks.

Through it all, she rubbed her hands up and down his back. Whispered soft words of love against his throat. She held a magnifying glass up to the most hidden parts of his soul and still smiled, happy to simply know him.

"Indira," he said, pulling his head back to look at her. She looked back—his safe soul. His happy place. His tether.

"Thank you for . . ." He paused, searching for the right words. None would be good enough. "Thank you for being you," he said, pressing a kiss to her neck, feeling her pulse against his lips. "I'm on my way back."

Indira smiled, eyes glistening. "I know."

"And . . . I love you."

"I know that too."

CHAPTER 30

Indira

∞

"I'm going to kill this motherfucker."

Indira looked at her mom, Angela, silently agreeing with the sentiment.

"I should have known he'd pull a stunt like this," Angela continued, talking in hushed tones out of the side of her mouth as the pair hovered in the back of the barn at Collin's wedding rehearsal.

The space was breathtaking, glowing lights strung across the lofted ceiling and down supporting beams, a large, arched window framing the mountain view that Collin and Jeremy would stand in front of the next day to take their vows.

Everything was perfect.

Except for Indira's father yet again fulfilling his role as the ultimate disappointment.

"I'm so sorry," Natalie, the venue owner and coordinator, said as she approached Indira and Angela. "But I'm not sure we can delay the rehearsal much longer. I have a different appointment to get to in forty-five minutes."

"I understand," Angela said. "I'll talk to Collin."

Natalie offered a sad smile before nodding and walking off.

Indira and Angela watched Collin pacing at the opposite end of the space, Jeremy and Jude standing helplessly nearby.

Angela shook her head. "I thought Greg's done unforgivable things in the past, but this is a new low."

With a sigh, the women approached Collin.

"Just a few more minutes," Collin said, his face strained but voice casual. "I'm sure Dad will be here any second. Probably a flight delay or something."

"Collin," Angela whispered, stepping toward her son. So many sentiments were embedded in the way she said his name. *There were no delays. There's no point in waiting. The man isn't coming.*

Indira's hands shook and her stomach roiled, a queasy, dizzy type of anger boiling in her. The shiftiness of Collin's eyes felt like a knife twisting in her chest.

"Collin, we—" Indira's voice was cut off at the trill of a phone.

Collin's face bloomed in hope as he hastily fished it out of his pocket, a relieved grin breaking across his face. "It's him. Told you he's coming."

"He's not," Indira said softly, shaking her head. She wanted to tear that phone out of Collin's hand and chuck it off the side of the mountain. Destroy any objects that helped carry Greg's empty promises.

"Hey, Dad!" Collin said, answering the call. "I know being fashionably late is a thing, but this might be a bit next level." Collin's voice was light. Breezy. But it cracked with the forced laugh at the end.

Indira recognized that voice; it was the same one she'd used with her dad for so many years as a teenager and even in her early twenties. It was cool but earnest. Calm but keen. It was reined-in excitement drenched in pitiful desperation to say the right thing in exactly the right way and then, maybe then, it would click things into place. Win Dad over. Make him eager to change.

Indira's heart squeezed in pain for sweet Collin.

"Oh," Collin said, face falling. He turned from the group, striding away. "No, of course!" Indira heard as he retreated. "Oh my gosh, absolutely. I totally understand. Don't worry . . ."

Jeremy trailed close behind his fiancé.

Indira didn't even realize she was crying until Jude was in front of her, wiping the tears from her cheeks with his thumbs.

"Hey," he whispered, cupping her face and angling it so she'd look at him. "I'm so sorry."

Indira crumpled into him, wet eyes pressed against the spot right above his heart, fingers twisting into the front of his shirt. Jude's hands soothed over her hunched back, and he whispered gentle words into her hair.

"I need to go check on him," she said, pulling away.

Jude nodded. "I'll be right here." He leaned in closer, lips grazing the shell of her ear. "I love you so much."

Indira blinked a few times to collect herself, and her mom's face came into focus over Jude's shoulder—mouth dangling open and eyes wide as she stared at the way Jude was embracing her.

Oops. Indira had wanted to tell her mom in person about her and Jude, but the day had been such a whirlwind of driving and setting up that there hadn't been an ideal moment.

"I'll explain later," Indira whispered as she walked over to her mom.

Angela placed a hand on her wrist, eyes glinting. "Oh yes you will, missy."

Indira's cheeks warmed—all of her warmed, really—as she imagined telling her mom just how in love she was with Jude. She wanted to tell everybody.

But Collin came first.

"Should we talk to him together?" Angela asked, walking with Indira toward the door Collin had disappeared through.

Indira thought about it for a moment. "Let me feel him out first," she said. She knew Collin had a tendency to put on a brave face around their mom, never wanting to worry her. "Then you can move in with the big hugs and cuddles."

"My forte," Angela said, pausing to demonstrate on Indira. Indira hugged her mom back, breathing in the familiar, warm scent of her.

"Be right back," she said, untangling herself and continuing her search for Collin.

She found him on the couch in one of the getting-ready rooms, silent tears rolling down his cheeks, his usually smiling mouth unrecognizable with its deep frown and hurt lines bracketing the corners.

Jeremy was sitting next to him, rubbing his back.

Indira had the urge to rip her father's head off. No one should be allowed to make Collin hurt this badly.

"Hi," she said softly, approaching them.

"Hey, Dira," Collin said, nose stuffy and eyes red. He dragged the heels of his hands across his cheeks.

Jeremy smiled sadly up at her. "I'll give you two a minute to talk," he said, standing up and patting Indira on the shoulder before leaving the room.

Indira sat down next to Collin, giving him a moment to adjust to her presence. She reached out, giving his hand a squeeze, and he collapsed against her, crying against her shoulder.

"I'm fine. Totally fine," Collin choked out as he sobbed.

"Could've fooled me," Indira said softly, rubbing circles along his back.

Collin took a shaky breath, pulling away to dab a tissue against his eyes.

"What did he say?" Indira asked, trying to sound calm. She failed.

"It's seriously not a big deal," Collin said, rolling his eyes to the ceiling and taking a deep breath. "I'm being dramatic. The stress of the wedding just has me extra sensitive."

Indira squeezed Collin's hand again. "Are you lying to me or yourself?"

Collin chuckled lightly at that before a hiccupping sob tore from his throat.

"He's not coming," he admitted after another rattling breath.

"Something came up, I guess, and he can't make it. He sounded really upset, though. At least there's that."

Right. Because putting on a sad voice was all it took to justify this man's toxic actions and constant empty promises. The bar for fatherhood was on the ground, and Greg always showed up with a shovel.

"He did say that he thinks he'll be able to make a visit up here soon. Maybe in the new year."

Indira wanted to scream at the note of optimism in her brother's voice. But she understood. That little bait—that easy, promising phrase of wanting to see them soon that Greg dangled like a carrot in front of his children—never failed to make either of their hopeful hearts bite.

"Collin," Indira said, swallowing back her own tears. "I'm so fucking sorry. That piece of shit."

Collin waved his hand. "Seriously, it's okay. It's fine. I honestly should have seen this coming. You were right," he said with a shrug.

Indira had never wished to be wrong more than she did in this moment. She didn't have words to tell Collin how sorry she was, so she hugged him instead, holding him close. He held her back.

"Can I ask you a favor?" Collin asked after a few minutes.

"Of course."

"Would you be willing to walk me down the aisle with Mom? You are two of the most important people in the world to me. It should always have been you two giving me away."

Indira started properly crying, shoulders shaking and snot pouring out of her nose. "Nothing would make me happier," she said through her sobs.

"It's going to fuck up the symmetry of the—"

"It doesn't matter," Indira said, hugging him again. She felt Collin nod in agreement.

A few minutes later, there was a soft tap on the door, Angela poking her head in. "You two okay?" she asked, crossing the room to her children.

They shot their mom similar, pointed looks.

"I'm sorry," she said, sitting on the other side of Collin and wrapping her arms around her kids.

"It's not your fault, Mom. You have nothing to be sorry for."

"He doesn't deserve you two," Angela said, her voice thick with emotion. "And I love you so much."

Another tap at the door interrupted their moment.

"I'm so, *so* sorry," Jeremy said, repeating the phrase of the moment. "But Natalie is about to ditch us if we don't do the rehearsal now."

"I'd rather die than lose Natalie," Collin said, pushing to stand. He smiled down at them. "Come on, you two. We have an aisle to walk down."

* * *

The rest of the rehearsal went smoothly (thank God) and was wrapped up in about twenty minutes, the wedding party filing out of the barn and packing into cars to head to the dinner.

"Give me a minute?" Indira asked, pressing a kiss to Jude's cheek.

"Take your time," he said, rubbing the end of a strand of her hair between his fingers before letting her go.

Indira walked around to the side of the barn, tucking into a corner to avoid the wind, the heat of her anger burning her from the inside.

Indira didn't like feeling angry. It was an uncomfortable, swollen feeling that took up too much space in her chest when it finally broke free from the lockbox she tried to keep it trapped in.

Due to the busyness of the past two weeks and travel for the wedding, Indira had, regrettably, needed to cancel a few therapy sessions. She'd told Dr. Koh about the trickle of worry in her chest about not having their sessions to untangle her emotions for a bit, especially with the looming interaction with her father. Dr. Koh had smiled, a true, broad smile.

"It's okay to sit with the feelings that don't feel good," Dr. Koh had said. "It means your body is digesting them, taking what it needs from the sensation and processing the rest to leave you, or guide you on what to do to honor those feelings. Express them to others. And our sessions will be ready and waiting for you as soon as you're back."

With fumbling, angry fingers, she unlocked her phone and jabbed out a number, blood pounding in her ears as it rang.

"Indira?" her dad's smooth voice answered. "Hi, sweetheart! It's been awhile. How are you?"

"You aren't coming to Collin's wedding." It wasn't a question, but Indira still wanted to make him admit it.

He let out a forlorn sigh. "It breaks my heart, you have no idea. But Brooke-Anne has this big product launch and needs me—"

"I don't give a flying fuck what your current wife is launching on Instagram. This wedding has been planned for over a year, and you've known that. You are actively prioritizing changeable things over your son's wedding day. There's no excuse for that."

Greg sighed again. "Oh, Dira. No. It's not like that. Brooke-Anne feels awful too, don't be mad at her—"

"I'm not mad at Brooke-Anne," Indira said, angry tears pricking her eyes. "I'm mad at *you*. *You* are the only one failing their children right now."

"What was I supposed to do, Dira?" Greg asked, his voice perfectly pitched to sound so devastated. So torn up. Fucking liar. "My hands are tied here. You have to believe me, I'm just as upset as you and your brother that I won't be there. It breaks my heart."

Indira tried to say something, but a treacherous sob broke from her throat instead. She hated being an angry crier.

"Indira, sweetie, don't cry," her dad cooed. "Please. I'm going to make it up to Collin. I promise."

All of a sudden, Indira was eight years old again, sitting on the staircase of her childhood home as she watched her dad pack up his shirts and shoes and watches. *Don't cry*, he'd said then, giving his daughter a placating smile as her world fractured apart, her entire body shaking with the fury of her heartbeat and the confusion of her thoughts. *I'll see you and Collin all the time. I promise.*

"Are you really this deluded?" Indira said, her voice rising. "You really think you can make up for something like this? Missing a moment like this? Especially when you've missed *every* moment?"

"Don't use that tone with me, Indira," her dad scolded. "I'm still your father."

"You're not," Indira said, voice finding a steadiness that didn't match the way her heart was collapsing in on itself. "Fathers make an effort. Fathers care about their kids. Their feelings. Fathers do everything they can to make it to graduations, remember birthdays, even just fucking check in with how their kids are doing. You are a mouthpiece for empty promises and I'm done listening."

"Dira, that's unfair. I've tried my best. I know I'm not perfect, I'll be the first to admit that. But I do try."

Indira's mouth dangled open.

He actually believed that. Her father—the man who had willfully missed it all while he built other trial families—really, truly believed he was doing his best.

Finally, *finally*, it clicked into place. He would never understand how much he'd failed his children. He would never acknowledge the hurt he'd caused them. And yelling or crying or opening herself up to him wouldn't do anything to change that.

Indira didn't need him. She didn't need her dad's approval or his presence or even his love. She didn't need to chase after the idea of a man who made her work so hard for affection.

Indira was worthy of love just as she was. And she needed to start loving herself too, let go of the things that hurt her.

"I need you to know something," Indira said, cutting him off as he continued to defend himself. "When we hang up this call, I am going to do everything in my power to let you go. I am going to unpack all this shit, week after week. I'm going to sit in therapy sessions and speak truth to what a shitty dad you've been. Every broken vow. Every time you left your children wondering why they weren't good enough for your love. And I am going to heal. I am going to surround myself with people that love me. Cherish me. Know I'm enough. But you? You're going to get old. And you're going to go through more wives. Have more kids. And you'll still end up dying alone, suffocating under the weight of the hurt you've caused so many people. And then, I hope, you'll finally understand."

"Indira—"

"Don't contact me again."

CHAPTER 31

Indira

∞

Collin and Jeremy's wedding was as close to perfect as a day could get.

Indira walked her brother down the aisle with a lump in her throat, emotion pressing through every inch of her, as Collin held tightly to her hand on one side, their mother's on the other.

And the entire time they moved toward that altar, Jude's eyes were on Indira, raw and honest, filled with an openness she once thought she'd never see again in him.

Indira silently cried through most of the ceremony, happy tears rolling down her cheeks as Jeremy and Collin promised their love. She couldn't have picked a better man for her brother.

* * *

"I fucking love weddings," Lizzie said a few hours later, sipping a glass of wine with Rake's arm draped over her shoulder. "An entire day celebrating love? That's some dope shit."

Indira, Thu, Harper, and their partners snorted at Lizzie's tipsy declaration. They were situated around a table toward the back that Harper had snagged for them, far enough from the speakers and dance floor that the noise wasn't too overwhelming.

"You outdid yourself with the cake," Dan, Harper's boyfriend, said, giving Lizzie a tiny salute.

She bowed. "I was explicitly told not to make it explicit," she said, rolling her eyes. "Apparently, this is a classy event and a dick-shaped cake blowing a load didn't fit the bill."

Dan laughed so hard he choked on his bite. Harper giggled with him, patting him on the back. He grabbed her hand and placed a kiss to her palm when he finally recovered, smiling at her like she was the sun.

"Oh, Alex! This is our song," Thu said, patting her boyfriend's knee as the DJ played a new track. "Let's dance."

"Thu, this is 'Disturbia' by Rihanna," Harper said, scrunching up her nose.

"Cute, right?" Thu said, pulling Alex behind her, his cheeks rosy and smile dopey. He'd follow wherever Thu led.

Indira nestled closer into Jude's chest, his arms wrapped around her from behind as they watched the dancing from afar. He pressed a kiss to the top of her head. "I'm gonna go get a little bit of air," he whispered into her ear.

"Need me to come with you?" she asked, turning to look at him. Jude definitely wasn't at his most comfortable with all the noise and people, but he was managing it well, taking lots of breaks and walks when a spark of anxiety would hit him.

"Nah, stay here with your friends," he said, smiling as he brushed his thumb across her cheek. "I won't be long."

She gave him a soft kiss, then untangled herself from him, watching him walk away. When she turned back to the table, she realized Lizzie and Rake were also missing.

A loud laugh drew her attention to a doorway right as the pair disappeared through it, Lizzie smacking Rake on the ass for good measure. Harper caught Indira's eye, and they shared a knowing look before erupting into giggles.

"Some things never change," Harper said, cheeks flooded with color.

"Thank God for that." Indira clinked her glass against Harper's and Dan's before taking a sip.

"All right, my dear, you've got some explaining to do," a familiar voice said next to Indira.

She looked up, smiling at her mom. "Who? Me?"

Angela sat down, grabbing her daughter's hand. "Yes, you. The girl who was just snuggled awfully close to Jude Bailey. The same Jude Bailey you once tried to push in front of my car when I was leaving to go to the grocery store."

"That was an accident!" Indira lied.

Angela gave her a knowing look.

"He'd just stolen my bike," Indira grumbled.

"When did this happen?" her mom asked, eyes sparkling as she leaned close. "Or maybe a better question is how?"

Indira laughed, dropping her head to her hands. "You know the old adage—keep your childhood nemesis close."

Angela smacked her on the thigh. "Details, Dira!"

"I don't really know," Indira said, looking up at her mom, her cheeks heating at just the thought of Jude being hers. "We were kind of helping each other deal with stuff and . . ." Indira made a goofy, flappy move with her hands.

Her mom grinned. "Are you happy?"

Indira nodded. "Yeah. I really am."

"That's all I've ever wanted for you."

Angela wrapped her in a big hug, Indira inhaling the familiar clean scent of her. There was nothing quite like a hug from her mom.

"Mama Papadakis?" Jeremy interrupted with a light clearing of his throat, appearing by their side. "May I have this dance?" He reached out a hand, smile wide and wonderful.

Angela beamed. "Of course, sweetheart," she said, taking his proffered hand. "We'll talk more later," she added, winking at her daughter.

Indira rolled her eyes but smiled, watching as Jeremy walked Angela to the dance floor. He led her in a slow dance, the pair talking and laughing the entire time while shooting frequent glances at Collin, who was animatedly talking to a group of guests on the side. Alex and Thu had continued dancing, holding each other tightly, Thu's head resting on his shoulder as Alex smiled.

Harper and Dan were still at the table, leaning close. Dan fed Harper a bite of cake, and she beamed, licking her lips and saying something that made him laugh.

"Dira?"

Indira jumped at the closeness of the voice. She turned, taking in Chris towering over her.

"Oh boy," Indira said, frowning up at him.

"Mind if I sit for a minute?" he asked, gesturing at the open seat next to her.

Indira gave him a dull look but eventually waved her hand. "Be my guest."

Chris clumsily pulled out the chair, fidgeting as he sat, eyes shifty and knee bouncing.

"I—uh—How are you?" Chris asked, coughing.

Indira looked at him, forcing him to meet her gaze. "I'm really good," she said, meaning it.

Chris nodded a few times, pressing his lips together in a tight line. "Good. Good," he said, still nodding.

Indira let the awkward silence linger, studying him.

"I, uh, I just wanted to say I'm sorry," Chris blurted out, glancing at her, then looking away again.

More silence.

"I'm sorry for cheating on you," Chris said, a bit softer this time, finally looking at her. "For hurting you."

"Where's this coming from?" Indira asked tersely.

Chris let out a pained laugh. "Well, the truth doesn't make me any less of an asshole, but seeing how happy you and Jude are together . . . it stung a bit. And then it was kind of a wake-up call to how shitty I was with how I handled everything. And I'm sorry."

Indira sucked her bottom lip into her mouth, turning that over.

She looked at him, at the man she'd thought she loved. The person she'd wanted so badly to be content with.

They'd never stood a chance.

"I forgive you," she said, meaning it. "It fucking sucked to walk in on something like that, but all's well that ends well, I guess."

She didn't want to carry that anger anymore; it took more work to sustain than she was interested in putting into it. Her life felt too full for any more ill will toward him. They sat together in comfortable silence, watching the party unfold.

"Don't do this to anyone else," Indira said, eyes landing on Lauren across the room as she braided the flower girl's hair. "Don't hurt someone by cheating on them ever again. It's not fair. It's not right."

Chris nodded, gaze dropping to his lap. "I promise."

Indira let the silence sit for a beat before clearing her throat and changing her tone. "Lauren looks really nice tonight. She's way out of your league."

Chris laughed, looking across the room. His lips twitched up at the corners. "I agree."

"You seem different with Jude," Chris said after a moment, nodding at the person in question as he reentered the barn at the opposite end, scanning the scene.

"What do you mean?" Indira asked, her gaze fixed on Jude's handsome face, the sharp lines of his suit creating a devastating effect.

Jude's eyes finally landed on Indira, and he smiled, starting toward her. She almost laughed when Jude noticed Chris sitting next to her, his brow furrowing and pace doubling.

Chris shrugged, taking a sip of his drink. "When you look at him . . . there's just sort of, I don't know, a spark in you. You look at him like he's the most special person in the world, and he looks back at you with the exact same expression. It's . . . uh . . . I'm happy for you."

She glanced at Chris for a moment before her eyes fixed back on Jude. "I'm happy for me too," she said, smile unfettered. "Excuse me."

Indira stood up, walking toward Jude, wanting to kiss that ridiculously cute face and whisper sarcastic comments into his too-big ears. Laugh and hug him and pour all her happiness into him.

Jude looked at her like he wanted to do the exact same thing.

But the feeling of someone watching her pulled her out of her focus, and Indira caught Lauren nervously watching her as she approached.

Oh God. Did the poor woman think Indira was about to charge her? Indira wanted to ignore her, but something poked at her ribs, and before she knew what was happening she was making a beeline to Lauren, who had finished with the flower girl's braids and was now standing alone.

"Hey," Indira said, standing a few feet away.

"Hi," Lauren responded, tucking her hair behind her ears. "You look really nice," she added. "That's a great dress."

"Thanks. It has pockets," Indira said, tucking her hands into the folds of fabric to prove the point.

Lauren nodded in appreciation.

They stood in awkward silence for a moment, gazes flicking around the room.

"Do you hate me?" Lauren blurted out, red blotches staining her cheeks.

Indira blinked. "No, I don't hate you," she said. Lauren wasn't exactly Indira's favorite person in the world, but she also wasn't the one who had cheated on her. "I mean, I can't say I necessarily like you or want to hang out with you and Chris once this wedding is over, but no, I don't hate you."

Lauren nodded, biting down on her lip. "That's fair. I . . . I am sorry, though. For playing a role in everything."

It was Indira's turn to nod. "I'm sorry for not being particularly kind to you at the events leading up to this," she said, gesturing around the room.

They stood there for a moment, letting the dust settle. Indira glanced over her shoulder, seeing Jude hovering nearby, waiting for her.

"I hope, whatever happens," Indira said, dragging her eyes away from Jude, "you end up happy. That's what matters."

Lauren blinked rapidly, lips parting. "You too," she whispered.

Indira nodded at her and walked away.

Walked to Jude, burrowing into his arms for a tight hug.

"Everything okay?" he asked, voice rough and on edge. Indira squeezed him tighter.

"Perfect."

Jude kissed the top of her head, and they swayed together for a few moments to the music around them.

"Dance with me?" he asked, pulling back and arching an eyebrow.

Indira glanced at the crowded dance floor, lips pursing. "Really?" she asked. "It looks a bit packed even for me."

Jude smiled, leaning forward to press his forehead against hers. "Come with me."

Braiding his fingers through hers, he led her out a side door.

The cool November night hit Indira instantly, sending a sparkly rush through her as her breath pushed out in a white puff. Jude let go of her hand, taking off his suit jacket and draping it over her shoulders. He tucked it around her, then moved his hand to her chin, tilting her face up and brushing his thumb across her bottom lip. Indira's eyes closed at the ripple of sensation that traveled through her.

Jude's lips came next—gentle, adoring, a hint of hunger—the heat of the kiss spearing straight through to her chest.

One hand moved to her waist, the other to the back of her head, twining in her hair and taking the kiss deeper. The tinkle of music drifted around them on the cool night, humming into their bones as they swayed together under the inky-black sky.

"You're a shockingly good dancer," Indira said against Jude's lips. A laugh rumbled in his chest, and Indira pressed closer to the sound, feeling the vibration in her own.

"I think the kissing distracts you from my two left feet," he whispered back.

"Whatever it is, I don't want you to stop," she said, looking up at him.

His eyes were deep pools of emotion, creased at the corners with a smile as he looked at her. "Like I could deny you anything," he said.

Then he kissed her again, holding her close as they danced under the moonlight.

CHAPTER 32

Indira

∞

"The only thing that still bothers me," Indira said a few hours later back in their small cabin on the outskirts of the property, staring up at the ceiling, arms clasped behind her head, "is the astronomical cleanup that amount of peanut butter would require. Is there really any type of sexual gratification that would be worth that mess? Think about how hard it is to lick a spoonful of peanut butter, then add in some skin and pubes?" She did a full-body shiver.

Jude turned his head to look at her, brow furrowed like he was deep in thought. Then a smile cracked along his stern mouth, a loud laugh escaping.

"You're so weird," Jude said, pulling her close. "I love you."

They giggled together for a moment.

"What did your mom have to say about us?" he asked, wrapping one of her corkscrew curls around his finger while trying to sound casual. Indira caught the adorable twinge of trepidation in his voice and she smiled.

"She was wondering if I'd been the victim of any curses or recruited into any cults recently. Pretty standard reaction, I'd say."

Jude tickled her side, making her squeal. "I'm serious!" he said, pressing closer to her.

"She's happy I'm happy," Indira said, turning to face him, wrapping an arm and a leg over his body and nuzzling into his neck. "Shocked. But happy."

Jude laughed, a soft puff of amusement dancing over her cheek. "Well, for lack of better phrasing, that makes me happy."

"Never pegged you as a poet, little love gremlin."

He let out a forlorn sigh. "Really think it's time for you to give up on the pet names."

"You didn't like that one, my pantie pirate?"

"How do they keep getting worse?" he whined, pressing his lips to her hair.

They held each other for a while, the quietness of their little space wrapping like a blanket around them. Indira was content—overwhelmingly comfortable—but a small, sharp prick of fear wormed between her ribs and up her throat.

"What happens when you go back?" she whispered.

Jude's entire body went rigid like she'd electrocuted him, his breath locking in his throat. Indira reached out her hand, cupping the angle of his jaw. All the air whooshed from his lungs, his shoulders curling as he melted into her touch.

As Indira's eyes traced over the sadness in his—all those shadows and lines that sharpened his features—she wondered what a heart looked like when it broke.

Was it a slow, subtle fissure that separated the chambers, cutting off blood and oxygen? Or a shattering? An explosion of a million shards embedding into the surrounding tissue and bone?

Based on the pain in Indira's chest, she decided it was a combination of both.

"Jude?"

"I'll go back," Jude said softly, his voice dancing on a razor's edge. "I'll finish my thirteen months. I'll write and call and video-chat you every fucking chance I get, if you'll let me. And then I'll come home."

Indira swallowed, picturing that bleak reality, the invisible weight of it pressing down on them.

"And I'll do whatever it takes to be with you. I don't feel right asking you to wait for me. But I hope . . . I hope you'll have me when I come back."

Hot tears started rolling down Indira's cheeks, over the tip of her nose and plunking onto the bed.

"Silly man," she said, pressing her forehead to his. "I'm yours whether you're here or somewhere across the globe. That was never my question."

"Then what was?" Jude's voice cracked as his shoulders sagged in relief, moving closer to her still.

"What happens to *you*, Jude? How can you keep doing this? Put yourself back in a situation that hurts you so badly?"

Jude swallowed, scratching his thumb across his forehead. "It'll be fine, Dira," he said, voice shaky. "It's one more year. Then I'll come home and I'll . . ."

"You'll what? Have an even heavier weight on your shoulders? More pain and trauma?"

"I don't want to have this conversation," Jude said, sitting up on the edge of the bed, facing away from her.

Indira watched him, eyes tracing over the stiff muscles of his back, the sharp jabs of his inhales and exhales.

"There's nothing I can do," he said, voice flat. Foreign. Indira hated how detached it was. "I made a commitment. I signed the paperwork. And none of this was some altruistic selflessness. I'm coming out ahead, without any debt. I owe GHCO one more year. And then I'm free."

Will you be, though? Indira wanted to ask. Wanted to scream at him. Was there any real freedom with all the trauma he internalized?

"But I can't—I fucking *can't*—sit here and waste the time we have left together thinking about all of that. I want to absorb every second with you."

He turned around, eyes flashing with hurt and heat and hunger. He reached out, pulling Indira onto his lap, holding her closely. She wrapped her arms around his neck, wishing she could dissolve into him.

"You're so damn precious to me, Dira," he whispered, brushing his lips along her skin before pressing a kiss to her pounding pulse at the base of her throat. "I love holding you. I don't ever want to let you go."

Indira raked her hands through his hair, tenderness shimmering from the center of her chest out through her fingertips.

"For tonight, at least," she whispered into the shell of his ear, feeling the shiver run through him, "you don't have to."

Indira's kiss ghosted across his cheek, down his jaw, hovering so close over his mouth she could feel the heat of him on her lips. She held there, drawing out every sweet, sharp moment of wanting. Of longing.

Anticipation swelled deep in her belly, blooming into something wild and beautiful.

Their chests crashed together with their labored breaths, and Indira wasn't sure how much longer she could hold back, could keep herself from claiming his mouth. Feeling his body.

Finally—*finally*—Jude closed the distance. The movement was slow, intentional, sipping at her lips and shocking every nerve ending until her heart jumped in her chest.

Then he pressed his teeth into her lip, biting lightly, pulling a gasp, then a moan from her throat as he kissed her like a drowning man finding air.

Indira moved, pushing Jude against the bed, while she straddled over him, kissing him with everything she had. His soft and fractured grunts of satisfaction filled her blood with an effervescent fizz.

"I'll never get over the feel of kissing you," Jude said, grabbing the hem of Indira's T-shirt and ripping it over her head, letting no more than half a second pass between kisses.

She was glad they'd changed out of their wedding attire and into comfier clothes as soon as they got back; it made the rest of getting undressed much more efficient.

Jude flipped their positions, hovering over Indira, his legs tangling with hers. Indira dragged the arch of her foot over his calf, loving the feel of his rough leg hair against her.

"Look at you," Jude said, palm splayed over her heart. He dragged his hand down, cupping her breast, rolling his thumb over her nipple, before following the path to her stomach, then her hip. Jude toyed with her, dragging the backs of his fingers up and down her inner thighs. Indira sucked in a breath, trying to press closer into his touch. He looked up at her, eyes pitch black and filled with molten heat. "I've never seen anything so beautiful."

Indira groaned, head falling against the mattress. It felt like a fever was building under her skin, threatening to burn her alive.

"Let me kiss you here?" Jude dipped a finger into her. "*Fuck*, you're wet," he murmured, dragging his other hand against his mouth, then pressing his knuckles against his teeth.

Indira pressed up onto her elbows. "I want to taste *you*," she said, reaching greedy hands for his hot and hard length. "Can I?"

His hips bucked as she dragged her thumb over the head, then stroked down. Her mouth watered, want coursing through her as she imagined him coming undone.

Color was high on Jude's cheeks, his eyes wide and breaths sharp as he nodded rapidly.

"No objections here," he choked out as she stroked him again with the amount of pressure she knew he loved.

"That's a first," she said. Their eyes locked. And, like a pair of lovestruck fools, they giggled.

Indira pushed Jude down, dragging her open mouth along his torso, tasting and licking and biting him until she had him panting and fisting his hand in her hair, guiding her head. She resisted for a moment, dragging her teeth over his hip bone and fondling below.

"I can't—I can't—"

"Can't what, baby?" Indira said, looking up at him with wide, innocent eyes before licking the length of him and taking him in her mouth.

"Get enough of you," Jude breathed out, head falling back as Indira sucked him deeper. She hummed, loving the taste of him, the closeness. She couldn't keep her eyes off his face, lips parted, body open to her. Trusting her so thoroughly. So completely.

"You're so good," he whispered, voice hoarse and fracturing as she moved up and down his length. "So perfect." His hand, still knotted in her hair, started moving faster.

Indira pulled back for a moment, focusing on the tip, reveling in his grunts.

"Wait. Wait. I'm not ready yet," Jude said, shifting back a bit and pulling from Indira's attention. She pouted at him.

"Come here," he said, gripping her hips and pulling her up his body. Indira was pliant, drunk on the pleasure coursing through her blood. "Like this," he instructed, turning her until she hovered over his mouth, facing his legs.

It took her a moment in her haze, but Indira caught on quickly, looking over her shoulder to give him a decadently wicked smile.

"Okay?" he asked, gripping her ass, spreading her for him.

Indira let out a choked *yes*, back arching and hands fisting in the comforter as he lifted his head, tasting her desire. Indira leaned forward, dragging her tongue over him again, swirling at the tip before sucking him deep.

"Fuck," he growled, pulling his head back and pushing two fingers into her. "Perfect and tight and absolutely soaked, just from sucking my cock. You're so good, Indira."

She gasped around him as Jude curled his fingers in her, the noise so whiny and needy and desperate that his dick hardened further in her mouth.

"Yeah?" he asked, pressing at the spot again.

She replaced her mouth with her hands, stroking him. "Yes. Yes. *Please*," she said, jaw clenched and body coiled tight with need.

"I love it when you say please," Jude whispered against her before moving his mouth to her clit, flicking his tongue over her.

They found their rhythm, sucking and loving and fucking each other until they were both shaking.

"Just like that," Jude grunted as Indira moved her hips over his mouth and chin, her own lips wet and stretched around his length. "It's so good. Don't stop."

She didn't. Couldn't. His words and his touch and his taste and his building pleasure, it all pushed Indira into a fever pitch of need. Her orgasm hit her hard. Fast. Electric desire zapping from her scalp down to her toes.

She cried out, trying to keep pleasuring Jude with her hand, but she was beyond coordinated movement.

"That's it," Jude said as her body bucked with the shock waves. "So perfect."

Indira's arms gave out, and she collapsed down, rolling to her side and letting out a giggle at the sparkling rush through her body.

"I think about the taste of you on my tongue all day. Dream about it," Jude said, shifting until he was lying next to her.

Another helpless giggle escaped her, and she grabbed Jude, rolling them so he was on top of her. "I want more," she said, reaching up to kiss him, tasting herself on his mouth.

Jude's eyes bordered on frantic, his movements almost clumsy as he did as she asked, pressing her knees apart and dragging the head of his cock along her wetness for a moment before pushing all the way in, making them both cry out.

Hips working in a fast rhythm, Jude kissed Indira's breasts, sucking on her until she arched into him and groaned.

"Your greedy little moans drive me so wild I can't think straight," he said, his voice so low and rough, Indira almost didn't hear him. She never wanted to miss a word out of that wicked mouth.

Indira cried out in satisfaction when Jude found that spot deep inside her that flashed stars across her vision, a hot and wicked type of pleasure zipping up and down her spine, pooling low in her belly, curling her toes, pressing against every muscle and joint until she thought she might shatter from it.

She watched where Jude moved in and out of her, the rough grip of his hands on her hips, moving her body in counterpoint to his every thrust. The frantic rise and fall of his chest matched her own, a jagged rhythm as they fought for every breath, chased the pleasure that felt too raw, too consuming to be real. When her eyes finally made it to his face, he was staring right at her, pupils blown, teeth gritted.

"I love you so fucking much," he growled, thrusting into her, deep and hard, then holding there, grinding against her, the pad of his thumb moving to her clit.

Indira's head pressed into the pillow, spine arching and neck muscles taut as a sharp spark of pleasure lit her nerves on fire. She couldn't take it. Couldn't survive it. It was too good, she thought she'd die from it.

"Look at me," Jude commanded, giving her a spank that caused all the air to leave her lungs at the exquisite decadence of it—the sharp bite mixing with the pleasure, pumping her blood to a fever pitch. "Look at me when you come, Indira. I want to see every feeling in those eyes."

"Harder," she begged, as Jude started moving his hips again, the sound of their skin slapping together punctuating every thrust.

"Yes," he gritted out, one hand hooking under her knee, draping her leg over his shoulder, the other moving to her breast, plumping it as he bent his head to bite her nipple.

Indira screamed, thrusting her hands in his hair, pulling at the strands, then dragging her nails down his neck. His back. Marking him.

She wanted him to mark her right back.

Indira felt Jude pulse in her, pressing his face into her neck with a hoarse groan as he held her as close as he could in those final moments.

The silence that followed was beautiful in its softness. The comfort of it.

Jude rolled them to their sides, bodies still connected.

Dragging one hand through the mass of her sweaty hair, he kissed the tip of her nose. Her eyebrow. Her chin.

He kissed her until his breathing was so soft, so gentle and languid, he fell asleep in her arms.

Indira wasn't surprised at the tears that rolled down her cheeks as she held the man she loved.

She was terrified of what came next. Of losing him. Of Jude not making it back to her.

But the future wasn't here. It wasn't now. Jude was with her. His skin was slick against hers, breath warming her cheek, scent enveloping her.

She didn't want to think about the goodbye. About losing him—not the distance, but the pain that would seep back into his bones. The walls he would reconstruct.

So, she held him tighter, and fell asleep too.

CHAPTER 33

Jude

Jude was doing great.

So, *so* great.

Except for the moments he was doing terribly.

Like, right now, for example.

"When the armed suspects are detained, the med team will move into location," Dr. Huang, the lead coordinator of GHCO's emergency response team, said. He pointed to the map of the organization's campus, a central building marked with a star as he continued to direct the group on the latest active shooter protocols for when GHCO providers were on location.

"We'll use the dining hall to set up a medical triage. There will be simulated patients with various injuries at the site waiting for treatment. Make sense?"

The various medical team members in the briefing nodded. Jude was a few seconds behind in his response, his neck stiff and brain clouded as he remembered two separate occasions where he'd had to put this training to use. His stomach twisted so tightly he couldn't suck down a breath.

He was a week out from leaving for his next assignment—the

location still being determined by higher-ups—and each hour that ticked by squirted a fresh dose of adrenaline over his fried nerves.

Where medicine once was his greatest thrill, his guiding purpose, now he wanted to run in the opposite direction of his calling. Sprint from it until he outpaced all the memories that haunted him.

But he couldn't do that. The next thirteen months were inevitable, unavoidable. Jude would do well to remember that and suck it up. Numb himself out.

He hoisted his emergency bag over his shoulder, following the line of his coworkers out of the clinic to wait on the lawn near the dining hall.

And that's when the alarms started blaring.

The noise was shrill and repetitive and punched haunting memories of his worst days straight to the front of Jude's mind—weeks turning into months in a war-torn city, random explosions and blasts, displaced people and the constant, devastating need that extended beyond anything Jude's hands were capable of.

His vision tunneled and knees buckled, jolting him off balance and into the medic in front of him, creating a domino effect.

Dr. Huang turned, frowning at Jude. "Focus up, Dr. Bailey."

Jude could only stare at Dr. Huang, images of patients' final moments creeping in at the edges. The alarms continued screeching, and people began toting injured mannequins out of the dining hall and setting them on the grass a few yards away.

The raw fear must have shown on Jude's face, because Dr. Huang looked around, his own body tensing.

"Easy, Bailey. It's just a drill," he said, turning back to Jude with a look of stern confusion. Jude couldn't speak, but he managed to nod.

Huang stared at him for a beat longer before shaking his head, moving into action with the rest of the team.

Just a drill. Just a drill, Jude repeated to himself, the sentiment lost under the piercing sirens both around the base and through Jude's nervous system, his brain jolting and muscles locking.

People funneled around him, feet and legs moving in coordinated sync as they ebbed and flowed to the dining hall. Commands were spoken, hand gestures given, all of it tunneling in and out of Jude's spotty vision. Adrenaline pumped through him, pooling in his palms, pressing at his knees and hips. Wanting him to move. God, he wished he could.

Simulated gunshots echoed around them, each sound wave going straight to his spine, ricocheting up and down every nerve ending.

Just a drill. Just a drill. Just a drill, he tried again.

It didn't do any good.

Nurses and doctors darted from injured mannequin to injured mannequin, orders crackling over their radios, fake blood and wounds obvious on the dummies from where Jude stood.

Jude knew this was his cue. His directive to move in and set up a medical triage. Tend to the wounds of those who needed him the most. But when he tried to take a step, his knees buckled again under the weight of the memories. He no longer felt the sharp chill of the November day. Couldn't hear the periodic automated voice over the loudspeakers announcing the drill was in progress.

Jude stood alone on his spot of frozen grass, the world around him morphing and bending until he was torn between reality and haunting memories.

He remembered overfilled clinics amid an epidemic. Devastation after a natural disaster. The fear that radiated out of a war-torn town.

He could feel the waves of heat pressing on his back as he moved from body to body. Hear the raw panic as everyone scrambled in the chaos. And the smell. God, he could still smell the mix of blood and smoke and desperation.

Jude finally got his legs to work in the real world, but instead of moving forward to perform his duty, he turned, sprinting back toward the office building.

He collapsed inside, chest heaving and head swimming as he tried to find peace, calm, in the sensory nightmare unfolding around him. Everything felt like a Rorschach test, a meaningless blot of ink his brain latched onto and twisted into horrible memories. Jude was helpless to do anything but succumb to the distress. All the pain, all the violence he'd been witness to felt like tiny rips of his soul, all culminating in its total disfigurement.

He was a failure. A complete and utter failure that couldn't do the one thing he was supposed to be an expert in: helping people. Saving them.

How was he supposed to do that?

He couldn't even save himself.

CHAPTER 34

Jude

∞

Jude had no memories of driving away from GHCO headquarters. He didn't register stoplights or other cars or merging lanes. He didn't realize that he drove around and around Philadelphia for hours until he was parked out front of Indira's building, the dark night settled coolly around him.

He glanced at his phone, multiple texts and missed calls from Indira lighting up the screen. Jude blew out a long breath through his nose and pressed the back of his skull into the headrest.

A new notification buzzed through, and Jude glanced at the screen.

New Email
Subject: URGENT Assignment decision and travel details

Jude closed his eyes, gripping his phone in his fist. He couldn't open that email. Couldn't see the next glimpse of his dark future, the strands of his life slipping through his fingers.

How was he supposed to go inside? How was he supposed to go to Indira, broken and hopeless and know where their upcoming goodbye would take him?

He managed to unfurl his stiff limbs from the car, locking it behind him and letting himself into her building.

Jude stood in front of Indira's door, the gentle hum of her voice audible through the wood. Numbness ebbed through him, spreading like ink in water. Numbness was good. Jude had become too comfortable feeling anything besides numbness. Numbness was the only way he could stay whole.

He let himself into her place.

Indira was pacing around the living room, cell phone plastered to her ear, Grammy watching her trek from the arm of the couch.

Indira whipped around at the sound of Jude shutting the door.

"Fuck, you scared me," she said, her eyes red. Then, into her phone, "He just walked in, Collin." Pause. "Yeah. I'll keep you posted."

She ended the call.

Silence thumped around them, but Indira didn't let it linger.

"Where the hell were you?" she said, voice angry. But she still crossed the space between them, pulling Jude into a tight hug. Jude couldn't bring himself to hug her back.

"You had me worried sick," she said into his chest. "It's eleven. Why didn't you call? Did you go out with friends?"

Jude shook his head, slipping out of her grip and slinking to the kitchen. He opened the fridge, staring into the harsh white light as the cooled air hit his cheeks.

"Jude. Talk to me, dammit," Indira said over his shoulder.

He sighed, grabbing a bottle of water and turning to face her.

Jude looked at Indira, unable to school his features or straighten his spine. His limbs were almost as heavy as his heart as he stood there, staring at the woman he loved, feeling an ocean of distance growing between them.

"What happened?" Indira said, two tears rolling down her cheeks. "You're scaring me."

That rattled Jude enough for him to blink. "I'm sorry," he said, his voice rough and harsh. "I . . . I had a hard day. Lost track of time."

Silence lingered as Indira studied him, those eyes boring into him.

"I got my next assignment," Jude said, a dull cadence to his voice as he tried to say the words without feeling them.

Indira was still, terrifyingly still, eyes wide and face drawn taut.

"You can't keep doing this." Her voice was a whisper.

Jude wished she'd yelled it. Maybe then it wouldn't hurt as much.

"Doing what?" he asked, being purposefully obtuse. With shaky hands, he opened the water bottle, taking a tiny sip that was hard to get down.

"Forcing yourself to do the thing that's slowly killing you." Indira stepped forward, jaw set as she looked at him.

"That's so dramatic." Jude turned his head away. "It's not killing me."

"It *is*, Jude," Indira snapped, her voice cracking like a whip through the room, her face crumpling with tears rolling down her cheeks. "It's killing you and I'm sitting here watching it. When you get stuck in those dark, terrifying places, that isn't you. That's a tormented version of you that has to endure for even longer."

"No . . . I . . . No." Maybe if Jude denied it for long enough, it would stop it from being true.

"Don't lie to me. Don't lie to yourself."

"What do you want from me?" Jude said, stepping away from her, slamming the bottle on the counter.

"I want you to stay," Indira cried. "I want you to find a therapist. I want you to have a stable home. With me. I want us to work together to actually build something that can last."

"Oh. Sure. Fuck all my obligations then, right?"

"Yes. Fuck your obligations. Fuck your scholarship. Fuck it all." She stepped toward him again. "You're so dead set on perpetuating this cycle of self-harm out of guilt that you aren't even willing to fight for other options."

"Because there aren't other options!" He flung his hands out at his sides. "Not for me. It's a contract, this legally binding fucking agreement. I don't even know where I would start to get out of it. And I . . ." Jude's throat locked up, a choked gasp escaping him.

"You what?" Indira said, voice soft.

Jude closed his eyes, shaking his head like he could empty it of the memories. That would never happen.

"I've watched too many people suffer," Jude said, voice low. "Too many people die on my table for me to take some easy way out."

Indira was silent for a moment before clearing her throat.

"Living—fully, unabashedly, fearlessly living—isn't the easy way out, Jude," she said. "It's the hardest thing you'll ever fucking do. Numbing yourself is the easy part. Hiding in self-loathing is the escape. You want to make those losses worth it? Then fucking choose yourself, Jude. Choose us. Choose your health. It's okay to let go of something that's hurting you. That won't ever change the love you had for it. If anything, it will let you preserve that love. But you can move away from something that doesn't serve you. That doesn't make you weak, that makes you brave."

Jude rested his hands on the counter, his head hanging as he tried to catch his breath.

"We're on the same team here," Indira whispered. "We can work through this together. We have to." She placed her hand on his back, and Jude flinched away.

"Stop. Just fucking stop. You're making this so much harder. This isn't some puzzle for you to solve. I'm not some patient for you to fix, Indira."

The usual transparency in Indira's eyes shuttered closed as his words hit her. She dropped her gaze to look at the floor, and Jude could almost hear the thoughts whirring through her mind.

"You're right," she said after what felt like an eternity. Her eyes flicked back to Jude's, but the vulnerability was back in them. With a fresh look of determination that scared him shitless.

"You aren't my patient. You aren't a diagnosis. You aren't a case file. You're the person I love. You're the person I would do anything for. I'm not here to fix you, Jude. I'm not. And I never was. No one can single-handedly fix another person. We all hurtle through life, getting bumped and cracked and broken along the way, but we are solely responsible for our own healing."

Her voice fractured, eyes red-rimmed as she stared at him.

"And it's work," she said through gritted teeth. "It's fucking hard. I will never know what it was like for you to see the things you did, experience the trauma you did, and I can never take that experience away from you."

Indira took another tentative step toward him, gently taking his hand and holding it to her chest.

"But I do know what it's like to feel broken and unlovable," she said, tears falling down her cheeks. "I know what it feels like to think you're unworthy of someone's care and support, that you don't deserve to lean on others while you get your shit together. But I also know it's possible to change that thought process. We tell ourselves lies over and over again, the brain this fickle organ that sometimes likes to hurt us. But just because we tell ourselves something, doesn't make it true. I'm not here to change you or heal you."

She took a shaky breath, ducking her head to press a kiss to his knuckles. "I'm here to support you. To love you. Every step of the way. Let me help you. Let's figure a way out of this."

Jude pulled his hand away, the world collapsing around him. He couldn't think. Couldn't breathe.

He felt so overwhelmingly hopeless and lost and broken, he was surprised he was still standing upright.

And Indira. His Indira. Seeing the tears streak down her cheeks felt like someone had lodged a hook deep into his chest and pulled until his bones cracked. He did that to her. Him and his shitty choices and his inability to cope.

He couldn't stay and keep hurting her.

"I need to leave," Jude said gruffly, moving to the door in quick strides.

"Jude."

The sound of his name on Indira's lips always seemed to stop the earth from spinning, changing its entire axis with her cadence.

He looked at her over his shoulder, hand poised on the doorknob.

Tears still marked her face, but her shoulders were squared, chin set. "Get the air you need. But when you come back, we go forward together."

Jude swallowed, turning his face away in shame and anger and sadness.

Holding back a sob that threatened to crumble his body to dust, he ripped open the door and left the apartment.

Out on the street, he started to walk, Indira's words looping around and around his skull. *When you come back, we go forward together.*

Maybe he shouldn't go back. Maybe he should walk and walk and walk until his feet were bloody and his body broken. Leave Indira to be happy and loved and free of his complications. He wanted her future to be as bright and warm and wonderful as she was.

The problem was, the past three years had robbed Jude of the ability to imagine a better life for himself, a future that wasn't as fractured as the people he lost. If those people couldn't have a happy future, why should he?

Jude had an ocean of guilt that it felt like he'd drown in.

He cut into a small, dark park, resting one hand on the rough bark of a tree. He concentrated on the texture beneath his palm, pressing his skin harder into it as he tried to catch his breath.

But pressure built in his throat and behind his eyes and his heart thrummed. And then he was crying.

Sobbing in anger. Fear. Devastation. Pain. He slid to the ground, pressing his back into the trunk of the tree as he continued to cry in the cold darkness. He cried until his eyes were swollen and his throat raw. He cried until he couldn't cry anymore.

As the stillness of the fall night gently stopped the out-of-control spinning of his mind, he sucked in a deep breath. Jude pulled out his phone, Indira's smiling face lighting up his screen. He unlocked it, going to his pictures. Indira liked to steal his phone and take hundreds of photos, catching Jude off guard while she fixed her features into a goofy look—her face smooshed against his while he was falling asleep, the flash catching his sleepy features. A surprise selfie when he sat on the couch, brow furrowed as he tried to find something for them to watch, Indira crossing one eye and sticking out her tongue.

So many moments of her smiling face, her giant hair, those gorgeous eyes.

With Jude right there with her.

He didn't have to imagine a better future, because he was actively experiencing the best he could have ever wanted. He was with a woman he loved, adored, cherished beyond measure. And, by some cosmic magical blessing, she loved him too. Ferociously.

His future was here.

Now.

He'd forgotten that happiness wasn't a banging, violent emotion like all the others that bombarded him every moment. Happiness was soft. Uneventful. It was holding Indira's hand. Sitting next to her on the couch and listening to her talk. It was a quiet cup of coffee with her next to him reading a magazine. It was teasing her, being goofy and pretending to pass out after sniffing her feet, making her shriek in outrage and giggle. Happiness was them.

And he was not about to forsake any of that for a lie his brain kept telling him. Indira deserved better. *Jude* deserved better.

He pushed to his feet, pocketing his phone and taking off in a sprint back to her place. He couldn't waste another second.

When he got to her door, he worked to catch his breath before rifling through his key ring and finding the spare Indira had given him. Inside, he stripped off his jacket, listening for any sounds of Indira still being up. All was quiet.

"Jude?"

He wondered if the sound of her voice would ever stop vibrating happiness through his chest like the plucking of a harp string.

Jude walked toward the sound, then stood in the doorway of her bedroom looking at Indira. His heart turned itself inside out just at the sight of her. She held his gaze for a weighted moment, a sadness still lining her eyes. Then her face morphed into a smile. It wasn't a smile of radiant, unabashed happiness, but one of soft hope. An invitation for Jude to hope too.

In a flash, she ducked under the covers and huddled beneath them until she looked like a little burrito lump on the bed.

Even though she couldn't see it, Jude smiled too. He knew this gesture like a siren's call and he was useless to resist. He toed off his shoes and shucked off his pants, then walked over and burrowed himself under the covers with her.

This had become their safe space, their perfect nest to talk and cry and laugh and kiss. They'd spent late nights and lazy mornings tucked beneath those covers as they discussed fears and bridged intimacy. If heaven existed on earth, it was in a blanket fort with Indira Papadakis.

They squirmed closer under the white comforter, almost nose to nose as their world turned warm and soft and amber. In their little cocoon, anything felt possible.

"I'm not going anywhere," she said, reaching out and dragging her finger down the bridge of his nose. Tracing his lips. "It's you, Jude. You and me. We'll get through this."

"I'm scared I don't deserve release from these feelings," he whispered. "I don't deserve absolution or a clear conscience." Words started tumbling out of him, fast and raw and escaping from his throat like it was their last chance to be heard.

"When I drop my guard," Jude said, "even for a moment, I feel so much that it's like a knife slicing through my chest, splitting me in two. It hurts so badly it seems impossible sometimes. I don't understand these feelings. This body. How can I hurt, how can I do awful things, but still feel so much love for you? How can I want forgiveness for the things I've done, when they can't be reversed? It feels selfish."

"It's not selfish, Jude," Indira said, pulling back to look at him, forcing his eyes to meet hers. "You want that because you deserve that. Trauma and happy endings aren't mutually exclusive. They aren't even separate entities that have to be experienced at different seasons of life. You can hurt. You can struggle and suffer and learn to heal while doing it. You can stare into the face of your pain and also choose to love. That's how I love you and I know you love me too. I want you to feel, Jude. Feel everything and do it with abandon. Because no matter what you feel, what rises up from all of that, you will always have a safe space in my heart. I will always, *always* be here, loving you through it all."

"What if I don't deserve that?"

"Everyone deserves that," Indira said simply. "That's what makes love so beautiful. We don't have to be perfect. I know I can fall apart with you, I can thrash and struggle and slog through my demons and your arms will always hold me. Let me be that for you too."

Jude continued to stare at her for a moment before closing his eyes and nodding. He felt Indira press her lips softly against his forehead.

"What comes next?" he asked, not fearing the answer as much as he expected to.

Indira bit her lip, eyes roaming across his features. "I think the most important thing is you find help. Someone to talk to. A psychologist. Maybe even group therapy. Being around people who *know* what it's like. Have experienced situations similar to yours. It could be really validating to share in that kind of space. Help you learn to love yourself like you deserve."

Jude's body jolted like she'd electrocuted him.

Is that . . . is that what he needed? The idea felt almost lewd. Gratuitous. Something he didn't deserve.

And Indira, never missing a thought that flicked through Jude's brain, seemed to read the sentiment on his features. She traced her thumb over his cheek as she looked at him.

"Loving yourself isn't a sin, Jude. Giving yourself love won't diminish the love and caring you give to others. In fact, it's one of the best things you can do for the people in your life."

"How?"

She smiled at him. "When you love yourself, you commit to knowing yourself," Indira said, moving her hands to play with his hair. "And when you know yourself, you also know your needs. Space. Attention. Help. Tenderness. Being able to acknowledge these needs in yourself lets you voice them to others and also understand more fully when others voice their needs to you. It allows you to experience your emotions more fully. Be more present in each one with the people you love."

For some reason, her words felt like a punch to the throat, a strong surge of emotion threatening to smash him to pieces. He felt vulnerable. Overwhelmed. He felt . . . Well, wasn't that what Indira was already telling him? To fully feel. To share that with her.

"I want that," he said, dragging his hand through her hair, curls twisting between his fingers. "I want that with you."

"Then that's what we'll do," she said with firm, lovely determination.

And Jude believed her. Indira would never lie to him. Sharply honest, terrifyingly hopeful. If Indira said something was true, Jude would believe her. He'd do everything in his power to make it so.

CHAPTER 35

Jude

∞

For a man who had spent most of his life convincing himself and others he was infallible, it was only moderately earth-shattering for Jude to admit he couldn't do what was being asked of him. He'd always been quick to flex his skills, his capabilities, signing up for extra rotations in med school, taking on extra shifts during residency, doing all of it without breaking a sweat.

Admitting something was outside of his capabilities still had a bitter taste of shame burning his tongue, but Jude was learning to swallow past it.

After a series of emails, Jude finally secured a meeting with his direct supervisor and assignment coordinator, Dr. Nora Prince.

He sat outside her office, knee bouncing in time with her assistant's ceaseless typing as a nervous pang squeezed his heart and prickled up to his shoulder, shooting down to the tips of his fingers.

Fuck. Feeling things was hard.

"Hi, Jude?" Dr. Prince said, opening her office door at last.

"Hi. Yes. Hi," Jude babbled out, fumbling with the button of his suit coat as he stood and moved toward her. "Thank you for taking the time to meet with me so soon."

"Of course," she said, ushering him into her office and taking a seat behind a large mahogany desk. "But, in all honesty, the tone of your emails didn't leave me much choice. They seemed increasingly distressed about your upcoming assignment."

Jude's cheeks heated a little but he nodded. It was true. He was desperate and distressed and spent most of the night pacing his room in worry about the ticking clock.

"I think that's a fair assessment," Jude said, voice tight.

"Is there an issue with your travel arrangements?" Dr. Prince asked, glancing at her computer as it dinged with a notification.

"No. Not exactly. It's—"

"Accommodations, then? I know there's a level of uncertainty on housing at your new spot, but I assure you we'll get it ironed out before you land or at least within a few days of arrival. You know how things go." She started typing something, eyes firmly fixed on the computer screen now.

Jude let out a humorless laugh. "I certainly do."

"And I hope this doesn't come off as rude, but there are other people that are better points of contact than myself when it comes to issues of this type. But you've been with GHCO long enough to know that many aspects of assignments are beyond our control. Sort of occupational hazards, if you will."

Jude blinked rapidly. She was talking so fast, he couldn't keep up with her, couldn't get his fuzzy brain and thick tongue to push out all the things he wanted to say.

"In fact, let me give you the coordinating associate's name. He should be able to help you with—"

"I'm sick," Jude blurted out, his voice a bit too loud. A bit too rough. It did at least get Dr. Prince to look at him.

"I'm sorry?" she said, head tilting and eyebrows furrowed.

Jude closed his eyes for a moment, sucking in a rattling breath that didn't do much to calm his racing heart. He looked at her again.

"I am mentally very ill," he admitted, saying the words slowly, enunciating every syllable. "I am unwell and hurting and I worry that sending me on another assignment would be a massive liability for not only myself, but those I'd be there to treat. I need—" His throat clamped tight, sweat pricking his skin.

He could do this. He could say the words. Admit the truth.

"I need help."

CHAPTER 36

Jude

Jude had his first therapy session a few days before his official hearing with GHCO's board regarding his future.

"Yay, therapy buds," Indira had said that morning, giving him a high five and a kiss when they realized they had sessions at nearly the same time. He'd felt something close to excitement when he'd talked about it with her earlier.

But now as he sat in the therapist's office, Jude felt more like a bundle of nerves and knots shoved into a human suit than he did an actual person, but if ever there was a time to learn to talk about his feelings . . .

"What are you thinking?" José, Jude's new counselor, asked.

Jude had given a rather thorough overview of the amount of trauma he'd witnessed over the past three years, and had dissolved into a contemplative silence as he relived some of the moments.

He ducked his head, staring at his shoes as he forced out the next words.

"I'm thinking that I'm kind of dumb."

There was a beat. "What makes you say that?" José asked, his voice soft. Genuine.

Jude let out a harsh, humorless laugh. "I truly believed I wouldn't feel any different going from an operating room at a public hospital here to one in active conflict zones or areas devastated by disasters . . . Isn't that fucking stupid? How was I so fucking stupid?"

Jude paused, finding the courage to glance up. He was genuinely curious for an answer.

José looked at him, letting the silence linger for a few seconds. "I don't think there's anything stupid about that," he said at last. "You were young and facing the reality of enormous student debt. No one wants to be burdened by that for the rest of their lives. And then you were trained for your medical career in a certain environment that offered you a great deal of control. Granted, there's always uncontrollable aspects to surgery, and medicine in general, but your formative training in standard teaching hospitals helped to minimize barriers."

Jude glanced away, leg bouncing.

"Of course being in the field was a shock," José said, leaning forward in his chair. "It's not something you could ever fully prepare for. Even conceptually understanding the kind of trauma you would witness wouldn't have prepared you for the emotional impact of that."

Jude nodded, knotting his hands together in his lap. "There's—I don't know how to explain it—a fundamental difference between cutting open a body to save it, and seeing one opened by a force of war."

There was that silence again. Jude never expected therapy to be composed of so much silence. Jude glanced at José, who gave him a soft nod of encouragement.

"The memories that haunt me the most, the ones I can't get over," Jude continued, the words pulled from the very center of his chest before his mind could even fully process them, "are the people that landed on my table from some sort of human-inflicted cruelty. All that pain and suffering wasn't by chance. Those injuries weren't from a random car accident. An unfortunate but uncontrollable embolism. None of it was some designless cosmic cruelty. It's war. It's humans fighting each other. Hurting each other. And people in nice suits sitting at desks in nice offices in safe cities get to decide when and where to send people to hurt each other, for purposes none of us ever get to know."

Jude didn't understand what was happening to him. These weren't cognizant thoughts he'd had before. They were shadows of doubt and anger that he'd never allowed to fully form in his consciousness. Scared that putting words to the truth would break him entirely.

"And I feel like such a fucking asshole all the time," Jude continued, his voice rough but strong as he dragged his hand through his hair. "Who am I to make it out of those places alive? Why do I get to enjoy food or a comfortable bed or laugh with my girlfriend when I failed so many people on their last day on earth?"

"That's your guilt trying to tie you down," José said after a few moments of silence. "Surviving, like so many other aspects of life, isn't a meritocracy. Someone's good deeds or their bad ones don't determine when or how they die. Your internalized perception of your worth, or lack thereof, doesn't change the fact that you are here. You are now. And you have the choice to do with it what you will."

Sharp tears pricked at Jude's eyes, and he tried to blink them away, sucking in a deep breath.

"I think it's also important to note," José continued, "how a great deal of our perceptions of our experiences and the trauma we've been a part of creates these fantasies of alternative paths our lives could have taken. We preserve worlds of what could have been. Worlds of what-ifs. It's easy to get trapped there. What if I hadn't decided to become a doctor? What if I'd chosen debt over the scholarship? What if I'd been standing there instead of the person I'm now trying to resuscitate?

"These alternative realities can claw at us almost as much as the memories of what really happened. But we have to find those sticking points. Ease our brains away from them. What we have is the present moment. We have our feelings and emotions and the best thing we can do is honor those pieces of ourselves. We can't change our participation in the past, but we can pave the way for a healthier, mindful future."

Jude was properly crying. And it was okay. It hurt—his chest ached and throat burned and every muscle in his body tensed as he sobbed—but it was the type of sharp pain that came with healing.

And that was the best he could do.

Eventually, he collected himself and left the office, confirming his appointment time for the next week. And the one after.

As Jude was walking to Indira's apartment, his phone rang, Collin's name lighting up the screen with a FaceTime call. Jude smiled as he answered.

"Hello?"

"Greetings from Costa Rica!" Collin cheered, holding up a giant frozen drink, his smile and the ocean behind him sparkling in the sun.

"Wow, weather looks awful," Jude deadpanned. "Bet you wish you were home." He flipped the screen for a moment, showing off the bleak gray darkness of November in Philadelphia.

"Yeah, this much sunshine is certainly hard to stomach," Collin said before taking a giant gulp of his drink.

Jude laughed. "Are you having fun?"

"Oh my god, we're having the best time," Collin said, facing lighting up. "We went hiking today and swam in this lagoon waterfall thing. And the food, dude. I can't stop stuffing my face. This is heaven on earth."

Jude's heart swelled at the happiness in his best friend's voice.

"I can't talk for long," Collin said, taking another sip. "But I just wanted to check in with you. I know tomorrow is a big day."

Jude bit back a sigh, nodding. He hadn't wanted to burden Collin with everything going on—shocking absolutely no one, requesting discharge from a program that had invested over half a million dollars in him and relied on his work to function meant a fuckton of paperwork and a plethora of invasive interviews to determine the "validity" of Jude's claim—but Indira had encouraged him to be honest with his friend.

"I'm nervous," Jude admitted, gaze darting up the street before he crossed an intersection. "But I'm ready to get tomorrow over with. Rip the Band-Aid off."

"I'm proud of you," Collin said, voice deep with emotion. "And, um, I'm really fucking sorry."

Jude stopped walking, giving his full attention to the call. "For what?"

Collin squinted to the side, biting his lip for a moment. "Jude, I've pretty much massively failed you as a friend."

Jude's frown deepened. "I seriously don't know what you're talking about."

"I should have known." Collin's usually smiling face crumpled, tears threatening to spill from his eyes. "I should have known you were hurting as badly as you were. Done more to help you. Find out what's going on. I knew something was up with you but I brushed it off. Convinced myself you were more or less fine. I—"

"Collin." Jude's voice cracked on his best friend's name as he cut him off. "I want to emphasize something to you: I didn't want you to know. I didn't want you to notice how different I was. I didn't want you to bring it up or push me to talk about it or anything like that. I was hiding the hurt because I was scared of it. Terrified. All I wanted was to seem normal as we celebrated your wedding."

Collin shook his head, dragging a hand down his face. "A real friend would have noticed. I was so caught up in my own stuff. I'm sorry."

Jude wanted to reach through the phone and shake Collin, make him understand.

"Collin, no. You know I don't bullshit people or say things to spare people's feelings—" Collin let out a wet laugh at that horribly accurate description. "And the same goes for you. Hiding what I was going through was some destructive attempt at self-preservation, but it was what I wanted. I will never, ever fault you for being swept up in your wedding. Enjoying it as fully as you did. That's all I ever wanted for you. And Jeremy. The two of you to be ridiculously happy. I didn't want you to see my hurt and have it distract from your wedding."

Collin was quiet for a second, blinking up at the sky. "Indira saw it," Collin said, a tinge of something close to jealousy in his voice. "I'm supposed to know you better than she does."

Jude let out a loud laugh at that. "That's only because the damn woman wouldn't let me hide. She pretty much forced the feelings out of me. You know how hardheaded she is."

Collin laughed too, the sound familiar and comforting. "I'm glad she did," he said after a moment, giving Jude a tiny smile.

It was Jude's turn to blink back tears. He loved her so much it was impossible to think about her without his heart getting so overwhelmed it wanted to burst from his chest. "I am too."

They were quiet for a moment before Jude cleared his throat. "I, uh, I can't tell you how thankful I am to know you."

Collin beamed at him, a few tears rolling down his cheeks as love and tenderness radiated between them.

"Oh fuck, I'm not supposed to cry on my honeymoon," Collin said at last, breaking the tension as he waved a hand in front of his face.

Jude laughed. "No, you're not. So you better get back to Jeremy and all that sunshine and perfect beaches. What a trial for you."

"Truly," Collin said, clearing his throat. They were quiet for another moment. "Love you," Collin said, smiling at Jude.

Jude smiled back. "Love you back."

CHAPTER 37

Jude

∞

"All you can do is be honest," Indira said in bed a few hours later as they talked about the next day's evaluation. She was lying on him with her deadweight, stretching out her arms and legs to match his. The world's loveliest weighted blanket.

"I'm scared honesty won't be enough for them," Jude admitted, sliding his arms out from under hers to wrap them around her waist.

Indira shifted her head, resting her chin on Jude's sternum and looking up at him. "I'm trying to think of something really profound and poignant to say right now to take all your stress away," she said at last, a small smile dancing on her lips. "But none of the metaphors I'm coming up with make much sense."

"*Shocker,*" Jude whispered, plucking at one of her curls as he teased her. Indira bent her head and bit his pec, making him laugh.

"Okay, ass," she said, rolling off him. Jude rolled too, both of them lying on their sides, facing each other. "I'll leave it at: no matter what happens tomorrow, we'll figure out what comes after."

Jude nodded, dragging his palm to her lower back and pulling her closer.

"And," Indira added, threading her fingers in his hair, "I'm really fucking proud of you."

Jude let out a deep breath, pressing his forehead against hers. "I love you so much," he said, kissing her. She was his safe soul. His happy place. His tether.

"Love ya back, Jude the dude with the attitude."

"Thank you," he said after a few moments.

"For what?"

Jude brushed her curls off her cheeks, tucking them behind her ear, then dragging the backs of his fingers across her skin.

"For everything."

*   *   *

Indira insisted on driving Jude to the hearing. She pulled up to the large, intimidating building in the center of GHCO's industrial park, cutting the engine and staring straight ahead. Jude watched her, memorizing her profile, the soft curve of her nose, the intricate folds of her ear, the way her lashes swept her cheeks every time she blinked. Tiny examples of perfection that he'd hold on to—use to center himself—when the next few hours got hard.

Indira and Jude walked into the building hand in hand, their steps echoing across the marble floors. They waited on the bench outside the conference room, both stealing glances at each other, eventually smiling and letting out an uncontrolled snort of giggles like two tweens caught making heart eyes. The moments ahead felt far too serious for Jude not to laugh at least once.

It wasn't long before his name was called, and he stood, heading toward the receptionist who had called him.

"One sec," Indira said, standing too. She couldn't go in with him, but she was stubbornly determined to wait for him there. "I love you," she said, pressing a kiss to his cheek and a piece of paper into his palm. Jude closed his fingers around the slip, blinking rapidly to stop the onslaught of emotions.

Love you too, he mouthed, before turning and walking through the door. He followed the woman down a series of hallways, Indira's note still clutched in his hand.

"Right through here," the woman said, stopping in front of a large set of dark, wooden doors.

Jude nodded, but turned away from her. He needed to steal one more moment with Indira before he walked into the lion's den.

He unfolded the piece of paper with shaking fingers, eyes tracing over the familiar shape of her handwriting, every swoop and curve of a letter like a map to his heart.

You're so brave

Jude closed his eyes, pulling in a deep breath. He pressed a quick kiss to the paper, then folded it back up and dropped it in his pocket. If Jude was brave, then Indira was indomitable.

He turned back around, walking through the doors with his back straight and head held high.

And was immediately overwhelmed. Bless his heart.

He was ushered to a seat across from three high-level administrators: Dr. Raymond Schwartz, the CEO of GHCO; Dr. Nora Prince, Jude's direct supervisor; and a man who introduced himself as Dr. Parrish, a board member with a psychiatric background brought in to lead the questioning.

All three of them opened leather portfolios, pulling out expensive-looking pens and turning a few pages in their legal pads.

Hot needles prickled along Jude's skin as he sat there, staring at the stern-faced group whose decision would dictate the next year of his life.

It wasn't that he didn't want to work—he'd always loved surgery, always garnered a thrill from it—but he couldn't heal patients if he continued to harm himself in the process. He was open to alternatives, he just had no idea what that would look like.

"The record states," Parrish said, opening a second large binder filled with documents, "that Dr. Bailey approached Dr. Prince with a request for evaluation of discharge due to claims of PTSD."

Jude nodded. "That's correct."

"I see," Parrish said slowly, sizing Jude up. The other two looked at Jude similarly, calculating the best approach to their questioning. Schwartz started clicking his pen. Slowly. Loudly. Each snap of the spring like a lash down Jude's spinal column.

"Well," Parrish said, leaning back and opening his arms in front of him. "Please go ahead and share with us your perspective on why you're here."

Jude cleared his throat once. Twice. Coughed. *Good Lord, Jude, get it together and say some words, please.*

"As you know," Jude finally managed, his voice surprisingly steady. "I've been stationed as an emergency physician at a myriad of clinics—Sierra Leone, Syria, Yemen, Ukraine—all of which were— are—experiencing humanitarian crises."

"Which is the crux of our mission at GHCO," Dr. Prince said.

"Yes," Jude agreed. "And so much good is done, and I have the utmost respect for the work that you all do. But pretty early on I struggled with the violence and trauma I was witnessing on a daily basis, the culmination changing me on a fundamental level. I've been experiencing tremendous emotional and mental distress. Severe and stressful flashbacks. Emotional outbursts. Confusion. All of these have made me . . . They've affected my ability to perform as a sur-geon even in the most controlled of environments."

Be honest, Jude repeated to himself, forcing the next words out. "I have serious concerns about my ability to help anyone if I'm placed back in a high-stress zone."

They all scribbled on their notepads, looking bored.

Parrish sighed, resting his elbows on the table as he looked at Jude. "Many of our doctors experience hardships while on assign-ments. It's an occupational hazard, if you will, that we try to make all GHCO physicians aware of before they start their service," he said, tilting his head as he looked at Jude.

"I was twenty-two years old when I signed the scholarship con-tract with GHCO," Jude said, voice rising. "I was a child with no

concept of what a humanitarian crisis actually looked like. I was naive and privileged enough to not have a firm grasp on some of the
horrors that happen in this world."

"Regardless, what you're describing doesn't sound particularly serious or out of the norm. Not grounds for medical discharge, at least."

A swell of anger roared in Jude's ears, his vision going blurry with
red. Not serious? Not fucking serious? A chunk of his soul was left in
every clinic he'd worked in, rotting and decaying away. Jude would
never get that back.

What wasn't serious about him clawing and fighting his way to
rebuild? Raging against every impulse to either numb himself to
death or explode from the terror that he was stuck in.

José had warned Jude that they might be harsh or rude through
this process, make him prove his invisible illness. But the actual experience of laying his trauma, his pain, out on the table to be analyzed
and dismissed was so much worse than he could have imagined.

Jude wanted to walk out. Actually, he wanted to flip the table,
break Schwartz's fucking pen that he kept clicking, *then* walk out.

But Dira was out there waiting for him. And she believed in
him. She pushed him and pressed him and annoyed him and loved
him with such consistent patience and intensity, Jude was certain
anything was possible.

Jude reached into his pocket, dragging his thumb over the fine
edge of Indira's note.

She'd told him he was brave, so brave he would be.

"With all due respect, sir," Jude said, reaching for his water, hand
trembling as he took a sip then set the glass back down. Good. Jude
let his hands tremble. If they wanted to see his pain, he'd wear it like
a badge of honor. "It's incredibly serious."

They looked at him dully.

"I'm a surgeon," Jude began, gripping the armrests of his chair.
"An emergency medicine professional. My training for this profession means I've seen the human body in countless broken ways. I've

seen bones shattered, hearts fail, insides ripped to the outsides. I've listened to howls of pain and silent pleas. I've heard sighs of relief when morphine hits, seen tears of joy when a surgery is completed and someone comes through. I, for a living, put a human body back together again."

Jude paused, taking a deep breath, trying not to let what he was saying get lost in the jumble of his fear.

"But healing doesn't end at the reconstruction of a facial fracture or the setting of a femur—that's just where it starts. We look at these patients who wear their trauma on their body, and instinctively know they need to heal. We can visualize their brokenness and grant them the grace of bed rest. Of physical therapy. Of time to recover.

"We honor the human body. Respect it. But we take the mind for granted. We ignore the invisible illnesses that plague countless people every single day." Jude's voice gained volume. Determination.

"We ignore their need for healing, we demand their absolute best when the most essential organ in their body isn't working at its optimal capacity. We tell them that an ill brain does not grant them grace or compassion. But, sir, I can attest to the torture that we inflict on people when we minimize the impact of a hurting mind.

"There are times I can't eat, can't sleep, due to an unfounded sense of absolute fear pounding through my body. If I do sleep, sometimes I wake up and don't know where I am. I jump to action like bombs are being dropped on me or I lock up, absolutely paralyzed and unable to move for *hours*. My brain gets stuck. It gets stuck and I'm back in these moments that shaped this fear, inspired this trauma, and I'm shaking and scared and no longer fully myself." Jude's voice cracked on the last words, and he took a deep breath, trying to steady himself.

"I cannot heal another human's body if my own is controlled by this fear. It's a type of stuck you can't understand until you experience it. Until you wake up from the nightmares and can't immediately grab on to reality. Until you get a flashback at work and the past and present merge into a state you can't function in.

"It's serious and it's changed me and there's no going back. I'm healing, but it's slow and painful. It's the most difficult thing I've ever done. And I worry that if I'm sent back to the environment that was the backdrop to this trauma, I won't only lose myself, I'll lose others. And I'm not willing to live with that on my conscience."

The room was silent. Waiting.

Jude cleared his throat. "So, I guess, the question is: Are you?"

The silence only grew, and Jude's body continued to quiver over the tension in the room.

After what felt like an eternity, Dr. Prince cleared her throat, leaning forward. "I am not," she said simply. "So what are the options?" She looked to the men on either side of her.

"Really, there's two courses of action we can take with this based on the stipulations of your scholarship and the precedent set by similar situations in the past," Schwartz said with a bored sigh, flipping through his portfolio.

"You can opt to go through psychological testing, both through GHCO's psychiatric team and outside practitioners for a comprehensive evaluation," he said, tracing his finger over a page. "Going this route would mean all benefits and pay are suspended until the final determination is granted. Historically, this process has taken anywhere from six months to two years. If the final report is in your favor, you will be discharged from the program without the expectation that you pay back that final year's worth of work."

Jude's hands curled into fists, his nails digging into his skin. In his favor? Did this guy really think that undergoing exhaustive psych evals for two years to be told, yeah, he's a fucked-up mess, was really a ruling in his *favor*?

"And the other option?" Jude said, voice dark.

"You pay back the GHCO for the amount of time you did not serve out on your contract."

Big, scary numbers danced across Jude's brain. He nodded slowly.

"I think it's important to note," Parrish chimed in, "that your contract stipulates that any breach in agreed-upon time served will result in a mandatory financial repayment twice what was granted for tuition and living fees plus the amount of interest that would have accumulated had you gone through government student loans; about six percent per year since graduation."

Schwartz steepled his hands on the table. "Take a second to think about that, Dr. Bailey. Are you really willing to take on that financial burden to get out of thirteen months of work?"

A weighted silence wrapped tightly around them.

"A third option," Schwartz said, voice low and calm, "is we leave this room and carry on as planned with your next assignment. Maybe we can even find a way to negotiate a shorter term, since your service has been excellent thus far. Maybe even just eleven months? Because, really, what's a year in the grand scheme of life?"

Jude blinked, his pulse punching against his chest as words and phrases swooped around his already crowded brain.

"The choice is yours, Dr. Bailey," Schwartz said. "What will it be?"

CHAPTER 38

Indira

Indira respected the silence on the car ride home, letting Jude think while all she wanted to do was ask him a million questions.

She couldn't hold back any longer, though, when they got into the comfort of her apartment.

"What did they say?" she asked, trying to hide the tang of anxiety saturating every word.

"They offered me a choice," Jude said, dragging his hands over his face. He laid out the options for her.

"And?" Indira's heart was in her throat.

Jude let out a deep breath, the tension in his shoulders leaving as he drooped and swayed where he stood.

"I guess I need to start saving," he said, looking at her with tired eyes but a hopeful smile.

Indira collapsed into him, throwing her arms around his neck as she let out a choked sob. "Thank God."

"You aren't mad?" he asked, squeezing her tightly.

Indira pulled back, face twisted up in a question. "Mad? Why the hell would I be mad?" she said, dragging her hand down his cheek, then wrapping her fist around his chin.

"I didn't talk to you about the choices. Trying to go the evaluation route. I . . . That's a lot of money I'll be paying back and it might impact our future. But I couldn't . . . I can't prolong this process for years. Even this was so exhausting and I—"

Indira cut him off, pressing her mouth to his, silencing his runaway thoughts. "You made the exact choice I would want for you."

"Really?"

"Yes. Because the choice I want for you is the one you want for yourself."

Jude dropped his forehead to hers, hands diving into her hair. He laughed, tears rolling down his cheeks. Indira laughed too. It was a sharp, fractured, curly sound. The sound of relief.

"Indira," he said, voice low. "I need you to know something. It's important."

"What?" she asked, pressing forward to lightly press a kiss to his jaw.

Jude took a deep breath, then looked straight into her eyes.

"I am not healed," he said, eyes steady, dark pools Indira could drown in. "I am not fixed. I can't promise you I ever will be. But I do promise to work on it. Every day. Every single day. And I think it started with wanting to be with you, but it changed. Morphed." Jude sucked in another gasping breath.

"I *like* feeling happy," he said, a smile breaking across his stern mouth. "And I want that for myself. For us. And I'm going to do whatever I can to make that happen."

"You're allowed to be broken," she said, taking his hands and kissing his knuckles. "And you're allowed to be repaired. I love every piece of you and however they fit together."

They held each other tightly for a few minutes, swaying back and forth. Wrung out and exhausted, Jude and Indira eventually let go long enough to gather armfuls of snacks and retreat to her bed, spending the next few hours in a daze of watching TV, kissing, and eating, letting themselves relax for the first time in days.

There were countless things to figure out, work to be done, but they knew work would never be successful without necessary rest.

Here, now—with the *Bob's Burgers* Thanksgiving special playing on loop and chip seasoning dusting their fingers as they laughed and held each other—they had their first page to a new beginning.

A FEW MONTHS LATER

"Ready?" Indira asked Jude as they stood outside an intricately carved wooden door.

Jude turned to her, smile wide and boyish. "Let's do it."

With a deep breath, Indira opened the door and led the way into their first couples therapy session.

After they filled out some paperwork, their new therapist, Dr. Brosta, greeted them and ushered them into her bright office.

"Why don't we start with why you've decided to come to couples therapy," she said, taking a seat on her plush chair. "What do you hope to gain from this experience?"

Jude and Indira glanced at each other, hands clasped as they sat on the small, comfortable couch. Jude nodded at Indira to start.

"We've both been through some shit," Indira said, giving Dr. Brosta a goofy smile and shrug. "Like, a lot of shit, actually. And while a lot of that occurred outside of our relationship, we want to make sure that it doesn't . . . I'm not sure exactly how to phrase it."

Indira glanced at Jude again.

"We're really happy in our relationship," he said, picking up her thread. "And we don't want to lose that."

Dr. Brosta nodded, offering them a warm smile.

"That's really wonderful to hear," she said. "Relationships are work, and we all enter into them with our own hurts, our own wounds, weights we carry around. Consider this a space where you can open the windows to your relationship and air out the things that no longer serve you as a couple."

"That's exactly what we want to do," Indira said, her heart beating up into her throat. They'd come so far. She couldn't wait to see all the places they still had to go.

Another smile from Dr. Brosta. "Then let's begin."

*　*　*

Indira and Jude both knew that healing wasn't linear, and they held hands through every loop and hill their paths took.

They both continued their personal therapy journeys, Indira meeting with Dr. Koh weekly as she learned to find value in who she was and not in the problems she could fix for others.

"I used to think being truly in love would be the thing that fixes me," Indira had told Dr. Koh one sunny spring afternoon. "It's old and antiquated and ridiculous, but I thought it would be the thing to stitch up my wounds."

Dr. Koh had nodded in that quiet, knowing way of hers. Indira no longer minded her silence.

"But it's so different." A few tears holding a microcosm of feelings rolled down her cheeks. "Being in love doesn't fix anything. It doesn't make me more whole or human than when I was single. But it is a safe, quiet space where I feel brave enough to look at those wounds . . . Stitch them up myself, no matter how long it takes."

And that's what she and Jude continued to do each day.

They took themselves apart, thread by thread, analyzing every piece, and decided what they wanted to weave back into the tapestry of their life—their opposite colors and differing textures looping together into something beautiful.

That didn't mean they weren't without their problems. They fought and bickered and had bad days with all their good. Some of the bad days were exacerbated by the increasing burnout Indira was feeling at her job.

"They keep cutting funding," Indira said one night, sitting on the floor in her PJs with takeout containers surrounding her. "I feel like they've lost sight of the whole point of what we're doing. The kids we're trying to help."

"Are you thinking about looking for a new job?" Jude asked, grabbing some noodles for his plate.

Indira shrugged as she chewed on a spring roll. "I toy with the idea pretty much every day," she said. "But the unknown is scary. And the job market isn't great."

Jude nodded. "I need to start looking for something new too, I think."

Indira sent him a questioning glance as she took another bite. "I thought you loved your job," she said through a mouthful.

Jude reached over, brushing crumbs off the corner of her mouth before kissing the spot. Indira beamed at him.

"I do really like it," he said, playing with his chopsticks. "But . . . I don't know. The money kind of sucks and I guess part of me . . ." He let out a deep sigh, dragging a hand over his hair. "Part of me misses medicine."

Indira swallowed. "Are you thinking of practicing again?"

Although Jude's contractual break from GHCO had no impact on his license or ability to practice medicine outside of their organization, he'd recognized that continuing to work as a surgeon would have been hugely fucking triggering and disastrous. The choice to take a break had crushed Jude a bit—it was a unique type of pain to love something and not have it love you back—but he was learning it was okay to let go of things you love if they no longer serve you.

He'd spent the past few months working at a bookstore. It was a completely random left turn from the career he'd worked so hard for, and most of his paycheck went directly to his GHCO repayments, but he found peace in the job, a quiet comfort as he surrounded himself with stories.

Indira's heart thrummed as she waited for his answer. She wanted Jude to do what made him happy, but she also didn't want him pushing himself into something he wasn't ready for.

"No, I don't think so," he said, fiddling with his chopsticks. "I'm not sure I'm ready for that. Or if I'll ever be. But I was kind of thinking about some sort of administrative role? For a hospital or clinic?

Help coordinate care and management and stuff. Get to be around medicine without the parts that trigger me quite as much."

"You'd be good at that."

Jude shot her a frown. "A compliment, Indira? Have we lost our spark so soon?"

She threw back her head and laughed, leaning over to punch Jude on the shoulder.

"It'd be cool if we started a clinic together," she said, popping another sushi roll in her mouth.

Jude's eyes snapped up to her. "What?"

Indira shrugged, holding up a finger as she chewed. "Like a non-profit," she said after swallowing. "Offering treatment to victims of trauma, maybe. Have medical services and psychiatric treatments."

Jude continued to stare at her.

"We could run it. You have your GHCO experience that could be a solid foundation for systems management. We could coordinate care, work with social workers. Could really do some good."

"Are you serious?" Jude said, his voice rough.

Indira frowned at him. "Yeah? It's not stupid, I don't know why you're acting so scandalized, you weirdo."

Jude pounced on her, grabbing her cheeks between his hands and peppering kisses all over her face. "Stupid?" Jude said, kissing her lips. "Of course it's not stupid. It's the best idea I've ever heard."

Indira's eyes lit up. "Wait. Are *you* serious?" she said. "If you're being sarcastic, it isn't funny."

"Yes. I'm one hundred percent serious. Indira, let's do it. Let's start our own clinic. Help those so often left behind in medical systems."

Indira's lips parted, then spread into a grin of pure excitement. "Do you think we could actually pull it off?" she asked. The idea was overwhelming and daunting and the most exciting thing she'd ever considered.

"There's nothing you can't do," Jude said, kissing her again. "I'm all in if you are."

CHAPTER 39

Indira

A year and a half later—after countless *Oh shit, what are we doing?* moments, plenty of tears, and, ironically enough, some loans—Indira and Jude had a fully functioning clinic and their names on the lease.

As with many nonprofits, Hope Renewed Care Clinic's resources were limited and their patients' needs great, but Indira and Jude both showed up every day at work and felt truly and utterly fulfilled. Together.

The clinic's mission was focused on helping immigrants establish care. Indira headed the mental health initiatives, hiring on two additional practitioners to meet their patients' needs. She worked directly with children, offering various therapy modalities for kids given a rough start to life.

Jude oversaw the broader operations of their nonprofit clinic, and discovered a deep passion in problem-solving the administrative aspects of medicine. He liked everything from the intricacies of helping a patient gain easier access to health care with coordinated transportation and wide-reaching translation services to the expansive creativity of guiding their practice to total sustainability.

They were slowly expanding Hope Renewed's network, partnering with similar nonprofits in other countries. They'd recently started sponsoring overseas clinics dedicated to treating refugees and trauma survivors and directing funds into organizations that helped strengthen community resources in destabilized areas. They were building connections with people across the globe with the same mission of helping others.

Jude and Indira's setup wasn't glamorous by any means. Every penny was precious as they allocated funds, and the pair shared a cramped office space that catalyzed plenty of bickering that ended in laughter and kisses. The room often looked like a neon explosion, all the surfaces plastered with Post-its. Important reminders. Goofy drawings. Little flirtatious notes. It was undeniably theirs.

"I have a surprise for you," Jude said one day as they finished up lunch on the picnic table at the back of the clinic.

Indira scrunched her nose into a question mark, mouth full of food.

He reached into his backpack, sliding a plastic cylinder across the bench.

"You're such a dick!" she screeched, spraying him with food. She cackled, snatching up the small jar of peanut butter and pretending to throw it at him.

"Excuse me for wanting to spice things up!" Jude said, slapping a hand to his chest.

Indira continued to giggle.

"Okay, I have an *actual* surprise for you," he said. "Come on, I'll show you."

Jude bit back a smile as he stood, gathering up their trash and depositing it in the bin. He brushed off his hands, then grabbed Indira's.

"What's the surprise for?" Indira asked, effervescent happiness fizzing in her chest as he led her inside.

"To surprise you."

Indira whacked him on the shoulder, making him laugh.

"What's the bane of your existence?" Jude asked, stopping outside their office door.

"My desk chair," she answered without hesitation. Indira imagined medieval stretching racks were more comfortable than the (affordable) monstrosities Jude had bought for them. "You're a close second," she added, giving him a wink.

"Lovely," he said. "Really makes me excited to present you with a gift."

"Oh my God, the suspense is killing me," Indira said, bouncing on her toes a bit.

Without further ado, Jude reached for the door handle, revealing their office.

And a giant, brand-new office chair sitting in the center.

Indira's mouth dropped open.

It was bright orange, crushed velvet stretched over a wide, heavily padded seat with tassels dangling along the edge.

It was the desk chair of Indira's dreams.

"That's for me?" Indira asked, whipping her eyes to Jude.

"Well, we can't risk the well-being of the clinic's president's ass now, can we?" Jude said, giving Indira a playful slap on the butt.

Indira let out a *yip* of excitement, launching herself into the chair. She spun around, legs kicking as she squealed in excitement. Jude beamed at her, his face blurring as she continued spinning.

After a few more seconds, he shut the door and walked over, catching the arms of the chair and stopping her rotations, swinging her to face him. He leaned in close, and Indira's heart did a loop-de-loop in her chest.

"Do you like it, Madame President?" he asked, his voice a loving, rough whisper.

"It will suffice, Mr. President," Indira sniffed, tilting her head up in a way she hoped looked haughty. The twitch of his smile told her it did. "So boring and conventional," she added dryly, rubbing her fingers over the soft velvet of her vibrant orange chair.

Jude nodded. "Had to get something that matched your personality."

Indira's lip curled in mock outrage, making Jude laugh.

In one smooth motion, he grabbed her hand, pulled her from the seat, sat down himself, and plunked Indira on his lap.

"Thank you," Indira said, kissing the words into his neck. "I love it."

"Of course," Jude said, hitching her closer, rocking them back and forth a bit with his foot.

"This thing is like a small couch," Indira said, shifting on his lap. Then getting a brilliant idea.

"It is a bit big," Jude said with a tiny frown, looking down at the wide base.

Indira put her fingers under his chin, tilting his face to meet hers. She let every thought play across her face as she moved to straddle his thighs.

"Extremely practical, if you ask me," she whispered, pressing her mouth against his. She kissed him deeply, licking at the seam of his lips, tongue tangling with his after the briefest hesitation on his part.

"What are you doing?" Jude asked slyly, his clever hands already snaking under her shirt.

"Let's call it a surprise of your own," Indira said, fingers diving to the button of Jude's pants, smiling with primal delight to feel him already hard.

"We can't," Jude hissed as she freed him from his pants, giving him a long, firm stroke that had his head rolling back. "We're at work."

"Lunch lasts for another twenty minutes," Indira said, brushing her thumb over the tip of his penis. Jude groaned, and he started tugging at the hem of her top.

"What if someone comes back early and catches us?" he asked, tossing her shirt behind his back and pulling the straps of her bra off her shoulders.

"We'll be quiet," Indira whispered, grinding herself against his lap and undoing the buttons of his shirt. "You don't have to worry about getting in trouble," she added, giving him another, dirty kiss. "I'm on good terms with the boss."

Jude let out a rough laugh, then they both focused on their task, awkwardly fumbling to get pants down and bodies closer.

They both sighed in relief as he entered her, Indira biting down on her lip as she started rocking against him.

"Fuck, you feel good," Jude said into her ear, pulling her closer.

Indira picked up her speed, loving the way her body perfectly ground against his, how he hissed out her name when she moaned.

One thing she didn't love was how her gorgeous new desk chair made an absurdly loud squeak every time she bounced against Jude. So much for being quiet.

"This chair"—*squeak*—"is"—*squeak*—"really"—*squeak*—"loud," Indira panted out.

Jude let out a noise of disbelief, giving her a quick spank before gripping her ass. Pressing her more firmly down on him.

"Is that what you're thinking about right now?" he growled, pressing up harder into her. "So ungrateful," he added, repositioning his hips and hitting a spot that made Indira whimper. "Ah, that's better. Good girl."

Indira bucked at the combination of his praise and his touch, Jude always knowing just what to do to build her up.

It didn't take long for them both to tumble over that edge of pleasure, cherishing the minutes where they held each other after.

"I love my new chair," Indira said as they cleaned up, righting their clothing and giggling at their naughty little secret.

"I'll buy you a thousand more chairs," Jude said, buttoning up his shirt. "An entire warehouse if that's the kind of thanks I get."

Indira snorted, sitting primly at her new orange throne and turning to her desk, waking up her computer. "All right, no more sweet-talking. It's work time."

"Yes, boss," Jude said, giving her a peck on the cheek, then sitting at his own desk.

They fell into a comfortable silence, their keyboards clacking as they worked. Indira was looking over encounter notes for a new patient when an email dinged through. She grinned as she saw who it was from.

FROM: Bailey, Jude <jude.bailey@gmail.com>
TO: Papadakis, Indira <indpapadakis@gmail.com>
DATE: September 30, 1:18 p.m.
SUBJECT:

I love you.

She wasted no time typing out a response.

FROM: Papadakis, Indira <indpapadakis@gmail.com>
TO: Bailey, Jude <jude.bailey@gmail.com>
DATE: September 30, 1:19 p.m.
SUBJECT: RE:

I love you too ♥

EPILOGUE

TWO YEARS LATER

"This next one is going to be *the one*," Lizzie said, taking a sip from her champagne flute.

"Right. Because everyone knows the fifty-seventh time is always the charm," Harper said.

"The longer she takes, the more free champagne we get, so I hope she never finds the perfect one," Indira added, plopping down on the plush white couch next to her friends after refilling her own glass.

"Oh shit. I look good as hell," Thu said from inside her dressing room. With a grand flourish, she whipped back the cream curtain, posing dramatically in a gorgeous white wedding dress hugging her every curve. "What do you think?"

All three friends were silent for a moment. Then they all started screaming.

"Umm, excuse me, who's the fucking model and what she'd do with Thu?" Lizzie said, leading the charge to grab Thu and thrust her on the elevated platform in front of the floor-length mirrors. Thu grinned, sliding her hands over her hips as she looked at herself in the mirror.

"This is so on brand for you, Thu," Indira said, admiring the exceptionally low cut of the back of the dress. "Trying to give Alex a heart attack on your wedding day. Touché, my dear."

"You look so pretty," Harper said, dabbing at her eyes with a tissue.

"Aww, Harpy," Thu said, blinking rapidly and grabbing her friend for a side hug. "I think this is the one," Thu added.

Indira, Lizzie, and Harper all muttered some version of *yeah, no fucking duh* in unison, then wrapped their arms around each other, Thu in the center. They stayed like that for a beat, cherishing the moment. Their friendship. Their over-the-top, can't-be-beat love for one another.

"I'm really loving being the center of all this attention," Thu finally said, "but you all won't even be allowed to breathe too close to me come wedding day. I'm not risking any wrinkles."

They all giggled, untangling themselves. After each guzzling down another glass of free champagne, Thu bought her wedding dress, adding a dramatic veil into the mix. As one does.

The friends piled into Indira's car after that, driving away from Center City and to Lizzie and Rake's home in West Philly. The pair had bought their Victorian duplex during Lizzie's second pregnancy, wanting at least some type of yard for their daughters to frolic in.

When the ladies filed through the house and out to the rickety patio, they were immediately greeted by Rake, who had plump baby Phoebe strapped to his chest and was dancing with toddler Evie standing on his feet, singing at the top of her lungs.

"No wonder you had a second one," Thu said after a pause, all four women requiring a moment to compose themselves at the sight of a giant, gorgeous man being a really good dad.

Alex, Dan, and Jude weren't doing too bad at looking extra hot either.

Dan had a tiny pair of fairy wings strapped to his back, pretending to play an accompanying flute for Evie's singing while music streamed from his phone. Harper's face broke into a grin, pink high on her cheeks, as she walked over and sat down next to him. He paused his pretend playing to give her a soft kiss.

Alex and Jude hovered around the grill, also wearing toddler-sized fairy wings. Jude even had a bonnet smashed on his head. He set down a plate of roasted veggies, then went to Indira, wrapping her in a hug.

"How'd it go?" he asked her, looking on as Thu animatedly talked to Alex. Alex looked at her like she was the only person in the world.

"She's gonna be a stone-cold stunner on her wedding day, I'll tell you that much," Indira said, smiling at her recently engaged friend.

"I have no doubt you will too," Jude whispered, toying with the engagement ring on Indira's finger, lighting up sparklers in her chest.

"Hi, hi! Sorry we're late! We have no excuse!" Jeremy called, bursting from the house with Collin in tow. "I'm going to blame Collin for it anyway."

Indira giggled, moving to give them hugs as they made their rounds with the group.

After a few more minutes, the food was ready, and they all swarmed the picnic table.

"How's the new job going, Harper?" Collin asked around a bite of burger.

"Really great," Harper said, taking a sip of iced tea. "It felt weird, at first, being back but not as a student. I'm more used to it now and I'm loving it." Harper had been offered a chair position at Callowhill's oral surgery clinic. She was teaching and mentoring students in the dental school, while also regularly performing groundbreaking head and neck surgeries in the hospital.

"Gonna be as hard on the students as our teachers were on us?" Thu asked.

"Oh, sure," Harper said, dryly. "Belittling and dehumanizing has always been my nature." Dan snorted, pressing a kiss to her temple.

After they finished eating, Lizzie brought out a gorgeous meringue dessert, white and topped with deep red and blue berries.

"A pavlova for my great Australian brute," she said, cutting into it and serving Rake. Rake rolled his eyes and beamed at her, accepting the plate.

"No titties or vulvas tonight, Lizzie?" Jeremy asked, obviously upset. Lizzie's erotic bakery, specializing in the yonic form, was a smashing success. She was even considering opening up a second location.

"Don't worry, Rake will get some of that too. *After our guests are gone*," she stage-whispered to Rake, making him choke on his bite and blush hot pink. Lizzie smacked him on the back while she giggled.

The warm summer night wrapped around the group of friends, twinkles of stars illuminating the happy little corner of the world they'd carved out as they all laughed and talked for hours. Wine flowing. Babies carried off to bed. Couples snuggled close. Memories shared.

Life wasn't perfect for any of them, and it never would be.

But this moment? Well, it felt pretty damn close.

AUTHOR'S NOTE

Thank you so much for reading! Jude and Indira's journey is one so near and dear to my heart, and I appreciate you spending your time with them.

I came to this story a bit bruised and battered, and there were many times I felt this book would never come to fruition. No matter how hard we try to suppress hurt, it has a way of bubbling to the surface, demanding we see it. Recognize it. Honor it. Hurt serves a purpose; a stepping stone to healing. An amplifier of happiness. Without hurt, joy and laughter and love wouldn't be so poignantly wonderful.

There is no easy or comfortable way to admit it, but I was a victim of abuse during my teenage years. As a result, I've lived with PTSD for the better part of a decade. I say this not in search of pity but because, for the first time in my life, I feel empowered to state the truth of my experiences and the reality of what I've dealt with and how it's influenced the mental health representation in this story. Writing has always been a place for me to unravel pesky feelings, and some of the hurt I've carried came out of me during Jude's journey.

While this book is entirely fictional, I found catharsis in looking at trauma through my characters' eyes and witnessing their raw determination to heal. It was a way to explore the hardship of PTSD, and the beauty of opening yourself up to healing, no matter how nonlinear that path may be. Recovery from trauma is vast and nuanced, and this story shows only one lens of that healing process. I feel incredibly grateful for the opportunity to write this book, and the others in the series, and find my own little bit of healing along the way.

For anyone who may ever need it:

Crisis Text Line: Text HOME to 741741 to be put in touch with a crisis counselor

National Domestic Violence Hotline: 800-799-7233

Suicide Prevention Hotline: 800-273-8255

ACKNOWLEDGMENTS

This book exists due to the endless support and help of the people around me, and I am wildly lucky to have so many to thank.

First and foremost, thank you to my editor, Eileen Rothschild, for recognizing what this book was trying to be in early drafts and helping me write the story it was meant to be in the end. Despite my many, *many* melodramatic emails of defeat, you always made me feel supported and invigorated to keep going. Thank you for championing this series. Working with you is a true privilege.

Thank you to my outstanding agent, Courtney Miller-Callihan, for *also* putting up with my melodramatic emails and phone calls. You are a force to be reckoned with and make this industry a better place. You constantly inspire me to be a better person, and I'm so grateful to work with you.

Megan Stillwell and Chloe Liese. Who would I be without you two? It is an exceptional gift to find friends like you, and, to put it eloquently, I cherish the fuck out of you. You are steady and constant in my best moments and my worst (and my drunkest, but we don't need to go into *those* details), and I'm endlessly grateful for all that you do and the absurd amount of laughter and joy you bring to my life.

Mae. You are the best CP and friend a person could ask for, and I will never be able to express what your help and support meant to me as I rewrote this book. Your ideas were invaluable, and I'm so thankful for you.

Thank you, Saniya Walawalkar and Emily Minarik, for your endless support and friendship. I'm not sure what I'd do without your voice memos and the deep analyses on J*e Alw*n's ass crack. Our group chat is my favorite place in the world.

I'm incredibly grateful for the support and friendship of Katie Holt, Ava Wilder, Kaitlyn Hill, Sarah Hogle, Esther Reid, Stacia Woods, Elizabeth Everett, Libby Hubscher, and Ali Hazelwood. I'm constantly stunned at your ceaseless compassion, humor, and love. I'M JUST REALLY GLAD TO KNOW YA'LL OKAY??

Thank you to my team at SMP. Lisa Bonvissuto, Alyssa Gammello, Brant Janeway, Alexis Neuville, Marissa Sangiacomo, Dori Weintraub, and Layla Yuro, I appreciate your work and all the hidden things you've done to bring this book into existence. Thank you to Kerri Resnick for designing yet another stunning cover; I'll never stop being awed by your talent.

Mom, Dad, Eric, Grammy, Uncle Beel, Sara, Uncle Doug, Aunt Robyn, Uncle Pat, Aunt Ronelle: thank you so much for supporting me in this wild writing thing and reading my books (which the reality of still makes me want to rip my skin off in embarrassment, but is still greatly appreciated). I'm oddly fortunate to have a family so ready and willing to discuss the value of face-sitting in romance novels at a very public brunch. I'll forward you my therapy bills.

A huge, never-ending thank you to all the booksellers, librarians, Bookstagrammers, bloggers, and BookTokkers out there who have shared my books. I can't tell you what a difference you make in authors' lives, and I'm so thankful for your hard work and passion.

Ben. Where do I even begin with you? You're my favorite person in the world, and I'm not sure I'd be able to write about romance and love without you inspiring me daily. You make me feel loved on my darkest days and my brightest, and your unwavering support in my dreams has pushed me to keep going even when I felt all was lost. Thank you for always buying me food when I'm stressed out and crying at my laptop. You make me laugh even when I'm trying my hardest to be grumpy.

And, finally, my greatest thanks to you, dear reader. Sharing the journeys of Harper, Lizzie, Indira, and Thu has been one of the brightest spots of my life, and I'm constantly humbled and moved by your love for them. It's always a bit terrifying to write about mental health, but your messages of support and kindness inspire me to be brave, and I can never thank you enough for reading my books. I wish you nothing but love and your very own happy ending.

Ben Eisdorfer

MAZEY EDDINGS is a neurodiverse author, dentist, and (most importantly) stage mom to her cats, Yaya and Zadie. She can most often be found reading romance novels under her weighted blanket and asking her boyfriend to bring her snacks. She has made it her personal mission in life to destigmatize mental health issues and write love stories for every brain. With roots in Ohio and Philadelphia, she now calls Asheville, North Carolina home. She is the author of *A Brush with Love* and *Lizzie Blake's Best Mistake*.

Fall in love with Mazey Eddings on audio!

"Harper and Dan found the perfect narrators . . . in Emily Lawrence and Vikas Adam."
—*The Infinite Limits of Love*

"Summer Morton and Will Peters . . . gave voice to the main characters and made the book come alive for me."
—*Carla Loves to Read*

What starts out as a fake wedding date turns into something these childhood enemies never expected.

Read by Joe Arden and Imani Jade Powers

Visit MacmillanAudio.com for audio samples and more!
Follow us on Facebook, Instagram, and Twitter.

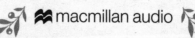 macmillan audio